About the Author

BILL FAWCETT is the author and editor of more than a dozen books, including *You Did What?* and *How to Lose a Battle*. He is also the author and editor of three historical mystery series and two oral histories of the U.S. Navy SEALs. He lives in Illinois.

OVAL OFFICE ODDITIES

AN IRREVERENT COLLECTION OF PRESIDENTIAL FACTS, FOLLIES, AND FOIBLES

★

BILL FAWCETT

HARPER

NEW YORK · LONDON · TORONTO · SYDNEY

HARPER

OVAL OFFICE ODDITIES. Copyright © 2008 by Bill Fawcett & Associates. All rights reserved. Printed in the United States of America. No part of this book may be used or reproduced in any manner whatsoever without written permission except in the case of brief quotations embodied in critical articles and reviews. For information address HarperCollins Publishers, 10 East 53rd Street, New York, NY 10022.

HarperCollins books may be purchased for educational, business, or sales promotional use. For information please write: Special Markets Department, HarperCollins Publishers, 10 East 53rd Street, New York, NY 10022.

FIRST EDITION

Designed by Nancy Singer Olaguera

Illustrations by Charles D. Moissant

Photo on page 290 courtesy of the Presidential Pet Museum.

Photos on pages 299, 301, 306, and 307 used with the permission of the Naval Historical Foundation.

Library of Congress Cataloging-in-Publication Data is available upon request.

ISBN: 978-0-06-134617-0

08 09 10 11 12   OV/RRD   10 9 8 7 6 5 4 3 2 1

CONTENTS

INTRODUCTION

*T*his is not a book about politics, issues, or lessons from history. What you have here is a book about the U.S. presidents and those around them. The presidents have had an immense impact on the nation and its history. Before you get the impression there is any redeeming social or educational value to *Oval Office Oddities*, be warned there isn't. But if you are occasionally tired of the political drama and the false promises, we have a treat for you. You are cordially invited to chuckle at one president who was denser than a box of rocks and was only put into office by his wife or at half a dozen really licentious past national leaders, each of whom made Bill Clinton look like an angel.

So here you have it: hundreds of glimpses of the American presidents, first ladies, even vice presidents as flawed, loving, hating, and burping human beings. This book is in hundreds of short sections so it can be read in little bits during brief breaks or in big gulps that will keep you entertained on a long flight or drive. So when you can't stand one more campaign commercial or empty promise, pick up this book and smile knowingly.

A FIELD GUIDE TO PAST AMERICAN PRESIDENTS, 1789 TO 1933

A word of explanation on this first section is in order. The fact is that just about everyone reading this book already knows a lot about George Washington, Abraham Lincoln, FDR, JFK, and a few of the other most renowned presidents. But what do you know about Franklin Pierce? So, what follows is a crib sheet. Each president is listed and there is actually a bit more about the more obscure, often deservedly obscure, national leaders than those few with whom we are most familiar. If you are at a nice snobby party full of historians and pseudo-historians, keep this list handy and astound your fellow guests. It is rather unlikely they will contest a single insightful statement you make about Franklin Pierce or even the relatively recent William Howard Taft.

GEORGE WASHINGTON 1789–1797
George Washington started poor and ambitious, married for money, led the American Revolution and, almost single hand-edly, set the standard and pattern for all future presidents. He is also the first president to order American soldiers against other Americans to put down a revolt, a distinction only he and Abraham Lincoln, who led the entire nation in the Civil War, share.

JOHN ADAMS 1797–1801

A revolutionary leader who distrusted the masses. John Adams was brilliant and one of the chief philosophical leaders of the new nation. He also was not very good at day-to-day politicking and was overwhelmed by infighting. Abigail Adams was one of the first true feminists to appear in the nation, wife to one president and mother to another.

THOMAS JEFFERSON 1801–1809

Almost certainly the most intelligent and creative man ever to hold the office. He was a renaissance man whose only real flaw was being a great host who entertained himself into poverty. He was also the president who made the Louisiana Purchase, which doubled the size of the nation and opened the continent. So much can be said about him that he has his own chapter in this book.

JAMES MADISON 1809–1817

An author and the chief supporter of the Constitution. He wrote extensively, helping to get the document accepted. He was analytical, cautious, and logical. His views on government molded the United States and are reflected in the nature of the nation even today.

JAMES MONROE 1817–1825

President Monroe was the first of the "foreign policy presidents." He could be concerned with such things because matters were going smoothly inside the still-new nation. Perhaps his greatest accomplishment was the Monroe Doctrine, which basically told foreign powers to stay out of the Western Hemisphere. The irony of this is that it was mostly enforced by the British, who actually had a navy, not the United States, which really didn't.

JOHN QUINCY ADAMS 1825–1829

Son of John Adams, he spent sixty-six years in government service. He was a determined and skilled negotiator before becoming president, but somewhere along the way he lost his drive. His term was lackluster, and he failed to be reelected.

ANDREW JACKSON   1829–1837

The first of the people's presidents, Jackson was from the then frontier state of Tennessee. He was rough-hewn, took offense easily, and was said to have fought, and survived, a hundred duels and certainly did fight more than most. He was against a central bank and other reforms we now take for granted. He was also the military hero of his day, having beaten both American Indians and then the British in battle. His victory at New Orleans energized the nation and helped restore its self-confidence.

MARTIN VAN BUREN   1837–1841

Van Buren was the campaign organizer who put Andrew Jackson into office. In repayment, Jackson named him his successor and that seems to have been enough to get him elected. Where Jackson was all rough edges and frontier attitudes, Van Buren was a politician full of street smarts. He had the misfortune to be president during one of the worst depressions in the nation's history, and though he did form the national bank, he failed to really deal with the problem. Jackson was a tough act to follow, and Van Buren was simply not equipped to do that.

WILLIAM HENRY HARRISON   1841

He was the first candidate to run what we would recognize today as being an actual campaign for the presidency. Being the oldest president elected up to that time, he wanted to prove how robust he was by delivering his hour-long inaugural speech without wearing a coat on a very cold and damp day. He did, and the resulting illnesses killed him a month later.

JOHN TYLER   1841–1845

Succeeded to the presidency when Harrison died. The program for replacing a dead president hadn't really been set, and by just taking the office and daring others to challenge him, Tyler settled what could have been a very messy issue. He was not popular with Congress and did not get many of his programs passed. He was the first president to have his veto overridden. He also actively helped to get Texas admitted as a state. Tyler was always troubled by the North-South split and once headed a peace commission, but eventually saw all efforts fail. He served as a senator for the Confederate States of America, where he was the only U.S. president to swear an oath to a nation at war with the United States.

JAMES KNOX POLK   1845–1849

This president was a strict Methodist who forbade drinking and dancing in the White House. He was a major force in the expansion of the United States through the addition of the western and southwestern portions of the continent to the still-young nation. The Mexican-American War was fought during his term. He was never very popular, but historians have been much kinder to his presidency than his contemporaries were.

ZACHARY TAYLOR   1849–1850

Win a war, get elected president. A good slogan helps, as it earlier did for General Harrison, who led the battle of Tippecanoe. Winning the Mexican-American War worked for Zachary Taylor, too, along with presidents from Washington to Eisenhower. Taylor was president for only sixteen months, much to the relief of the party that elected him. No one knew his politics when he was elected, and though he was from Virginia, he took an anti-slavery stand, bringing California in as a free state and upsetting the balance. His few months in office actually started the skid that ended with the American Civil War.

MILLARD FILLMORE   1850–1853
Inheriting the office upon the death of Taylor, Millard Fillmore may not be a household name, but is there anyone today who has not at least chuckled at the name itself? It has become something of a joke name and with good cause. Taking over for Taylor, Fillmore accomplished little except bringing in a new and bigger bathtub to the White House. Strong of character personally, he was too legalistic and doctrinaire and too poor a politician to slow the slide to war. He was the first of three presidents whose inaction led to the struggle.

FRANKLIN PIERCE   1853–1857
Though from New England, Pierce never forgot that Southern votes helped put him in office. What Pierce did regarding slavery invariably made things worse, even while pleasing his slave-owning supporters. He was often clinically depressed and this robbed him of much of his effectiveness at a time when the nation needed a strong leader.

JAMES BUCHANAN   1857–1861
Buchanan is often rated one of the worst presidents, deservedly so. He was a good lawyer and a really bad president. He failed to do anything at all about the divide growing over slavery and was no more effective at dealing with a financial depression in 1857 that certainly made everything worse. People forget that Buchanan, not Lincoln, was president when Fort Sumter was fired on and the Confederacy seceded.

ABRAHAM LINCOLN   1861–1865
He seems to have been as wise, concerned, humanitarian, determined, and caring as he is portrayed. Lincoln overcame much personal tragedy and was the strong commander-in-chief needed to preserve the Union and, afterward, the caring leader who wanted to heal the nation's wounds quickly. He fought

the Civil War with great determination and just as quickly pardoned all but a few of the rebel leaders. His assassination has to rank as one of the worst tragedies in American history, and it changed the course of the nation.

ANDREW JOHNSON　1865–1869

One of the reasons we so mourn Lincoln is that his successor was a total disaster in a time when strong leadership was needed. Andrew Johnson was on the ticket to appeal to the border states and offer hope for conciliation to the Southern states once they were defeated. Historians today sometimes concede that Johnson meant well, but all agree his incompetence and style made for disaster.

ULYSSES SIMPSON GRANT　1869–1877

As presidents go, Grant was a good general. He was an abysmal businessman who managed to go broke for a fourth or fifth time, depending how you count, after leaving office. Grant was better at the business of the nation than handling his own money. When he took over the government, the money floated to pay for the Civil War was still causing massive inflation. By the time he left office, the nation was on a hard money policy that lead it to decades of prosperity. As president, Grant was betrayed by many of his corrupt appointees and mired in scandal, but no one questioned his personal integrity. He was, particularly by those who had fought under him, highly regarded even after his death. Though Grant was born and raised in Illinois, Grant's Tomb, where he and his wife are buried, is in Manhattan.

RUTHERFORD BIRCHARD HAYES　1877–1881

Don't you just love those old names? Hayes was in some ways the first modern president. He strongly rebuilt the power of the presidency and was himself progressive, with concern for the growing financial difference between the rich and poor and for prison reform. This was the beginning of the age of the great industrial robber barons, such as Carnegie and Rockefeller. Perhaps what he left the nation more than anything else was a massive reform of the civil service system, replacing patronage with competence.

JAMES GARFIELD   1881

Inaugurated in March. Shot in July. Spent the next eighty days suffering and died in September. For the short time he did serve as president, there was not only a lack of need for any drastic actions, but his philosophy that government "was to keep the peace and stand outside the sunshine of the people," that is, do as little as possible and let the people handle things. This would have made major decisions unlikely. He was greatly mourned and is now mostly forgotten.

CHESTER ALAN ARTHUR   1881–1885

Like those of all presidents of the era, Arthur's whiskers were impressive. Not much else about his more than three years as president was. He is known for two accomplishments. The first is to carry on the work of professionalizing the federal employees. The second is that he can be considered the father of the modern U.S. Navy. As he was neither impressively bright nor that astute a politician, there is not much more to say about him.

GROVER CLEVELAND   1885–1889 AND 1893–1897

He was born Steven Grover Cleveland, so he must have preferred Grover to Steven. He is the only president to be elected twice but not in a row. He had an illegitimate son whom he devotedly supported, and when this became an election issue, politicians were shocked to find the people approved of his being supportive of the child. His problems when president were often financial in nature, and he handled them well, maintaining and restoring prosperity. His terms were times of great unrest, including massive strikes and riots. Cleveland often sided with the businessmen and during the Pullman Strike placed Chicago under martial law.

BENJAMIN HARRISON   1889–1893

This president was also a war hero during the Civil War. It is not that Benjamin Harrison was a bad president—he wasn't. It was just that a hostile Congress made most of this president's four years not very memorable. He felt that the nation was getting away from the rule of law and, as a very successful lawyer, promised to rectify this. In many ways he did, strengthening the courts and enforcing laws. Harrison was also more concerned with foreign affairs. He greatly strengthened pan-American relationships, and dealt at various times with near-war crises involving Britain, Germany, Italy, and even Chile.

WILLIAM MCKINLEY   1897–1901

This president was always rumored, mostly unfairly, to be the tool of political boss Mark Hanna. McKinley was a devout Methodist and a bit old-fashioned; he entertained guests by reading Bible passages. He did have a thing for cigars and the very occasional glass of wine. One legacy he has left us is the special relationship the United States has with Britain. It was under his administration that this was solidified by a series of cooperative efforts and it has remained a part of both nations' policies for over a century.

THEODORE ROOSEVELT   1901–1909

The term colorful should be defined as "like Teddy Roosevelt." Born to money, he was a cowboy, soldier, big game hunter, police chief, environmentalist, writer, and just about everything else that made him bigger then life. He was, almost without question, the most colorful president. He was also a jingoistic expansionist who was never afraid to exert a little military muscle. The first time he sent the newly built and modern Great

White Fleet off to foreign, hostile waters was when he was just the assistant secretary of the navy, and the secretary had taken the day off. A young reformer, he was banished to the vice presidency to get him out of New York. Once president, he lived large and fostered a sense of national greatness.

WILLIAM HOWARD TAFT   1909–1913

Taft was born to be a judge. He was extremely good at it, which is more than you can say about his being president. Anyone following Teddy Roosevelt would seem bland, but Taft was simply very competent and had none of the over-the-top behaviors of his predecessor. He did great work modernizing the American judiciary and, often he left office, was given the position he had always coveted much more than being president: Chief Justice of the Supreme Court.

THOMAS WOODROW WILSON   1913–1921

There is a good chance that if you had met Woodrow Wilson you would not have liked him. He was not a nasty person—we have had presidents who were—but he did have a tendency to let you know he was your intellectual superior. When not making an effort to be charming, Wilson tended to talk down to his audience, even to preach. He had no problem getting involved in other nation's affairs, sending U.S. troops into Mexico in both 1914 and 1916, and had the marines invade Haiti in 1915. Even though he ran for reelection on the platform "He kept us out of war," President Wilson saw and prepared for the day America joined in World War I. We won the war, but his lasting peace plans for the League of Nations and the Fourteen Points were a total disaster, with neither the allies nor the Senate cooperating.

WARREN GAMALIEL HARDING   1921–1923

May have been the least competent person ever to be president. His main asset was to have married his wife, Florence, who ran his every campaign and had all the brains and political acumen. Neither of the Hardings were good judges of character and his administration was rocked by scandal. Warren Harding's legacy was only kept somewhat untarnished by his unexpected death after less than two years in office.

JOHN CALVIN COOLIDGE   1923–1929

Silent Cal, as the president was known, really was a man of few words. He was actually honest, pushing for reform of the bureaucracy, modest, and a competent manager. Perhaps his greatest accomplishment was to avoid any situation so grave he would be remembered today for dealing with it. He was more cautious than conservative and more concerned with foreign affairs than most in an era when isolationism was a very real force. Yet another president who used his middle name.

HERBERT CLARK HOOVER   1929–1933

This president was a hero of the siege of Tientsin (as portrayed in *55 Days in Peking*, the hit movie starring Charlton Heston), as was his wife. He was also a top engineer and self-made millionaire by age forty. During World War I he personally supervised the escape of American citizens from Europe, often using his own fortune to buy them passage. A brilliant man and known humanitarian, Hoover, it seemed, would make an excellent president. And, for a while, this is how it was. Then came the Great Depression in 1929. Being a good Republican of his day, Herbert Hoover believed that it was not the place of government to meddle in the economy. So he did little to alleviate the problems or poverty that followed. His popularity fell and the shantytowns became known as "Hoovervilles."

2

CAMPAIGN PROMISES

*"Under democracy one party always devotes its chief
energies to trying to prove that the other party is unfit to
rule — and both commonly succeed, and are right."*
H. L. Mencken, 1956

*T*he president campaigns, sometimes for years, to be elected
to the position. Because of the electoral college, this is not
as straightforward as it sounds. It can be a lot of fun to watch if
you have the right attitude.

REAL WASHINGTON OUTSIDERS

In this age, when it seems to be a political asset to *not* be an experienced Washington figure, William Henry Harrison, the ninth president, likely holds the record for the biggest jump in Civil Service
position. A successful and popular general, Harrison chose after the
War of 1812 to retire to his farm near Cincinnati. While he had pre-
viously served as governor of the Northwest Territory (those states
that we now call the upper Midwest) he chose for a while to have
a less stressful life. After retiring, the only office he held was that of
clerk of the courts. But in 1840 the Whig Party was looking for a
military hero to run for president. Harrison won in what became
known as the Log Cabin and Hard Cider campaign. He went directly
from local court clerk to president of the United States.

Grover Cleveland spent almost all of his life in Erie County, New York. His first elected office was sheriff in Buffalo, New York. It wasn't until three years before being elected that the twenty-second and twenty-fourth president traveled substantially outside the county. His first trip to Washington, D.C., was for his own inaugural.

ROLE MODEL

Andrew Jackson had real problems with the way that the nation's finances were handled. He disliked the federal banks and their monopoly on issuing money. He also was just plain old-fashioned about money. He was the first president to accomplish something that none of us has seen in our lifetimes: Jackson paid off the entire national debt and turned a technically solvent nation over to his chosen successor, Martin Van Buren.

CALIFORNIA DREAMING

No president visited California until Rutherford B. Hayes in 1880. It didn't have as many electoral votes in those days. But the entire West Coast was growing quickly in both population and economic importance. The journey from Washington, D.C., to California took several days on the transcontinental railroad and Hayes's presence in the far west was a major novelty. He drew large crowds and often gave impromptu speeches.

CHADS REDUX

Close elections are not the sole property of George W. Bush and Al Gore. In 1880, James Garfield defeated Winfield Hancock by the narrow margin of only 9,464 votes nationally to become the twentieth president. Al Gore actually got half a million more votes than George W. Bush in 2000, fifty times more than the difference between Garfield and Hancock. Then there is what may be the most infamous election ever, that of 1876. That year, those in power engineered what would today be considered a coup, when three very Democratic voting states were excluded from the Electoral College. This allowed Republican Hayes to be elected by a single electoral vote. And you thought Florida seemed unfair.

CLINTON REDUX

When he had barely started his campaign, Grover Cleveland publicly admitted that he had once had an affair with a lady from New York named Maria Halpin. It was also public knowledge that her son was likely his. It had very little effect on the campaign, this being before the days of TV and blogs. Unlike the Monica Lewinsky affair, where President Clinton hedged, stalled, and lied, Cleveland came clean early and that made all the difference in keeping the faith of the American people.

AND WITHOUT A TELEPROMPTER

The news crews that follow candidates and elected officials often hear the same speech so often they can recite it better than the candidate. They sit there just waiting for some new sentence or paragraph in the canned talk that will give them something to write or talk about. This may be one reason they always look so bored when the audience is shown. There was one time when this definitely was not the case. One of our brightest and most scholarly presidents was Benjamin Harrison. Even his enemies acknowledged that he was a brilliant orator. Perhaps his most noteworthy achievement in this regard occurred on a thirty-day tour of the Pacific Coast states. He gave about 140 speeches, and each one was original. Some were written in advance, by Harrison in most cases; others were given on just a few minutes' notice when a crowd had gathered spontaneously. Today's news staff can only look back with envy.

LOSERS

The men who became president did not all have a smooth rise to power. A surprising number of them lost one or even several elections before attaining the nation's highest office.

Lincoln	Lost race to become U.S. senator from Illinois
Jackson	Lost his first presidential race
Nixon	Lost the presidency to Kennedy and his race for governor of California two years later
Benjamin Harrison	Was defeated running for both governor and senator of Indiana
Polk	Twice defeated when running for governor of Tennessee
McKinley	After fourteen years, lost the election to serve his eighth term in Congress
Harding	Defeated running for governor of Ohio
Fillmore	Lost a run at governor of New York
Coolidge	Couldn't get elected to the school board in Northampton, Massachusetts
Cleveland	Lost a bid to become the prosecuting attorney for Buffalo, New York

| Teddy Roosevelt | Was beaten when running for mayor of New York City |
| Franklin Roosevelt | Ran for vice president and lost |

SELECTED CAMPAIGN SLOGANS

Slogans became popular when the nation expanded and the ability of the people to know the candidates diminished. At first they referred to specific issues or promises. Lately they seem to have become more generalized propaganda.

1840   William Henry Harrison, "Tippecanoe and Tyler, Too"

1844   James K. Polk, "54–40 or Fight"—This involved a dispute with Britain over the Canadian border and also annexation of Texas.

1844   Henry Clay, "Who is James K. Polk?"—The next president, as it turned out.

1848   Zachary Taylor, "For President of the People"

1856   John C. Fremont, "Free Soil, Free Labor, Free Speech, Free Men, and Fremont"—Lots of free stuff, but Buchanan won.

1860   Abraham Lincoln, "Vote Yourself a Farm"

1864   Abraham Lincoln, "Don't Swap Horses in the Middle of the Stream"

1884   Grover Cleveland, "Blaine, Blaine, James G. Blaine, the Continental Liar from the State of Maine"—Note that negative ads have a long history.

1884   James Blaine, "Ma, Ma, Where's My Pa?" This was in reference to Cleveland's out-of-wedlock child. After winning, Democrats responded: "Gone to the White House, Ha, Ha, Ha!"—Mud throwing is not a modern development.

1896   William McKinley, "Patriotism, Protection, and Prosperity"

1900   William McKinley, "A Full Dinner Pail"

1916   Woodrow Wilson, "He Kept Us Out of War"—And he did, until 1917 anyhow. . . .

1920   Warren G. Harding, "Return to Normalcy"—No, that was not a real word yet.

1924   Calvin Coolidge, "Keep Cool and Keep Coolidge"— Well, this *was* before air conditioners.

1928   Herbert Hoover, "A Chicken in Every Pot and a Car in Every Garage"—In 1929, the Depression hit, and the American people never forgave Hoover, calling their shanty towns "Hoovervilles."

1952   Dwight Eisenhower, "I Like Ike"—War heroes do not need issues.

1960   Richard Nixon, "For the Future"—Lost to Kennedy.

1964   Barry Goldwater, "In your heart you know he's right"—But not many did.

1968   Richard Nixon, "Nixon's the One"—He certainly was. . . .

1972   George McGovern, "Come Home, America"

1976   Gerald Ford, "He's Making Us Proud Again"

1976   Jimmy Carter, "Not Just Peanuts," and later, "Leader, for a Change"

1980   Ronald Reagan, "Are You Better Off Than You Were Four Years Ago?"

1984   Walter Mondale, "America Needs a Change"—Most Americans didn't think so.

1988   George Bush, "Kinder, Gentler Nation"

1992   Bill Clinton, "Don't Stop Thinking About Tomorrow"

1992   Bill Clinton, "Putting People First"—And under the desk?

1996   Bill Clinton, "Building a Bridge to the Twenty-first Century"

1996   Bob Dole, "The Better Man for a Better America"

2000   Al Gore, "Prosperity and Progress"—Global warming came later.

2000   George W. Bush, "Compassionate Conservatism" (except to Saddam Hussein) and also "Leave No Child Behind" (2000), "Real Plans for Real People" (2000), and "Reformer with Results" (2000, too).

2004   Ralph Nader "Government of, by, and for the People . . . Not the Monied Interests"—He got two percent of the vote.

2004   John Kerry "Let America Be America Again"

2004   George W. Bush "Yes, America Can!"

ALL FIFTY STATES

Early in his campaign in 1960, Richard Nixon vowed to be the president of all the people and to campaign in all fifty states. This included the relatively new and distant state of Alaska, with a paltry three electoral votes. Considering what came later, and maybe even a bit because of this, with just a few days before the voting and the race with Kennedy too close to call, Nixon spent a full day on a side trip to campaign in Alaska, the only state he had not yet been in. Kennedy spent that same day in the major states and later won. It wasn't good politics, but Nixon kept his word.

LOG CABIN SYRUPS

It was a common claim by politicians in the nineteenth century that they had been born in a log cabin. This helped to portray them as just being one of the people. In six cases, presidents actually *were* born in log cabins. These six are Jackson, Taylor, Fillmore, Buchanan, Lincoln, and Garfield. One of the most adamant of the claimants was William Henry Harrison, who was actually born in a rather large Southern mansion on the James River. But he got away with it until the biographers began checking.

CAMPAIGN MANAGER

The campaign manager who got Andrew Jackson elected was Martin Van Buren. There was a much smaller gulf in those days between the campaign and the politicians. Van Buren convinced Andrew Jackson to do one very unusual thing that probably got him elected president. This was an era when politics were very rough and tumble and two issues split the country in different ways. The first issue was slavery. This caused a split between the Northern and Southern states. The other issue was money: who could print it and what banks could issue it. This was an important pocketbook concern for many voters, since those settling new land or starting a business needed "easy money," while the established money interests wanted to protect the value of their assets. So the country was split between social classes, and also frontier versus older states, on money. The result was a series of vicious congressional sessions. Tempers were high enough to result in physical violence. And don't forget it was the time when duels still took place, though illegal. What Van Buren did was to get Andrew Jackson to resign from the U.S. Senate. By doing this, he was able to return to his estate in Tennessee and avoid being part of the partisan bickering. This meant his reputation as a victorious general and statesman remained intact, since he was less of a target than those voting in Congress. By the time it was apparent that Jackson was going to run for president, and he had become a target of the really dirty politics of that day, his position with the voters was secure. By avoiding the fights in Washington, he managed to appear to stand above them. While the election was hard fought and his enemies diligent in their efforts after he had won, Andrew Jackson was elected to two terms.

The genius campaign manager was even able to convince several dozen congressmen to pledge their personal fortunes in order to set up printing presses used to further Old Hickory's campaign. That's something we are not likely to see the equivalent of today. Jackson rewarded Van Buren, whom he called a political genius, by naming him as the man he wanted to succeed him and, in 1836, after Jackson retired, Van Buren won. So by leaving his job as senator from Tennessee, Andrew Jackson was able to become president.

FINANCIAL FLIP-FLOP

While being shown to be a "flip-flopper" condemns today's politicians, there are a number of presidential flip-flops that served the country well. One of these involved the biggest sale of land in history. Knowing that Napoleon was short on money, Thomas Jefferson sent a delegation headed by John Adams and Robert Livingston to Paris with an offer. The offer was to rent or purchase the right for American traders to move freely through New Orleans, which was becoming vital to businesses in what are now the Midwestern states. To the delegates' amazement, Napoleon offered them the entire territory at a large but bargain price. Now, this was not all generosity. The French navy had been virtually driven from the seas and there was a good chance he would lose the territory, which had just been recovered from Spain, to the British anyhow. Better to sell the lands to the Americans who could defend it than to simply lose it to the Redcoats.

But there was a problem. One of the most adamantly-stated portions of Thomas Jefferson's campaign was that the United States was not going to borrow any money. (Heaven knows how the Founding Father would react to today's deficit spending.) But the new nation did not have enough money to complete the purchase. Deciding that obtaining nearly a third of the present U.S. area was more important, Jefferson flip-flopped and quickly urged the Senate to buy Louisiana from Napoleon. Except for certain low-lying neighborhoods in New Orleans, it still looks like one of the wisest flip-flops ever performed.

FROM THE BIRDS

Millard Fillmore ran for vice president and made few promises. This is probably a good thing, because when he took office upon

Taylor's death, his list of accomplishments was short. Almost every action he took or desired was held hostage to the slave/free state debate. His first accomplishment was bringing California into the Union. This was marred by the Fugitive Slave Act, which greatly expanded federal involvement in returning slaves who had escaped to free states. His second accomplishment was to send Admiral Perry to open up trade with Japan. This worked, though some say the eventual result of how this was handled was Pearl Harbor. Finally Millard Fillmore's big diplomatic accomplishment was to negotiate a treaty with Peru that gave the United States access to the Guano Islands. These islands proved an invaluable source of nitrogen-rich materials. Nitrogen is used to manufacture explosives and ammunition. The actual source of this nitrogen, and Fillmore's diplomatic accomplishment, is yards-deep piles of bird droppings that have accumulated over thousands of years on the Pacific islands.

FREEDOM TO FLIP-FLOP

When Abraham Lincoln campaigned in 1860, he promised many times that the Federal government under his leadership would not interfere with the right to hold slaves. The reason was to attract Southern voters. The ploy didn't work. Its failure was called the American Civil War. On January 1, 1863, he flip-flopped and signed the Emancipation Proclamation. This had no immediate effect on slavery in the South, but helped to turn the war into a Crusade to Free the Slaves, making liberals and many European governments happy.

FDR'S BIG FLOP

Franklin Delano Roosevelt campaigned on the idea that one of the main reasons for the Great Depression was the deficit spending of the Federal government. Rather soon after taking office, this was forgotten and he began borrowing and spending on a massive level in an effort, only partially effective, to end the

FRANKLIN D. ROOSEVELT
1933–1945

financial crisis. (World War II spending finished the recovery.) Had he kept his promise, the United States might well have not been in a position to be victorious in World War II.

PROFILE IN COURAGE

While Andrew Johnson, who became president upon Lincoln's assassination, was a bigot, made a less than competent president, and managed to antagonize nearly everyone, he also demonstrated great personal courage. When the Southern states, including his own Tennessee, were deciding to secede, he was just about the only major Southern politician to publicly oppose the popular action. Because of this, he was often at risk of attack or worse. While traveling by train through Virginia, which lies between Tennessee and Washington, D.C., Johnson once had to force a mob of irate secessionists off the train with a loaded pistol. This didn't work twice and a more determined mob of Virginians did manage to drag Andrew Johnson off a train and beat him badly. There appears also to have been a serious debate as to whether or not to hang him as a traitor as well. The most likely reason that this did not happen was that the mob did not want to take the fun away from the secessionists in Tennessee, who had first call on hanging their former governor. After these incidents, Johnson felt it was necessary to keep a gun near him while delivering his anti-secession speeches.

Abraham Lincoln appreciated his brave pro-Union stand and made Johnson his vice president in hopes of gaining credibility among the Southern, or at least border, states.

329

There was a major scandal that outraged the nation while Grant was president. Okay, actually there were several scandals while Grant was president, but this one was a doozy and included many congressmen and senators among the guilty. The scandal was named after the company involved, the Crédit Mobilier, and involved government contracts, stock manipulation, kickbacks, and insider trading on a grand scale. When the dust settled, it appeared that, out of the tens of millions involved, James Garfield had received stock dividends from the Crédit Mobilier to the total of a paltry $329. There was really nothing to show Garfield was actually involved, but that did not stop his opponents in the 1880 election from scrawling the number 329 in every wall and barn roof they could find. They were hoping to label the twentieth president as corrupt. Though I have to suspect (perhaps it is my Chicago upbringing) that there was also an element of disdain. People stole millions of dollars in the railroad scandals, and all Garfield got was a lousy $329.

SUBSTITUTE

At this time there is great debate over how honorably George W. Bush or John Kerry served in the military. It appears that such service a hundred years ago was less important to being elected. During the Civil War, the Union Army was concerned with filling its ranks and not at all with who filled them. With a war on, being a soldier was not only inconvenient but dangerous. Civil War casualties totaled in the hundreds of thousands. A common practice during the American Civil War was the purchase of a substitute. If someone who had money was drafted, it was perfectly legal to pay another person to serve instead of you. Think of it as the ultimate student deferment. This is what Grover Cleveland did. When he got the notice he was going to have to report to the army, he had very little desire to go. This was likely less a question of courage or patriotism than a reflection of his attitude that all exercise was at best unfortunate and to be avoided. Certainly being part of an army that marched hundreds of miles carrying heavy packs was out. The twenty-second (and twenty-fourth) president hired a Polish immigrant to serve in his place. This cost him the sum of $150, less than $5,000 in today's money.

FRONT-PORCH CAMPAIGN

It took eight ballots for the Republicans to nominate Benjamin Harrison at their 1888 convention. He then sat for office rather than ran for it. Harrison conducted what became known as his "front-porch campaign" by spending most of the election in Indiana on his front porch, where he gave speeches and met with those who came to see him. He was the grandson of President William Henry Harrison of the battle of Tippecanoe fame.

BONAFIDES

Because of her ill health, Ida McKinley rarely campaigned or appeared with her husband. This was fairly well known around Washington, but if you think things are vicious today, around the turn of the century everything was fair game with any lie that could be passed. Those opposing McKinley in 1896 began to spread the rumor first that Ida was some sort of freak, then that she was reported to be a spy, and eventually that she was hiding bruises from spousal abuse. None of the stories were true and eventually the Republican Party published her biography to show the voters what Ida was really like. It was the first time that information on a future First Lady became part of the official campaign.

WILSON'S FLIP

The campaign motto that helped reelect Woodrow Wilson in 1916 was "He Kept Us Out of War." Two years later there were almost a million American doughboys in the trenches of France. But since we won that war, all was forgiven. Pity he lost the peace afterward by conceding the vindictive terms on the Treaty of Versailles in exchange for support for the stillborn League of Nations.

THE LOSER WINNER

You may think the poll numbers reached an all-time low in Bill Clinton's or George W's second term, but those are percentages in the mid-thirties. In the 1912 election the incumbent president, William Howard Taft, got a pitiful twenty-three percent of the vote, losing to both McKinley and Theodore Roosevelt.

SILENT CAL

Calvin Coolidge seemed to value every word and hold them to himself like a miser. His nickname of "Silent Cal" was well earned. Normally when a candidate holds a press conference they say a lot, even if they do not have a lot to say. This is not how it was with Calvin Coolidge. A few lines from a press conference he held in 1924 shows this better than any of my words.

Reporter:	Have you any statement from the campaign?
Silent Cal:	No.
Reporter:	Can you tell us something about the world situation?
Silent Cal:	No.

Reporter: Any information about Prohibition?

Silent Cal: No.

To add insult to injury, as the reporters left, likely wondering just what they could write to justify their pay for that day, the candidate also reminded them not to quote him. It seems likely they didn't.

One quote about Calvin Coolidge comes from the famous author Dorothy Parker, a regular among the famous wits of the Algonquin Roundtable: when it was announced that the somniferous and silent former president had died, her comment was "How could they tell?"

AS PROMISED

Although Calvin Coolidge fulfilled the promise he made when taking office as president to rid the government of the graft and corruption that had marked the Harding presidency, there was a lot he didn't tell John Q. Public about his own people that came back and bit him later. It seems Silent Cal was a fan of big money and big business. He introduced a massive tax cut for the very rich, but vetoed any legislation meant to help the poorer segments of the population. The result was that wealth became concentrated more than ever and the economy began the slide into what was later known as the Great Depression. Much more than Hoover, who was mostly guilty of inaction, this economic disaster can be attributed to Calvin Coolidge's policies. This is a time when government was not supposed to get involved in the business of America, but the thirtieth president raised that policy to an indolent, but eventually disastrous, extreme.

FIRST TIME LUCKY

Herbert Hoover had not only never run for national office when he became the Republican candidate for the presidency in 1928, but he had never run for any office in his life, except class treasurer when attending Stanford University. He defeated the Democrat Al Smith decisively in what turned out to be the only time Hoover ever campaigned for any office.

ACADEMICALLY AVERAGE

Dwight D. Eisenhower, who command the Allied armies in Europe during World War II and spent two terms as president, just barely graduated in the top half of his class at West Point. He finished eighty-first out of 164.

NEVER, WELL HARDLY EVER

When both parties first approached General Eisenhower to be their candidate for president, he was less than receptive. His exact words were, "I cannot conceive of any circumstance that could drag out of me permission to consider me for any political post from dogcatcher to grand high king of the universe." The World War II war hero later changed his mind and became the thirty-fourth president.

SECOND TIME LUCKY

John Kennedy was only the second Catholic to ever run for the presidency.

The first Catholic candidate was Al Smith, who lost badly in 1928. JFK was also the first man to hold the office who was born in the twentieth century.

OWN FAULT

There is no question that JFK acted heroically after his boat, PT109, was struck and sunk by a Japanese destroyer. One of the reasons he had to do what he did to save an injured crew member was because, against regulations, there was no life-boat on PT109. Like many of the courageous commanders of the Patrol Boat *Torpedo*, JFK modified his boat to improve its combat ability. In this case, he replaced the PT boat's only life-boat with a .50-caliber machine gun. Such changes on the crew's initiative were both common and illegal during World War II. Many smaller ships and planes, including freighters and even bombers, had guns added by those who manned them. As commander of the modified PT boat, JFK could have been found by the navy to be partially at fault for the very problem of his men being in the water, in addition to being a hero for how he handled the disaster. Though, as the son of the highly connected Joseph P. Kennedy, it was most unlikely the Navy Board would find against him. And he did save the crew, personally carrying one man to safety, so if at fault, he was also a true hero.

A DEAL HE COULD NOT REFUSE

At least some of the stories about JFK and the mob have substance in fact. Before the 1960 election, Joseph P. Kennedy, JFK's father, not only met with the notoriously corrupt Judge Touhy, but attending the same meeting making sure Jack Kennedy was elected was Sam Giancana, the head of the Mafia in Chicago. At this time many of the unions were controlled by the mob (some say many still are) and Giancana promised and delivered the union vote and thousands of union member workers for the JFK campaign. Of course there is no record of what the rest of the deal made with the mob was. After the election, the attorney general chose not to investigate the rumors. The new attorney general was Bobby Kennedy.

MOBBED UP

Jack Kennedy was a womanizer at a level almost bordering on addiction. This caused him to have another up close and personal connection to Mob boss Sam Giancana. It seems that both men were intimately involved with the same very attractive woman, divorcee Judith Exner. Now it is likely one of the few men who could play around with the Chicago don's girl and get away with it would be the president of the United States. Then again, maybe JFK wasn't so sure of that himself. When informed by the FBI of her other relationship, he ended the affair.

TRICKY DICK

Richard Nixon didn't begin playing dirty with Watergate. He won his first two elections as representative, and then senator, from California by wrongly accusing his opponents of being communists. He described one as "pink down to her panties." Okay, he was a sexist, too. These tactics worked because he was good at making allies that could help spread any message he chose, some being in the mob. His ability to smear others is what, early in his political career, earned him the nickname "Tricky Dick."

AT WHOSE EXPENSE?

Most people forget that what raised Richard Nixon above the crowd and earned him the VP spot with Dwight Eisenhower were his actions on the now discredited and downright embarrassing House Un-American Activities Committee, working closely with, and just as rabidly as, the now discredited Senator Joe McCarthy. More than anything else, it was Nixon's determined and dogged pursuit of Alger Hiss, a government official who had held several important positions under FDR and was accused of being a Communist, that got him the job.

BUSH OR DOLE IN 2008?

Since 1976, there has not been a Republican presidential ticket that did not have on it someone named Bush or Dole. Here is how that breaks down:

1976   Dole for vice president
1980   George H. W. Bush for vice president

1984 George H. W. Bush for vice president
1988 George H. W. Bush for vice president
1992 George H. W. Bush for president
1996 Dole for president
2000 George W. Bush for president
2004 George W. Bush for president

UNKNOWN

When the mother of then dark horse and nationally unknown candidate Jimmy Carter heard he was running for president, her first response was to ask, "President of what?"

A WHAT?

For most of his life Ronald Reagan was not only a Democrat but a serious New Deal–loving Roosevelt Democrat at that. In 1938, the future president played with the idea of joining the American Communist Party and may even have been turned down for not being one of the party's true believers. When head of the Screen Actors Guild from 1947 to 1954, he supported Democratic candidates. But by the 1960s he had become a Republican. Reagan's speech at the 1964 Republican convention in support of nominee Barry Goldwater was so well received that it instantly elevated him to the attention of that party's leaders. (You have to wonder why they were surprised that a man who had acted in fifty-one movies, made an ape look good in one of them, and been "the dying Gipper" in another could deliver a speech well.) Ronald Reagan was soon elected governor of California and was considered a likely alternative to the incumbent Gerald Ford in 1976. Jimmy Carter beat Ford, mostly due to his unpopular pardon of Richard Nixon. Reagan was the nominee in 1980 and got revenge, trouncing Carter. You have to wonder what the young Reagan's hero, FDR, would have thought about it.

UPSTAGED

After the Nixon-Kennedy debates, where Kennedy's appearance and poise won over the TV audience and had a decisive effect on the election, the events have been considered make or break for any candidate. They are preceded by rehearsals and even posture and speech lessons. An overemphatic sigh on one debate that was caught on camera may well have lost Al Gore the election. Bush was speaking and the camera panned to Gore who theatrically and audibly sighed. The air of superiority this gave Gore was thought to have cost him support in many states where he lost by only a few thousand votes. Then again, the debates didn't intimidate every candidate. When Ronald Reagan was asked if he was nervous about debating the current president, Jimmy Carter, he answered, "No, not at all. I've been on the same stage with John Wayne."

3

PRESIDENTIAL FIRSTS

To the memory of the Man, first in war, first in peace, and
first in the hearts of his countrymen.
Henry Lee (1756–1818), referring to George Washington

DAY OFF
It was the first president, George Washington, who created the
Thanksgiving holiday in 1789.

DUBIOUS DISTINCTION
The first president to die in office was William Henry Harrison. In an age when 50 was considered old, Harrison was sixty-
eight when he took office. He died within a month of taking his
oath, leaving Vice President John Tyler to take over the office.
For several decades, the short-termed president's grave went
unmarked after a very impressive Washington, D.C., funeral.

THREE CAPITALS
In its history, the United States has had three capital cities. The
first was New York City. This was soon changed to Philadelphia.
Philly was replaced by the new city created specifically just to be
the nation's capital: Washington, in the District of Columbia.
George Washington lived to see the creation of Washington,
D.C., but not to serve there. The first president inaugurated in
Washington, D.C., was Thomas Jefferson.

CITIZENSHIP REQUIREMENT

The first president to be born an American citizen, not a British subject, was Martin Van Buren. All those born before the American Revolution began life as subjects of the king.

FIRST AMERICAN **BORN** PRESIDENT
MARTIN VAN BUREN
1837-1841

SHIPPED OUT

The age of steam was just beginning when James Monroe took a ride on the *Savannah* and became the first president ever to ride on a steamship. Not long after hosting Monroe, the *Savannah* became the first American steamship to sail across the Atlantic.

RAILROADED

The first time a president rode on one of those dangerous new railroad machines was in 1833, when Andrew Jackson took a ride. At the time it was speculated that the human body could not survive speeds over 60 mph.

OKAY?

When Martin Van Buren ran for president, this nickname was derived from the town he had been born and raised in: Kinderhook, New York. His nickname was OK, which stood for Old Kinderhook, and this OK was used as his political slogan as well, being spread across the country. Some scholars feel this was the start of the slang phrase "okay" used so frequently today. Next time you say it, think of our eighth, and often otherwise ignored, president.

UNOPPOSED

The first and only time a president ran for reelection and had no opponent was James Monroe in 1820.

SMILE

The first president to have his photo taken was William Henry Harrison in 1841. In those days you often had to sit perfectly still for several minutes for the image to come out. By the age of Lincoln, twenty years later, great strides had been made and photos could even be taken on the battlefield, if everything stood still for several seconds.

EFFIGY

It is a dubious distinction at best, but John Tyler was the first president to be burned in effigy on the White House lawn. It was all over money. There was an economic crisis in 1842 and, being against federal intervention into economic affairs, the president had refused to sign a series of bank bills meant to clean up the economy and make money easier to obtain. Most of his own cabinet and the Congress were also upset, but not as much as the angry mob that appeared when word got out. The large crowd hissed the president and then burned him in effigy.

I DO

The first president to be married while in office was John Tyler, his second marriage, in 1844. Two other presidents have tied the knot in the White House. These are Grover Cleveland in 1886 and Woodrow Wilson, who married his second wife in 1915.

DOORMEN: THE START OF THE SECRET SERVICE

Early in his term, John Tyler managed to alienate the Democrats in Congress. When he split with his party over the National Bank, he was disowned also by the only other major party of his time, the Whigs. Suddenly the tenth president, who had taken over after being Harrison's vice president and was not elected to the office, became one of the most hated men in America. The bank, and other issues he still took strong stands on, more than angered many large groups of citizens. Those on the frontier were particularly upset over the central bank concept, which would have the ability to control the amount of money in circulation. Prior to this time, even local banks would issue their own currency and this made money easy to borrow. With money controlled by a distant central bank, the prosperity of the Western farmers was threatened by both higher interest rates and a scarcity of the physical money itself. All Americans, but especially those hardy frontier settlers, were rather used to grabbing a gun as the resolution to their disputes. (The dueling Andrew Jackson was only three presidents back.) Death threats and bombs threats were a daily event. Eventually, even the hostile Congress became worried that the nation's leader might be killed, to the embarrassment of all. To assist with the president's security, four men were assigned to act as presidential bodyguards. They wore plain clothes and never ran alongside Tyler's carriage. Officially the four were listed on the government payroll as being "doormen" for the White House.

LITTLE FIRST FAMILY FEET

The first girl born in the White House was the granddaughter of John Tyler. Letitia Tyler was born to his son Robert's wife, Priscilla.

WASHINGTON OUTSIDER

Abraham Lincoln was the first man elected president who was born outside the original thirteen colonies.

TURKEY DAY

Did you wonder how the president of the United States ever got into the business of pardoning a turkey on Thanksgiving? Well, it all started with Abraham Lincoln. A few weeks before Thanksgiving, a supporter sent the president a turkey to be used for Thanksgiving dinner. In a era when refrigeration was primitive, animals were kept alive until used. But Lincoln's son, Tad, took a liking to the bird and often fed it. Within a week, the turkey was following the young boy around the White House like a house pet. But as Thanksgiving approached Tad began to realize the fate of his new pet. Reacting as only a young child can, he became quite upset over the impending fate of his new animal friend. This was during the Civil War, and President Lincoln was in a meeting when Tad burst in, able to wait no longer. The boy insisted that his father act immediately to save the turkey. Rather than leave the meeting, Lincoln scribbled an order giving the turkey a reprieve. His son happily rushed the note to the cook and the bird was spared. It remained a pet, among many others, living at the White House. Since then, other presidents

have formalized the process created by the hurried note, turning it into one of the most popular White House traditions.

LATE STARTER

The first time Zachary Taylor ever voted was at the age of sixty-two. This can be attributed mostly to the fact that Taylor was a career military man who spent virtually all his life on various frontier posts. Most of these were so far out that an election would be settled before any record of their votes could arrive at the territorial capital, so why bother? He was asked by the Whigs to be their candidate for president because he commanded

ZACHARY TAYLOR
1849–1850

the army when the United States invaded Mexico. When they asked if he was a Whig, Taylor said he didn't know. This bothered no one and he easily won the election.

FIRST TIME FOR EVERYTHING

The first time Zachary Taylor ever voted for anyone to be president, it was for himself. He won.

FIRST SECRETARY, THEN PRESIDENT

The distinction of being the first secretary of the United States has to go to James Madison. He used a form of shorthand he had developed for himself—modern shorthand dates from much later—to record the events of the Constitutional Convention. After actively participating in and also recording the discussions and debates, Madison spent much of each night transcribing in long hand his shorthand notes. Because of his efforts we have a near complete record of this historic gathering.

LITERACY TEST?

There was no library in the White House until Millard Fillmore finally had one installed in 1850. What makes this more than a bit surprising was that this president had never had a formal education and was self-taught. He didn't even see a map of the United States until he was nineteen years old. Even so, he developed a lifelong interest in learning, even marrying a teacher named Abigail Powers.

LOVE STORY

There is a rather tragic and touching love story involving James Buchanan. As a young man, he feel deeply in love and was engaged to be married. But her family and other forces prevented the match and eventually the engagement was broken off. Not long after this, Buchanan's one love died. There were rumors of suicide, but no investigation. James Buchanan sent a letter pleading to be allowed to view the body and attend the funeral. His letter was returned by her father unopened. Perhaps this left just too much unresolved for the young man. He lived another forty-four years, but is the only president never to marry. When Buchanan died, a packet of love letters from the young woman was found in his safe.

HAIR RAISING

Take a look at the pictures. Up until Abraham Lincoln and his famous beard, all the presidents were clean shaven. Not a permanent beard or mustache among them. After Andrew Johnson, who succeeded Lincoln upon his assassination, most of the next presidents had served as officers in the Civil War. In the war it had been the custom that officers had a beard, mustache, or both. So Grant, Hayes, Garfield, and Harrison all had full beards. After that, the trend ran to mustaches. Teddy Roosevelt and Taft had them. Then the clean shaven Wilson won, and all the Presidents since then have gone back to the old way and been themselves clean shaven.

LICENSED

The first saloon license ever granted a future president went to Abraham Lincoln in 1833. Liquor was served at the Lincoln and Berry store in Illinois. He sold out to his partner, William Berry, later that year.

CHANGE OF HEART

In 1865, the Congress of the United States impeached President Andrew Johnson. This is one of the two times in all of the nation's history that a president has been impeached. He was acquitted (an impeachment is like an indictment, not a conviction) by just one vote. The story of this vote is brilliantly portrayed in John F. Kennedy's book *Profiles in Courage*. But only a decade later, the Senate had a change of heart. Andrew Johnson was elected senator from Tennessee in 1875, and he was not only welcomed into the Senate with open arms, but was presented with a bouquet of flowers when he arrived. He lived only a few months after taking office. He was the first and only former president to later become a senator.

TREATED LIKE ROYALTY

The first time a queen ever met with a president was when Queen Emma of the Sandwich Isles met with Andrew Johnson in 1866. The Sandwich Isles are now called Hawaii. At the time, the islands were independent. In 1898, they were annexed by the United States, primarily at the request of the Dole company, and in 1900 they became a territory.

DUBIOUS DISTINCTION

The first president to die in office was William Henry Harrison in 1841. This led to the first state funeral for a serving national executive. In Europe, where kings ruled until they died, such funerals were resplendent and relatively common. The still-young nation was determined to give him as singular a send-off. The result was a most impressive funeral, with twenty-six pallbearers and a two-mile-long funeral procession, in which an estimated ten thousand mourners marched.

FLAG DAY

In 1889, President Benjamin Harrison visited New York City to officiate at a reenactment of Washington's inauguration held there a century before. At this time Wall Street was the heart of the city and not just the financial district. While attending, President Harrison was greatly impressed by the multitude of American flags that graced the Federal Hall and buildings near it, so much so that when he returned to Washington he instituted the custom that all federal buildings fly the national colors.

PRESSING QUESTION

President William McKinley was one of the most open and personable men ever to hold the office. As a result, he was very popular with the press who covered the White House and who almost always wrote favorably of the president and his policies. It is a reflection of the cordial relationship between the president and the reporters that it was during McKinley's administration that the now famous press room was added to the White House. This was not only more convenient for all concerned, but on another level, greatly aided the president in controlling the information released to the press. The location used then is not that of the current press room. The briefing room was moved by Richard Nixon to be located today over the pool (hopefully drained) that LBJ once liked to swim naked in.

A LAST AND FIRST

The twenty-fifth president, William McKinley, was the last president to be elected who was a Civil War veteran. He was also the first to have his inauguration recorded by the latest technology in mass communications: the movie camera.

KIDS

The youngest president at the time of his inauguration was Theodore Roosevelt. He succeeded to office when William McKinley was assassinated. He was just forty-two at that time. Kennedy was forty-three when he became president in 1960. The next youngest were William Clinton and U. S. Grant, both at forty-six. The oldest president at his inauguration was Ronald Reagan at sixty-nine. He just barely beat out William Henry Harrison, sixty-eight.

WEAK BUT STRONG HEART

Teddy Roosevelt was a sickly child and an aftereffect of his illnesses was to be left with a weak heart. This never slowed the adventurous war hero down. He is, so far as I can tell, the first and likely the only president to climb the Matterhorn in Switzerland, while honeymooning in 1881 with his first wife, Alice.

EASY RIDER

The first president to ride in a motorcar to his inauguration was Warren Harding in 1921.

IN STYLE

Times changed and so did transportation. By the time Taft was president, the automobile had become a practical, and stylish, means of travel. Congress, after refusing once and being embarrassed by the First Lady, gave the president $12,000 for the purpose of buying cars. While at least one of the vehicles, a monstrosity known as the White Steamer, seated seven and ran on steam, the others were the more normal gasoline-powered engines. The driver became a chauffeur and soon the president had four vehicles to choose from. President Taft's favorite way to ride was alone in the back seat so he could catch a nap.

PLAY BALL

The venerable tradition of throwing out the first ball of the baseball season dates back to 1910, when William Howard Taft threw out the first pitch in a game between Washington and Philadelphia.

OUT OF TOWN

The first president to leave the United States while in office was Theodore Roosevelt, who was carried by the Navy to Panama on a battleship. He was there to inspect how far along the digging and construction on one of his pet projects, the Panama Canal, had got.

STAYED BEHIND

Of all the presidents, only one is actually buried in Washington, D.C. (Kennedy's grave and the perpetual flame are at the National Cemetery in Bethesda, Maryland.) The one who stayed in Washington permanently is Woodrow Wilson. He is buried in the National Cathedral.

YANKEE DOODLE DANDY

The only president born on the Fourth of July was Calvin Coolidge.

SILVER SCREEN

Even before Reagan, presidents were intrigued by movies. It is thought that the first movie to be shown in the White House was projected about 1912. After that, movies were regularly shown to family and guests. This was the era of the silent picture, so politicians, who have always favored the sound of their own voices, rarely made use of the medium. The first president to appear on film was Calvin Coolidge, who read his 1928 Thanksgiving proclamation into a Newsreel microphone. On the other hand, Herbert Hoover appears never to have attended the theater during his entire four years as president.

ABOUT TIME

The only surprise in this presidential first was that it took so long to happen. Warren Harding was not one of the better presidents and his control of his cabinet was less than total. It was during Harding's administration that the Tea Pot Dome scandal outraged the nation. This involved the leasing of oil reserves in Wyoming (a "dome" is an oil formation) to certain well-placed and overly generous businessmen. Some of their generosity went to Albert B. Fall, who was Harding's secretary of the interior. He became the first serving presidential cabinet member to go to jail.

GO WEST, YOUNG MAN

The first president to have been born west of the Mississippi was Herbert Hoover, born in West Branch, Iowa.

SCHEDULED EVENT

When Franklin Delano Roosevelt was sworn in for his second term as president on January 20, 1937, this was the first inauguration on the now set January 20 date. All presidents before that time was were inaugurated on March 4.

THIRD TIME LUCKY

The only president to serve more than two terms was Franklin Delano Roosevelt. No one had done so before him, and since the Twenty-second Amendment to the Constitution was passed in 1951, no one can ever do it again. FDR broke with tradition due to America already being deeply involved in World War II, even though the nation was not yet at war. While the decision was overwhelmingly popular, the event also spurred action on the amendment to make a two-term limit as president into a law. There is, as voters are seeing now in 2007, no restriction on a former First Lady subsequently serving two terms as well. This loophole has been abused in South American nations to allow presidents of those nations to effectively have four terms. Though, considering just how forceful Eleanor was, had she been elected she might have been the one running the country. FDR served as president for a total of twelve years and forty days, a record that is unlikely ever to be broken.

TWO BATHROOMS NOW

The first woman to serve as a member of the cabinet was Frances Perkins. She was the secretary of labor for Franklin Delano Roosevelt during the trying years of the Depression. It was under her that child labor was finally abolished and both a minimum wage and standard work week (forty-four hours) were instituted. She was appointed in 1933 and held the position until FDR died in 1945.

OVER THERE

While today it is not uncommon for a sitting president to visit the troops in time of war, travel was much slower and riskier in the past and this discouraged the practice. It wasn't until World War II and Franklin Roosevelt that an incumbent president traveled outside the United States during a war.

TV NEWS

While the first presidential debate on TV didn't occur until the famous 1960 meeting between Nixon and Kennedy, other presidents have recognized television's potential. The first TV broadcast from the White House was made in 1947 by Harry Truman. At that time few people actually had televisions, so there were not many viewers watching. But, then, there wasn't much competition, since Milton Berle's groundbreaking show hadn't started yet. It's a fair bet he would have come out on top in the ratings, if there were any.

DIRTY FINGERNAILS

Harry Truman was the first president since U.S. Grant to have been a farmer and later been elected president. He was much more successful than President Grant, who went bankrupt at agribusiness.

DUBIOUS FIRST

Not only was John Fitzgerald Kennedy the youngest man ever to be elected president (the youngest president, at forty-two, was Teddy Roosevelt, who succeeded to the office from vice president), JFK has the distinction of dying at the youngest age of any president as well.

PRIZE WINNING PREZ

The first and only president to have been awarded the Pulitzer Prize for Literature was John F. Kennedy for *Profiles in Courage*. Wonder how much that cost old Joe Kennedy?

SORRY FIRST

In a first that he most likely would gladly have avoided, Lyndon Johnson has the dubious distinction of being the first and, so far, only vice president to be present at the assassination of his predecessor. JFK was in LBJ's home state of Texas when shot. As his host and a popular local, Johnson was also in the motorcade through Dallas that ended in tragedy. Another first, a direct result of the assassination, was that LBJ became the first president to be sworn in by a woman: District Judge Sarah T. Hughes. The ceremony was performed on Air Force One.

OVERACHIEVER

Having been in the Senate and wise in its ways, Lyndon Johnson was quite successful in pushing through his massive social program called "The Great Society." Because of his skill and political acumen, he has the distinction of signing more major bills during his first two years in office than any other president. The one who comes closest happened to be LBJ's mentor, Franklin Roosevelt.

BUT WAS SHE THE CENTERFOLD?

The first and only child of a president to pose in the nude for a major magazine was Patti Reagan, whose revealing photos appeared in *Playboy*.

SECOND TIMER

Only two presidents have ever been impeached. The first was Andrew Johnson, impeached for disobeying new laws the Congress had passed to take away most of the office of the president's power at the peak of emotions about post–American Civil War reconstruction and integration. The second was William Jefferson Clinton, for lying to cover up an affair he had with a presidential intern. Impeached means accused, not convicted, and Bill Clinton was "impeached" by the House of Representatives for lying under oath at their hearings. But the judges of an impeachment proceeding are the U.S. Senate. They did not find the president guilty. So Clinton was impeached, but found not guilty. It all comes down to the definition of impeachment.

MR. SCHOLAR

To date, Woodrow Wilson is the only president to have earned a PhD.

THE FIRST DEGREE

Surprisingly with the dominance of business in America and the number of highly educated scholars that have occupied the Oval Office, President George W. Bush is the first president to have an MBA, not that his business history indicates he made much use of the learning he got at Yale.

4

PRESIDENTIAL PECULIARITIES

We sometime lose sight of the fact, perhaps because we would prefer not to think about it, that presidents are also people with all the flaws and eccentricities that entails. Much of what follows says a lot about the presidents as people. Then again, several entries are here because they are just too much fun not to pass on.

DIGNITY, ALWAYS DIGNITY

There is no question that John Quincy Adams was among the most dignified and eloquent men ever to serve as president. He was also the victim of perhaps the first outright theft and certainly one of the most embarrassing thefts in presidential history. The story is that the sixth president was also an athlete in the style of Teddy Roosevelt. Among his exercise regimes was to walk from the White House early every morning and swim in the Potomac River. (It was a *lot* less polluted in those days.) When doing this, he simply took off his clothes and dived in. Since this was long before the days when there was a Secret Service, or any other bodyguards, the clothes sat unattended on the riverbank. Someone out walking found the fine clothes and money on the bank and helped himself. The result was, at the end of his swim, the president of the United States was bare naked and alone. To retain what dignity he had left, Adams retreated back into the water. When a young boy walked past with a fishing pole, he convinced the lad to run to the White

House and tell the First Lady to bring him some clothes. There is no record of what the lad thought about this errand and who it was for.

THE BIG BLOCK OF CHEESE

There is an episode of *The West Wing* where the chief of staff, Leo McGarry, gives what they call his "big block of cheese speech." The fictional character talks about how Andrew Jackson not only had an open door policy but also kept a big block of cheese in the foyer of the White House for visitors to nibble on. The real story is even more bizarre.

It was toward the end of Jackson's term in office. He was quite popular with the farmer and rural voters. Some of the wealthier ones decided to reward Jackson for a job well done with a wagon-size block of cheese, estimated to weigh about fourteen hundred pounds. With only a few months left in office, Jackson realized that this generous gift was a bit of over-kill. He could eat more than twenty pounds of cheese a day and there still would be some when he left the White House. So the

egalitarian president announced, just as the TV story went, that anyone visiting could have a piece of cheese. The trouble came because Andrew Jackson was not very easy to get along with and had, as president, made a lot of enemies in town. When they heard about his generous offer, they decided to spoil the gesture. Through word of mouth the invitation for free cheese spread quickly and the next day the lobby of the White House had what was probably the first, and only, politically motivated cheese riot in the august building's history. Several thousand people lined up and pushed into the building. Some carried knives and plates, most cheerfully dug out a piece of cheese with their hands. The crush was so great that Andrew Jackson was forced against a wall. When the rush subsided a few hours later and the doors were closed, Jackson was likely pleased to see that there was still more than enough cheese left for his use.

CLOSING THE OPEN DOOR

For more than a century the door to the White House had been open to anyone who wished to make an appointment to see the president. Every weekday at 12:30, the line of often several hundred people would begin walking though the office of the last president to honor this tradition, Calvin Coolidge. It is strange that the often abrupt and short-spoken president was the final one to observe the custom, but he made a great effort to be present at the meetings, though he often lamented the long-winded nature of his guests. Herbert Hoover ended the practice when he took office in 1929.

FEEL GOOD PRESIDENT

Though, personally, James Monroe was not at all a "feel good" type, his administration benefited from two major trends. The first was the heady feeling that the new nation had stood up to Britain and held its own. It is hard to calculate just how much this added to the sense of national identity, but it established the national optimism that led to Manifest Destiny and the expansion across to the Pacific. The second factor was the economy was booming. Not everything was sweetness and light, there was the 1819 recession scare and some scandals, but the sense that the United States had come of age as a nation changed history.

GOOD PREPARATION

Most of the first presidents went to school at the best universities. Then along came Andrew Jackson. He sprang from an area on the border between the Carolinas that was literally dirt poor. Most of those living in this Waxhaws region were farmers making a living on marginal, rocky land. No one had much money and there was a marked lack of schools. If anyone was trained instead at the school of hard knocks it was Andy Jackson. By the age of fourteen, Andy had already survived a bout of smallpox (yes, his face did have pock marks, but they got left off the portrait on the $20 bill). During the Revolution he had been captured by the British. Worse yet, his mother and two brothers were killed in the conflict. He then went on to become a renowned Indian fighter and to lead some of the toughest frontier men of his age, the Tennessee Riflemen. With such a rough and tumble background, he had little formal education. But it did prepare him for some of the nastiest and most vicious infighting possible: working with Congress. Jackson later studied law—let's just say he was less than studious—and even served as a prosecutor in Tennessee.

FAIR AND SQUARE

While John Quincy Adams accepted a *fait accompli* when General Andrew Jackson sort of accidentally took over Florida while chasing the Seminoles there, the record for biggest land grabber has to be James Polk. The eleventh president got elected by supporting statehood for Texas and this instilled a desire to grab even more Mexican land. As a result, when there was a border dispute over whether the Nueces River or the Rio Grande was the southern boundary of the new state, he ignored the evidence and insisted it be the Rio Grande. To enforce his decision he sent the future president, General Zachary Taylor, with a large body of troops to "protect" the border. Once Taylor's forces crossed the Nueces, they were attacked by Mexican troops, who saw them as invaders. Polk then pressured Congress to declare war on the grounds that American soldiers had been attacked on American soil. They did and, in the war that followed, not only did Polk's government take the land between the Nueces River and the Rio Grande, but also lands that are now most of the states of New Mexico, Arizona, Colorado, Nevada, and California.

Anyone else notice a pattern? Jackson grabs Florida and later is president. Taylor leads another army and takes most of northern Mexico and soon he also becomes president. Maybe the best way to get elected is to invade Canada? Nah, some of 'em speak French.

FIRE FIGHTERS

Things were a bit more casual in Washington and presidents mixed more in everyday life. Two presidents personally helped to fight major fires while in office. The first was John Quincy Adams. The treasury building, not far down Pennsylvania Avenue from the White House, caught fire. Adams organized and directed the bucket brigade that helped fight the fire. When the Congressional Library was burning in 1851, Millard Fillmore joined in as a volunteer to help put out the blaze.

A side note is that this may have been the only time that Fillmore was more successful than Adams. The Treasury Building had to be replaced during the administration of Andrew Jackson, the next president. There was a good deal of dispute over where to put the new Treasury Building, even though plans were complete. Finally, President Jackson got disgusted, poked his cane in the ground, and instructed the workers to put the cornerstone at that location. Unlike Washington and Lincoln, he was not much of a surveyor. They built the new Treasury Building as and where instructed, but the location meant it intruded into Pennsylvania Avenue. Even today, the otherwise straight road is forced to curve around it.

THE ADAMS FAMILY

Charles Francis Adams was appointed by Abraham Lincoln minister to France. It was a time of strained relations, as France was sympathetic to the Confederacy. Charles Adams was a good choice; there was quite a family tradition of holding this particular ministry. Charles's father and grandfather had each also been minister to France, something often overlooked since his dad, John Quincy Adams, and his grandfather, John Adams, both went on to become president.

HANGMAN

There appears to be only one president who is officially recorded as having actually hanged a man. This was Grover Cleveland. The first office that the twice-elected president held was that of sheriff for Buffalo, New York. One of his duties involved presiding and pulling the lever at the hanging of a murderer. Rather than delegate this distasteful duty, Cleveland took it on himself. You have to suppose this means that the murderer also has the distinction of being the only person to be personally hanged by a future president, but he probably would have passed on the honor if asked.

ICEBERG

In today's media age you need to have a great personality to get elected. One errant sigh on national TV can cost you an election. This was not always the case. Few early voters actually had any direct contact with the president except to see him give a speech. Elected in 1889, Benjamin Harrison was the opposite of personable and appealing. In fact, Harrison was generally unpleasant to deal with. Mostly, though, he was unfeeling. His nickname was "The White House Iceberg" based upon the way that he treated nearly everyone. You do have to credit him for being consistent to the end. He even left his own children out of his will.

MARCHING MUSIC

The reception line at many presidential events is quite long and often a strain for a busy president. Generally at such events classical music is played by the Marine Band to lend an air of sophistication and harmony. Whenever President Teddy Roosevelt found the line too long or had something else he needed to do, he would order the Marine Band to play instead a medley of marches. This invariably picked up the pace.

WASHINGTON BULL

While image is amusing today, it is likely most people in 1841 hardly noticed when William Henry Harrison personally drove a cow, which he had just purchased, across the city to the White House. This was an era when most homes provided as much of their own food as possible and the White House was no exception. Since he discovered that they needed a cow, President Harrison went to the livestock market and purchased one. It was a Durham, and the farmer assisted the president in driving the cow through the main streets of Washington to the White House stables. Though he did not drive the animal through the streets, President Taft enjoyed fresh milk and in 1910 allowed a cow to pasture on the White House lawn. This seemed to surprise and amuse foreign dignitaries. There is still a lot of bull traveling through Washington, but this seems to be the last presidential cow to be famous.

WORKAHOLIC

President Grover Cleveland was a firm believer in the Protestant work ethic and, no matter what, endeavored to do each day's work. This meant that on his wedding day he worked until almost 7 p.m. and then emerged for the wedding.

KAISER ROLLED

There is no question that Theodore Roosevelt immensely enjoyed his time at war with the Rough Riders. He often spoke of how he went hand to hand with a Spanish soldier and won. What is less known is that he came very close, and seemingly was quite willing, to start a war between the United States and Germany while he was president.

The reason behind this action is the Monroe Doctrine. Under President Monroe, with the support of the much more powerful England, the United States issued a doctrine that basically told the European nations to keep their hands off the Western Hemisphere. There were exceptions for areas already controlled, such as a number of Caribbean islands and the Guianas, but basically it stated no new incursions were going to be allowed. Almost a century later, the government of Germany was threatening to seize a large portion of Venezuela. The Germans had valid claims against the Venezuelan government, and the Kaiser was getting no satisfaction. The German emperor's stated intention was to hold the lands to guarantee the payment of what was due. The reality was that Germany, having started late as a major European nation, was feeling the need to have a foreign empire like England, France, and even tiny Belgium. They were grabbing or had grabbed areas of Africa and the Pacific islands, and had turned their attention to the Americas.

Teddy Roosevelt heard about the Kaiser's intentions and called the German minister in. He stated that if the German emperor did not call off the invasion of Venezuela and accept arbitration, which he would kindly handle, the president would order Admiral Dewey to the Venezuelan coast to prevent any landings. That would be, in effect, a *casus belli*, a declaration of war between the United States and Germany. Roosevelt gave the Germans ten days to agree.

The minister was said to have been Teutonically outraged and insisted the Kaiser would never accept such a demand. Just to keep the pressure on, seven days later Teddy called the same ambassador in and changed the time limit from three more days to two more days. Again the German ambassador sputtered and protested, but passed on the new deadline. With less than twelve hours left before Dewey sailed, the German ambassador appeared at the White House and briefly stated that the Kaiser had agreed to call off the troops and accept arbitration.

An even less well-known footnote was that, as a likely result of the this confrontation, the German General Staff drew up plans for the German invasion of the United States. It called for a landing in New York City and the gradual expansion of the territory held along the East Coast. This today seems ludicrous, but at that time the German army was one of the largest and best in the world and the American army was small, badly equipped, trained mostly for fighting American Indians, and reliant on state militias to fill out its ranks in the event of a major conflict. Had fifty thousand Germans actually landed, there is no question they could have taken New York City and a number of others. Also, the German fleet was at least as large and modern as the United States' Great White Fleet. Fortunately, the Kaiser's interests turned elsewhere and the German invasion never went beyond planning.

TWENTY-YEAR CURSE

There has been talk of a twenty-year curse on the presidency. Almost everyone has heard that whoever is elected in a year that ends in a zero is doomed to an early death. The first presidents elected on the zero had no problems. Thomas Jefferson lived nineteen more years after leaving office and James Monroe another six years. The pattern *seemed* to have been broken by

Franklin Roosevelt, who made it to his next term, being elected for a fourth time in 1944. But then he *did* die while still in office. Here are the fates of the presidents elected on the twenty-year periods from 1840 to 1960. Fortunately, Ronald Reagan seems to have broken the pattern for good, having been elected in 1980 and lived on many years after his presidency.

Year	President	Fate
1840	Harrison	Died a month into his term
1860	Lincoln	Assassinated during his second term
1880	Garfield	Assassinated
1900	McKinley	Assassinated
1920	Harding	Died in office
1940	FDR	Died in office during his fourth term
1960	Kennedy	Assassinated

BAD DEBT

As a side note, for no reason anyone now can determine, Congress stiffed the New Elberon funeral director the considerable cost of Garfield's funeral. But then, that was just one of three full-scale funerals held for the assassinated president. The bill remains unpaid to this day.

THE OTHER SIDE OF THE COIN

When he was president, Theodore Roosevelt lobbied, unsuccessfully, to have "In God We Trust" removed from U.S. coins. Today we would attribute such an action to activist atheists. But TR's reasons were just the opposite. He felt that having God on currency that was being used to pay for alcohol and even women was blasphemy.

HANGMAN

Abraham Lincoln is remembered as a man who defended minorities and preached mercy. This was often so, but he also approved the largest mass hanging in America's history. The cause of this was an 1862 Sioux attack on settlements in Minnesota. The reason for this attack was that corrupt officials and the distractions of the Civil War meant that the Indians and their families were being literally starved to death. In reaction, they killed more than eight hundred men, women, and children. It took a unit of the Union Army to put down the virtual revolt, and more than three hundred Indians were captured. A military court tried all 307 captives and found them all guilty. Each and every one was condemned to be hanged. The sheer numbers involved attracted the president's attention and he personally reviewed each of the 307 cases. In the end, he commuted all but thirty-eight of the sentences. The remaining captives were consigned to the noose. In front of four thousand spectators in Mankato, Minnesota, they were all hung. So, depending on your view, Abraham Lincoln either saved 269 from the gallows, or allowed the single largest hanging in history to be perpetrated on the starving Sioux.

SECOND TIME AROUND

Of the forty-three presidents, Grover Cleveland has a particular distinction. He was both the twenty-second *and* the twenty-fourth president. Cleveland was first elected in 1884 and again in 1892, the term in between going to Benjamin Harrison. The second time was not a charm. While Cleveland's "less is more" attitude towards government served him well during the relatively placid times of his first tenure, the second time things got more than a bit bad. The United States was hit by a massive depression and doing nothing served Cleveland about as well as it did Hoover forty years later—horribly. You would think Hoover might have studied his history and known better. At least now *you* do.

STRIKE BREAKER

Cal Coolidge was no friend of labor. He often sided with the big companies. By 1923, when Harding died and Coolidge became president, he felt strongly that there had been more than enough reform legislation passed, and it was time for him as the new president to put an end to more. When once asked by Samuel Gompers, leader of the AFL, to help make sure that striking Boston Police officers be hired back, Coolidge replied "There is no right to strike against the public safety by anybody, anywhere, any time." And Coolidge was not alone, as many in the United States felt that by 1924 the government had become unwieldy and top heavy, and the "he who governs least, governs best" attitude made Silent Cal popular. You have to wonder what he would make of today's ungainly federal structure and bureaucracy.

FIRST AND LAST

The marriage between Eleanor Roosevelt and FDR may never have been idyllic. Who is to blame can be debated. The first time the split became public was in 1918. In one of those "oh no" moments, Eleanor discovered the love letters that were still being written between Franklin and his mistress, one Lucy Mercer. She went off on the future president and even threatened to divorce him, which would have crippled his political career, if he did not stop seeing Lucy immediately. Just to make certain he straightened up, FDR's mother, Sara, joined the argument with the threat to cut her son off from the family money if he didn't clean up his act. The result of all this was two-fold. Firstly, FDR broke off with Lucy Mercer and soon replaced her with a new mistress. The second effect was the almost-total emotional alienation between Eleanor and Franklin. It is likely that from that point on the couple were never again physically close. FDR's new mistress, Missy LeHand, remained with him until she died in 1944. FDR then returned to the arms of Lucy Mercer, and was with her at the Calabogie Gardens resort in Georgia when he died. Knowing of Eleanor Roosevelt's antipathy, all traces of Lucy's presence had been removed before the grieving widow arrived.

OTHER SIDE OF THE COIN

Once the marriage between Eleanor and Franklin D. Roosevelt became loveless, both turned to others for companionship. Eleanor developed a very close relationship with a reporter named Lorena Hickok, who moved into the White House, into a bedroom directly across from that of the First Lady. It was well known that they were both emotionally and physically close. But even though Lorena was herself a reporter, there was virtually no mention by any of the papers or radio commentators about the two women. Strange as it may seem to the modern reader, this was due to a gentleman's agreement between presidents and press that kept such things out of the news until the new journalism of the sixties.

AN S BY ANY OTHER NAME

Due to a disagreement on what to name him, Harry S. Truman had no middle name. All the records and his birth certificate have only the letter S. Eventually the dispute over which name the letter stood for was forgotten or ignored. No name was ever assigned to the letter and the S remained undefined all his life.

AIR FORCE FUN

Before there was an Air Force One, President Truman had at his disposal a C4 fitted for travel. The name of this aircraft was Sacred Cow, which would be the name they used when contacting a tower. At one time, Truman was able to cajole the pilot into buzzing the White House. Trouble is, no one radioed ahead to warn the First Family or security staff of what they planned. The result was that when the large aircraft roared low over the building, his wife and daughter were rushed to a safe spot and the Air Force scrambled to intercept the plane they thought had been hijacked by assassins. Fortunately the plane's real occupants were made known before it was shot down.

DRIVING MISS, ER, SOMERSBY

While commanding the Allied Forces in Europe, General Eisenhower was constantly chauffeured around. He was assigned one driver, the very attractive Kay Somersby, whose driving and other skills he seems to have greatly appreciated. She became his permanent driver and by all accounts, including hers, also something much closer.

I LIKE IKE

Dwight Eisenhower was not the only Eisenhower child to go by the nickname "Ike," though he was certainly the best known. Ike, it seems, was a sort of generic nickname used by the entire family, including his five brothers.

ENOUGH SAID

At least *some* of the stories about JFK and Marilyn Monroe were true. Also, according to her, you could throw in Bobby as well. Jealous?

BESTSELLER

The famous and still-selling book by John F. Kennedy, *Profiles in Courage*, was actually his second bestseller. A younger JFK turned his senior thesis into a book entitled *While England Slept*, which was a study of how Britain failed to prepare for World War II. The book was not exactly Pulitzer material, with factual errors and less-than-inspired writing. It was an instant bestseller, but only because his father bought thirty thousand copies that ended up in storage.

MATA HURRY

In the second year of his presidency, John Kennedy was involved for some months with Ellen Rometach. She was the wife of the military attaché at the East German embassy. She was also one of the most expensive prostitutes serving the better class of clients in Washington, D.C. It appears, not very surprisingly, that Ellen Rometach was also working as a spy for the East Germans. When her espionage connection was discovered by Kennedy enemy J. Edgar Hoover, the State Department deported her so quickly that no one was able to question her about any of her high-placed customers, including the president.

TIME OUT

With all his energy, LBJ often had little patience for meetings he did not feel were productive. Loving technological gadgets, he wore a watch that also contained an alarm clock. In meetings, his alarm would go off and the president would hurry out. There were occasional suspicions that those alarms had been set by the president just minutes before going off.

MONO-MONOGRAMS

The entire Johnson family had the same initials, even the daughters. Lady Bird Johnson, Lyndon Baines Johnson, Lucy Baines Johnson, and Lynda Byrd Johnson. All were LBJs. Did the girls get to steal Daddy's monogrammed shirts?

TRUE SUCCESSOR

LBJ was very much the successor of Jack Kennedy in a number of ways. It seems this president, too, was quite a womanizer. Lady Bird and Lyndon slept apart. Lyndon often did not sleep alone. He had two longtime mistresses. One affair lasted, non-exclusively, for twenty-one years. LBJ gave her cars and even a house. Another was a woman who shared his liberal views and bed for upwards of thirty years. But Johnson was almost always looking for a young, well-built conquest. If the president liked them enough, he even brought them back to Washington from Texas. The girls, often totally unqualified, were given make-work jobs during the day and performed their patriotic duty nights. LBJ was a philanderer, but not a complete cad. Once the president tired of one of these young women, he made sure they were sent to a new government position, but one that was far from the White House and his new companion. It seems likely that the hanky-panky was not limited to the presidential suite. Johnson had a buzzer installed in the Oval Office that gave warning when Lady Bird was approaching. If you were president, could you resist doing it there?

THE KING

Nixon acted like he was a king, but not the time he met "The King." One of the most famous presidential photos is a shot of Nixon and Elvis Presley arm in arm and smiling broadly. Elvis collected badges and was there to get the president to give him one for the narcotics feds. To sweeten the offer, just before the photo he presented Richard Nixon with a gold-plated .45-caliber handgun. The ironies here are too many to list, but start with Elvis asking for a badge from the people who arrested drug users.

GERALD FORD WAS NOT A KLUTZ

When in college Gerald Ford played center on scholarship for the University of Michigan. He was not only a team leader, but was also so good at football he was voted one year's most valuable player. The many tales of his being a klutz began in almost a joking manner and took on lives of their own. Part of the reporting may have been a reflection of the dissatisfaction everyone felt when he pardoned Richard Nixon. Another part comes from the fact that President Ford still skied and practiced other sports with enthusiasm. But when he fell while skiing down an advanced slope it made the news. You have to wonder how many other people wiped out skiing that winter day.

HUNK

How about a president who when young was a state athlete and so good looking he was a model in a photo spread on "Beautiful People" for *Look* magazine and on the cover of *Cosmopolitan*? We had one—Gerald Ford.

OUT THERE

While at a Lions Club meeting in 1969, the later-President Jimmy Carter and several others saw a UFO. Carter was sure enough of what he saw—a flying object as bright as that night's moon which flew to within about a third of a mile of where he stood—that he sent in a written report. He is the only president to have reported a UFO. When elected there was some excitement among UFO buffs that he might expose the whole government "cover-up." Why the thirty-ninth president did not was a matter of much speculation and disappointment. We are still waiting for our guided tours of Area 51.

LONG PASS

Jimmy Carter liked his privacy and to get totally away from the job of being president when he returned home for a vacation. He was also very casual and often negative about things military, even though he was himself a naval veteran. Occasionally he took this attitude to a dangerous extreme. There was, and still is, a military officer who escorts the president with a device that resembles a football. That device is the only way the launch codes for nuclear missiles are released in the case of an attack. President Carter did not want the man carrying the launch codes to stay with or near him while he was home in Plains, Georgia. This meant that the football sat ten miles away in Americus, Georgia, every time Jimmy went home. Since the window for a successful retaliation to a Russian first strike was less than the almost fifteen minutes it would have taken to bring the codes to the president, let's all be happy the Russians never pulled the trigger while Jimmy was on break.

BAD TREE

Ronald Reagan did really once state that trees caused eighty percent of the world's pollution. He was quickly corrected and no trees were lost.

STAR POWER

When things feel out of control, people will look in the strangest places for security. Such was the case toward the end of the Reagan Administration. Frightened by the assassination attempt on her husband, Nancy Reagan turned to an astrologer, Joan Quigley, for advice on keeping her husband safe. Very soon White House schedules, event times, even the time at which Air Force One would take off and land, were being dictated by the astrologer. Ms. Quigley's star charts became a major factor in everything the president did. His chief of staff would often peruse the charts to determine when the president would be available to make crucial decisions.

5

GEORGE WASHINGTON

"The Aggregate happiness of society, which is best promoted by the practice of a virtuous policy, is, or ought to be, the end of all government."
George Washington

FIRST IN WAR

The first and only president to muster an army himself and lead it personally was George Washington. This army was not mustered against the British, pirates, Indians, or any other external threat. The purpose of the army was to put down what has since been called the "Whiskey Rebellion." The year was 1791, and the nation had just gotten started. One of the genuine problems Washington faced was to make the United States into a real nation and his administration into a real government. One of the unfortunate side effects of being a government was the need for money. Under Washington the Congress enacted a number of taxes. The trouble was that this close to the American Revolution there was still a lot of bad feeling toward any central government and especially toward new taxes.

The tax that brought this to a head was a seven-cents-per-gallon tax on each gallon of whiskey sold anywhere in the nation. This was wildly unpopular in the counties of western Pennsylvania. The four counties south of Pittsburgh erupted into violence and outright revolt. The homes and offices of the federal tax collectors were attacked and even burned. Hundreds of local whiskey makers simply refused to pay the tax and defied Washington to do anything about it.

In response, the first president sent out a call for volunteers in Virginia, Maryland, and nearby eastern Pennsylvania. The lure of this was great for both those who had served with Washington in the Revolution and those who were too young and could now join up. Over twelve thousand men joined the ranks and were formed into companies. This massive army, Washington at its head for the first six days, then marched toward Pittsburgh. As the president likely expected, the show of force was enough. Those with land or assets realized that this was serious and quickly changed their attitudes. Those who still could not stomach the tax picked up and moved beyond the frontier into Tennessee and Kentucky. Many of their descendants today likely are among those who still refuse to pay whiskey taxes and run moonshine in a family tradition started by Washington's army over two centuries ago.

TOOTHY TALE

George Washington lost his teeth fairly early in life. This was common in the eighteenth century. He wore numerous replacements, none of them wood. No one really used wooden teeth. It just wasn't practical. Wood decays quickly when exposed to the acid of saliva, it has splinters, and it is relatively soft even before rotting in your mouth. Washington's teeth were mostly carved from bone. He may also have worn bone teeth taken from cadavers; ghoulish as this may sound today, it was common practice three hundred years ago. Exotic materials were tried. In those days teeth were made from any animal bone or horn that was large enough to carve, including porcelain. There is a record that Washington used a set of teeth carved from a hippo bone. But hippopotamus bone proved very porous and when the first president imbibed his favorite port wine they were quickly stained black and discarded.

FATHER ONLY OF THE COUNTRY

At the age of seventeen, George Washington was sick simultaneously with both malaria and small pox. There was no way to check either in the eighteenth century, but there is a good chance that the effect of the combined illnesses was to render the future president sterile. While he doted on Martha's children from an earlier marriage, Washington never had any of his own. This, strangely, was one of the reasons everyone considered him the perfect candidate to become the first president. To understand this you have to realize two things. One is that the colonies had just finished a revolution, and it was an era when the rule of kings had a negative reputation. The year Washington was elected saw the beginning of the French Revolution. The second consideration was that there was no real precedent for how the president would act or what the office would be like. When you combine this with the overwhelming popularity Washington enjoyed, there could and would be a concern that the presidency might become a "royal" office held by Washington and passed through his family in the same way the Caesars ruled. "Divine right" was a lot more familiar to most people than "will of the masses."

Because George Washington had no blood descendants, there was no risk of this happening. So his lack of a true heir actually was considered a major plus in the minds of the revolutionaries who were now forming the new government.

THE GREAT PROGRESS

Everyone who has visited the original thirteen colonies has seen more than one "Washington Slept Here" sign. Most of us tend to discount the veracity of these signs due to their sheer number. Actually it is likely that most of them are accurate, for at least one night's stay. As the first president, Washington insightfully believed that a big part of his job was to help solidify into a nation thirteen rival colonies that each had their own government already in place. To do this the people had to think of themselves as citizens of the United States first and of their state second. He did this in a number of ways.

One way was to have a presence in each state. That meant to go to that state and be seen there, meet with the people, the local leaders, the merchants, and let everyone know he was their leader. To do this Washington traveled extensively during his eight years as president. The tradition of a ruler moving around the country was an old one. For hundreds of years kings and queens had made a circuit of their countries, staying with and being hosted by their kingdom's nobles along the way. This could be a very expensive proposition for their host as the royal Progress often included a few hundred nobles, guards, and support personnel who also had to be housed and fed. In fact there are records of where a king or queen was unhappy with a noble and so would show up and cost their temporary host a fortune by simply sticking around for days or even weeks. What the Progress did accomplish was to let people all over the kingdom see that their sovereign was not only aware of them, but had been in their area. Washington used his travels as president for the same purpose, but in a much more friendly way. He traveled with a relatively small retinue and, especially in the smaller towns, often stayed in rooming houses or private homes each night. This meant that over the months he would have gone to a town, met with the people there, and then spent the night in hundreds of locations all over the original states. So when you see those "Slept Here" plaques and wall signs, there is a good chance he did, at least for one night.

HE DID NOT HAVE SEX WITH THAT WOMAN

One of the most intriguing aspects of Washington the man is his relationship with Sally Fairfax. The beautiful Sally Fairfax was the sister-in-law of his half-brother Lawrence Washington. In the interest of promoting Lawrence's interests with the much richer and more prestigious Fairfax family, young George would often visit the Fairfax estate. There he met and befriended an older man named George William. He also became completely enamored with the woman that George William soon married, Sally Fairfax. Eventually George Washington was also married—to Sally's best friend Martha Custis. Martha was a rich and socially important widow, which gave Washington the status and wealth he desired. The two couples often met socially and traveled in the same social circles until about 1773. Although over the years Sally and Washington exchanged many letters, it shows something about his personal sense of honor and high standards that the relationship went no farther. This is not to say that there was no passion, but more that nothing came of it. You get a sense of both the restraint and the depth of feeling from this excerpt from a letter from Washington to Sally:

> Tis true I profess myself a votary to Love. I acknowledge that a Lady is in the case; and, further, I confess that this lady is known to you. Yes, Madam, as well as she is to one who is too sensible of her Charms to deny the Power whose influence he feels and must ever

submit to. . . . You have drawn me, my dear Madam, or rather I have drawn myself, into an honest confession of a Simple Fact. Misconstrue not my meaning, 'tis obvious; doubt it not or expose it. The world has no business to know the object of my love, declared in this manner to—you, when I want to conceal it. One thing above all things, in this World I wish to know, and only one person of your acquaintance can solve me that or guess my meaning—but adieu to this till happier times, if ever I shall see them.

Even many years later his feelings remained, though all through his life Washington remained the faithful and devoted husband of Martha:

> . . . never been able to eradicate from my mind those happy moments, the happiest in my life, which I have enjoyed in your company.

There is a final irony to the story. George William was a Tory and was forced to flee after losing most of his wealth. He planned to return to Virginia after the insurrection was put down, but when Independence occurred instead, like many who had supported the king, he could not and never did return. He died in 1787 and Sally remained alone in England for another twenty-four years.

HE DIDN'T DO IT

Never in his life did George Washington throw a dollar across the Rappahannock River, which runs through Virginia. Nor did he ever cut down a cherry tree and then tell his father he had done it. In the early years, the United States was still finding itself. There was a need for bigger-than-life heroes and the first president was one of these already. Both of these stories appeared in a book, purported to be a biography of George Washington, by Mason Locke Weems. This book, *A History of the Life and Death Virtues and Exploits of General George Washington* (yep, the title was that long), included not only actual stories of Washington's leadership, but also made-up stories used to make him a near mythic figure and role model. The book was a success and since then, when someone thinks of a young Washington, they remember Weems's two stories. That's a pity since he was an ambitious young man who started in the middle class and rose through his own efforts to become the "Father of His Country" after fighting in two wars and leading a revolt against the most powerful empire in the world.

WITH A WHIMPER

After surviving being a surveyor in the wilderness, two wars, Valley Forge, and years of politics, the first president succumbed to a "sore throat" that was really an oedematous affection of the windpipe on December 14, 1799, only three years after leaving office. He might well have survived except for what was done and not done to treat him. At first he did nothing after contracting the illness from being chilled while riding in a snow storm. When the illness got worse the doctors will called in. Because he was important and a public figure, his doctors were particularly aggressive in their efforts. The problem was that, at that point in time, medicine had taken a few wrong turns. First, the doctors bled the ill president four times. Then, the weakened leader was given a concoction of molasses, butter, and vinegar. When he did not improve dramatically, they took the next step and fed him a strong laxative. Washington spent his last hours of life dealing with the effects of that ill-conceived medication. He likely spent most of his last day on earth squatting over the chamber pot, or worse, until his weakened system succumbed not only to the illness, but to the cure.

6

BEFORE AND AFTER

It may or may not be significant that two of our greatest presidents, Washington and Lincoln, were both surveyors when young. This was an extremely challenging position even in Lincoln's day, where the land they surveyed could be lawless frontier or even land claimed by Native Americans who resented their presence. Still, so far surveyors are two for two in producing great presidents.

Of the first thirty presidents (up to Hoover), most were lawyers. Twenty-three of the thirty practiced law or were involved in some way in the legal profession. Four were professionally trained soldiers—Washington (who was also a plantation owner), Grant (who was a very bad businessman), Harrison, and Taylor. Warren Harding ran a newspaper and edited it as well. Woodrow Wilson had been a college president, while Herbert Hoover was a mining engineer. Andrew Johnson started his political career as a tailor. After Hoover, they get harder to classify effectively, since many of the recent presidents were professional officeholders, but not all. Eisenhower was another soldier. Carter a peanut farmer, a distinction always made from farmer since peanut growing is heavily subsidized and regulated and he was really more of a businessman than a man of the soil. Reagan, of course, was an actor and radio announcer.

SENIORITY

The first job future President John Quincy Adams held was at the age of fourteen. He went to Russia to serve as the secretary to the United States minister there. Of course, as the son of the second president, John Adams, he did have a few connections getting the position. From this point, J. Q. Adams was in service to the government for the next sixty-six years. He was still a member of the House of Representatives when he died at age eighty. All that time and there were no government pensions yet.

JUST LIKE A LAWYER?

Benjamin Harrison has the distinction of being one of the least likable and most irritating men to ever hold the office of president. While he could inspire thousands with his speeches, when meeting with individuals one to one, he invariably managed to antagonize them. Even members of his own cabinet were known to go out of their way to avoid meeting with this president. His abrasive conversational style never hurt his career. Not only was he nominated and elected president, but upon leaving office he became one of the most successful lawyers in the nation, earning annually what today would be millions of dollars in fees. Why do I have the sudden urge to do a lawyer joke?

PREACHING TO THE CONGRESS

Certain jobs may better prepare a man to be president than others. James A. Garfield held such a job. He studied at, and eventually became, president of Hiram College near Cleveland, Ohio. During this time he also became an ordained minister in the Church of Christ. It is recorded that his sermons made him a popular preacher at the camp meetings and revivals that were common during his time. Even while president of the United States, Garfield regularly took the opportunity to preach at local churches. Again his eloquence and presentation made him popular and welcome. He also, as is almost expected, had become a lawyer, though he went directly into politics and practiced little law.

NAMESAKES

There is a certain irony in the image of Andrew Jackson on the twenty dollar bill. As a general and president, Jackson wore himself out and spent a good deal of his own money. He left the White House less well-off than when he entered it. Having picked his successor, the popular ex-president spent a few extra weeks in Washington before leaving for Tennessee, enjoying the adulation of the crowds and attending several social events. He also stayed because the roads to Tennessee were difficult. It was very early spring and the former general had never fully recovered from a pistol ball that was lodged in his lungs from being shot in a duel with Charles Dickinson, so he wanted to leave rested. Even after the delay, the weather was atrocious and the journey to his home, the Hermitage, took over a month. When Jackson left Washington he took with him the remaining money he had there, just several hundred dollars. This was diminished along the way, not only by travel expenses but by an honor Andrew Jackson felt he was required to acknowledge. Jackson had been very popular with the people during his two terms, and many babies born at this time were named after the president. Whenever Andy Jackson was presented with one of his namesakes among the crowds that cheered him along the road, he gave the child one of three hundred silver half-dollars he had brought for that very purpose. He often told the mothers the coins were for the baby to "teethe on." By the time he arrived home, the former president was down to under one hundred dollars. Fortunately his plantation was profitable and Jackson was able to rebuild his savings.

SORE LOSER

With Washington, D.C., being the center of the government, it is hardly uncommon for an ex-president to return to the city. But there is one man who made a point of never returning. This was John Adams. Thomas Jefferson defeated Adams's attempt to be reelected and the Founding Father took this very badly. On the morning of his last day as president, March 4, 1801, John Adams woke early and rode out of town. This allowed him to avoid riding in the parade with Jefferson. Adams remained bitter the rest of his life and never once returned to the capital of the nation he helped to form.

BAD DAY

You would think the Fourth of July would be a lucky day for the Founding Fathers. This was certainly not the case for three of the first five presidents. Three former presidents died on July fourth—an amazing coincidence. These were John Adams, Thomas Jefferson, and James Monroe. Two of the presidents who died on the Fourth of July did so on the same day, July 4, 1826. It was the fiftieth anniversary of the signing of the document both men were best known for: the Declaration of Independence. Also coincidentally, all three were key leaders in the American Revolution. Monroe was the last president of the three. He died in 1831. Did some cranky British general curse them, or is it just one of those random timings that litter history?

OLD FRIENDS, SORT OF

No one can make you more angry than your friends. Such was the case with John Adams and Thomas Jefferson. The two men were not only leaders among the Founding Fathers, but worked together on the Declaration of Independence. Thomas Jefferson actually wrote the document and John Adams was its best and most adamant advocate. It was Adams more than anyone else who convinced the representatives of the thirteen colonies to sign what was, at that point, an act of treason.

The problems began when Jefferson was secretary of state and Adams was vice president under George Washington. Things came to a head when Adams ran for reelection in 1800 and Jefferson ran

against him. Adams was outraged, and even more upset when Jefferson won. The two men became enemies and rivals. It did not help that Jefferson succeeded where Adams had failed and won reelection in 1804. What had been a close friendship ended.

It was not until years after both men had left office that mutual friends managed to at least get the two ex-presidents to communicate civilly again. This resulted in an exchange of letters that is fascinating and unique. In 1826, John Adams, living near Boston, was ninety and Jefferson, in Virginia, was eighty-four. Both men were in poor health and knew they were dying. A bit of their old rivalry must have remained, however. Both men hung on, evidently wanting to outlive the other. When John Adams awakened on the Fourth of July he heard cannons being fired in the distance celebrating the anniversary. When asked by a friend if he knew what day it was, the dying Adams correctly said it was the "glorious Fourth." He then went on to add, in a final gesture to their friendship and rivalry, "But my old friend Thomas Jefferson still lives." He died a short time later without knowing he had, in fact, lived longer. Jefferson had died about two hours earlier. But since it took a message much longer than that to travel by horseback between Boston and Washington, D.C., neither knew the time of the other's death, or that they shared the day, the anniversary of their great accomplishment.

GOOD TRAINING
Three presidents were the sons of ministers: Chester A. Arthur, Grover Cleveland, and Woodrow Wilson.

BETTER TRAINING
After decades of dominance by Army officers in the presidency, the U.S. Navy finally came into its own when John F. Kennedy was elected. They were on a roll, and the next four presidents, too, were Navy vets: Johnson, Nixon, Ford, and Carter.

UNDERGRADS?
Nine presidents never went to college. Among them are some of the greatest presidents ever—and Millard Fillmore. The other eight are Washington, Jackson, Van Buren, Taylor (who had no formal education), Lincoln, Andrew Johnson, Cleveland, and Truman.

SECOND TRY
Before John Adams helped write the U.S. Constitution, he wrote the Constitution of the Commonwealth of Massachusetts. Which means that state is operating under a constitution that is even older than that of the nation it is in.

JUST LIKE WITH CONGRESS
If you want to visit a different spot from the others that honor incidents in Abraham Lincoln's life, try the riverbank just below the "Rustic Mill" in New Salem, Illinois. It is on this spot that, in 1831, a young Lincoln ran aground while poling a flatboat of pigs. As part of his 1860 campaign, posters were made showing Lincoln guiding the ship of state, again poling a flatboat, but no squealing pigs this time.

FUNERAL PROCESSION

Abraham Lincoln was, by the end of the Civil War, held very dear by many Americans. When he died from the assassin's gunshot on April 15, 1865, the nation mourned. The Civil War had also marked the beginning of the golden age for train travel. The movement of troops and supplies by train was one of the major reasons the North was victorious. The actual funeral was delayed until April 21, after which the casket was placed on a special train that would take Lincoln to his final resting place in Springfield, Illinois. Also on the train for the same reason was the small casket of his son, Willie, who had died of smallpox in 1862. To bring the president full circle, in a sense, three men who had accompanied Lincoln on his train trip to Washington, D.C., on the way to take office were allowed to accompany the body back as well.

The train ride itself was not very direct. Everyone wanted to say goodbye. The first stop was New York City, where the casket was left open and people walked past all night. The streets around the site were packed all night. Beginning at midnight, a chorus of seventy singers from the German community sang for several hours. The procession to return the beloved president's casket to the train included just about every important politician, organization, and military unit that could get there. At the last minute, a group of two hundred recently freed slaves asked to march as well. They were given a position, though fear that their being in the march might cause a riot meant that they were preceded and followed by strong police units. Not only was there no problem, but in a spirit Lincoln would have approved of, they were applauded in several locations. The entire funeral procession was recorded as taking more than four hours to pass by any one spot.

Every time the funeral train entered a town or city, it was met by large crowds. Often the tracks were lined by those saying goodbye as well. As the train approached each town, the bells were rung and guns fired. The telegraph wired ahead so everyone would know the exact time the train would reach the next black-and-crepe-covered station. Bonfires lined the route of the train every night and even heavy rain failed to prevent thousands from lining the tracks as it passed every day. Eventually the long journey to his final resting place brought Lincoln's casket through Baltimore, Harrisburg, Philadelphia, New York City, Albany, Syracuse, Rochester, Buffalo, Cleveland, Columbus, Indianapolis, Chicago, and hundreds of small towns where the train did not stop. Finally, eighteen days later, now in a less-than-presentable condition, the casket arrived in Springfield, where it remains today beneath a massive and well-visited memorial.

ANOTHER JULY 4 DEATH

On July 4, 1850, there was a long and well-attended ceremony for the laying of the cornerstone of the Washington Monument. It was a typical July day in Washington, D.C.: the heat was intense and the humidity stifling. For hours on end, Zachary Taylor sat under the sun on the open reviewing stand. By the time the ceremony had ended, the former general was near collapse. He was driven back in a buggy to the White House. To recover, Taylor helped himself to large quantities of cool milk and fresh cherries. Five days later, he died. The diagnosis? Cholera, which he may have caught from the cherries and was too weak to fight off. Cholera is spread by contaminated food and has an incubation period of two to three days. Taylor had served just eighteen months of his term as president.

ARLINGTON

Though many presidents have served in the military, only two are buried in the national cemetery at Arlington, Virginia. These are William Howard Taft and John F. Kennedy. The Arlington cemetery was established during the American Civil War on land confiscated from the family of Robert E. Lee.

SWM

With the exception of those whose spouses are still alive, almost every president is buried with his wife. The one exception to this is James Buchanan, who was a lifelong bachelor and is buried alone in Lancaster, Pennsylvania.

BLACKMAIL ATTEMPT

The year is 1876, and this is one of those examples of stupid criminals and not much more adept detectives. A gang of three counterfeiters has been broken up because one of them has been caught and is now in prison. The other two search for a way to get their partner freed. They decide that the best way is to kidnap Abraham Lincoln's body. The plan is to break into the tomb at night when it is unguarded, take Lincoln's casket and body, and then hide it in the Indiana Dunes. They then intend to ask as ransom the freedom of their friend.

Now the stupid crook part. So the twosome search around for an expert at grave robbing to help them. Their inquiries get a response, but it is from a Pinkerton agent *posing* as a grave robber. He agrees to join them and assist. The three all board a train to Springfield, Illinois. Unknown to the counterfeiters, the rest of the train is swarming with Pinkerton agents.

Before the train arrives at the Springfield station, it passes through a train yard and they all get off and hurry to Lincoln's tomb. The tomb and memorial they planned to rob had been completed only two years earlier and dedicated with great fanfare. The two crooks and the agent divide up the duties and split up to get ready. One crook gets the tools, the second cases the tomb (and does not notice the Pinkertons), and the agent is to get a horse and wagon to carry the casket away.

Initially the agent's next job is to be lookout. So he has made plans to light his cigar to alert the other agents to close in and make the arrest. This would be visible on the dark night in the unlit Oak Ridge Cemetery. But as plans tend to, this one doesn't work out. The effort to break loose and lift the coffin is so difficult that the two counterfeiters call the agent in to hold the light. This means the agent is inside the tomb where no one will see his cigar. It isn't until probably several very nervous minutes later that Lincoln's casket is jammed part way out of a window and that the agent is sent to get the wagon. He then lights up and the other Pinkertons close in.

They find the casket, still hanging part way out of the window, but no crooks. It seems the two men are so exhausted from the effort of freeing and moving the large coffin that they have gone outside to cool off and are resting under some nearby bushes. They get away, but not cleanly since the Pinkertons know who they are. A few days later both are captured in Chicago.

The trial also had its comedic aspects. It was discovered that there was no Illinois law against kidnapping a body or grave robbing. And since the two men did not actually manage to take the body, all they could be charged with was breaking the lock on the door to the tomb. For this they got one year in prison each.

COWBOY TRAGEDY

Did you ever wonder why rich and well-educated Teddy Roosevelt ended up in the Badlands as a cowboy? He was not exactly the typical cowboy, most of whom were barely literate and worked long lonely hours for low pay. Teddy was a Harvard graduate, had questionable health, and more wealth than most of the ranchers. The reason he left his comfortable New York existence for life in the open spaces could be a daytime drama or tear-jerking movie. While he had always loved the West and visited it many times, the reason he just up and moved west in 1884 at the age of twenty-six was that on the same day both his beloved wife and his mother died.

NICE TRADITION

On his twenty-first birthday, Jack Kennedy was given the gift of one million dollars by his father. Some say years later his dad bought him a lot of votes as well and it wasn't even his birthday.

BABY BOOMER

The first president who was born after the end of World War II was Bill Clinton. His predecessor, George H. W. Bush, whose reelection he prevented, was old enough to have been a decorated combat pilot and war hero who fought in the Pacific Theater.

INTESTATE

Considering they had attorney generals working for them, there was no excuse for four of the presidents dying without a will. But they did. They were Lincoln, Andrew Johnson, Grant, and Garfield.

INSOLVENT

Four presidents were known to be broke or in debt when they died. They were Jefferson, Monroe, William Henry Harrison, and U. S. Grant. Published after his death, Grant's memoirs did set his widow up for life.

7

THOMAS THE THINK ENGINE

"Never did a prisoner released from his chains feel such relief as I shall upon shaking off the shackles of power."
President Thomas Jefferson

Thomas Jefferson, the third president, was renowned during his age and is even now for being quite a renaissance man. In addition to helping to found the nation and becoming President, Thomas Jefferson was noted as a linguist, author, astronomer, and musician. Jefferson spoke French, German, Spanish, and Greek. His talent for the violin was not as great as his aptitude for politics, but enough to make his playing well worth listening to. He also shared with Benjamin Franklin the distinction of being one of the foremost inventors of his day.

A TOAST

When JFK was speaking at a formal dinner where he was entertaining a gathering of highly esteemed Nobel Prize winners, he welcomed them as the most distinguished gathering of intellectual talent to have been in the White House since Thomas Jefferson dined there alone. Any one of them who was knowledgeable in the history of science would not have protested the comparison and there is no record anyone did.

A FEW FIRSTS

Thomas Jefferson was the first U.S. president to shake hands rather than following the European tradition of bowing. He was the first president to have a grandchild born in the White House. He was the first president to be inaugurated in the city of Washington, D.C.

FOR THE BOOK

In this case, you *can* judge a president by a book's cover. Most of those who knew Thomas Jefferson were sure he was at best an agnostic, or maybe an atheist, in what was still a very religious age. Just about everyone was amazed to find that the former president had made a major effort to create his own, personalized Bible. Thomas Jefferson had cut out sections of the Gospels, mostly the various sayings of Jesus, and pasted them into a blank book. The sayings he collected were those relating to how to treat your fellow man and none of those regarding faith. So was he religious? Probably not in the traditional sense, but the president certainly put great store in Christian values.

AND HIS BOOKS

The United States had a few setbacks during the War of 1812. One of them was a British landing that resulted in the burning of several government buildings in Washington in 1814. At the time, the Library of Congress was being rebuilt, and there was a need for one other component: books.

Thomas Jefferson had spent fifty years putting together one of the most complete and impressive libraries in the Americas. He had spent extensively and the almost six-thousand-five-hundred-book library contained the latest reference, scientific, historical, and philosophical titles. Now retired, Jefferson generously offered to sell the government the books he had spent most of his life accumulating. The offer was quickly accepted and, for just under $24,000, purchased. A short time later, twelve wagonloads of books arrived at the newly finished library building. Even today you can find Thomas Jefferson's personal stamp on many titles in the rare books room.

VINTAGE

Our third president, Thomas Jefferson, was a Virginia aristocrat and preferred to live like one. He made every effort to make the Executive Mansion as comfortable as his elegant home, Monticello, on which he personally had done much of the labor. Among his actions was to bring with him, at his own expense, about a dozen servants, and to have a well-stocked larder and wine cellar. The wine bill for his two terms in office exceeded $10,000, a very large sum for that time.

A NERD?

While unquestionably brilliant and an astute politician, Jefferson was also a bit eccentric. One of his habits, that of greeting foreign emissaries while still wearing his pajamas, rankled the dignity and occasionally seriously upset such distinguished visitors.

HOME SWEAT HOME

Thomas Jefferson took a very direct hand in the construction of his famous mansion, Monticello. He helped to cut the timbers, worked at making the bricks used, helped build the walls, and even supervised the making of the nails used on the plantation. Those whitewashing the presidents will stop there and not add that most of the rest of the labor was performed by his slaves. This was not a small task, the house having a total of thirty-three rooms, including twelve bedrooms and what we would call a "finished" basement, with ten rooms in it. This is a large place for just one widower to live in, even with Sally Hemmings sharing it. But the president entertained and often had his children and grandchildren there to fill the place up. Monticello was also a modern home, even by today's definitions. It made use of solar heating, natural air flows, advanced plumbing, interior shutters for privacy, insulated walls, an attached greenhouse to provide extra warmth from the sun, and many other advances that we are just rediscovering as energy prices rise.

NOT ALL HIS SWEAT

In his first draft of the Declaration of Independence, Thomas Jefferson included a scathing attack on the institution of slavery. In order to ensure the Southern states' support, that part was later deleted. Jefferson was verbally a staunch opponent of slavery. Yet all his life, including when he was writing the Declaration of Independence, he was also a slave *owner*. Which leads to one question: Was he guilty of hypocrisy? Even after Jefferson retired from the presidency, Monticello was one of the largest slave-operated estates in the entire nation. But Jefferson, for what it is worth, tried to be as humane as possible and freed several. Due to financial problems during his later years, Jefferson died over $100,000 in debt. His estate made up some of the debt by selling off all of Monticello's slaves.

A STREET CAR NAMED JEFFERSON

Every time you get on a bus or streetcar and the doors fold open, you are looking at something that was modeled on plans created by Thomas Jefferson. Those doors you use every day take their basic design from an idea that Jefferson had two hundred years ago. Most of the third president's inventions were of a practical nature. He invented a highly efficient letter copying press, both a swivel and a folding chair, a hemp machine that broke apart the fibers so that hemp could be used to make cloth and paper, and one of the first folding ladders. It wasn't just here that Jefferson's genius was acknowledged. He created a plow that took first prize at the Paris Exposition and that is the ancestor of the modern plow in use today.

Thomas Jefferson liked to turn to science to solve problems. He liked long walks and often wondered how far they took him. To find out, he invented a pedometer. He had an interest in weather and not only kept records to look for patterns, but when he built Monticello he included a cunningly placed weather vane that could be seen from both inside and outside the mansion. As an amateur astronomer, he was able to calculate correctly the date and time of an eclipse and built one of the first telescopes to be used in the United States.

PLAIN MONEY

It was Thomas Jefferson, striving for mathematical simplicity, who devised our decimal system of dimes and dollars so that the arithmetic of money would be easy to calculate. The British monetary system of this period, like most European systems, was much more complicated, having evolved over a long period and often combining several earlier systems.

PEN PAL

Thomas Jefferson was an inveterate letter writer. Before the days of telegraph or phones, this was the only way to keep in contact. Letters by the president and Founding Father are fairly common in the collector's market for one reason: it is estimated that over his lifetime Jefferson wrote and sent around twenty-five thousand letters. Of course, keeping up with what he said and promised in such a massive volume of correspondence was also a challenge. The inventor Jefferson triumphed here with a letter press that made copies of his letters before they were sent. These were kept on file and could be referred to when necessary. The bulk of the letters were sent after Jefferson retired to his estate of Monticello. He considered it a point of honor to answer every letter he received. Beyond friends, statesmen, scientists, and those wanting favors, the former president often received correspondence whose main purpose was simply to get a letter and, as a result, an autograph back. Jefferson never used a secretary and every one of the thousands of letters was written by hand.

SINGULAR HONOR

Thomas Jefferson is the only U.S. vice president who was next elected president who was also voted into a second term as president.

TOP HOST

After his long career serving the United States as congressman, senator, vice president, president, and diplomat to a foreign nation, Thomas Jefferson finally retired to Monticello. There he became the consummate host, entertaining in great style until it hurt. When Jefferson retired, he was a fairly rich man. Monticello had a dozen bedrooms and it was rare, except when the weather closed the roads, for any of them to be unoccupied. Not only did old friends often visit, but many "new friends" also appeared at his door. Few were ever turned away. Some wanted to share some of the founding father's glory, others were sincere friends and supporters, but a number were there simply to take advantage of the proud and generous former president. After years of being the most hospitable host in Virginia, the financial strain took its toll. The final straw was when Jefferson cosigned a note for what was then the very large sum of $20,000. The friend he had signed for defaulted and Jefferson had to use most of his remaining funds to pay off the debt. Fortunately, Thomas Jefferson also had many true friends who rallied to help him financially. Without their help it is likely the genius of Monticello would have died in poverty. Instead, with his hospitality toned down a good deal, he remained comfortable in his mansion for the rest of his years.

HE DID HAVE SEX WITH THAT WOMAN

Thomas Jefferson was single at the time his close friend John Walker was sent to New York, several hard travel days away, to negotiate a treaty. It appears that the future president took his promise to take care of the very beautiful Betsy Walker a bit too literally. They were discreet and only years later did an outraged John Walker find out about the couple's indiscretions.

In a later day, Thomas Jefferson would have been called a "Bohemian" for his free thinking and free love attitudes. (You have to wonder if he learned them from Ben Franklin, whose exploits were notorious even in his day.) While a widower in Paris as the U.S. minister to France, he was seen to actively pursue, but probably without success, a married woman named Maria Cosway. At one point, showing off while strolling, the young Jefferson jumped over a fence—and promptly broke his wrist. All his life Thomas Jefferson called himself a "natural philosopher" when asked about religion. It seems this fit with his philosophy of doing what comes natural, even if the other woman was married.

UNIVERSITY OF VIRGINIA

When you are as dynamic as Thomas Jefferson a little thing like retirement, or being eighty-two in an era when men normally died in their fifties, doesn't slow you down. At that late age he decided to establish a university For most people, this would involve chairing a committee and hiring lots of specialists, but not Thomas Jefferson. He sited the school in Charlottesville, only four miles from Monticello. This made it easy for him to do much of the work himself. The former president supervised virtually all of the construction, making suggestions regularly. If the weather was too rough for him to make the buggy ride, Jefferson would use his telescope to watch the work from his home. He also played a large part in the design of the buildings and layout of the campus. Some of the campus features, such as the serpentine wall, are considered architectural masterpieces. Even starting at that age, Jefferson lived to see the campus of the University of Virginia finished and filled with students. He took great pride in the school and his central role in its creation. He also often enjoyed hosting students at Monticello and dispensing his unquestioned wisdom to them.

SPY GAME

We sometimes read about attachés at embassies actually being spies. In the good old days it was often the ambassador himself. Such was the case with Thomas Jefferson while minister to France. This was a period also when agriculture was the main source of wealth for most of the world. This meant that a superior plant or new crop was as much a state asset as high-tech computer chips can be today. Jefferson was himself a landowner and as a result was always on the lookout for something that would help America's farmers. He found one such plant in the south of France. There he came across a form of rice that was generally considered superior to that being grown in the United States at the time. The problem was that it was being eaten and preferred in southern France, but came from Italy.

This Italian rice was also considered a state secret in Lombardy, the part of Italy closest to France that grew it. But this did not deter Thomas Jefferson, who literally stuffed his pockets with the seeds. He later hired a mule driver to smuggle bags of seeds into France, from which point Jefferson could send them on to America. His efforts worked. The new Italian rice was a hit and is still grown today under several names.

THE BIG SCANDAL

It all started in 1802. Thomas Jefferson was president, and presidents make enemies. This one was named James Thomson Callender. As revenge for Jefferson and his party attacking him in the papers, Callender publicized the relationship, to be polite, between Thomas Jefferson and one of his slaves. The slave was Sally Hemmings, who was likely also the half-sister of Jefferson's deceased wife. There is nothing like a good scandal to catch the eye of the American public, then or now. This one was a doozy and has appeared and reappeared for over two centuries. Just recently there was a new burst of interest when the descendants of Sally Hemmings all applied to join a society whose membership requirement is that you be descended from Thomas Jefferson. DNA evidence has proven at least one, if not five, of Sally Hemmings' children had been fathered by Jefferson.

One of the reasons the decades-long affair raised such a furor was that it involved one of the more embarrassing aspects of slavery, the sexual exploitation of the slaves. It was a constant, but rarely discussed, part of the slave-holding culture. The even less discussed side of this was that if you had sex with a slave and she had a child, you would end up owning your own son or daughter as a slave and a slave that was of mixed race, referred to then as a mulatto, at that. So what they had was the forbidden combined with the unspoken.

When Martha Jefferson died, Thomas Jefferson was only forty-eight. But that made him considerably older than the seventeen-year-old Sally Hemmings. Their affair is known to have continued off and on until he died thirty-three years later. It was surprising that even in his will Jefferson freed five of his slaves, but not Sally Hemmings. Only later did Martha Randolph, Jefferson's daughter who inherited her, set her free.

TOMBSTONE

The following was written before his death by Thomas Jefferson to be inscribed on his tombstone:

Here was buried
Thomas Jefferson
Author of the Declaration of Independence
of the Statute of Virginia for Religious Freedom
& Father of the University of Virginia

Now that is an impressive list of accomplishments, but did you notice what he left out? How about being president of the United States?

8

PRESIDENTS AS PEOPLE

Studying the men who have been president gives a certain perspective. Among the many benefits is that you realize that some of the men who led the United States were brilliant while a surprising number were incompetent, others were clinically depressed, and a few apparently didn't care. Yet despite all this, the nation has gone on and prospered. This can be most reassuring while watching the candidates gyrate on TV as they try to get elected.

NOT READY FOR GQ

President James Monroe was very proud of having fought in the Revolution. He was wounded and decorated. Perhaps this was why while president he always wore the same style of clothes he had worn forty years earlier. To get the equivalent picture, imagine the current president wearing a gold chain, paisley, and a Nehru jacket. The cocked hat Monroe wore had been out of style for decades, as were his coats and breeches.

JAMES MONROE
1817–1825

PROUD TO SERVE

After he had been president, some of John Quincy Adams's colleagues chastised him for "demeaning" himself by returning to the Congress as a representative. His reply was to state that no man could be degraded by serving the people. He was sitting in the House of Representatives when he collapsed while working at his desk, at the age of eighty. Adams died two days later. A small plaque commemorates the location, which is in today's Statuary Hall. If you visit, the exact point where the bronze plate sits is also on a "whisper spot"—where a soft word can be heard clearly at another focus spot across the room, but not a few feet away.

BEQUEST

In 1826 James Smithson, an Englishman and scientist, fascinated by the new country, left to the U.S. government a substantial bequest (a lot of money) expressly for the "increase and diffusion of knowledge." Now, any government can always find a use for more money, but John Quincy Adams spent years passionately defending the fund and fending off attempts to raid it. He succeeded, and eventually all the money was used to found the Smithsonian Institution. Yes, our national museums were started with a gift from the British.

"P" AND THAT STANDS FOR POOL

After eight years of the presidency of "Old Hickory" Andrew Jackson, maybe the nation was just not ready for the abrupt change in style that came with his hand-picked successor, Martin Van Buren. Where Jackson had been used to frontier living, and rather left the White House reflecting this, the next president was a polished sophisticate with tastes to match. While personal friends with his predecessor, Van Buren found the condition of the White House to be unsuitable as both his home and the residence of a national leader. Almost the day after entering office, the eighth president began remodeling. He quickly convinced Congress to give him $27,000 to pay for repairs, new furniture, and decorations. (That would be would be $648,000 in 2007 dollars.) Many people were just not ready for serious elegance. They raised a cry over the fact that the cut glass and china to be used at state banquets was imported. Another complaint was the fact that a "foreign" chef now cooked the presidential meals. The silverware became a specific target with a barrage of accusations stating that Van Buren ate with a "golden spoon," which was what such autocrats as the czar of Russia used. But the final straw that everyone agreed illustrated the decadence of the new president was that fact that he included in the new furnishings a billiard table. Martin Van Buren did not take the criticism lightly or well. Too many times in the first year of his administration did a guest return to Ohio or Tennessee with quickly-printed tales of the president's extravagance. During the later part of his term, only select friends were invited into the White House and state receptions were kept to a minimum. Even though this all happened almost two centuries ago, doesn't it sound very much like something that would happen today?

AS A HOUSEKEEPER, ZACHARY TAYLOR WAS A GOOD GENERAL

President Zachary Taylor was a field general in an era when that meant rough living on the edge of the wilderness. Both he and his wife were much more comfortable in a fort than at the White House. So they basically treated the Executive Mansion as if it were part of a frontier fort. Zachary smoked and chewed. Mostly he spit tobacco and rarely hit the spittoon, if he even tried. The First Lady chain-smoked a pipe, and not always with the smoothest tobaccos. When you add to that the dirt—Washington still had mostly dirt roads—and the general lack of consideration for the building and its furniture, you have one awful mess. The carpets were stained, many beyond hope, and the walls coated with smoke and dirt. Many of the former presidents had used several pieces of their own furniture to fill out the White House rooms, often leaving them upon departing. The Taylors, having learned to live light on the frontier and at army posts, had none to move in. They entertained less, perhaps for obvious reasons, than most presidents and had little interest or incentive to keep the mansion up. When Millard Fillmore moved in, he found the White House was a serious "fixer upper." Beyond stains, dirt, and rooms used as stalls, there was little furniture and most of it was unsalvageable, and the Blue Room floor was completely covered with straw. It took weeks to render the building what the Fillmores considered habitable and even then the place was a mess. Rotting tobacco juice smells strongly. The new president's father, a man of almost eighty, once visited and departed much earlier than planned. When asked why not stay longer he responded, "No, no, I will go. I don't like it here. It isn't a good place to live. It ain't a good place for Millard either. I wish he was at home in Buffalo." Considering how undistinguished Millard Fillmore's presidency was, maybe he should have listened to Dad.

JOB SECURITY

At one time in 1880, due to being elected while still holding a previous office, James Garfield was simultaneously a member of the Ohio House of Representatives, senator-elect from Ohio, and president-elect. Perhaps there was a politician shortage in Ohio that year?

THE GREAT PRESIDENTIAL YARD SALE

The whole thing began because Chester A. Arthur had become president after Garfield's death. The real cause was the fact that the two presidents were very different men. President Garfield was, to be kind, less than a good housekeeper. Under Garfield, and to a lesser degree the earlier presidents, the White House had been more used and abused than maintained. The carpets were soiled, the furniture worn and stained, and even the inside walls covered with smoke stains and mold. Beyond this, the

storage areas of the White House were packed with discards
and boxes going back to the Madison presidency. A few of the
items were valuable, but most were simply junk that the departing presidents did not feel were worth taking with them when
they left office. President Arthur was a scrupulous man who
had high standards of both cleanliness and presentability in a
residence. He chose to stay in his own home until the White
House could be cleaned and new furniture provided. The process eventually included the removal of enough boxes, furniture, and old clothing to fill twenty-four wagons.

Everything was then offered for bid at an open auction. Many
items were simply trash, but others ranged from trivial to authentic
pieces of history. No matter, everything must go, and it did. Items
sold included pants and a tall silk hat that belonged to Lincoln, the
rat trap which caught a rat that once ate part of a pair of Lincoln's
pants, an elaborate and well-carved sideboard that the Woman's
Christian Temperance Union had given to President Hayes. The

irony of that last sale is that the sideboard was bought by a prominent saloon owner who used it in his Washington establishment. Fortunately, being so placed it was unlikely any of the original contributors ever saw it stacked high with liquor and wines. Historians swarmed over the items. The last time such White House items had been offered to the public was under Buchanan and there was never another sale like it. Prices were high and bidding strong. A total of three thousand dollars was raised by the White House rummage auction, a considerable sum for the day. Even the rat trap sold for a relatively large amount.

LEFT OVER VACATION DAYS

If President George W. Bush is setting a record the for most days off while president, James K. Polk has the record for the opposite. In the times before air conditioning, Washington, D.C., was virtually uninhabitable during the hot summer months. Not very long before, the city had been just a swamp, and the humidity that environment generated still remains. But Polk had a work ethic that just would not quit. He was the first president to stay in Washington, D.C., and continue working during the summer. In fact, over his four-year term he was out of the city no more than a total of six weeks. Isn't that about how long President Bush was on his ranch last year?

PRESIDENTIAL PARLOR TRICK

It is hard to determine exactly why he developed the skill, but James Garfield could simultaneously write in Latin with one hand and Greek with the other. He developed the skill while a "classics man" in college. I wonder if there was extra credit?

RUNAWAY

In the nineteenth century it was still common for an apprentice to sign himself into servitude in exchange for the support and training of the master. Such was the case for the often maligned and hapless seventeenth president, Andrew Johnson. At one point he found such a life in North Carolina unbearable and became a poor and homeless runaway apprentice.

JUST SHOP TALK

Before he ran for office, the self-made and self-educated Andrew Johnson was a tailor. It was more than just a job to the seventeenth president. In fact, considering the muddle he made of being president, you could speculate he remembered his days as a tailor as the good times. He was, it was said, a very good tailor. Even when he was president, Andrew Johnson simply could not walk by a tailor shop. If he happened to pass by one, he would drop in and talk shop with the owner and staff. While serving as governor of Tennessee, Andrew Johnson personally made a suit for the governor of Kentucky. That governor had once been a blacksmith and returned the favor by sending Governor Johnson a shovel and tongs he had made. So, all in all, when you examine the presidency of Andrew Johnson, it is safe to say that as a president he was a good tailor.

GOOD OL' PREZ

Grover Cleveland had a tendency to do, and overdo, anything he enjoyed. Chief among his interests were food and beer. While he disliked exercise, he knew he needed more and eventually took an avid interest in hunting and fishing. A sign of his enthusiasm was the name he gave his hunting rifle, which he called "Death and Destruction."

GROVER CLEVELAND
1885–1889, 1893–1897

BAD LUCK

For a modern leader known for being progressive, Franklin Delano Roosevelt was surprisingly superstitious. He held strongly to the World War I superstition that three on a match was bad luck. The reality of this was that in the trenches during World War I each side had snipers who watched across no-man's-land for targets on the other side. It took time to find and aim at a light or movement. The time it took was normally about the same time as it took to pass a lit match to a third smoker. While meaningless for a president, as a rule and not a superstition it made sense in that specific situation. Roosevelt also refused to sit down to any meal that had thirteen people at the table. In fact he was a triskaidekaphobic who feared and disliked the number thirteen. He refused to start a trip on any Friday, or do much of anything on a Friday the thirteenth. Only once was his no Fridays travel rule broken; under the circumstances, he could not object. The funeral train carrying FDR's body from Georgia to Washington, D.C., started its journey on a Friday the thirteenth.

SHADES OF BILL

Warren Harding's wife virtually put him in office. She was a woman of iron will and immense determination. The "Duchess" ran first his newspaper and then his campaign in 1920. She may have had another motive for having her husband run for office. It seems that, on a personal level, the Hardings were not very close. In fact, by the time he was president, they kept apart most of the time, including nights. For years before the presidential campaign, Warren Harding had been having a fairly public affair with one Carrie Fulton Phillips. Once he was running for president, that relationship had the potential for causing serious harm. When you combine this with the fact that the Duchess was actually the one running the campaign, it is not surprising that Carrie and her husband suddenly found themselves on a world tour. A tour whose expenses were all paid by the Republican Party.

But the Duchess's effort gave her only temporary respite. Once in office, Warren Harding developed a relationship with the much-younger Nan Briton. Great efforts were made to avoid suspicion or being seen by the Duchess. In what may be, but probably isn't, another first for Harding, he used his body guards to sneak his mistress into the White House. They were under orders to make sure that, at all costs, Harding's wife didn't see or suspect anything. In 1919, Nan Briton bore Harding a daughter, Elizabeth Christian, but he died before ever seeing the child.

If large parts of the above sound familiar, then just substitute Bill and Hillary for Warren and the Duchess. Bet you didn't realize Monica was just part of presidential tradition.

COOL HAND MCKINLEY

Shaking hands is one of those things that presidents have to suffer through. There is a certain prestige to having shaken the national leader's hand. Perhaps this goes back to when the king's touch was thought to cure disease. In any case, the desire and demand for a presidential handshake became even more strident after photographers were able to take a picture of the event. The out and out champion presidential handshaker has to be William McKinley, the twenty-fifth president. The last president of the nineteenth century was clocked at shaking an amazing two thousand five hundred hands per hour. This is not to say other presidents were slackers. The next president, Theodore Roosevelt, was recorded as having shaken hands with 8,100 New Year's Day White House visitors in 1902. In 1906, this number was still around 8,000 on a single New Year's Day. His personal best was the astonishing and hand wrenching total of shaking the hands of 8,513 New Year's visitors in 1907. Such handshaking extravaganzas often lasted all day and left the president's hand sore, though the show of support was surely gratifying.

TESTED IN BATTLE

Although he was a civil engineer, and a good one, and not a soldier, Herbert Hoover saw his share of conflict. In June 1900, Herbert and his wife, Lou, were in Tientsin when the Boxer

Rebellion broke out. He and several hundred other foreigners were trapped in one small part of the city. The incident was made into a hit movie titled *55 Days in Peking* starring Charlton Heston. Heston didn't play Hoover, but the future president had a vital part in the defense and survival of the enclave.

Herbert was in charge of food and supplies; Lou had the much more dangerous task of bringing supplies to the men defending the front lines of the besieged foreign quarter. This brought her under fire several times. Once, her tire was shot out. Another time she was thought lost and the Peking paper printed her obituary. Her reaction was to be thrilled that they had given her death three whole columns in that day's newspaper.

HUMANITARIAN

In America we remember Herbert Hoover as a failed president who was unable to slow or prevent the Great Depression. But Herbert Hoover is remembered very differently in Europe. During World War I, after making sure all American civilians were safely out of the war zone as a favor to the American consul general in France, he took charge of the program to provide food and necessities to the war-ravaged nations of Europe. Hoover personally ran the gauntlet of mined and submarine-infested waters forty times while crossing the North Sea and the English Channel while supervising the massive relief effort. Because of his program millions of British and French children and adults were saved from starvation.

BLUE RIBBON FOR BLUE LANGUAGE

Not since Andrew Jackson had there been as profane a president in the White House as Harry Truman. His down-to-earth language and occasional outbursts were renowned among those who worked with him. When told FDR had chosen him to be his vice president (being elected was virtually assured), his less-than-diplomatic response was "Tell him to go to hell." He later agreed. For a while he likely held the record for the president with the bluest language, but twenty years later the Nixon tapes left no question that the thirty-seventh president far exceeded in bad language even the most notorious efforts of Harry Truman. But not even the earthy Nixon could match Truman for obscene eloquence. President Nixon's use of racial epithets and constant use on his tapes of vulgar and obscene terms to describe anyone he disliked or distrusted, which was just about everyone, set a very high standard for disgustingly low speech.

LOCAL TRAFFIC LAWS

The LBJ Ranch was a big spread, even for Texas. Lyndon Johnson often drove himself when entertaining important visitors and the road that was, in essence, his driveway ran a good distance. Occasionally these rides could be quite an experience. Since he was effectively the law on his ranch, Johnson was known to drive at speeds up to ninety miles per hour with one hand on the wheel and a cup of scotch in the other. If that didn't shake up his guests enough, LBJ had another trick. He owned one of the world's few amphibious cars. But the vehicle looked only a little different from a normal vehicle. Johnson would take the guest he wished to terrify on a ride around the ranch in it and, when near a lake, would seem to lose control. Most guests panicked as they hit the water, which sent the president into fits of laughter.

THE LBJ TREATMENT

Lyndon Baines Johnson was one of the most determinedly energetic men to ever serve as president. When he was pursuing some legislation, the president could literally be tireless and seem—to those he wanted something from—sleepless. He would pursue his targets relentlessly and anywhere. LBJ was known to follow a man into the men's room to harangue him for his vote. Multiple late-night calls were common and there seemed to be little regard for time. If there was a major vote near, it was no surprise to many legislators if their phone rang at 3 a.m. and the president was on the line. The whole process was called by Beltway insiders the "LBJ Treatment" and it worked.

THE RIGHT SPOT

Having been from the South, well, Texas, and very socially aware, Lyndon Johnson was very conscious of the historic importance of the Voting Rights Act. He chose to have the signing ceremony for this law in the President's Room of the Capitol. In doing, so he was remembering another bill signed in that room on a similar subject more than a century earlier. Also signed in the exact same spot by Abraham Lincoln was the Emancipation Proclamation.

EGO

Perhaps nothing shows the massive egotism that eventually crippled the Nixon presidency more than two choices he made. One of these choices literally cost him the job. That was that, until subpoenaed, the White House tapes which eventually provided virtually all of the evidence that led to Richard Nixon's resignation were his personal property. As such he could have tossed a match in the storage room and likely never have been personally linked to Watergate by proof. But Nixon felt that the taped records of his Oval Office meetings were too important historically to destroy. Ironically, he was right, but for the wrong reason.

While in office, President Nixon decided he wanted a uniform for the White House police force that reflected his position. He personally designed their new uniforms that were a gaudy combination of gold trim, high-brimmed hats, and embroidery. When the new look was previewed, just about everyone but Nixon immediately realized they were so ostentatious that a banana republic dictator would find them embarrassing. The uniforms, which were already finished, did not go to waste. Somewhere in Iowa is a very well-dressed high school band that benefited from that particular burst of egotism.

NOT ALONE

While Richard Nixon won the popular vote in a landslide victory over George McGovern, he was never actually popular. There was something, and we found out what in the Watergate hearings, that just didn't let you trust the man. Even Eisenhower, who twice made him his vice president, had a negative opinion.

Truman:	"Nixon is a tricky, goddamned liar and people know it." So true.
Ike:	"This man will never be president. The people don't like him." Ooops, wrong twice.
Kissinger:	"The most dangerous of all the men running, to have as a president." Good judge of character wasn't he?
JFK:	"If I have done nothing else for this country, I've saved them from Dick Nixon." Well, delayed anyhow.

On one level, these quotes show just how unlikable and distrusted Tricky Dick was. On another, they show just how good a politician he was to overcome such antipathy and twice be elected president.

A TRUE MOVIE BUFF

Both Ronald Reagan and the First Lady, Nancy, were big movie fans. Sometimes the movies even affected his real world decisions. One of the Great Communicator's boldest offers was to guarantee the balance of power (or terror) by allowing the Russians access to the technology of his Star Wars anti-missile program. General Colin Powell has said that Reagan got the idea of sharing the program from the Michael Rennie character in *The Day the Earth Stood Still*.

SEARCHING FOR ONE GOOD MAN

If you have tired at this point of hearing about promiscuous presidents, then skip to the next entry. It seems that George H. W. Bush may not have been above following in the shoes of FDR, Kennedy, and Johnson when it came to sex in the White House. Close associates have confirmed (off the record) that the first President Bush did indeed have a number of affairs, including one with his secretary Jennifer Fitzgerald. It was that rumored affair that was lampooned in the movie *Dave*. But it is important to add that there has never been any proof of these rumors and you have to suppose that a wise man would have thought carefully before crossing the both greatly loved and formidable Barbara Bush.

KENNEDY'S SUCCESSOR

Bill Clinton liked to think and act as the true successor to JFK. The problem was one thing the two men shared was a near-addictive need for sex. Most certainly, Monica Lewinsky was a passing relationship compared to Bill Clinton's twenty-five-year arrangement with a lawyer named Dolly Kyle. Like Kennedy, the forty-second president seemed to have a need for constant intimacy with a wide range of women. And also like Kennedy and LBJ, he was willing to use his office, first as governor of Arkansas and later president, to seduce or aid others in procuring women to have sex with him. But there is one difference. The press consciously gave JFK, LBJ, and those who were president before a pass. This was not the case with Bill Clinton. One thing to also remember, a presidential affair is not illegal. What Clinton was lambasted and nearly impeached for was lying under oath about the affair, not the affair itself.

DRIVING DRUNK

Richard Nixon was known by his staff to occasionally get totally blitzed. The fact was that Dick Nixon was a cheap drunk and even a few wines could cause him to slur his words. Even if drunk, he would always exercise his presidential authority. There were several incidents where a sloshed Nixon would have caused worldwide destruction if his drunken commands had been actually obeyed. Once while drunk, when the North Koreans shot down one of our spy planes, he ordered preparations for a nuclear attack. Since just getting the missiles out would likely have started World War III, it is a good thing he staff recognized his condition and ignored the order.

DRIVING MISS

Driving a car in Kennebunkport, Maine, can be hazardous to your political career. Now, this is not referring to the infamous time that Ted Kennedy ran a car off a bridge and killed his companion. It seems that in 1976, future President George W. Bush was stopped there for driving while intoxicated, was fined, and lost his license over the incident. This was later brought up as part of the attacks on candidate George W. Bush's character, but the attacks never got any traction. At the age of forty, the president had sworn off all alcohol and appears to have stuck with that promise.

WHO'S QUOTE?

This should sound familiar: "With riches have come inexcusable waste. We . . . have not stopped to conserve the exceeding bounty of nature. . . . We have been proud of our industrial achievements, but we have not hereto stopped thoughtfully enough to count the human cost." This is not a quote from Al Gore's latest ecological diatribe, but is taken from Woodrow Wilson's inaugural address given in 1913, almost a century ago!

LATE NIGHTS

Woodrow Wilson was another of those workaholic presidents. He put in long hours and was at his desk late most nights. Wilson made less use of staff compared to a modern president in that he drafted most of own his speeches, press releases, and important letters. He did this first in shorthand and then transcribed his own notes using a typewriter.

9

GRANT ME THIS

"My failures have been errors in judgment, not intent"
U. S. Grant

U. S. Grant's first name was not Ulysses. He was born Hiram Ulysses Grant. He had always disliked his first name of Hiram so when he signed up at West Point he used his middle name, Ulysses, and his mother's maiden name, Simpson. The ploy worked and he was always recognized and known by his chosen name after the change.

Ulysses Grant was by no definition one of the most important or effective presidents. He was in his way a colorful figure and in another way the embodiment of the American dream. He overcame failure in business, leaving the military under a cloud to return eventually as the commander of the Army of the Potomac, and then president of the United States. We have all heard of him, as Jim West's boss on the TV show and movie *Wild Wild West* if nothing else, but much of what you think you know about the man is likely wrong.

HE WHAT?

Okay let's start with a bit of a shocker. At one time, Grant bought and owned a slave. The slave's name was William Jones and he was thirty-five when purchased. Grant lived in Missouri, where slavery was legal. This happened only two years before the Civil

War. There are some records that show the future president was not very comfortable with the arrangement. Even though he was hurting for money, rather than sell William Jones off, Grant chose to free him in less than a year.

This was not the only time U. S. Grant owned slaves. His wife, Julia Dent, was from a Southern, slave-holding family. Since slaves were legal in Missouri at that time, she brought three of the family slaves with her when she moved into Grant's house. Again, he was not happy with the arrangement and eventually convinced her to return the three slaves to her family. Incidentally, most of her family was loyal to the Confederacy, causing Grant no end of trouble by giving ammunition to his political opponents and jealous generals.

WOOZY

There is good reason to believe that the general who ordered tens of thousands of men to their deaths could not personally deal with the sight of blood. The roots of this may lie in his childhood. Grant's father was a tanner. This meant that in his youth the future general and president was constantly exposed to newly cut and bloody hides. While serving in Mexico, U. S. Grant attended a bullfight and was so sickened by the blood that he left early. It has always been traditional that the commanding general tour hospitals after a battle to thank the wounded for their sacrifice. The Civil War was a particularly nasty period for such visits and the amputation of limbs was perhaps the most common surgery performed. Grant often had trouble visiting the hospitals and rarely lingered, even though he always had great concern for his men. A final note on blood went to the president's taste in meat: he insisted that his steaks be served only well done.

MISS JULIA

Julia Grant, often referred to as "Mrs. G" by her husband, was cross-eyed. She is the only First Lady to have been such. He was always most concerned with her well-being and how she suffered from his lack of financial acumen.

SKIN OF HIS TEETH
Grant was pushed into the spotlight because of his victory in capturing the well-defended city of Vicksburg. During that siege, he had more problems than just military ones. At one point, by mistake, a servant threw assorted garbage—and the future president's false teeth—into the Mississippi.

A PRESIDENT BY ANY OTHER NAME . . .
When he, reluctantly, attended West Point and his middle name was recorded incorrectly, he never bothered to change it. After being given a newspaper with a headline calling him "U. S. Grant," he saw the PR value and continued to use the incorrect "S." He never formally changed his middle name, though he was such a popular war hero (in the North anyhow) that no one cared.

EVERYONE IS A CRITIC
Even as president, Grant was not much for music. He may well have had a "tin ear" and echoed Admiral Nelson when he commented, "I only know two tunes. One of them is 'Yankee Doodle' and the other isn't." (For Nelson it was "God Save the King" and not.)

TIPPLER
Everyone has heard that Grant was a heavy drinker. Actually, records and his associates' memoirs show just the opposite. He was never a heavy drinker, though at one point early in his career he did have a problem with drinking. The root of that problem was not the quantity of alcohol that Ulysses Grant consumed. Basically it was because, as a young army officer, the future president was a cheap drunk. He could not hold

his liquor and was affected by a surprisingly small number of drinks. The rumors all stem from a time when young Grant, while stationed at Fort Humboldt, allowed himself a drink or two at the wrong time. He was found to be inebriated while on duty as the paymaster. Since this job involved handling large sums of money in an army that was kept poor by Congress, it was a serious offense. Grant was forced to resign his commission. This is what later led to rumors about General Grant being drunk or drinking while in command. These rumors were mostly spread by his political enemies and had no basis in truth. In fact, there is good evidence he didn't drink at all, or very rarely, during the war.

There is not a single record that Lincoln actually once said to find out what brand of whiskey Grant drank so he could send it to his other generals. There are records of similar sarcastic remarks dating back at least to the ancient Greeks.

BUT NOT THEM (OR THE IRISH)

As an officer Grant may well have been a bit anti-Semitic. While he had no trouble working with Jewish officers, he once issued an order regarding sutlers who sold goods to the troops that began, "The Jews, as a class violating every regulation of the trade established by the Treasury Department and also department orders, are hereby expelled from the department within twenty-four hours from the receipt of this order." The support of the Jewish community and the materials they provided to the army were considered vital and the order was blocked from Washington before it could be implemented. There are no records of his taking any anti-Semitic actions while he was U.S. president.

ANTI-WAR VOTE

What you might find to be another surprise is that Grant, in 1860, did not support nor did he vote for Abraham Lincoln.

Grant had served in the Mexican-American War and knew firsthand the horrors of battle. Like many soldiers, Grant did not want to see his country torn apart by war. He voted for Stephen Douglas, a Democrat who ran on a platform of compromise between the free and slave states—and warned Lincoln that he had done so when offered the command of the Army of the Potomac.

COST OF LIVING . . . IN THE WHITE HOUSE

President Grant received one of the larger pay raises for the era while in office. In 1873, his official salary was raised from $25,000 to $50,000. For the day, this was a very substantial amount, but in those days the president was expected to entertain and pay many of the White House expenses out of his own pocket.

AND THE HORSE HE RODE IN ON

President Ulysses Grant has the distinction of being the last president to receive a speeding ticket in the federal District of Columbia. The president loved fast horses and always had several stabled at the White House. He also may have been an average cadet academically, but held the record for high jumps while at West Point. It seems that after the war a number of new police officers were trained, many of them black. The new recruits took the laws seriously, so when a man sped through the city in his open carriage, he was stopped for going at an excessive rate. The man was President Grant, who accepted the ticket and complimented the officer for his diligence. He put up a $20 deposit, but did not show up for court and no one said anything. Hey, he was the president, and therefore both the judge and the officer's boss in the federal territory of Washington, D.C.

DEFICIT SPENDING

There are renaissance men who can be successful in business, as national leaders, soldiers, and even scientists. But these are rare and far between. President Grant was not one of these men. To give him credit, he was a great general and, despite the general impression, a competent president. What he never, ever was good at was finance or business. Before returning to the Army, U. S. Grant managed to fail miserably at several businesses. He left the army to become the eighteenth president and serve two terms. Once he retired from the presidency, old habits and problems returned. Among other things, Grant was roped into a fraud involving a New York City investment company. This was one of those pyramid schemes where the early investors, such as Grant, are paid dividends that are actually just some of the money gained from later investors. Many of those investors were wooed by the former president being one as well. Thinking all was well, Grant thought nothing when the head of the company appeared at his door in Spring of 1884 and asked the former president's help in raising a large sum, about $150,000, quickly. Grant went to William H. Vanderbilt and signed a note for the whole amount. He never saw that man or a penny of his money again. The whole scam collapsed with the man running the company and all the money gone. Grant was now on the hook for the massive loan to pay off Vanderbilt and had a total of $80 in his personal accounts. He soon did not have enough money even to pay his bills. To pay off the loan, as he felt honor required, Grant gave Vanderbilt all his real estate and personal belongings, even including the ceremonial swords and other memorabilia given him by the grateful government and citizens. In a desperate effort to recover from his spiraling debt, the former general wrote his own memoirs of the Civil War and presidency. Published after his death, the book was a bestseller and allowed the Civil War hero's widow to live her remaining years in cautious solvency.

FINAL BEQUEST

Ulysses Grant was one of the worst businessmen ever to occupy the White House. After resigning his commission, Grant failed

as both a farmer and then as a dry goods merchant. This was long before the day of presidential pensions and office allowances. Grant died broke and in debt.

In many other ways, Ulysses Grant was a very classy man. His presidency, mostly due to his trusting some of the worst thieves in the government's history (and that takes a lot!), is not remembered well by historians. But he was popular with the voters and the men who had served under him during the Civil War. When Grant was caught up in the bank scam described earlier, he knew many of the investors had been taken because they had trusted anything he was involved in. His efforts to even partially compensate those who had suffered left him insolvent. It was at about this time that Sam Clemens (who wrote as Mark Twain) approached Grant and offered him a very good royalty if he would write his autobiography. Now U. S. Grant was not a stylish writer, but his straightforward prose style and the numerous stories he could relate about not only the major political figures of his day but also about the men who fought the Civil War with and against him made the book fascinating and a good read even today.

But the Union general and president's literary success was not without its inherent tragedy. While working on the book and living very simply, Grant began to notice a sharp pain in his mouth. When the pain persisted he went to a doctor and received the shocking news that it was cancer. Further examination showed that the cancer had reached a point where there was no hope that nineteenth-century medicine could cure it. With the cancer growing and his death imminent, Grant continued to write. He was determined to complete the book and hoped he could provide for his widow in death better than he often had in life. For a while, he continued to dictate to a secretary, but as the cancer spread, his voice failed. Even then he continued writing out his remembrances. Soon Grant was so weak he could only sit up and write in short spurts. But the determined general was true to form and he completed the book as promised. A week later Grant was dead.

While he never lived to see the book published, you have to assume he would be very pleased. It became an instant bestseller and continued to sell well for years. Thanks to the high royalty rate and the book's popularity, the book earned over half a million dollars. This would be more than ten million dollars today and was more money than the leading general of the Civil War and two-term president had earned during his entire lifetime.

10

DIGNITY, ALWAYS DIGNITY

*A*t times you have to give into the temptation to have a serious belly laugh at something a past president has done or said. Certainly they have presented many opportunities, just ask the writers of *Saturday Night Live* for whom modern presidents have unintentionally provided a bounty of material weekly. Somehow, even after looking at every presidential pratfall and pimple, you come away with an amazing regard for the office and even the men who hold it.

SETTING THE STANDARD

When George Washington became the first president, there were no guidelines as to how to act or how he should be treated. The closest examples anyone had were the kings and queens in Europe, and that did not sit well with anyone. After all, we had just fought a revolution to get rid of arbitrary rule. Few cared that the arbitrary actions came more from the British parliament than the king; he supported it (when sane). The quandary was that, while the people did not want anyone to act, well, *royally*, they did want someone who would be given the respect a head of state of a major nation deserved.

We owe a lot of the more egalitarian aspects of the presidency to Washington and his political allies. For a start, the name. Many in the Senate wanted the official way to address the U.S. president to be "His Highness" or even, in the tradition of naming all of a king's titles, the rather large mouthful of "His Highness, the President of the United States of America, and the Protector of Their Liberties." But George Washington preferred "Mister President" and this prevailed. He also set a pattern of talking to the people. This again was not the standard for either the king or the prime minister of England.

MARKED SUCCESS

There are those historians and scholars who say that one of the first president's greatest accomplishments was that he succeeded in keeping Alexander Hamilton and Thomas Jefferson from killing each other. This is not as frivolous a comment as it seems. You have to remember that not only did the men often disagree vehemently and on a basic level about a wide range of important issues, but that both were also competitive, very intelligent, and well-spoken. When you add to this the fact that duels were still being fought, then you see just how much the steady hand of Washington achieved. Though each normally respected the other, Jefferson once accused Alexander Hamilton of misusing public funds while Treasury Secretary under Washington. It was investigated and Hamilton was acquitted. Even though Hamilton was influential in Jefferson eventually becoming president, most of the time they just did not play well together and it was only the diplomatic skill of George Washington that allowed the young nation to have the services of both men.

THE WINNER

There were a lot of ways to maintain your dignity in early America. One of the more popular routes was the duel. Gentlemen dueled over honor, women, and perceived slights. Since the occasional outcome of these duels was the death of one or both parties, you would think they would be officially disapproved of. This was hardly the case back then. Andrew Jackson fought many duels. His skill with sword and pistol is shown by the fact that he survived them all. When anyone made a disparaging remark about his deceased wife, Andy was quick to the challenge. His noted skill almost always meant a rapid retraction and apology. Back then, the president could shoot it out with a senator who mouthed off; today you can't even smoke in the cloakroom. Certainly the recent presidents would probably see a time when you could shoot your opponents as the good old days.

THE DUEL OF THE CENTURY

Most of us have heard something about the infamous duel between Aaron Burr and Alexander Hamilton. What we often don't realize was that it was the direct result of a presidential election. Burr and Hamilton went way back. They had once been law partners in New York City. Where Hamilton was constantly considered a statesman and leader, Burr at first had a very hard time getting elected to anything. Finally Burr was appointed attorney general of New York and parleyed that into being elected U.S. Senator. He also built up what was the first

of many patronage machines in New York City. Hamilton by this time was serving in the national government under Washington. Along comes the election of 1800. Now, at this time the Electoral College had a lot more latitude. Primaries hadn't been invented yet and even when state legislatures sent electors with instructions, these rarely extended beyond the first few votes. This often left the electors free to indulge in old-fashioned deal-making and that was the case in 1800.

It was more or less agreed that the Democratic ticket would be Jefferson as president and Aaron Burr, a tribute to the fact that his New York machine virtually guaranteed them the election, as vice president. The procedure in those days was that the person with the most votes from the Electoral College was president and the runner up became vice president. But in this election there was a hitch. Both Thomas Jefferson and Aaron Burr received exactly seventy-three votes. They tied. And since they already did not like each other, neither man was willing to concede the one vote needed by the other to become president. The other political force involved was Alexander Hamilton, who had used his influence to support Jefferson, whom he respected, if often disagreed with. Thomas Jefferson was elected the third president of the United States and Aaron Burr became the vice president, whose duties were pretty well restricted to flooring motions and voting in case of ties in the Senate. Burr blamed Hamilton for his loss to Jefferson and was aggressively antagonistic to the Founding Father from then on. The famed duel took place in 1804. Alexander Hamilton was wounded and died the next day. Aaron Burr was accused in 1807 of a plot to cause and take advantage of a war with Spain, and while acquitted, he left the United States for Europe. There he tried to convince the British government to support him in creating a revolution against Spain in Mexico and was eventually thrown out of that nation. He traveled to Sweden, Denmark, and Germany before ending up in Paris. No one was interested in financing his revolution, not even Napoleon. He ran out of money in Paris and could not even get back to New York City. When he finally did get to leave it was on a French ship that was promptly captured by the Royal Navy. Burr spent the better part of a year in Britain before finally being allowed to return to New York City and his law practice.

COLORFUL

When you become president and you are like Andrew Jackson as a youth or even a grown man, this makes you colorful and mischievous. Otherwise, there is the opinion of many of his contemporaries in Washington and elsewhere that he was just a little bit crazy. While a law student, he and his buds decided to destroy the inn they were getting drunk in. They proceeded to first destroy all the glassware, then started on the furniture, and finally torched the building. Colorful. One time, when asked to organize a ball for his dance school (required if you wanted to be a gentleman), Jackson did a great job, except for the part where he invited two of the town's more notorious whores. As a prosecutor, his patience was also limited. It is on record that he once picked up a piece of wood and knocked out a tax dodger he was prosecuting. In 1813, General Jackson was in Nashville when he met one Thomas Benton in the street. Benton had been bad mouthing Jackson for having the bad judgment of allowing his younger brother to duel another officer. Jackson set onto Benton with a whip, and the brawl exploded into a real battle featuring knives and guns. The fight tore up the first floor of a hotel and Jackson received two bullet wounds, one of which nearly cost him his arm. When you add to all this his numerous duels, which he professed to really enjoy, and two terms as the seventh president, you get colorful. And I'll bet you thought Bill Clinton was a little wild.

THE ALIEN AND SEDITION ACTS

The current spate of laws intended to increase national security is not the first such attempt at the expense of individual rights.

The first was back at the very beginning of the United States when John Adams was the second president. One of the reasons that the man who wrote the Constitution and should have known better promoted and signed laws that made it illegal to criticize the new country, either verbally or in print, was his ongoing rivalry with Thomas Jefferson. It seems that during a scandal later known as the XYZ Affair, France's foreign minister tried to bribe a team of American envoys. Somehow it appeared to Adams that Jefferson was involved and could even be working, while vice president, for the French. So he signed some stringent laws that made all of the post-9/11 acts look mild. Thomas Jefferson repealed them when he became president.

JUST PLAIN CRANKY

If you have the impression from other sections of this book that John Adams, the revered author of the Constitution and the second president, was a bit hard to get along with, you are correct. Here is how some of his contemporaries described Adams:

" . . . vain, irritable, and a bad calculator of the force and the probable effect of the motives which govern men." —Thomas Jefferson, whom you must remember had a long running feud with his predecessor

" . . . a certain irritability which has sometimes thrown you off your guard." —Abigail Adams to her husband

" . . . sometimes absolutely mad." —Ben Franklin

When James Henry was fired as Secretary of War, he went on to say that he thought the president was "actually insane."

CLEANING OUT THE CABINET

James Monroe was a man of strong opinions and decisive action. When his Secretary of the Treasury went too far in disagreeing with the president, he chased the man from the White House using a pair of heavy fire tongs.

NOT ONE OF US

The people of the United States adored Andrew Jackson as one of their own. He, too, saw himself as a man of the people. He was less well-received by the society of aristocratic Washington, D.C. One of Jackson's favorite past times, sitting under a White House tree and smoking his pipe, tended to outrage those who drank tea correctly. His interest in horse racing, cockfights, and just about any competitive sport, also set him apart. His impatience with protocol and ceremonies regularly offended those who put great store in them. Regardless of these differences with the Washington elite, or even perhaps because of them, Jackson was reelected in 1832 and served two terms.

DON'T YOU WISH

In the first decades of the republic, things were more personal. Those looking for a federal position often met directly with the president to state their case and ask for the job. This could be tiring, and occasionally dangerous, as most of the time the president would have to say no. Such was the case with Andrew Jackson. An office-seeker, refused the position he wanted, reached across and twisted the president's nose.

NOT IN GQ

Perhaps the worst-dressed president ever was Zachary Taylor. The first presidents had all come from the colonial upper classes and maintained a high standard of apparel. Even homespun Andrew Jackson dressed reasonably well. But Zachary Taylor was simply and totally unconcerned with his personal dress. He often sported clothes that were worn, even torn and patched, if they were comfortable. He wore a broad-brimmed hat made of woven palmetto leaves, and in his choice of what to wear held little regard for color or style. On more than one occasion, he was mistaken for a farmer because of his rough clothes and casual nature.

NOT THE STEREOTYPE

There is an image we measure our presidents against. This is a statesman with youthful zest, graying hair, and the impression of gravitas. Zachary Taylor was perhaps not only the worst-dressed president ever but also the least presidential in physical appearance. Taylor had a thick body but thin arms and legs. His face was permanently tanned to the shade of leather and to a similar consistency from his years in the elements while serving in the army. His legs also were bowed and so short that he was, while an excellent rider once on the horse, unable to mount it without assistance. With his long arms and short legs, it was inevitable that the twelfth president's political enemies and cartoonists often compared him to an ape.

OPPOSITION

If the twelfth president was perhaps the ugliest man to hold that office, then the thirteenth president made up for it. When Taylor died in the second year of his term, Millard Fillmore became president. As presidents go, Fillmore was rather a bust, but he did look the part. Queen Victoria once commented he was the handsomest man she had ever seen.

DEGREE OF HUMILITY

Millard Fillmore was a self-educated man. Two years after being president, he traveled to Britain. At Oxford University, as is their tradition with visiting heads of state, Fillmore was offered an honorary degree. He turned down this prestigious offer by saying "no man should, in my judgment, accept a degree he cannot read." Oxford degrees are written in Latin.

DUFFERS

Ulysses S. Grant was dragged to the golf course by a friend who wanted to interest the president in the (even then) trendy sport. He agreed, after being told that the game was good exercise. On the first tee, the party stood and watch a beginning golfer swinging away with no effect. Grant was heard to observe, "That does look like good exercise, but what is the little white ball for?"

Golf is game that respects no office. It wasn't until 1968, in Palm Springs, that fanatic golfer Dwight D. Eisenhower finally got a hole in one. We are sure his secret service agents, who had followed him around for hundreds of rounds of golf, cheered loudly.

NO SECRET SERVICE YET

John Quincy Adams's son on occasion acted as a sort of assistant to his father. He had a longstanding feud with a Washington newspaper editor named Russell Jarvis. (No he was not at the *Washington Post*!) Regardless of how his son felt about the editor, President Adams felt required to invite Jarvis to some of the White House receptions. At one of these, the editor was publicly insulted by the president's son. Remember, this is still the era when duels were fought. Presumably to avoid conflict with the father, Russell Jarvis reacted little at the time. But a short time later, Jarvis made a point of meeting young John inside the Capitol building while the young man was on his way to deliver a message to Congress. He slapped the president's son, embarrassing and annoying the young man. His father, too, was upset and a Congressional investigation ensued. No report or conclusion was ever brought to Congress, which was most likely happy not being further involved.

WHERE WAS THAT SECRET SERVICE AGAIN?

The White House is normally considered fairly secure, but this wasn't always so. Security could be quite lax in the first years. Once, when attending a reception held at the White House by President

John Quincy Adams, General Winfield Scott had his pocket picked. The thief seems to have escaped, at least there is no record he was apprehended, and he got away with eight hundred dollars of the general's money. That's over $50,000 by today's standards.

VACATION

At one time during his presidency, John Adams became angry at his own party, Congress, and nearly everyone else. He decided he'd had enough and simply stopped functioning as president. For three months, the nation ran itself with no one acting in the top office. And you thought those two-week Texas ranch vacations were a first?

PRESIDENTIAL NICKNAMES

Most presidential nicknames refer to something the man had done. There was, especially in the first years of the republic, a much greater tendency to assign nicknames. Even today, most soldiers have some name for their commanders, even the ones who became commander in chief.

President Washington: "The Old Fox," "Father of Our Country"
> The first refers to Washington's skill at out-foxing the British as a general. And yes, they used the father nickname while he was still alive.

John Adams: "His Rotundity," the "Duke of Braintree"
> Neither of these is friendly. The Rotundity nickname came when, as VP, Adams cast the tie vote determining that the official address would be Mr. President and not something much more flamboyant and noble-sounding. Those losing resented the tie-breaking votes Adams cast on this and other matters, and the way he ran the Senate.

Jefferson: "Sage of Monticello"
> And he was...

Madison: "Father of the Constitution"
Say no more.

Monroe: "Last Cocked Hat"
Monroe liked to recall the days when he fought in the Revolution. He was a true war hero and tended to dress as he had in 1776, including in the completely-out-of-style tricorn hat.

J. Q. Adams: "Old Man Eloquent"
John Quincy Adams was one of the best spoken and most intellectual pesidents of all time.

Jackson: "Old Hickory" by his friends and "King Andrew the First" by his many political opponents.

Van Buren: "The Little Magician," "Little Van," "Old Kinderhook"
"The Magician" referred to his ability to get men elected, including Andrew Jackson. "Little Van" was also respectful, as he was physically small. His enemies often called him "Martin Van Ruin."

W. H. Harrison: He was the "Tippecanoe" of "Tippecanoe and Tyler too."
This referred to a famous battle against Indians he won as commander. Those less friendly referred to him as "Old Granny."

Tyler: "And Tyler too."
He was the first vice president to succeed to the presidency when Harrison died very early in his term. Opponents, some of whom rejected the concept that the vice president should even replace a lost president for the rest of his term (the law was vague, succession laws really weren't fixed for almost another century) called him "His Accidency."

Polk: "Young Hickory"
He was really best known for his mullet hair style.

Taylor: "Old Rough and Ready"
Referring to his military career.

Fillmore: Another "His Accidency," for the same unfriendly reasons.

Pierce: "Old Hickory of the Granite Hills"
Everyone wanted to be thought of as being like Andy Jackson; none were. A Northerner with Southern sympathies, Pierce managed to antagonize just about everyone.

Buchanan: "Ten Cent Jimmy," "Old Buck"
A successful trial lawyer and a totally ineffective president, there is a good chance most of what he was called in Washington can't be printed here. The Ten Cents refers to a vote-buying scandal. They were cheaper in those days.

Lincoln: "Honest Abe"
Well, sort of. He was a consummate politician as well as statesman. Also "The Great Emancipator." Confederates often likened him to an ape during the war.

A. Johnson: "King Andy," "Sir Veto"
He was as unpopular as these sound.

Grant: "Useless Grant," "The Hero of Appomattox"
"Useless Grant" to his enemies, "The Hero of Appomattox" to his many supporters. During the war he was "Unconditional Surrender" Grant due to a typo in a newspaper headline.

Hayes: "Rutherfraud Hayes," "His Fraudulency"
He actually lost the popular vote by over 250,000 votes and his enemies never let anyone forget it. Hmmm, sounds familiar. . . .

Garfield: "The Preacher"
Deeply religious and a minister, he often did preach on Sundays while president. Popular, his lingering death after being shot made him the "Martyr President."

Arthur: "Elegant Arthur"

This referred to the fact that Chester A. Arthur was a clothes horse and took great efforts to dress fashionably. His elegant lifestyle also earned him the sobriquet "Prince Arthur."

Cleveland: "His Obstinacy," "Buffalo Hangman"

Cleveland is our only president who personally hanged a man.

B. Harrison: "Little Ben," "The White House Iceberg"

This guy was cold and not very personable. He even cut his children out of his will. After four years of him, the nation went back and elected Grover Cleveland to be president again.

McKinley: His supporters called him the "Idol of Ohio," where they loved him and had elected him to several offices; his enemies normally used "Wobbly Willy."

T. Roosevelt: "Hero of San Juan Hill," "The Bull Moose," but most people just affectionately called him "TR."

Taft: "Big Bill"

What else can you say about a three-hundred-plus pound president?

Wilson: "The Schoolmaster"

This was more a reference to his style than his background as the former president of Princeton University.

Harding: "Wobbly Warren"

He was personable, pleasant, popular, and endearing. The "Wobbly" refers to the fact that Harding was also way above his Peter Principle position and was often taken advantage of by less-than-well-meaning politicians and outright scoundrels.

Coolidge: "Silent Cal"

He rarely spoke and did so in concise terms. At one time, a guest at the White House came upon the notoriously reticent president and announced that he had a bet that he could get Calvin Coolidge to say more than two words. The president answered simply "You lose" and walked away.

Hoover: "The Great Engineer"

Before he was elected president, Herbert Hoover was a very successful engineer and businessman. He had built up a personal fortune of over a million dollars by age forty. That would be fourteen million today. This was admired in good time. When the Great Depression hit, the shantytowns were called Hoovervilles and he, for some very good reasons, got much of the blame for the economic collapse. After that, few cared how good an engineer he was.

F. D. Roosevelt: "FDR," "The New Dealer"

The New Deal was the name given the series of economic policies Roosevelt introduced to end the Depression.

Truman: "Give 'em Hell Harry," the "Haberdasher"

The first referred to his tendency to use profanity. Until Nixon, he held the potty mouth presidential record.

Eisenhower: "Ike"

When you command the armies in Europe and win, "Ike" is all you need.

Kennedy: "JFK," "Jack"

Not imaginative names, but people related to him personally and that is what "Jack" showed.

L. B. Johnson: "LBJ," "Big Daddy"

People did not relate to LBJ personally; by the end, few even liked him.

Nixon: "Tricky Dick"

With that nickname, you can't say we weren't warned. The nickname came from his very dubious, but successful, campaign practices while running for Congress in California.

Ford: "Jerry"

Carter: "Jimmy"

Reagan: "Dutch," his boyhood nickname; "The Gipper," from his movie part of that name; "The Great Communicator"

> Ronald Reagan was better able to use his skills to rally the masses than almost any other president in the nation's history. His popularity is reflected in the fact that he is the first modern president with non-derogatory, real nicknames.

G. H. W. Bush: "Poppy," a rarely used family name.

Clinton: "Bubba," "Slick Willy," the "Comeback Kid"

> He had nicknames, but not positive ones except maybe "Comeback Kid," a tribute to his political talents.

G. W. Bush: "W," "Dubya," "Junior"

11

BODY POLITIC

Everyone is interested in the president's health. It now appears that most of the time we knew very little about any problems a president might have had. Today, with modern media, we can all take an interest in the president's health, something that once was only the concern of the vice president and the First Lady. So let's take a look at the presidents, short, tall, wild, and wounded.

IN SHAPE

President John Quincy Adams was a health nut. If ever there was a man for whom health clubs would have been nirvana, he was it. The sixth president believed that ice cold baths made his system stronger. After his bath, he would scrub himself with a horsehair brush. We use horsehair brushes to scrape rust off metal. Even while president, he would walk up to six miles each day. For a long time, like Monroe, he would swim nude, but once John Quincy Adams discovered how much harder swimming fully dressed was, he changed to doing that. All this exercise may have been good for this president's health, but getting to it nearly killed him. While rowing across the Potomac River to his chosen swimming spot, John Quincy Adams and a servant were caught in a sudden storm. The river was wide and churned by the weather. The light canoe they were in sank and both men barely made it ashore.

DUCK!

Future President James Monroe was wounded in the Battle of Trenton, a victory which likely saved the American Revolution. Of all the presidents who served in the armed services, only four—James Monroe, Rutherford B. Hayes, Jack Kennedy, and George H. W. Bush—were wounded while serving. James Monroe fought in several battles, some under the Marquis de Lafayette, during the American Revolution. He carried a bullet from that war in his shoulder for the rest of his life.

LONGEVITY

The average person in 1800 lived to about the age of fifty. Thomas Jefferson added another three decades to this total. He by no means took it easy and was known to work very long hours all his life. It appears that the secret of living to an old age for Thomas Jefferson was cold foot baths. He plunged his feet into cold water every morning for almost sixty years and to this attributed his longevity. There has to be an easier way.

THE COST

Since James Polk was the youngest president at the time that he took office in 1845, you would have thought his youthful vigor would protect him from the physical price most presidents pay due to stress and long hours. But even at forty-nine, President Polk managed to put in so much time and work such long days, often eighteen to twenty hours, that the cost to his health

was obvious even before the end of his term. You could even say that he worked himself to death. Only a few months after leaving office, former President Polk developed an intestinal ailment. Normally, the problem would not have been fatal, but the relatively young man's system was still so worn down that he died from it.

POLITICAL FIRST

Before the election of William Henry Harrison, actually *campaigning* to get elected when running for a major office, particularly president, was just not done. Andrew Jackson's mechanisms aside, you let others speak for you and get the vote out while the candidate appeared to the public to be "standing," not running, for office. Under the tutelage of Henry Clay, this changed and Harrison was the first man to actively campaign to be elected president. That this worked was evident, since he won and became the ninth president in 1841. Harrison also died from illness only a month after taking office. Still, his success meant that every candidate since has "run" for the presidency. So while you wonder who to blame for the interminable commercials on every TV channel, at least some your anger should be addressed to William Henry Harrison and Henry Clay's Whig Party for starting the entire months-long campaign circus.

BAD CHOICE OF WORDS

The speech William Henry Harrison gave at his inaugural had many of the right words—just too many of them. The newly elected president gave the longest address ever, lasting an hour and three-quarters. Also, to prove how robust he was, or some such macho silliness, the new president shunned the warm and sensible garb that everyone else wore and chose not to wear a coat or gloves. Within a few days, he was ill and his system weakened. He seemed to recover, but never really did. A few weeks later, Harrison was unable to attend a cabinet meeting; he was suffering from chills and other symptoms. He was then subjected to the "medicine" of his era which consisted of treatments that would get you imprisoned if you used them today. His weakened body succumbed to illness and abuse on April 4, 1841. The nation avidly followed the news of his illness and mourned his loss.

PAYING THE PRICE

Andrew Jackson, the seventh president, was known for his robust health and energy while leading troops. But by the time he was in his second term as president, the hard living, many wounds, and bad habits had taken their toll. Today, the news media covers every aspect of the president's health, whether it's a small clot or an irregular heartbeat. But the list of illnesses Jackson suffered from was never publicly known. These included aches from numerous wounds, persistent headaches (some speculate he had frontal lobe damage), regularly occurring diarrhea, coughing spells that brought up quantities of material from his lungs, extremities swollen so badly he could not walk, and finally, rotting teeth. To keep going in spite of all these problems, the old general regularly imbibed alcoholic "tonics," along with smoking constantly. But Old Hickory really was that tough, he lived nine years after serving two terms as president, dying at the age of seventy-eight.

BIG TIME

The president is said to be most powerful individual in the world; one of them was a big man by any definition. William Howard Taft. The twenty-seventh President stood about six feet tall and weighed in at a hefty three hundred forty pounds. Once when he wired to Elihu Root that he had just taken a twenty-five-mile horseback ride, the secretary of state wired back only the query "How is the horse?" Strangely, Taft never really wanted to be president and wasn't very happy with the job. Later, when appointed Chief Justice of the Supreme Court, he publicly declared with glee, "In my present life I don't remember that I ever was president."

PLEASE BE SEATED

When the very large William Taft was offered the "Chair of Law" at Yale he did not take it. When asked why, he replied that "a Sofa of Law" would have fit someone his size better.

SMALL TIME

With all the comments about Napoleon complexes and the image of the bantyweight, Ross Perot, it is surprising that there have really been very few short and small presidents. Without question, the shortest president was James Madison. Never healthy, he had to quit Princeton due to major health problems and was never really that fit. As a result, when not being president of the United States, Madison lived with his father most of his life and rarely engaged in any activity that earned him an income, except when elected. The fourth president was five foot four inches and weighed less than a hundred pounds. Despite his small stature and sickly nature, James Madison lived to the age of eighty-five. He was, incidentally, two inches shorter than another famously short person of his day— Napoleon Bonaparte.

SLOW STARTER

Though he grew into one of the most macho presidents and generals the nation ever had, Andrew Jackson got off to a physically tough start as he was known for drooling and slobbering into his teen years.

STARTING POSITION

Until the last century it was much more common to be born at home than in a hospital. From what records can be found, it is likely that no president was born in a hospital until Jimmy Carter was delivered at Wise Hospital in his later famous hometown of Plains, Georgia.

GREEN ROOM

One of the delights of the White House in the dark first years of the American Civil War was the presence of Willie Lincoln. The happy child brought a smile and solace to the beleaguered president during the war's darkest days. Young Willie was popular with the staff and enjoyed playing in the various rooms of the executive mansion. He was also popular with the troops and accompanied his father to many military reviews. In 1862, Willie was stricken by smallpox and died at the age of eleven. Abraham Lincoln, upon his death, observed, "My poor boy. He was too good for this earth. God has called him home. I know that he is much better off in heaven, but then we loved him so. It is hard, hard to have him die!" All Washington mourned. The scene was described by Elizabeth Keckley, family friend and seamstress: "The funeral was very touching. Of the entertainments in the East Room, the boy had been a most life-giving variation. . . . He was his father's favorite. They were intimates—often seen hand in hand. And there sat the man, with a burden on the brain at which the world marvels—bent now with the load both at heart and brain—staggering under a blow like the taking from him of his child." The young boy's body lay in state in the Green Room and hundreds passed by. From that time on President Lincoln could never again bring himself to even walk into the Green Room.

WWAD NEXT?

Until the stress of his presidency and the Civil War seriously degraded Abraham Lincoln's health, he was known for his robust constitution and athletic ability. Having been raised doing physical labor, the president was actually quite strong. Perhaps the best indication of just how personally tough Lincoln was is shown by his almost-legendary skill as a wrestler. Now, wresting in Illinois was not exactly the polite Greco-Roman competition you see in the Olympics. Illinois was on the western edge of "civilization" in Lincoln's time and a rough place. Wrestling there was a much more of a wide-open brawl that would quickly determine who was the toughest, fastest, and strongest. While a shopkeeper, before running for office, Lincoln ran afoul of a gang of toughs. This was hardly unusual, since the frontier towns attracted a rougher sort of man. He determined the best way to deal with them was to challenge their leader to a wrestling match. It is not even a sure thing that Lincoln won, but it can be certain he impressed the gang. From that time on they became Abe's biggest fans. The whole gang would make a point of showing up for all of Lincoln's rallies, and pity the poor heckler once they caught him.

SEEING THE ELEPHANT

While he was president during the Civil War, Abraham Lincoln actually witnessed shots fired in anger during the entire war only once. This happened when he was at Fort Stevens in 1864. The fort is about seven miles from Washington and was attacked by rebel forces. He was recorded as standing on the walls "impassive" until a Union officer was killed only a few feet away. Only after Major General Horatio Wright literally tugged at Lincoln's sleeve did he move to a safer spot.

SURGEON GENERAL'S WARNING

With all the rumors, and facts, regarding U. S. Grant's problems with alcohol, it wasn't the booze or even the stress of the presidency that got him. The habit that *did* do him in was smoking. You never saw General or President Grant without a cigar while he was awake. He chain-smoked cigars whenever he could afford them. This habit was well-known even by those who never were close enough to notice the strong tobacco odor that lingered on his clothes and anywhere he had resided. When the war was looking bad for the Union, General Grant won a major victory by taking Fort Donelson. This did wonders for the nation's morale, not to mention Lincoln's. Grateful Union citizens from all over the country responded by sending General Grant somewhere in the range of ten thousand boxes of cigars. There is no record of his giving most of these cigars away. Ulysses Grant died from a form of cancer of the throat that we know today can be directly attributed to tobacco use.

BAD RAP

For years, his critics and most of the nation were sure that his large meals and lavish parties were the reason that Chester A. Arthur was the epitome of the do-nothing president. It was not until he died nine months after leaving office that everyone learned he had been suffering from Bright's disease, an inflammation of the kidney. Bright's, combined with a resurgence of his malaria, did him in. It seems that his lethargy and lack of energy were

CHESTER A. ARTHUR
1881–1885

real and not character flaws. Then again, if he was so sick, you have to wonder about all those parties, drinking, and late hours.

SINISTER NEWS

The first left-handed president was Rutherford B. Hayes, elected in 1876. Righties dominated for almost all of the first century of the nation.

SNOOZE

William Howard Taft was not only a big man, weighing in at more than three hundred pounds, but a most hearty eater. He tended to have large meals several times a day. These meals tended to make the president drowsy and he often fell asleep during conversations and even cabinet meetings. The common reaction to this was simply to wait, as President Taft normally woke up after fifteen or twenty minutes and resumed any conversation as if there had been no interruption.

President Taft was such a large man, in fact, that he had trouble using the existing bathtub in the White House. After an embarrassing incident where he had to call for help to be extricated from the normal-sized tub, the president had a much larger tub installed. History does not record what his successor, the much slighter and lighter Wilson, thought of the massive appliance.

TALLPOX

Biological warfare is not a new development. Catapulting diseased animals and human bodies into cities under siege goes back to ancient timies. Surprisingly, it was used successfully against Abraham Lincoln during the Civil War. The presidency was seen as much more an office of the people at this time and those with grievances, or those seeking office, were often able to meet directly with the president. One female Confederate sympathizer went directly from being with a man who was infected with smallpox to such a meeting in the hope she would spread the disease, and without the president the nation would lose its resolve. Lincoln soon developed the disease and was laid up for several weeks. In keeping with the long tradition of never telling the public the truth about any presidential illness, his doctors stated Honest Abe was suffering from a mild case of the far less serious varioloid. The president eventually recovered fully.

SELF-INFLICTED WOUND

Theodore Roosevelt was one of the most physically adventurous men ever to serve as president. He was extremely aware of one weakness: his poor eyesight. While a Rough Rider he was known to carry as many as six pairs of glasses with him.

Teddy Roosevelt's eyesight got a lot worse while he was president. Always a very athletic man, he often engaged in contact sports, mostly boxing and jujitsu, while in office. He was always looking for a good boxing opponent and often fought much younger military personnel or professional boxers. One suspects that some of the young army and navy officers might not have worked too hard to beat the commander in chief, but he insisted they give him a good fight. During one boxing match in 1904, President Theodore Roosevelt didn't quite duck quickly enough and took a glancing blow to his left eye. Now, who did this has been a bit vague. Most attribute the blow to a young naval officer. But Teddy also was known to say it came from the current heavyweight champion, whom he also fought. Given this president's ego, the actual opponent was likely the naval officer; claiming it was the champion made the wound more acceptable.

Whoever actually landed the blow, the truth is the real damage was done by Teddy himself. A few hours after the fight, floating spots appeared in the president's vision. They were caused by blood leaking from ruptured blood vessels. Normally this was not a major problem. The patient makes sure not to jar the head and rests the eye a lot and the vessels seal up. But the president could never be described as patient. He announced that he could not rest his eyes since he had another boxing match and also his jujitsu lesson that day. He kept up this intense regimen for the rest of his term in office. All sight in Teddy's left eye was gone by late 1908; of course, the president didn't admit publicly to the loss until a decade later when he wanted to raise a regiment to fight in World War I.

MOUTHING THE WORDS

In this age of TV candidates, a quick mouth and resonant voice are a real asset. Grover Cleveland actually lost his. In early 1893, at the start of his second term, President Cleveland was given the shocking news that he had a cancerous growth on the top of his mouth. There was no chemotherapy at the end of the nineteenth century. U. S. Grant had died of cancer less than a decade earlier and untreated cancers were a death sentence. But President Cleveland had another concern. The United States was at the peak of a major financial crisis. He had been reelected to solve the problems causing it and even a hint that he might be unable to continue as president would likely cause a panic.

So the president chose, as several other presidents have before and since, to keep what was happening from the public. At the end of June, President Cleveland completed an appearance in New York City, then boarded a friend's boat to take a "six-day cruise" around Long Island. The reality was that the yacht had been equipped with an operating theater and doctors waited on board. A portion of the president's upper jaw and palate was removed in a way that left no visible scar. When the yacht landed in Buzzard's Bay, the president walked ashore without help and no one was the wiser. A few weeks later, a follow-up operation removed a much smaller area of cancer that had been missed at the edge of the growth. Then a dentist put in a rubber fixture that replaced the lost bone. The operation and the new palate were a success. There was little change in the president's voice or appearance. Eventually the economy returned to normal, but it was not until after Grover Cleveland died ten years later that the American public learned of the president's cancer and operation.

HYPOCRITICAL OATH

There is a real tradition of hiding presidential disabilities. From Kennedy's multiple illnesses to FDR's legs, the American public rarely learns when their president has a problem. One of the worst examples of this was the collapse of Woodrow Wilson. After World War I, the scholarly Wilson was convinced that war could be ended if there was a forum at which international disputes could be settled. This was his beloved League of Nations. There was only one problem: a growing isolationist movement and questions about the League's structure meant that the treaty met with solid opposition in the Senate. In response, Woodrow Wilson went on an extensive and exhausting railroad tour of the Western states. He often made four or more speeches in a day and returned on the edge of collapse. On October 4, 1919, a few days after returning the to the White House, President Wilson was found unconscious on the floor of a bathroom.

When the doctors were able to bring Woodrow Wilson back to consciousness he appeared to have had a stroke and his entire left side was paralyzed. This was a major and serious condition, with the president not only incapacitated but in danger of dying. For his last five months as president, Wilson was barely, if at all, able to function. Only his wife and personal secretary were allowed to enter his room, with his wife reporting the president's "decisions" from his sickbed to awaiting staff. Yes, there is a question of who was actually making those decisions, but this was a more genteel era. Can you imagine what Rush Limbaugh would do with such a situation today?

To relax her husband, the First Lady turned to the newest media wonder of its day. Every afternoon, a movie was shown in the East Room for the benefit of the president. Many of the studios and producers cooperated, sending copies of their movies to be viewed by the president and his guests. Gradually, Wilson recovered, and in February of 1920, was able to make a short trip in his automobile. During all this time, even after Warren Harding became president, there was virtually no mention in the newspapers or on the radio that Woodrow Wilson, the president of the United States, was unable to function in the office.

A SHORT VISIT

The shortest celebrity likely to have visited the White House arrived during the administration of James Polk. This was the famous General Tom Thumb, star of P. T. Barnum's famous show. When he heard that the showman and the perfectly formed, but very short man (at this point standing about two feet six inches) arrived, President Polk adjourned a cabinet meeting to rush out to meet them. This visit went much better for the little person than one of his meetings with Queen Victoria, where he was attacked by her pet poodle.

TO THE RANCH WITH YOU, MR. PRESIDENT

The best way to describe Warren Harding's end was that he worked himself to death. The story of how this happened makes you want to encourage presidents to spend more time getting healthy, even on their ranch. To begin with, the thirtieth president knew he was not healthy. He had diabetes (before there were effective treatments for it), an enlarged heart, and his arteries were hardening by the day. But rather than take it easy, the president embarked on an intensive trip to the West Coast and Alaska.

It seems likely President Harding was aware of the risk he was taking and just how far he was pushing his body. Before leaving, the president made a will, sold some property, shifted investments, and generally put everything in order. His concerns must have been increased by a bad case of flu he was still recovering from, and which he constantly complained about as having left him weak. Yet he not only took a strenuous trip, but did so on a schedule that would exhaust a healthy twenty-year-old.

In the next months after his illness, Warren Harding traveled by train to fifty-four cities and delivered over eighty speeches. He also rarely repeated a speech, so he was constantly changing them, or creating new ones during the trip. In addition, he was featured at literally dozens of ceremonies ranging from giving Boy Scouts badges to laying a golden spike in Alaska. Even as he traveled between the various stops, the train was filled with local politicians, each one determined to have a few minutes with the president on what was likely their only chance to have such a meeting.

Weak and ailing, Harding carried on and never missed an appearance. It was only after he had come south from Alaska and was in Seattle that the toll of his efforts began to show. During a speech there, the president seemed to pause and almost collapse, but he managed to finish the speech. President Harding made it back to San Francisco before he was hospitalized, and soon died of pneumonia and a suspected brain hemorrhage. The simple fact was that Warren G. Harding worked himself to death.

BEST DRESSED
Perhaps JFK and Millard Fillmore could give him a run for his money, but the top candidate for Best Dressed President had to be Chester A. Arthur. In the era when most men owned "a suit," he had eighty pairs of pants, with matching coats and accessories. But then, the widowed twenty-first president needed to dress well, as he was a serious party animal. He regularly visited nightclubs and stayed in them late into the night.

FACING IT
Abraham Lincoln was many things, but by the standards of then or today handsome was not among his attributes. It is likely that in today's blow-dried, TV-dominated elections he could not get elected. The tall president may have had Marfan's syndrome, which would explain his unusual height, thin but strong physique, and long limbs. His arms were proportionally longer than normal, which is very long indeed for a man as tall as he was. Lincoln also had no illusions about his looks. He said it best himself. Once in a debate his opponent called him "two faced." The future president's quick reply was, "I leave it to my audience. If I had another face, do you think I would wear this one?"

MOST IMPORTANT MEAL OF THE DAY
In the tradition of Grover Cleveland, Theodore Roosevelt loved to eat. A typical breakfast for the active president consisted of up

to a dozen eggs, large amounts of coffee, and side dishes. Even his constant exercise and hikes could not totally reverse the effects of the twenty-sixth president's enormous appetite. To put it politely, in modern terms, Teddy developed a belly. A really large and noticeable belly. All that cholesterol every morning may have also had a second price. It is likely that Teddy died of arteriosclerosis and atherosclerosis (calcium and fat build up and blockage in the arteries).

PURPLE ABOUT EVERYTHING

While there have been other presidents who were injured, none can hold a candle to the sheer volume of abuse Theodore Roosevelt subjected his body to. A short list of his major accidents alone is impressive, even more so when you realize he died not from any of them but from clogged arteries.

Teddy was thrown through a glass window when a steamship he was in collided with another ship.

He lost the sight in one eye in a boxing match with a sailor at the White House.

Roosevelt broke an arm falling off his horse while riding to the hounds (a fox hunt).

His arm was broken again in a stick-fighting bout, which was a martial art fighting style from the Philippines he became trained in.

The president was almost killed when his carriage was hit by a trolley in Pittsfield, Massachusetts. A Secret Service agent did die and the bruise the president received on one leg was so bad that it became necrotic. Doctors cut away dead tissue all the way down to the bone.

In 1912, he was shot on his way to a Progressive "Bull Moose" Party rally in Milwaukee. The bullet was slowed when it first hit his eyeglass case, but it did penetrate the president. Everyone got ready to rush the former president to a hospital, but he was already at the rally and could hear the crowd as word of the shooting spread. Before leaving to be treated, Roosevelt got up on the stage and announced to a shocked and pleased audience,

"I do not know whether you fully understand that I have been shot, but it takes more than that to kill a Bull Moose."

THE TYPO OF LOVE

When Woodrow Wilson lost his wife to disease in 1914, he was overwhelmed with the loss and excessively depressed. For some time, there was concern that the nation might have its first presidential suicide. What helped pull Wilson out of his downer was Edith Boling Galt. The couple met and she quickly charmed the bereaved president. Soon they were dating, and since they married a year later, the *Washington Post* report of one of their first events may have been not untrue but only premature. The president escorted Edith Galt to a play. It must have been obvious that the couple paid more attention to each other than to the actors, but still the *Post* report appearing the next day was likely off, considering the very proper manner of both subjects of the piece. The article read, "the President spent most of his time entering Mrs. Galt." We *think* they meant "entertaining,"

SLEEPER

If Calvin Coolidge had a lifelong hobby, it has to be sleeping. He was by far the champion sleeper in a job that is characterized by sleepless nights. The thirtieth president rarely missed his 10 p.m. bedtime and slept at least eight, and often ten, hours each night. He also napped most afternoons. His proclivity for slumber was well-known. At a performance of *Animal Crackers*, the always-irreverent Groucho Marx once spotted the president and, in the middle of the show, faced the audience and asked, "Isn't this past your bedtime, Calvin?"

JFK AND FDR

While president, both Jack Kennedy and Franklin Roosevelt had a similar secret. Today, most people know that FDR was crippled and unable to walk without braces, but few even today realize that JFK had a similar problem. The thirty-fifth president had a bad back even when young. During his truly heroic efforts after the sinking of PT-109, he seriously aggravated the problem when he had to tow a wounded sailor some distance to a nearby island when their boat was rammed by a Japanese destroyer. Eventually, Kennedy had a steel plate placed in his back which later had to be removed. Because of his back, Jack Kennedy often used crutches to walk around the White House but, like Roosevelt, he never let the American people be aware of his many medical problems, much less see him use assistance to walk. Also like FDR, the press kept a gentleman's agreement, and neither wrote about nor took pictures of JFK using his crutches.

LEGACY

One of Jack Kennedy's doctors, Seymour Hersh, MD, has stated that he regularly treated the president for chlamydia, a nasty venereal infection that can leave a woman sterile. He went on to say that, with his promiscuous personal habits, JFK was constantly getting infected by STDs, as were his partners. The age of Camelot has long faded, but perhaps some of the STDs JFK passed on are still around.

GOTTA HAVE HEART

While a senator in 1955, long before he became president, Lyndon Baines Johnson had a severe heart attack. He made a complete recovery and was the Democratic Majority Leader of the Senate while Eisenhower was president.

ANOTHER SECRET SERVICE

President Gerald Ford had occasional problems with his lower intestinal tract. This tended to manifest itself by producing gas in large quantities, which was occasionally very loudly expelled. When this occurred while walking, President Ford would turn to his escorting agent and blame one of them for the unpresidential outburst.

MODEL PRESIDENT

One of Ronald Reagan's jobs while a student at the University of California was to pose, with just enough on for modesty, for the life drawing classes. Because of this, he was once voted "Most Nearly Perfect Male Figure." Maybe that was what Jane Wyman saw in him?

BUSHUSURU

It is not many men that have a word created from their name. For most who do it is a dubious distinction, just ask Boycott and Lynch. President George H. W. Bush achieved this distinction in one televised action. It was the night he vomited into the lap of the Japanese prime minister at a state banquet. The word Bushusuru quickly appeared in common use as a slang phrase in Japan and continues to be used to this day. As you might guess, the meaning is "to throw up."

12

PRESIDENTIAL POLITICS

"Hell, I never vote for anybody. I always vote against."
W. C. Fields

*T*he first presidential elections were very gentlemanly compared to today's mud-slinging fiascos. But chaotic politics and back-room agreements are hardly a new thing. The election of 1824 was a prime example of the republic still finding itself and the politics this spawned. The electors in the Electoral College were much more independent back then. In fact, the original intention was to see the electors, many of whom were appointed not elected, use their collective wisdom to select the best person to become president. There were, as you can see, a few of the Founding Fathers whose faith in general elections and the masses was less than total. But this led to the situation in 1824 where no one had even close to a majority and four men were striving to be elected to the office, regardless of the fact that Andrew Jackson had won the popular vote. Finally the election was, as per procedure, thrown to the House of Representatives. Henry Clay had lost badly in the voting, but was very influential in the Congress. He could no longer present himself as a viable candidate, but was in a position to choose who would win. He chose John Quincy Adams over the voters' choice of Andrew Jackson. In return, Henry Clay was appointed secretary of state, the number two executive office at that time. The uproar this caused basically crippled the J. Q. Adams presidency and not one of his major initiatives was passed. His was the first administration to be crippled by politics, though hardly the last.

A DUBIOUS TRADITION

Feeling he had been cheated out of being president in 1824, Andrew Jackson campaigned tirelessly in 1828. He was aided by a number of factors. The most important was the popular support he got for being the nation's best-known war hero and leader. But John Quincy Adams, running for a second term, was also a great help—to Jackson. Adams was a bit of an elitist who disliked campaigning, and it showed. He was also described as being arrogant and haughty, and had an immense dislike for casual conversation. When his negative attitude was combined with the failure his battle with Congress made of his first term, John Quincy Adams became only the second president in history to be defeated in his bid for reelection. Even more painful: his father, John Adams, was the first. This makes for a rather dubious family tradition.

"P" AND THAT RHYMES WITH POOL

John Quincy Adams was an elitist and hard to deal with, but he was scrupulously honest and kept accurate and highly-detailed records of everything. This served him very badly when he listed a billiards table as one of his personal purchases for use in the White House. While he did not use any government money for the purchase, the supporters of Andrew Jackson made a tremendous stink about the depravity of having a gaming table in the executive mansion.

THE WHAT PARTY?

When Andrew Jackson became president, he was a populist, the people's choice. His platform was to clean up Washington. He sounded then just like all the candidates now, including diatribes on elitists (read, "inside the Beltway") and influence peddlers

(read, "special interests"). And the result was just about the same—nothing. All he did was to fire those who had supported his opponent, former President J. Q. Adams, with his own patronage army. He then went on to take over the party established by Thomas Jefferson, which was then known as the Republican Party. But now that he was running it, the party got a new name to reflect his populist support, and the Republican Party became the Democratic Party. Those opposing Jackson found that they needed an organization, too. After all, he had just trounced them at the polls—and formed the Whig Party. So the Republicans became the Democrats who were opposed by the Whigs, who thirty years later ceded their role as the opposition to the new party whose candidate was Abraham Lincoln. Since the name was available, this new party called itself the Republican Party.

CONVENTIONAL CHOICE

The 1852, the Democratic National convention had a problem. Due to the split in its members between pro- and anti-slavery delegates, it was unable to select a candidate. After thirty-four ballots, everyone was ready to find someone, anyone, who could represent the party. By this point, it is safe to assume that not only exhaustion and embarrassment were at play. The cost of attending the greatly-extended convention was also adding up. So the Democrats settled on an unknown party loyalist who had two big advantages. He was well thought of, which meant no one objected to him, and he was a "Dogface." Dogfaces were Northern politicians with pro-slavery and Southern attitudes, and Franklin Pierce was one. Part of being a Dogface was the tradition (like Andrew Jackson) of states' rights. This policy maintained that the federal

FRANKLIN PIERCE 1853–1857

government should play a very narrow role in everything, and anything not stated as being a federal responsibility in the Constitution should be left to each state. This policy worked well for those states who wanted to maintain slavery. So in 1852, Franklin Pierce was elected president with little going for him, and an attitude that the government he led should do as little as possible. The presidency of Franklin Pierce proved such a disaster that when he strove to get the Democrats to nominate him for a second term, that party chose as a motto "Anybody but Pierce." He dropped out of the race.

CLOSE CALL

While his incompetent presidency likely contributed to starting the Civil War, former President Franklin Pierce maintained his states' rights and Southern sympathies. This angered those who bothered to remember the undistinguished president and his lackluster single term in office. Feelings were very high and hot after Abraham Lincoln was assassinated. Pierce made the mistake of not displaying an American flag during the period of mourning, something nearly every home in the North did. Seeing this, a mob formed, under the assumption that the insult to the memory of Lincoln, with whom Pierce differed on about every subject, was intentional. Only by grabbing a flag and then talking very quickly was the former president able to preserve health and home.

BLAME GAME

Politicians are always quick to assign blame. Slower, but more critical, are historians. Among the lowest, if not *the* lowest, rated by virtually all presidential scholars is James Buchanan. The real sin for which such a low rating comes is not something the fifteenth president did but rather what he *didn't* do. The nation was being torn apart politically by the slav-

JAMES BUCHANAN
1857–1861

ery and states' rights issues. Several opportunities arose where a decisive leader might have acted to defuse the conflict. Rather than provide leadership, Buchanan simply did nothing. Or rather what little he attempted, such as an abortive attempt for a constitution for Kansas, simply made things worse. Because of this incompetence and inaction, the nation sank deeper into antipathy and discord. His failures encouraged the rise of the relatively new anti-slavery party known as the Republicans. The Republican rhetoric and strength in the Northern states meant that the Southern states viewed a Republican election success as a threat to their society and economy. By the time the Republican Abraham Lincoln took office, there was no room for compromise left and the Southern states began to secede. The inaction and feeble leadership of James Buchanan, in a time when strong and courageous leadership was needed, led to the Civil War and hundreds of thousands of deaths.

DEFINITION

"What is conservatism? Is it not the adherence to the old and tried against the new and untried?"—Abraham Lincoln

COMPARED TO WHO?

John Lennon was not the first person to claim he was comparable to Jesus Christ himself. When Andrew Johnson, later the first president to be impeached, was responding to hecklers, he compared himself to Christ. He then went on to say that Lincoln may have been struck down by a deity who wanted *him* to become president. By 1868, no one even considered his running for reelection.

BETRAYAL

Chester A. Arthur became president after Garfield died from being shot and the botched treatments that followed. He had been given the vice presidency as a reward for his successful use of dubious ways of raising a very great amount of funds for the Republican Party and its candidates. This process of selling positions, threats, and using the power of the government to cajole money for those in power was known as the "spoils system." He was the crony of some of the most notorious politicians in New York history. Beyond his talent at raising money using any means necessary, there wasn't much to distinguish Arthur from hundreds of other political hacks. But after he became president, Chester A. Arthur had some sort of transformation. He suddenly became the chief proponent and enforcer of public honesty. Since he had been perhaps the worst and most knowledgeable of the offenders he now opposed, this made the twenty-first resident very effective at cleaning up a corrupt political system. Under his administration the Pendleton Act was passed, whose reforms made it impossible for the spoils system, and all of the many money raising techniques Arthur himself perfected, to continue.

A final note: it would be nice to say that the nation appreciated President Arthur's efforts and made him a hero who was reelected in a landslide. The reality was that even if he had handicapped their money-raising and other crooked practices, the party bosses were still in control of the Republican Party apparatus. Those bosses, now poorer but wiser, dropped their newly found reformer almost before the next nominating convention began.

PRECEDENT

Before recent times, three presidents were elected with less than a majority of the popular vote. These were:

1825
Andrew Jackson	153,544	
John Q. Adams	108, 740	winner by vote of the House of Representatives

1877
Rutherford B. Hayes	4,036,298	voted in by a special commission
Samuel Tilden	4,300,590	

1889
Grover Cleveland	5,540,309	
Benjamin Harrison	5,439,853	won more electoral votes

13

LEFT AND RIGHT . . .

OR, WHEN REPUBLICANS DO DEMOCRATIC THINGS AND VICE VERSA

By Brian M. Thomsen

"There are many men of principle in both parties in America, but there is no party of principle."
Alexis de Tocqueville

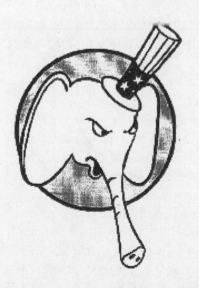

n his 2004 book, *The Great Game of Politics*, Dick Stoken mapped the presidential political cycle of history as a back-and-forth pendulum swing.

In each case a movement in one direction dictates a resultant and reactive movement in the other direction and over the course of the history of our great democracy these swings have grown wider and wider.

Initially, the Federalist swing to the right (John Adams being elected after Washington) was answered by the reactive leftward Jeffersonian swing. And over time each swing and the resultant period of left or right philosophy in power has increased, the two most prominent swings of the twentieth century being the FDR "New Deal" answer to the conservative pro-business Harding-Coolidge "New Era," and the Ronald Reagan-led "New Economy" that was an answer to the attitudes and practices of the "New Deal."

An oversimplified explication of this is that, when one party overreaches, there is citizen dissatisfaction that leads to a move toward supremacy of the opposite party—and in most cases these moves are led by a Democrat on the left and a Republican on the right.

Ergo, Democrats are on the left and Republicans are on the right.

Simple.

No, not really—and not so fast with that distinction.

Consider the following anomalies:

The Democratic Party is sometimes referred to as the party of Thomas Jefferson. Now, when you think of the Democratic Party, you tend to think of sweeping national programs that override the views of local governments, which has resulted in such legislative actions as those pertaining to civil rights, or legal decisions such as *Roe vs. Wade*. Yet when you look at Jefferson's platform, one must immediately realize that it was quite the opposite, as it was pro states' rights, anti national bank, and against tariffs/taxes imposed at the federal level.

Just as Jefferson is considered to be the initiating icon of the modern Democratic Party, Abraham Lincoln, the sixteenth president, has taken the mantle of patriarch of the modern Republican Party or, more precisely, Federalists 2.0.

So isn't it ironic that Lincoln was the first president to shift from strict constitutional constructionism to a more, dare I say "liberal" approach? Unlike his Federalist forefathers, Lincoln in his rhetoric and reasoning shifted the focus of American values away from the set-in-stone legalisms of the Constitution and back to the platitudes of the first American document, the Declaration of Independence. He claimed it provided the nation with the foundation of American political values or what he more precisely referred to as the "sheet anchor" of republicanism (freedom and liberty for all, at least metaphorically).

And what else is this Federalist 2.0 credited with?

Initiating the first United States income tax, of course— something staunch Republican talking heads such as anti-tax maven and ultra-conservative activist Grover Norquist always leave out in their diatribes about reducing taxes so that we can shrink the government to a size that would enable us to drown it in a bathtub.

Let's look at another issue on the Democratic side.

In a recent debate of the candidates running for the Republican nomination for the presidency in 2008, a questioner asked the gentlemen at hand, "Who believes in evolution?"

Such a question as this would have no real significance in the Democratic Party, but in recent years the schism over faith vs. science has widened, particularly among the evangelical wings of the Republican Party.

So the question is, which party has nominated the strongest opponent to the theory of evolution as their party's nominee?

No question about it.

The Democrats.

Huh?

Yup ... he never won, but they nominated him three times in 1896, 1900, and 1908. His name was William Jennings Bryan, and nowadays he is mostly remembered as being Clarence Darrow's opposing counsel in the so-called "Scopes/Monkey Trial" that was the basis for the popular play *Inherit the Wind*. To date, no Republican has been a stauncher anti-evolution advocate than Bryan.

Conversely, what president said the following?

"Leave the matter of religion to the family altar, the church, and the private school, supported entirely by private contributions. Keep the church and state forever separate."

Separation of church and state.

No federal funds for religious schools.

Obviously a Democrat.

Uh ... no.

That was Ulysses S. Grant, eighteenth president of the United States, who was a Republican.

What about other Republicans who have embraced supposed Democratic issues?

Well, let's see ... how about the environment?

Has there been a more seminally Democratic issue, even before Al Gore's Academy Award for *An Inconvenient Truth*? Whether it be the allocation of federal land for national parks or preserves, or the imposition of limits on industry in their selfish exploitation of such resources, Democrats have always led on this issue.

And who inaugurated this movement?

None other than Theodore Roosevelt, a Republican who not only championed the environment, but also opposed the moneyed interest of big business on a variety of issues that have now become planks in the platform of the Democratic Party.

But of course TR was not the first president to express his gratitude for the wonders of nature through the exercising of his presidential powers.

In 1891, the twenty-third president, through an executive order, set aside a tract of land in Wyoming as the nation's first forest reservation, the first unit in what eventually became the National Forest system.

That President was Benjamin Harrison.

You guessed it, another Republican.

Indeed, nowadays big business rather than big nature has become more synonymous with the Republican Party, with many opponents pointing out the overwhelming coziness between money men and Republican politicians who make them rich through huge defense contracts, resulting in a shadow government run by the so-called "Military-Industrial Complex" that trumps our democracy.

And who was the first president to warn the American people against the insidious "Military-Industrial Complex"? None other than Dwight David Eisenhower, a former military man and a Republican in good standing.

And who can forget the twenty-second president, who took a hard line on governmental hardship handouts, who maintained that "federal aid in such cases encourages the expectation of paternal care on the part of the Government and weakens the sturdiness of our national character" and as a result vetoed aid bills for drought-beset farmers and economically and physically challenged veterans. Indeed 22 exercised the veto pen more than any of his predecessors as a means to cut federal government handouts.

And what about the twenty-fourth president, who sent in federal troops to union bust and strike break the Eugene Debbs-led Pullman Strike that threatened to obstruct the nation's railways?

Both 22 and 24 sound awfully conservative and very Republican.

But the answer *is* both, though that is probably misleading, as 22 and 24 are the same man. Indeed the only person ever to serve two nonconsecutive terms as president.

That man was Grover Cleveland, a Democrat.

Herewith some more food for thought:

President number six, John Quincy Adams, son of president number two, John Adams, an ardent conservative in the Federalist vein.

Nowadays when we think of "Federalists" we think of strict constitutional constructionists, supporters of little government and even littler taxes.

So the question arises what was "Q" known for domestically (as opposed to internationally, since his five predecessors seemed more concerned with extra-American matters like defense, trade, and land acquisition)?

The answer: the first major American public works program which would be financed by the raising of tariffs (tariffs being taxes by any other name, though to be fair he never promised "Read my lips—no new tariffs!").

It was to be called "the American System" and it was to be composed of a program of internal improvements including road building, canal-digging, university endowing, and other pet projects, including a national observatory for astral studies and a national bank to encourage productive enterprise and form a national currency. It also included a number of pork projects.

So much for smaller government and limited taxes.

Now if we compare him to the next level-headed (thus skipping Andrew Jackson and his ineffective lackeys) Democrat president, we come to James K. Polk, the eleventh president.

Opposite party.

Opposite policy.

A Democrat through and through.

And what did he do?

He lowered the tariffs and is widely credited with actively supporting unrestricted free trade, thus ticking off the Northern protectionists who had flourished during the reign of the mad Whig Party.

In addition to his economic incentives, he also had a very non-Democratic idea of promulgating the expansion of U.S. holdings. Where previous expansion had occurred through diplomatic negotiation and economic expansion (both of which Polk also practiced), the eleventh president had another plan up his sleeve.

"If they don't want to negotiate . . . there are always alternatives." And in Polk's case this alternative wound up with a name: the Mexican-American War, where our *casus belli* was simple—they didn't want to give us what we wanted.

So when Mexican forces crossed the Rio Grande and killed eleven American troops, Polk announced that Mexicans had "invaded our territory and shed American blood upon the American soil." (More precisely *soon-to-be* American soil, as this territory was part of the real estate for which our "negotiations" were stymied.)

The result: a soon-to-be state named New Mexico. (It is worth noting that Polk tried the same sort of maneuver with Spain for Cuba. But the lack of a situational excuse like the Mexican incursion effectively neutralized his strategy, putting Cuba on the back-burner for a few more presidents to try and handle.)

The Mexican-American War contributed more than just territory to American history—it also gave us the war career of future President Pierce.

Franklin Pierce, the fourteenth president and an avowed Democrat, holds a true distinction among all presidents to date: thus far, he is the only president ever to have hailed from the great state of New Hampshire.

Now, the state slogan of New Hampshire, as anyone with access to New England license plates knows, is "Live Free or Die."

So since he was a Northern Democrat, what was his view on the slavery issue?

Ironically, the opposite of what one would expect, and indeed, by signing the Kansas-Nebraska Act, he pretty much undid the war-averting Missouri Compromise and thus allowed the further spread of slavery and laid the groundwork for the Civil War.

Recently, two new issues have risen to the forefront for the right-leaning Republicans:

1. the dismantlement of the federal civil service system to divorce it from political cronyism
2. immigration as a means to bring in "cheap labor" to feed our competitiveness in an international free market economy (without the obligation of a path to citizenship, of course)

Consider therefore the career of the twenty-first president of the United States Chester A. Arthur, who assumed the presidency upon the death of James Garfield.

The two hallmarks of his tenure in office were:

1. the passage of the 1883 Pendleton Act, which established the Civil Service Commission, which "stopped big businesses from giving out rebates and pooling with other companies, forbade levying political assessments against officeholders, and provided for a system that made certain government positions obtainable only through competitive written examinations and protected employees against removal for political reasons" (yes, the exact system that current Republicans are trying to dismantle)
2. the passage of the Chinese Exclusion Act, which allowed the United States to essentially block entry to Chinese immigrants solely on the basis that they were undercutting the ability of U.S. citizens to get jobs and also driving down the wages for said positions (passed largely in response to the numerous railroad labor construction jobs that were linked to the Gold Rush and seemed to be continually filled by low-cost laborers from the other side of the Pacific)

And what was Chester A. Arthur?
A staunch and conservative Republican, of course.

Indeed, things are never as simple as they seem, and ideas and ideologies seldom really split down party lines.

Possibly our most racist president was a Democrat, Woodrow Wilson.

This twenty-eighth president, though obviously a man of learning (he was a scholar and an Ivy League university president after all), was an ardent fan of the D. W. Griffith film *The Birth of a Nation*, which glorified the Reconstruction-era exploits of the Ku Klux Klan as a natural evolutionary reaction to post-Civil War events. (Indeed, one of Wilson's classmates penned the novel *The Klansman*, upon which the film was based.) It is even believed that he supported segregation in the Washington, D.C., governmental workplace, and actively discouraged minorities from applying to Princeton when he was president there.

But all of this, too, must be taken with a grain of salt.

After all, who is the only president known to have actually looked into joining the Communist party?

The fortieth president, Ronald Reagan, a Republican and the man credited by some with breaking the back of the Soviet menace.

Just as it took a Democratic president (Bill Clinton) to balance the budget and reform welfare, it sometimes takes a maverick in one party to implement a pragmatic approach to a process that, in essence, achieves the goals of the other party— usually to the betterment of the lot of the American people.

A great philosopher and social commentator once said, "Only Nixon could go to China," meaning that it takes a strong and bellicose anti-Communist to make peace with a strong and equally bellicose Communist.

Okay, that wasn't said by a great philosopher; it was said by Mr. Spock in *Star Trek VI*, but its wisdom still stands.

14

WHEN, WHO, AND HOW MUCH?

*"Politicians are people who, when they see light at the end
of the tunnel, go out and buy some more tunnel."*
John Quinton

Here are some fun facts on the statistics, numbers, and names related to the presidents.

The law states that a president has to be at least thirty-five years old. None have approached that youthful age. There is no upper limit.

PRESIDENT	IN OFFICE	BORN	AGE INAUGURATED	AGE AT DEATH
Washington	1789–1797	VA	Inaugurated age 57	Died 67
John Adams	1797–1801	MA	Inaugurated age 61	Died 90
Jefferson	1801–1809	VA	Inaugurated age 57	Died 83
Madison	1809–1817	VA	Inaugurated age 57	Died 85
Monroe	1817–1825	VA	Inaugurated age 58	Died 73

PRESIDENT	IN OFFICE	BORN	AGE INAUGURATED	AGE AT DEATH
J. Q. Adams	1825–1829	MA	Inaugurated age 57	Died 80
Jackson	1829–1837	SC	Inaugurated age 61	Died 78
Van Buren	1837–1841	NY	Inaugurated age 54	Died 79
W. H. Harrison	1841	VA	Inaugurated age 68	Died 68
Tyler	1841–1845	VA	Inaugurated age 51	Died 71
Polk	1845–1849	NC	Inaugurated age 49	Died 53
Taylor	1849–1850	VA	Inaugurated age 64	Died 65
Fillmore	1850–1853	NY	Inaugurated age 50	Died 74
Pierce	1853–1857	NH	Inaugurated age 48	Died 64
Buchanan	1857–1861	PA	Inaugurated age 65	Died 77
Lincoln	1861–1865	KY	Inaugurated age 52	Died 56
A. Johnson	1865–1869	NC	Inaugurated age 56	Died 66
Grant	1869–1877	OH	Inaugurated age 46	Died 63
Hayes	1877–1881	OH	Inaugurated age 54	Died 70

PRESIDENT	IN OFFICE	BORN	AGE INAUGURATED	AGE AT DEATH
Garfield	1881	OH	Inaugurated age 49	Died 49
Arthur	1881–1885	VT	Inaugurated age 50	Died 56
Cleveland	1885–1889	NJ	Inaugurated age 47	Died 71
B. Harrison	1889–1893	OH	Inaugurated age 55	Died 67
Cleveland	1893–1897	NJ	Inaugurated age 55	Died 71
McKinley	1897–1901	OH	Inaugurated age 54	Died 58
T. Roosevelt	1901–1909	NY	Inaugurated age 42	Died 60
Taft	1909–1913	OH	Inaugurated age 51	Died 72
Wilson	1913–1921	VA	Inaugurated age 56	Died 67
Harding	1921–1923	OH	Inaugurated age 55	Died 57
Coolidge	1923–1929	VT	Inaugurated age 51	Died 60
Hoover	1929–1933	IA	Inaugurated age 54	Died 90
F. D. Roosevelt	1933–1945	NY	Inaugurated age 51	Died 63
Truman	1945–1953	MO	Inaugurated age 60	Died 88

PRESIDENT	IN OFFICE	BORN	AGE INAUGURATED	AGE AT DEATH
Eisenhower	1953–1961	TX.	Inaugurated age 62	Died 78
Kennedy	1961–1963	MA	Inaugurated age 43	Died 46
L. B. Johnson	1963–1969	TX	Inaugurated age 55	Died 64
Nixon	1969–1974	CA	Inaugurated age 56	Died 81
Ford	1974–1977	NE	Inaugurated age 61	Died 93
Carter	1977–1981	GA	Inaugurated age 52	
Reagan	1981–1989	IL	Inaugurated age 69	Died 93
G. H. W. Bush	1989–1993	MA	Inaugurated age 64	
Clinton	1993–2001	AR.	Inaugurated age 46	
G. W. Bush	2001	CN	Inaugurated age 54	

Until modern times, the ex-president who lived the longest was Herbert Hoover, who likely enjoyed it the least. He was never forgiven by the nation for being in office when the Great Depression started, or for his bungled efforts to stop it. Also living to ninety was John Adams, who happily played the role of elder statesman. The two presidents who lived to the oldest age were Ronald Reagan and Gerald Ford. The youngest resident at death was the assassinated John Kennedy. The oldest president elected was Ronald Reagan. It is interesting to note that, through the first twelve presidencies, over half were born in Virginia. After Zachary Taylor, the next and latest Virginia-born president was Woodrow Wilson. From Grant in 1869 until Harding in 1921, Ohio became the state to be from. Half the fourteen presidents elected during this period were from Ohio. Of the last thirteen presidents, starting with Hoover, a majority (seven) were born west of the Mississippi River.

West   Truman, Ike, LBJ, Nixon, Ford and Reagan
East   Hoover, FDR, JFK, Carter, Bush 1, Clinton, Bush 2

THE "H" WORD

It probably means nothing, but there have been five Presidents whose name began with an "H." These were William Henry Harrison, Benjamin Harrison, Rutherford B. Hayes, Warren G. Harding, and Herbert Hoover. It probably means nothing, but if your name is Haig, or Harvey, or anything starting with an H, each and every one of these men was not reelected to a second term.

WILLIAM HENRY HARRISON
1841

MONEY TALKS

Of the eleven types of bills that were at any time circulated, presidents are on eight of them. The $100,000 bill was only used for Treasury purposes and also featured a president: Wilson. Note that two of the three exceptions were treasury secretaries, who control the Bureau of Engraving. All bills over $100 are no longer used.

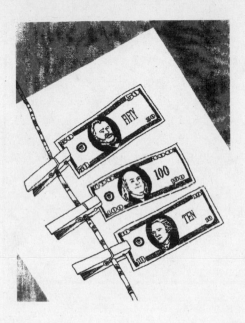

$1	George Washington	1st U.S. President
$2	Thomas Jefferson	3rd U.S. President
$5	Abraham Lincoln	16th U.S. President
$10	Alexander Hamilton	1st Secretary of the Treasury and never President
$20	Andrew Jackson	7th U.S. President
$50	Ulysses Grant	18th U.S. President
$100	Ben Franklin	Statesman and never President
$500	William McKinley	25th U.S. President
$1,000	Grover Cleveland	22nd & 24th U.S. President
$5,000	James Madison	4th U.S. President
$10,000	Salmon Chase	U.S. Treasury Secretary under Lincoln
$100,000	Woodrow Wilson	28th U.S. President

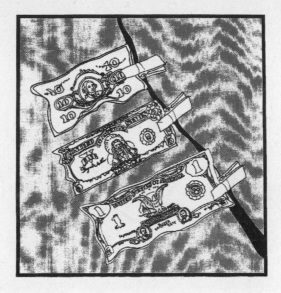

LIVING MONEY

Harkening back to the Roman Empire, when the reigning emperor put his own likeness on coins, only once in history has a living president been on money. This was when Calvin Coolidge appeared alongside George Washington on a special, sesquicentennial half dollar.

STARTING SALARY

While later presidents' salary suffered from the ravages of inflation and the cost of being the chief host for the nation, the first president, George Washington, was paid a really excellent salary that would translate today into a high six-figure amount. This was intended to, and did, allow him to act presidential, though no one was sure what that was yet. The closest they knew was royalty, so the budget was there to pay for a good deal of pomp. After all his years of sacrifice and field camps with the Continental Army, Washington rightly used his high pay to look and act like the leader of a sovereign nation. He traveled extensively, dressed well, entertained with style, and even bought his horses fancy robes made of such exotic materials as leopard skins. Some records show that more than five percent of the total he spent during his presidency went for the purchase of alcohol—though mostly for entertainment and not his personal use.

VP PAY

The honor was often dubious and no one knows why today anyone would want to be the vice president, but it is certain the vice presidents have never been after the job for the money. Though in real dollars it used to actually pay better than it does today, since in 1800 one dollar had the buying power of over sixteen of today's dollars, and in 1900 that had risen to twenty-six to one. Here is a quick look at what we pay our backup leaders:

1789	$5,000
1907	$10,000
1949	$30,000
1964	$43,000
1969	$62,500
2001	$171,500
2004	$192,600

The question is what changed to make the vice president worth three times as much today as in 1969?

CAN YOU SPARE ME A DIME?

Many of the first presidents and vice presidents were rich men. They were the leaders of their states and had to be well off enough to spend long periods governing. Many also were from what we today call "old money" and served because it was a family tradition. It did not matter to them that their paychecks were a bit slow in coming. This time it did. Vice President John Tyler had not yet received his first paycheck when a messenger arrived informing him that William Henry Harrison had died and he was to be the president. The vice president was at his home in Williamsburg and had never been financially well off. It was quickly discovered that he simply did not have enough money to get to Washington for his own inauguration. Several friends rallied to Tyler and loaned him the money for the trip. That was probably a very

safe loan, since now that he was president, they certainly knew where he lived.

LINCOLN PENNIES

For some reason, there is an impression that Abraham Lincoln was some sort of monkish figure who lived on good intentions and honor. The reality is that Lincoln was a rather good businessman. Unlike John Tyler, he was quite financially comfortable when he took office in 1861. One bank in Springfield, Illinois, owed him the proceeds of a note for almost $10,000. That would be $250,000 of today's money. While president, Lincoln often saved his salary, and in 1864 used those savings to purchase federal bonds totaling almost $68,000. After Lincoln's assassination, he left an estate valued at about $111,000, or the equivalent of well over two million dollars in today's money. Lincoln had not always been this well off. He made most of his money in his law practice. His attempt to become a grocer went almost as badly as that of U. S. Grant. One story goes that it took Honest Abe sixteen years to repay the whole grocery bill he ran up in the attempt. If it did, Lincoln must have had one patient creditor.

LOCAL HERO

Illinois is the only state whose toll ways accept pennies. While a bother for the authorities, and anyone behind a person throwing eighty pennies into the collector, there is a reason. President Lincoln is on every penny and Illinois is the state whose motto is "Land of Lincoln."

BUSINESS SENSE

When it comes to being a business failure, President U. S. Grant is generally the example we all remember. But he really has to contend for that dubious honor with James Monroe. Always bad with money, he even had trouble while president. Since all of Dolley Madison's new furniture was ruined when the White House was burned in 1812, President Madison received $50,000 from Congress to get the place back into shape. This is almost exactly double what Dolley spent. Trouble was, he didn't keep very good track of the money and his bookkeeper stole almost $20,000 of it. Then, his taste for Paris modern (okay, modern for 1817) was expensive. What developed was another presidential precedent now popular with defense contractors: the cost overrun. Congress bailed Monroe out, but when investigating they also discovered that he had sold to the White House, effectively himself, much of his own furniture for the then substantial sum of $9,000. None of this did Monroe any good in the long run. After his presidency, he seemed to never quite be able to earn a living. The nation was only a few decades old and James Monroe was the first president not to be personally very wealthy, so there simply were no procedures for supporting former presidents. There was no pension for former presidents yet, either, so they were left to live on what they could earn. In the years after he left office, Monroe bombarded the government with bills for expenses he had incurred while president and belatedly wanted reimbursement for. Only a few were actually honored by an annoyed Congress. Eventually James Monroe, the fifth president, had to move in with his daughter in New York City, where he died on July 4 in 1831, still broke.

HEIR APPARENT

Franklin Delano Roosevelt really was raised being fed with a silver spoon. His family was very well off and he inherited large sums from a number of relatives. His father left him $100,000 ($1.4 million in today's dollars) and his mother was worth close to a million dollars (read that as $14 million today) herself, and owned Hyde Park, a six-hundred-acre estate on the Hudson River not far from Poughkeepsie, New York. In addition, he was almost constantly employed in an elected or appointed position. While he was the president that dealt with the Great Depression of 1929, FDR certainly did not suffer because of it.

AND HE IS ON THE $500 BILL

In 1890, after seven terms in Congress, William McKinley, not yet president, found he had been defeated for reelection; in 1893, he was also informed that a massive note he had cosigned for a friend had defaulted. He was suddenly was out of work and out of money. The note was so large that paying it off took all of the family money and his wife's inheritance, wiping out over $100,000 they had accumulated. Still it was not enough and an additional $100,000 was raised by Mark Hanna (the machine boss) from McKinley's many friends. Though it basically left the former congressman destitute, he paid off the note. Three years later, his fortunes improved when the still financially stretched William McKinley was elected the twenty-fifth president of the United States in 1896.

GIFT OF HONESTY

As we live in a time when all ethical reforms have built-in loopholes, one past president should be an inspiration. James Buchanan was not that great a leader, but he was a most ethical one. In his time, as is sadly true now, gifts and contributions to those in office were common. Votes were not-too-subtly up for sale. In reaction, the fifteenth president had a rule. His secretary was to return all gifts immediately, even those from his personal friends and longtime supporters. He kept assiduously to this rule during his entire administration.

THICK AS A BRICK

If you are not up on your conspiracy theory, the Freemasons are taking over, or have taken over, the world. A large number of the Founding Fathers were members, as have been many other influential men in U.S. history. The real question is not if the Freemasons have taken over, but if they are in turn controlled by Skull and Bones. If you are curious, here is a list of the presidents who were Freemasons:

George Washington
James Monroe
Andrew Jackson
James Polk
James Buchanan
Andrew Johnson
James Garfield
William McKinley
Theodore Roosevelt
William Taft
Warren Harding
Franklin Delano Roosevelt
Harry Truman
Lyndon Johnson
Gerald Ford

Fifteen of the forty-three presidents were Freemasons. The list has several distinguished members, but if they are really in control, could the Masons not have done better than Polk, Buchanan, Andrew Johnson, and the short term of Garfield? Maybe they just were on a bad streak with these always low-rated or short-term presidents.

CORRUPTION CAUSED CASTRO

The administration of James Buchanan was marked by inaction and corruption. One of the worst scandals involved the theft of $870,000 by a relative of the secretary of state, John Floyd. (Multiply by twenty-five to see what that would be in today's dollars.) The secretary of state was clearly involved and the Congress livid. Part of the fallout of this scandal was that when this same John Floyd presented Congress with the opportunity to peacefully buy Cuba from Spain, they refused to trust him with the money. The chance was missed and it wasn't until decades later, after the Spanish-American War, that Cuba became free. If we had bought Cuba in 1860, it would likely have become part of the United States and its history would be very different. But due to the lack of trust for the corrupt Buchanan presidency, the opportunity was lost to have no Castro and no Bay of Pigs.

THE BLAME

The first income tax was instituted by Woodrow Wilson. At the time, it affected only the top one percent of all taxpayers with a tax rate ranging from one percent to six percent maximum. To get the new tax passed, he made the first joint session appearance before Congress that had occurred since John Adams was president. And yes, he promised Congress that the average worker would never have to pay income tax. He lied.

15

ON THE RECORD:
PRESIDENTIAL LIBRARIES

Presidential libraries, and the access to information they bring, are among the unique wonders of modern America. Few of us realize just how amazing it is to have access to almost all the records of what our leaders have done. Just as American is the fact that the presidential libraries are just as different and idiosyncratic as the men they commemorate.

One of the unique elements of the modern U.S. government is that the records of our recent presidents are available to the public and to scholars. You have to realize that the papers of European heads of state are almost never open to anyone. While we have recently made it a law that the official records of the presidency and Congress are retained and eventually made public, this was not always the case. At first, what paperwork and notes existed were considered the personal property of the president. As such, these papers were often sold by the family of former presidents, normally after their deaths. The records of George Washington's two terms were not owned by the government or available until they were bought by the government for $55,000 in the years before the Civil War. Three presidents' papers were lost in fires and can never be recovered, those of Zachary Taylor, John Tyler, and William Henry Harrison.

Perhaps the most striking example was that of Andrew

Johnson. His was not a happy term. Anyone succeeding Abraham Lincoln would probably have looked bad, but Johnson was often very ineffective. The embittered seventeenth president took the complete records of his administration with him when he left the White House. This included virtually every action of the period, including the complete files on his impeachment, which may explain why everything was taken.

WHO PAYS

On one level, the presidential libraries are one of the taxpayer's few bargains. No government money goes into their construction or preparation. Instead each one is financed by a private foundation that is controlled by the president while in office. Once the library is complete and the records moved into it, the building is taken over and run by the National Archives and Records Administration.

GOING ON THE RECORD

The trend to making presidential papers a national asset began with Franklin Delano Roosevelt. The thirty-second president ordered the National Archives to take possession of the records of his administration. Since these covered both the Great Depression and World War II, they have been invaluable to scholars. This was formalized by his successor, who created the first presidential library: Harry Truman. Every president since has helped with the creation of a library. This process was formalized when Congress passed the Presidential Libraries Act of 1955.

This process is not without its dark side, though. It means the sitting president has to raise millions of dollars in contributions for the creation of a building whose purpose is to immortalize him and his actions. Beyond the ego boost this must give, there is no oversight or limit on who can contribute to the library's fund. This means that even a lobbyist, who cannot buy a lunch for a congressman, is allowed to donate thousands or even millions of dollars directly to an organization that is run by the president and which has no other supervision. There is a potential for abuse, the selling of favors, or the awkward appearance of outright bribery. The result is generally wonderful for historians and even reporters, but the process is just asking for a scandal. One such scandal came at the end of the Clinton administration. Just before he left office, William Jefferson Clinton pardoned a number of individuals. One of these was a fugitive named Mark Rich. He was sought for significant financial crimes and a wanted man. His wife contributed $450,000 to the Bill Clinton Presidential Library Fund within days of when Clinton pardoned her husband. His reasons for pardoning a wanted man whose case had not been heard and who had been a fugitive for years were never revealed.

PERSONAL PREFERENCE

Since the president controls the design and creation of his own library, they tend to reflect both the man and his attitudes. When you compare, say, the Truman Library to the Kennedy Library you easily see the small-town Missouri background in the library of Harry Truman in comparison with the stylish building and

hip interior of Kennedy's or the massive size of Lyndon John-son's ostentatious and very Texas library building. Nixon, when president, was most concerned with foreign affairs (and getting reelected). His library reflects this in its famous Hall of Leaders with life-sized bronze statues of the world leaders he dealt with when president. Perhaps it says something about Bill Clinton, as well, that when you walk thought his library it is impossible to be more than a few feet from a speaker, and often a monitor, featur-ing some speech or appearance of the forty-second president. You have to judge for yourself if the Clinton library might also reflect another part of President Clinton's background. More than one commentator or architect has observed the strong resemblance between the Clinton Presidential Library and, very large mobile home. This is likely unkind or at least unintended by the archi-tect, but then again, for all his faults, Bill Clinton has a wonderful sense of humor. He couldn't have . . . could he?

COLLECTOR'S CHOICE
The first libraries contained what their president chose to send them. In 1978 the Congress passed the Presidential Records Act. This made the files of each president since then a nationally owned item. As such, everything now has to be passed on to the library. To allow the president access to what records he needs for personal use or memoirs, each president now has twelve years after leaving office before everything has to be submit-ted. This was significantly watered down by Executive Order 13233 issued in 2001, which cites national security. This order allows a sitting president to declare any limit he wants before the records of his administration or any previous administra-tion have to be turned over.

DIGGING THROUGH
One of the reason the contents of the libraries is left to the president is the sheer volume of the materials stored. You cer-

tainly need someone as familiar with what happened to find the right papers and information. There are twenty million pages of paper in the Ford Presidential Library!

WE DID SAY PERSONAL PREFERENCE

Another understated entry in a presidential library is that for the Bay of Pigs in the Kennedy Library. His last-minute abandonment of the Cuban rebels the CIA and military had supported and promised to assist was one of the really low points of the Age of Camelot. On the bright side, you can find an entire gallery extolling the virtues and accomplishments of the Peace Corps, which was founded and fostered under the JFK administration.

There is a mosaic made completely of jellybeans in the Reagan Library. It is a larger-than-life image of the fortieth president, who always kept of jar of his favorite candy on his desk in the oval office. But if you want to find out about the Iran Contra scandal, it will take some searching. It is mentioned only on a small text panel hidden away in a dark corner of the displays.

16

THE UNSINKABLE TEDDY ROOSEVELT

by Mike Resnick

> "No president ever enjoyed himself in
> the presidency as much as I did."
> *Theodore Roosevelt*

You cannot research the life of President Theodore Roosevelt without being carried away by the sheer exuberance and joy of life that characterized this exceptional man. He was not perfect and, by today's standard, a jingo and exploiter, but he was just somehow bigger than life, knew it, and enjoyed it.

His daughter, Alice, said it best: "He wanted to be the bride at every wedding and the corpse at every funeral."

But then he had a little something to say about his daughter, too. When various staff members complained that she was running wild through the White House, his response was, "Gentlemen, I can either run the country, or I can control Alice. I cannot do both."

He was Theodore Roosevelt, of course: statesman, politician, adventurer, naturalist, ornithologist, taxidermist, cowboy, police commissioner, explorer, writer, diplomat, boxer, and president of the United States.

John Fitzgerald Kennedy was widely quoted after inviting a dozen writers, artists, musicians and scientists to lunch at the White House when he announced that "this is the greatest assemblage of talent to eat here since Thomas Jefferson dined alone." It's a witty statement, but JFK must have thought Roosevelt ate all his meals out.

Roosevelt didn't begin life all that auspiciously. "Teedee" was a sickly child, his body weakened by asthma. It was his father who decided that he was not going to raise an invalid. Roosevelt was encouraged to swim, to take long hikes, to do everything he could to build up his body.

He was picked on by bullies, who took advantage of his weakened condition, so he asked his father to get him boxing lessons. They worked pretty well. By the time he entered Harvard he had the body and reactions of a trained athlete, and before long he was a member of the boxing team.

It was while fighting for the lightweight championship when an incident occurred that gave everyone an insight into Roosevelt's character. He was carrying the fight to his opponent, C. S. Hanks, the defending champion, when he slipped and fell to his knee. Hanks had launched a blow that he couldn't pull back, and he opened Roosevelt's nose, which began gushing blood. The crowd got ugly and started booing the champion, but Roosevelt held up his hand for silence, announced that it was an honest mistake, and shook hands with Hanks before the fight resumed.

It was his strength of character that led to his developing

an equally strong body. His doctor, W. Thompson, once told a friend: "Look out for Theodore. He's not strong, but he's all grit. He'll kill himself before he'll ever say he's tired."

In fifty-nine years of a vigorous, strenuous life, he never once admitted to being tired.

Roosevelt was always fascinated by nature, and in fact had seriously considered becoming a biologist or a naturalist before discovering politics. The young men sharing his lodgings at Harvard were probably less than thrilled with his interest. He kept a number of animals in his room. Not cute, cuddly ones, but rather snakes, lobsters, and a tortoise that was always escaping and scaring the life out of his landlady. Before long most of the young men in his building refused to go anywhere near his room.

Roosevelt "discovered" politics shortly after graduating Harvard (Phi Beta Kappa and summa cum laude, of course). He attacked the field with the same vigor he attacked everything else. The result? At twenty-four he became the youngest assemblyman in the New York State House, and the next year he became the youngest-ever minority leader.

He might have remained in New York politics for years, but something happened that changed his life. He had met and fallen in love with Alice Hathaway Lee while in college and married her very soon thereafter. His widowed mother lived with them.

And then, on February 14, 1884, Alice and his mother both died (Alice in childbirth, his mother of typhoid fever) twelve hours apart in the same house.

The blow was devastating to Roosevelt. He never mentioned Alice again and refused to allow her to be mentioned in his presence. He put his former life behind him and decided to lose himself in what was left of the Wild West.

He bought the Maltese Cross Ranch in the Dakota badlands. Then, because he was Theodore Roosevelt and couldn't do anything in a small way, he bought a second ranch, the Medora, less than forty miles from the first ranch. He spent a lot more time hunting than ranching, and more time writing and reading than hunting. (During his lifetime he wrote more than 150,000 letters, as well as close to thirty books.)

He'd outfitted himself with the best "Western" outfit money could buy back in New York, and of course he appeared to the locals to be a wealthy New York dandy. By now he was wearing glasses, and he took a lot of teasing over them; the sobriquet "Four Eyes" seemed destined to stick.

Until the night he found himself far from his Elkhorn Ranch and decided to rent a room at Nolan's Hotel in Mingusville, on the west bank of the Beaver River. After dinner he went down to the bar—it was the only gathering point in the entire town—and right after Roosevelt arrived, a huge drunk entered, causing a ruckus, shooting off his six-gun, and making himself generally obnoxious. When he saw Roosevelt, he announced that "Four Eyes" would buy drinks for everyone in the bar—or else. Roosevelt, who wasn't looking for a fight, tried to mollify him, but the drunk was having none of it. He insisted that the effete dandy put up his dukes and defend himself.

"Well, if I've got to, I've got to," muttered Roosevelt, getting up from his chair.

The bully took one swing. The boxer from Harvard ducked and bent the drunk in half with a one-two combination to the belly, then caught him flush on the jaw. He kept pummeling the drunk until the man was out cold, and then, with a little help from the appreciative onlookers, he carried the unconscious man to an outhouse behind the hotel and deposited him there for the night.

He was never "Four Eyes" again.

The dude from New York didn't limit himself to human bullies. No horse could scare him either.

During the roundup of 1884, he and his companions encountered a horse known only as "The Devil." He'd earned his name throwing one cowboy after another, and was generally considered to be the meanest horse in the badlands. Finally Roosevelt decided to match his will and skills against the stallion, and all the other cowboys gathered around the corral to watch the New Yorker get his comeuppance—and indeed, The Devil soon bucked him off.

Roosevelt got on again. And got bucked off again.

According to one observer, "With almost every other jump, we would see about twelve acres of bottom land between Roosevelt and the saddle." The Devil sent him flying a third and then a fourth time.

But Roosevelt wasn't about to quit. The Devil couldn't throw him a fifth time, and before long Roosevelt had him behaving "as meek as a rabbit," according to the same observer.

The next year there was an even wilder horse. The local cowboys knew him simply as "The Killer," but Roosevelt decided he was going to tame him, and a tame horse needed a better name than that, so he dubbed him "Ben Baxter." The cowboys, even those who had seen him break The Devil, urged him to keep away from The Killer, to have the horse destroyed. Roosevelt paid them no attention,

He tossed a blanket over Ben Baxter's head to keep him calm while putting on the saddle, an operation that was usually life-threatening in itself. Then he tightened the cinch, climbed onto the horse, and removed the blanket. And two seconds later Roosevelt was sprawling in the dirt of the corral.

A minute later, he was back in the saddle.

Five seconds later he was flying through the air again, to land with a bone-jarring *thud!*

They kept it up most of the afternoon, Roosevelt climbing back on every time he was thrown, and finally the fight was all gone from Ben Baxter. Roosevelt had broken his shoulder during one of his spills, but it hadn't kept him from mastering the horse. He kept Ben Baxter, and from that day forward "The Killer" became the gentlest horse on his ranch.

Is it any wonder that he never backed down from a political battle?

• • •

Having done everything else one could do in the badlands, Roosevelt became a deputy sheriff. And in March of 1886, he found out that it meant a little more than rounding up the town drunks on a Saturday night. It seems that a wild man named Mike Finnegan, who had a reputation for breaking laws and heads that stretched from one end of the badlands to the other, had gotten drunk and shot up the town of Medora, escaping —not that anyone dared to stop him—on a small flatboat with two confederates.

Anyone who's ever been in Dakota in March knows that it's still quite a few weeks away from the first signs of spring. Roosevelt, accompanied by Bill Sewell and Wilmot Dow, was ordered to bring Finnegan in, and took off after him on a raft a couple of days later. They negotiated the ice-filled river and finally came to the spot where the gang had made camp.

Roosevelt, the experienced hunter, managed to approach silently and unseen until the moment he stood up, rifle in hands, and announced that they were his prisoners. Not a shot had to be fired.

But capturing Finnegan and his friends was the easy part. They had to be transported overland more than 100 miles to the town of Dickenson, where they would stand trial. Within a couple of days the party of three lawmen and three outlaws was out of food. Finally Roosevelt set out on foot for a ranch—*any* ranch—and came back a day later with a small wagon filled with enough food to keep them alive on the long trek. The wagon had a single horse, and given the weather and conditions of the crude trails, the horse couldn't be expected pull all six men, so Sewell and Dow rode in the wagon while Roosevelt and the three captives walked behind it on an almost nonexistent trail, knee-deep in snow, in below-freezing weather. The closer they got to Dickenson, the more likely it was that Finnegan would attempt to escape, so Roosevelt didn't sleep the last two days and nights of the forced march.

But he delivered the outlaws, safe and reasonably sound.

He would be a lawman again in another nine years, but his turf would be as different from the badlands as night is from day.

He became the police commissioner of New York City.

New York was already a pretty crime-ridden city, even before the turn of the twentieth century. Roosevelt, who had already been a successful politician, lawman, lecturer, and author, was hired to change that—and change it he did.

He hired the best people he could find. That included the first woman on the New York police force—and the next few dozen as well. (Before long every station had police matrons around the clock, thus assuring that any female prisoner would be booked by a member of her own sex.)

Then came another innovation: Roosevelt decided that most of the cops couldn't hit the broad side of a barn with their side arms; target practice was not merely encouraged but made mandatory for the first time in the force's history.

When the rise of the automobile meant that police on foot could no longer catch some escaping lawbreakers, Roosevelt created a unit of bicycle police (who, in the 1890s, had no problem keeping up with the cars of that era, which were traversing streets that had not been created with automobiles in mind.)

He hired Democrats as well as Republicans, men who disliked him as well as men who worshipped him. All he cared about was that they were able to get the job done.

He was intolerant only of intolerance. When the famed anti-Semitic preacher from Berlin, Rector Ahlwardt, came to America, New York's Jewish population didn't want to allow him in the city. Roosevelt couldn't bar him, but he came up with the perfect solution: Ahlwardt's police bodyguard was composed entirely of very large, very unhappy Jewish cops whose presence convinced the bigot to forgo his anti-Semitic harangues while he was in the city.

Roosevelt announced that all promotions would be strictly

on merit and not political pull, then spent the next two years proving he meant what he said. He also invited the press into his office whenever he was there, and if a visiting politician tried to whisper a question so that the reporters couldn't hear it, Roosevelt would repeat and answer it in a loud, clear voice.

As police commissioner, Roosevelt felt the best way to make sure his police force was performing its duty was to go out in the field and see for himself. He didn't bother to do so during the day; the press and the public were more than happy to report on the doings of his policemen.

No, what he did was go out into the most dangerous neighborhoods, unannounced, between midnight and sunrise, usually with a reporter or two in tow, just in case things got out of hand. (Not that he thought they would help him physically, but he expected them to accurately report what happened if a misbehaving or loafing cop turned on him.)

The press dubbed these his "midnight rambles," and after a while the publicity alone caused almost all the police to stay at their posts and do their duty. They never knew when the commissioner might show up in their territory and either fire them on the spot or let the reporters who accompanied him expose them to public ridicule and condemnation.

Roosevelt began writing early and never stopped. You'd expect a man who was governor of New York and president of the United States to write about politics, and of course he did. But Roosevelt didn't like intellectual restrictions any more than he liked physical restrictions, and he wrote books—not just articles, mind you, but *books*—about anything that interested him.

While still in college he wrote *The Naval War of 1812*, which was considered at the time to be the definitive treatise on naval warfare.

Here's a partial list of the non-political books that followed, just to give you an indication of the breadth of Roosevelt's interests:

Hunting Trips of a Ranchman
The Wilderness Hunter
A Book-Lover's Holidays in the Open
The Winning of the West, Volumes 1–4
The Rough Riders
Literary Treats
Papers on Natural History
African Game Trails
Hero Tales from American History
Through the Brazilian Wilderness
The Strenuous Life
Ranch Life and the Hunting Trail

He'd be a pretty interesting guy to talk to. On any subject. In fact, it'd be hard to find one he hadn't written up.

A character as interesting and multifaceted as Roosevelt's had to be portrayed in film sooner or later, but surprisingly, the first truly memorable characterization was by John Alexander, who delivered a classic and hilarious portrayal of a harmless madman who *thinks* he's Teddy Roosevelt and constantly screams "Charge!" as he runs up the stairs, his version of San Juan Hill, in *Arsenic and Old Lace*.

Eventually there were more serious portrayals: Brian Keith, Tom Berenger, even Robin Williams. And word has it that, possibly by the time you read this, you'll be able to add Leonardo DiCaprio to the list.

Roosevelt believed in the active life, not just for himself but for his four sons—Kermit, Archie, Quentin, and Theodore Junior—and two daughters—Alice and Edith. He built Sagamore Hill, his rambling house on equally rambling acreage, and he often took the children—and any visiting dignitaries—on what he called "scrambles," cross-country hikes that were more obstacle course than anything else.

His motto: "Above or below, but never around." If you couldn't walk through it, you climbed over it or crawled under it, but you never ever circled it. This included not only hills, boulders, and thornbushes, but also rivers. And frequently he, the children, and the occasional visitor who didn't know what he was getting into, would come home soaking wet from swimming a river or stream with their clothes on, or covered with mud, or with their clothes torn to shreds from thorns.

Those wet, muddy, and torn clothes were their badges of honor. It meant that they hadn't walked around any obstacle.

"If I am to be any use in politics," Roosevelt wrote to a friend, "it is because I am supposed to be a man who does not preach what he fears to practice. For the year I have preached war with Spain . . ."

So it was inevitable that he should leave his job as undersecretary of the navy and enlist in the military. He instantly became Lieutenant Colonel Roosevelt, and began putting together a very special elite unit, one that perhaps only he could have assembled.

The Rough Riders consisted, among others, of cowboys, Indians, tennis stars, college athletes, the marshal of Dodge City, the master of the Chevy Chase hounds, and the man who was reputed to be the best quarterback ever to play for Harvard.

They were quite a crew, Colonel Roosevelt's Rough Riders. They captured the imagination of the public as had no other military unit in U.S. history. They also captured San Juan Hill in the face of some serious machine gun fire, and Roosevelt, who led the charge, returned home an even bigger hero than when he'd left.

While on a bear hunt in Mississippi, Colonel Roosevelt, as he liked to be called after San Juan Hill and Cuba, was told that a bear had been spotted a few miles away. When Roosevelt and his entourage—which always included the press—arrived, he found a small, undernourished, terrified bear tied to a tree. He refused to shoot it, and turned away in disgust, ordering a member of the party to put the poor creature out of its misery. His unwilling-ness to kill a helpless animal was captured by *Washington Post* cartoonist Clifford Berryman. It made him more popular than ever and before long toy companies were turning out replicas of cute little bears that the great Theodore Roosevelt would cer-tainly never kill, rather than ferocious game animals.

Just in case you ever wondered about the origin of the teddy bear.

Some thirty years ago, writer-director John Milius gave the public one of the truly great adventure films, *The Wind and the Lion*, in which the Raisuli (Sean Connery), known as the "Last of the Barbary Pirates," kidnapped an American woman, Eden Perdicaris (Candice Bergen) and her two children, and held them for ransom at his stronghold in Morocco. At which point President Theodore Roosevelt (Brian Keith, in probably the best representation of Roosevelt ever put on film) declared that America wanted "Perdicaris alive or Raisuli dead!" and sent the fleet to Morocco.

Wonderful film, beautifully photographed, well-written, well-acted, with a gorgeous musical score.

Would you like to know what *really* happened?

First of all, it wasn't *Eden* Perdicaris; it was *Ion* Perdicaris, a 64-year-old man. And he wasn't kidnapped with two small children, but with a grown stepson. And far from wanting to be rescued, he and the Raisuli became great friends.

Roosevelt felt the president of the United States had to pro-tect Americans abroad, so he sent a telegram to the Sultan of Morocco, the country in which the kidnapping took place, to the effect that America wanted Perdicaris alive or Raisuli dead. He also dispatched seven warships to Morocco.

So why wasn't there a war with Morocco?

Two reasons.

First, during the summer of 1904, shortly after the kidnapping and Roosevelt's telegram, the government learned something that was kept secret until after all the principals in the little drama—Roosevelt, Perdicaris, and the Raisuli—had been dead for years, and that was that Ion Perdicaris was *not* an American citizen. He had been born one, but he later renounced his citizenship and moved to Greece, years before the kidnapping.

The other reason? Perdicaris's dear friend, the Raisuli, set him free. Secretary of State John Hay knew full well that Perdicaris had been freed before the Republican convention convened, but he whipped the assembled delegates up with the "America wants Perdicaris alive or Raisuli dead!" slogan anyway, and Roosevelt was nominated in a landslide.

Roosevelt was as vigorous and active a president as he'd been in every previous position. Consider:

Even though the country was relatively empty, he could see land being gobbled up in great quantities by settlers and others, and he created the national park system.

He arranged for a revolt against the Venezuelan government, which resulted in the founding of the nation of Panama, which then supported his plan for the Panama Canal, which a century later is *still* vital to international shipping.

He took on J. P. Morgan and his cohorts, and became the greatest "trust buster" in our history, then created the Department of Commerce and the Department of Labor to make sure weaker presidents in the future didn't give up the ground he'd taken.

We were a regional power when he took office. Then he sent the Navy's "Great White Fleet" around the world on a "goodwill tour." By the time it returned home, we were, for the first time, a world power.

Because he never backed down from a fight, a lot of people thought of him as a warmonger—but he became the first American president to win the Nobel Peace Prize while still in office when he mediated a war between Japan and Russia.

He created and signed the Pure Food and Drug Act.

He became the first president to leave the United States while in office when he visited Panama to inspect the canal.

Roosevelt remained physically active throughout his life. He may or may not have been the only president to be blind in one eye, but he was the only who ever to go blind in one eye from injuries received in a boxing match *while serving as president.* Roosevelt frequently boxed, competed with martial artists and the like all through his time in office.

He also took years of jujitsu lessons while in office, and became quite proficient at it.

And, in keeping with daughter Alice's appraisal of him, he was the first president to fly in an airplane.

Roosevelt's last day in office was March 3, 1909.

He'd already been a cowboy, a rancher, a soldier, a marshal, a police commissioner, a governor, and a president. So did he finally slow down?

Just long enough to pack. Accompanied by his son, Kermit, and the ever-present journalists, on March 23 he boarded a ship that would take him to East Africa for his first organized safari on record. It was sponsored by the American Museum of Natural History and Smithsonian museums, which to this day display some of the trophies he shot and brought back. His two guides were F. C. Selous, widely considered to be the greatest hunter in African history and the inspiration for the classic fictional character Allan Quartermain, and Philip Percival, who was already a legend among Kenya's hunting fraternity.

What did Roosevelt manage to bag for the museums?

9 lions
9 elephants
5 hyenas
8 black rhinos

5 white rhinos
7 hippos
8 warthogs
6 Cape buffalo
3 pythons
And literally hundreds of antelope, gazelle, and other
    smaller herbivores

Is it any wonder that he needed five hundred uniformed porters? And since he paid as much attention to the mind as to the body, one of those porters carried sixty pounds of Roosevelt's favorite books on his back, and Roosevelt made sure he got in his reading every day, no matter what.

While hunting in Uganda, he ran into the noted rapscallion John Boyes and others who were poaching elephants in the Lado Enclave. According to Boyes's memoir, *The Company of Adventurers*, the poachers offered to put a force of fifty hunters and poachers at Roosevelt's disposal if he would like to take a shot at bringing American democracy, capitalism, and know-how to the Belgian Congo (not that they had any right to it, but from their point of view, neither did King Leopold of Belgium). Roosevelt admitted to being tempted, but he had decided that his chosen successor, William Howard Taft, was doing a lousy job as president and he'd made up his mind to run again.

But first, he wrote what remains one of the true classics of hunting literature, *African Game Trails*, which has remained in print for just short of a century as these words are written. (And half a dozen of the journalists sent *their* versions of the safari to the book publishers, whose readers simply couldn't get enough of Roosevelt.)

William Howard Taft, the sitting president (and Roosevelt's hand-picked successor), of course wanted to run for reelection. Roosevelt was the clear choice among the Republican rank and file, but the president controls the party's machinery, and due to a number of procedural moves Taft got the nomination.

Roosevelt, outraged at the backstage manipulations, decided to form a third party. Officially it was the Progressive Party, but after he mentioned that he felt "as fit as a bull moose," the public dubbed it the Bull Moose Party.

Not everyone was thrilled to see him run for a third term. (It would have been only his second election to the presidency; he became president in 1901 after McKinley's election and assassination, so though he'd only been elected once, he had served in the White House for seven years.) One such unhappy citizen was John F. Schrank.

On October 14, 1912, Roosevelt came out of Milwaukee's Hotel Gillespie to give a speech at a nearby auditorium. He climbed into an open car and waved to the crowd—and found himself face-to-face with Schrank, who raised his pistol and shot Roosevelt in the chest.

The crowd would have torn Schrank to pieces, but Roosevelt shouted: "Stand back! Don't touch that man!"

He had Schrank brought before him, stared at the man until the potential killer could no longer meet his gaze, then refused all immediate medical help. He wasn't coughing up blood, which convinced him that the wound wasn't fatal, and he insisted on giving his speech before going to the hospital.

He was a brave man, but he was also a politician and a showman, and he knew what the effect on the crowd would be when they saw the indestructible Roosevelt standing before them in a blood-soaked shirt, ignoring his wound to give them his vision of what he could do for America. "I shall ask you to be as quiet as possible," he began. "I don't know whether you fully understand that I have just been shot." He gave them the famous Roosevelt grin. "But it takes more than that to kill a Bull Moose!"

It brought the house down.

He lost the election to Woodrow Wilson—even Roosevelt couldn't win as a third-party candidate—but William Howard

Taft, the president of the United States, came in a distant third, capturing only eight electoral votes.

That was enough for one vigorous lifetime, right?

Not hardly.

Did you ever hear of the River of Doubt?

You can be excused if your answer is negative. It no longer exists on any map.

On February 27, 1914, at the request of the Brazilian government, Roosevelt and his party set off to map the River of Doubt. It turned out to be not quite the triumph that the African safari had been.

Early on they began running short of supplies. Then Roosevelt developed a severe infection in his leg. It got so bad that at one point he urged the party to leave him behind. Of course they didn't, and gradually his leg and his health improved to the point where he was finally able to continue the expedition.

Eventually they mapped all nine hundred miles of the river, and Roosevelt, upon returning home, wrote another bestseller, *Through the Brazilian Wilderness*. Shortly thereafter, the *Rio da Duvida* (River of Doubt) officially became the river you can now find on the maps, the *Rio Teodoro* (River Theodore).

He was a man in his mid-fifties, back when the average man's life expectancy was only fifty-five. He was just recovering from being shot in the chest (and was still walking around with the bullet inside his body). Unlike East Africa, where he would be hunting the same territory that Selous had hunted before and Percival knew like the back of his hand, no one had ever mapped the River of Doubt. It was uncharted jungle, with no support network for hundreds of miles.

So why did he agree to map it?

His answer is so typically Rooseveltian that it will serve as the end to this chapter:

"It was my last chance to be a boy again."

17

COMMANDER IN CHIEF

*T*hink about having to tell your neighbor to go somewhere where there is a good chance he will be shot and killed. And then he is. Tough? But multiply that by thousands and you have what most presidents have felt was the most difficult part of the job. In a time of near-constant warfare, here is a look at the past presidents who were commander in chief while the United States was at war.

SHIVER ME TIMBERS!
THOMAS JEFFERSON AND THE BARBARY PIRATES (1801–1805)

by Douglas Niles

The Barbary States were nations of North Africa to the west of Egypt, occupying the coast of the Mediterranean into the Atlantic. Named for the Berber tribes who made up most of their population, they included lands that would become the nations of Libya, Tunisia, Algeria, and Morocco, with their most significant ports being Tripoli, Tunis, and Algiers. They reached the height of their power during the 1600s, with each of the four nations being ruled by a strongman-type dictator who usually assumed power by violent elimination of his predecessor. Nominally a part of the Muslim Ottoman Empire, the Barbary states were more or less self-governed.

They became a steady menace to the shipping and commerce of European nations, raiding throughout the central and western Mediterranean, capturing ships and goods for their own use or trade, and holding captured crew for ransom, or selling them as slaves. The Barbary pirates relied upon galleys for their fleets until a Flemish outlaw, Simon Danzer, was able to convince them of the virtues of sail during the seventeenth-century. From then on their small, nimble vessels became the scourge of the seas. By 1650, more than 30,000 captives were held in Algiers alone!

Although the fleets of the European powers could have overcome the Barbary pirates, none of the countries being preyed upon desired to make the effort. Beginning with England, which signed a treaty with a Barbary state in 1662, the countries of Europe universally decided to pay tribute—usually in the form of a large initial payment followed by

annual supplemental bribes—to purchase safety for their ships. By making these payments, countries not only bought safety for their own fleets but they hoped to direct the pirate activities against their rivals.

Of course, it became an ever more expensive cycle, as the pirates were prone to changing the terms of the tribute, raising the price and then resuming their raids until the new, higher price was met. Still, the Europeans paid, and the Barbary pirates lived in high style.

Merchants in the American colonies traded extensively in the Mediterranean. Prior to the Revolutionary War, this trade was protected under the treaties between the pirates and the English. Shortly after gaining independence, however, the Americans found that their ships had become favored targets of the Barbary pirates. Obviously, this development was welcomed by the British, who believed that American trade in the Mediterranean Sea would be virtually eliminated. As one English official remarked, "The Americans cannot protect themselves—they cannot pretend to a navy!"

Indeed, U.S. trade pretty much ceased along the coastlines of the Barbary states within a few years after independence. The Continental Congress authorized a delegation in 1784, including Thomas Jefferson, Benjamin Franklin, and John Adams, to negotiate tribute with the Barbary states. They were authorized to spend a total of $80,000. In 1787, they concluded a reasonably successful tribute treaty with Morocco, making a one-time payment of $20,000. From this time on, the Moroccans more or less left American shipping alone.

Algiers was the most powerful of the Barbary States, however, and it would not be so easily dissuaded. Between 1785 and 1790, more than a dozen American ships and more than one hundred crewmen, were captured by pirates based out of Algiers. The ruler of that state, called the Dey, demanded ten times more tribute than the Americans were willing to pay. Ben

Franklin urged the nation to accept the Dey's demands, while Jefferson grew more and more convinced that the matter would need to be settled by force. By 1795, Congress authorized the construction of six warships, even as it also finally agreed to a payment of more than half a million dollars (money that had to be borrowed) plus regular deliveries of naval supplies, to buy peace with Algiers.

A few years later, less expensive treaties were reached with the pashas who ruled Tripoli and Tunis. Jefferson was convinced that all of these agreements were mere stopgaps, that the pirates would keep raising their prices and resuming their raiding until the new fees were paid. In this he was in agreement with William Eaton, the American consul at Tunis. Eaton wrote: "There is no access to the permanent friendship of these states without paving the way with gold or cannonballs; and the proper question is which method is preferable."

Jefferson was inaugurated as America's third president in March 1801, and he was determined to use cannonballs as his currency. However, the Barbary pirates were only one small matter in a host of important policy issues, many of them unprece dented, facing the man who was the author of the Declaration of Independence. As a leader of the Democratic-Republican party, Jefferson had soundly defeated his rival Alexander Hamilton's Federalist party, setting in motion the first inauguration that also represented a shift in party control. (Jefferson regarded Hamilton as an enemy of the republican style of government; Hamilton, in turn, thought Jefferson was a radical demagogue.)

Jefferson had barely assumed the mantle of office when he dispatched a squadron of four warships to the Mediterranean. Even before these ships arrived, the pasha of Tripoli had decided that the United States was not paying its bounty in a timely fashion, and he declared war on America (or American shipping, at least). Though the ships of the fledgling United States Navy did succeed in blockading Tripoli for a short time, over the first two years of the conflict they were not effective in bringing an end to the piracy.

At the same time, William Eaton, who was less than impressed by the lack of initiative and rather inept capabilities displayed by the navy commanders, began working on his own plot: he would attempt to overthrow the pasha and replace him with his exiled brother, who would presumably be more friendly toward American interests.

In 1803, a more aggressive U.S. Navy officer, Commodore Edward Preble, arrived on the scene with a fresh squadron of warships. He restored the blockade on Tripoli's harbor. Unfortunately, during this process, one of his frigates—the thirty-six-gun USS *Philadelphia*—ran aground. More than three hundred officers and crew were captured, and the pasha demanded $3 million for their release. Unwilling to leave the stranded frigate in the hands of the pirates, Preble authorized a daring raid: Lieutenant Stephen Decatur and seventy men sailed up to the stranded *Philadelphia* in a captured pirate vessel, boarded the frigate, overwhelmed the pirates on guard, and set her on fire. Decatur's party escaped with no casualties, escorted out of the harbor by the spectacular sight of the frigate exploding behind them.

Preble then concentrated all of his warships into a moderate-sized fleet and proceeded to firmly blockade Tripoli, and also to bombard its fortifications from the sea. In the meantime, William Eaton organized a force in Egypt, including mercenaries, Arab horsemen, and assorted criminal types. They marched hundreds of miles across the desert to attack one of the Tripoli pasha's lesser ports, Derna. Aided by gunnery support from several of Preble's frigates—as well as a contingent of United States Marines—Eaton's ad hoc force captured Derna and held it against the pasha's counterattack. (This event is memorialized in the famous "to the shores of Tripoli" line in the Hymn of the Marine Corps.)

Much to Eaton's disappointment, the United States finally

agreed to a treaty with the pasha. Even with the military successes of Preble's and Eaton's operations, the Americans paid $60,000 to secure the release of all American prisoners. At least this brought the war with Tripoli to a close and another stretch of the Barbary coast was rendered safe for American merchant ships. Jefferson then summoned the warships home from the Mediterranean, as conflict with England was growing sharper. (These tensions would soon result in the War of 1812.)

The last engagement between the United States and the Barbary pirates would not occur until the war with England was resolved. In 1814, the new Dey of Algiers renewed hostilities against American shipping, charging overdue tribute payments. President James Madison gained the authorization of Congress for a punitive expedition that was commanded by none other than the hero of Tripoli, Stephen Decatur (now a commodore). Commanding a squadron of nine ships, Decatur brazenly sailed into Algiers harbor, threatening the city with his guns. The Dey agreed to free all American prisoners, and actually paid a fee of $10,000 to get the Americans to go away! Decatur went on to leverage similar arrangements from Tunis and Tripoli before returning home to report that the Barbary pirates were no longer a threat to American commerce.

WHITE HOUSE BURNING
JAMES MADISON AND THE BRITISH RAID ON WASHINGTON (1814)

by Douglas Niles

The War of 1812 was a little sideshow of a conflict to England, which was deeply engaged in the effort to contain and eventually defeat Napoleonic France. To the Americans, however, it was a struggle for survival that resulted in displays of military ineptness and political bickering that could have torn the fledgling nation asunder. Not for the last time, it was a conflict in which part of the American population (deemed the "War Hawks") adamantly endorsed the war, while others (primarily of the Federalist Party) vehemently opposed it.

Elected to the presidency in 1808, after two terms as Thomas Jefferson's secretary of state, James Madison inherited a growing crisis between the United States and England. While it was not the sole cause of the war, the interruption of American commerce by the British Navy, and especially the capture of American sailors who were forced to serve aboard English warships ("impressment"), aroused fierce resentment in the young nation. Britain was involved in more or less constant war with France over the period from 1793 to 1815, and—as always—she relied upon her peerless navy to control the seas.

Furthermore, American merchants traded with both England and Europe, and the British were adamant about blockading the French-controlled European ports, which seriously curtailed U.S. business interests. In 1807, Britain issued orders requiring that any ships intending to sail for French ports first stop at an English port and pay duties. (In one of several ironic coincidences of timing in this war, the order was repealed by England the day before the United States declared war.)

Another source of conflict between the two countries involved Canadian support for Native American tribes on the frontier. On November 11, 1811, the Shawnee under Tecumseh were defeated at the Battle of Tippecanoe (in what would become the state of Indiana). The War Hawks included a number of aggressive congressmen from frontier districts, and they used this battle as an argument for carrying the war into Indian Territory, and against Canada (a British colony) itself. Some of these firebrands even began advocating the invasion and conquest of Canada. While this goal was never a realistic American objective, it became a rallying cry for those who favored war.

On the other side were the members of the Federalist Party, centered in New England and very pro-British. They were so much so, in fact, that when Britain blockaded American ports during the war, the ports in New England were allowed to function more or less unimpeded. Nevertheless, in light of the growing pro-war sentiment, and deeply insulted by arrogant British behavior on the high seas, President Madison and the Congress declared war on England—albeit by the smallest "yes" vote on a war declaration in American history.

However, it was soon revealed that the Americans were woefully unprepared for war. At first, President Madison put much faith in aging heroes of the Revolution, but these commanders proved almost universally inept. The British quickly captured forts on the sites of current day Detroit and Chicago. Not one but two American invasions of Canada were thwarted when mixed armies of regulars and militia reached the border; the regulars crossed over while the militiamen refused to leave American soil. The divided armies were easily dispatched by the British, while sulking commanders put their troops into barren winter quarters where the troops suffered severe hardships.

On the high seas, the Americans met with some individual successes (the USS *Constitution* earned her sobriquet, "Old Ironsides," early on) but British numbers put grave pressure on American shipping. In the Great Lakes, it became a matter of which side could build ships faster, and here the U.S. forces were able to gain control of Lake Erie long enough to land a force at York (now Toronto), where the Americans proceeded to loot and burn the place.

By 1814, the British controlled the waters off the American coast, and a fleet—with many soldiers aboard—sailed into Chesapeake during the summer of that year. President Madison's incompetent secretary of war, John Armstrong, refused to take his boss's counsel when Madison warned him about a potential threat to Washington, D.C. As a result, when the British sailed up the Patuxent River and put some five thousand men ashore in August, the Americans had only a force of some seven thousand untrained militia, commanded by the politically appointed General Winder, to oppose them.

The Battle of Bladensburg was fought on August 24, 1814. Some fifteen hundred British regulars, the advance force, completely and shamefully routed the militia in a short engagement, leaving the road to Washington undefended. The triumphant British troops quickly marched to Capitol Hill, taking fire only from some angry citizens in a house at the corner of Maryland and Constitution Avenues. The house was quickly destroyed, and the British troops encountered no more resistance.

But they were angry about the casualties they had taken, and also wished to avenge the sacking of York. Very quickly they set fire to the buildings of the Senate and House of Representatives (the classic rotunda of the modern Capitol building had not yet been built). The Library of Congress also went up in flames.

The next day the British commander, Admiral Cockburn, arrived on the scene with a personal grudge. A newspaper, the *National Intelligencer*, had aroused his ire with a series of articles branding him "the Ruffian." He intended to burn the paper's building, but was dissuaded by local residents who feared the fire would spread to their homes. Cockburn contented himself by having the newspaper building knocked down, and made sure that his troops got rid of every "C" for the typesetting presses—ostensibly so that the paper would not be able to write about him anymore.

Meanwhile, the victorious British troops started down Pennsylvania Avenue toward the executive mansion. Congress had already fled the city, the president himself seeking refuge in Virginia. Famously, his wife, Dolley Madison, stayed in the presidential mansion even after her personal bodyguards had fled. She saved a number of important documents and was able to remove the Lansdowne Portrait, a full-length image of George Washington. She fled the house out the back just before British troops charged in through the front.

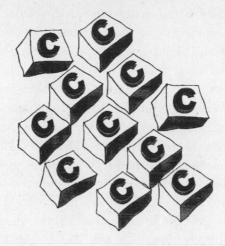

These soldiers must have been delighted to find the table set with a feast for forty people. They obligingly consumed the food before they started burning the building, throwing extra tinder on the blaze to make sure everything was incinerated. At the same time, the Treasury Building was burned, and the Americans themselves burned the Washington Navy Yard to keep several nearly-completed warships from falling into enemy hands. People as far away as Baltimore could see the flames from the massive conflagrations—although the British were persuaded to spare the United States Patent Office, convinced that those important records should be preserved.

The raid completed, the British withdrew to their ships and went on to raid Baltimore, where their bombardment of Fort McHenry would cause Francis Scott Key to observe that "our flag was still there" as he scribed the verses that would become the "Star-Spangled Banner."

The raid on Washington was not a strategic success, because the British held the city for only a matter of days, but it was a devastating blow to American pride. Even as the U.S. Army was beginning to show success on other fronts, the cost of the war was brought home with devastating symbolism. Even so, under

President Madison the army improved dramatically as he replaced incompetent aged commanders with younger, more vigorous leaders. (The average age of generals dropped from sixty in 1812 to thirty in 1814.)

Ever resentful of the war, and deeply tied to Britain, the New England states began to talk seriously of secession, meeting at the Hartford Convention (December 1814–January 1815) to draw up specific plans to break away from the United States. The convention never finished its business as, in the end, the Americans won just enough crucial victories, and both nations were consumed with such war weariness, that the Treaty of Ghent was signed on Christmas Eve 1814, ending hostilities. Because of policies viewed as seditious by most Americans, the Federalist Party was more or less destroyed by the war. Ironically, the greatest American land victory, a rout of British regulars by militia under Andrew Jackson at the Battle of New Orleans, occurred after the peace treaty had been signed but before word of the agreement could reach the troops.

MANIFEST DESTINY
JAMES POLK AND THE WAR WITH MEXICO (1846–1848)

by Douglas Niles

There are times, situations, conflicts when a person can just see that Big Trouble lies not too far over the horizon. One of these circumstances could have been found in Texas, circa 1836–1845, following the Texas Revolution. For this short decade, following the defeat of Santa Anna's army, Texas—in the eyes of Texans, Americans, and several European powers such as France and England—was a small, independent country.

To Mexico, however, Texas was a rebellious province that would eventually be returned to control of the central government. Santa Anna had been Sam Houston's prisoner when he signed the treaty granting Texas independence, so most Mexicans felt the document to be invalid.

The United States government treated both Texas and Mexico as neutral states, engaging in diplomacy and trade with both. The American population, however, viewed the state of affairs through no such diffuse goggles—to the vast majority of Americans, Texas was destined to become part of the United States, and the sooner the better. In 1845, Texas was annexed by the United States and became the twenty-eighth state in the Union. This was an intolerable insult to proud Mexicans, an insult further aggravated by the American contention that Texas territory extended all the way to the Rio Grande, whereas Mexico maintained that the border lay along the Nueces River.

The annexation of Texas was virtually the last act of John Tyler's presidency, but it was perfectly in keeping with newly elected President Polk's objectives. While the concept of Manifest Destiny—the God-given right of the American people to control North America from the Atlantic to the Pacific—was not new, no president before or since did so much to realize that grand ambition.

He was elected to office in November 1844 on the slimmest of margins, learning several weeks after the election that New York had gone to his Democratic party by around five thousand votes. Henry Clay and the Whigs were defeated. (It is said that when Polk received word of his victory, he strolled around his Tennessee hometown for an evening without telling anyone that he had been elected president.) The youngest man, at forty-nine, to be elected at the time, Polk had promised to limit himself to one term.

Although the showdown with Mexico was on the front burner from the first days of his administration, Polk could not be accused of singlemindedness. He was also determined to settle control of the vast "Oregon Territory" in America's favor. (At the time he was elected, the territory was claimed by both the United States and the British.) The negotiations with England grew so tense that, for several months, the United States was facing the prospect of a two-front war with Mexico in the southwest and Britain in the northwest. Some of the more radical fear-mongers actually saw a potential menace in a British alliance with an independent Texas, which could eventually link up to effectively block the United States from access to the Pacific!

Fortunately, matters with England were peaceably resolved after the United States agreed to give up Vancouver Island, freeing the government and army to direct its attention against Mexico. Future president Zachary Taylor, commanding about half the total regular force of the U.S. Army, moved from New Orleans into Texas after annexation. Marching southward, he crossed the Nueces River into territory Mexico regarded as not part of Texas. Setting up camp across the Rio Grande from the Mexican city of Matamoros, Taylor awaited developments. Not surprisingly, some skirmishing resulted.

At the same time, Polk was preparing a message to Congress asking for a declaration of war. His emissary to Mexico, John Slidell, had returned to Washington to report intolerably rude treatment at the hands of the Mexican government (which had changed hands several times during Slidell's mission). The diplomat had actually been dispatched on a secret mission, and had hoped to purchase California from Mexico. Such a sale was regarded as unacceptable by most Mexicans, and so no matter who held the reins of state, they had all refused to meet Slidell. It is likely that personal pride as much as diplomatic reality was at the root of Slidell's pique when he returned to Washington.

Polk was not at all sure that Congress was prepared to declare war, but an accident of timing rendered the issue a no-brainer. Even as Polk was writing the draft of his speech, he received a message from Taylor reporting on the skirmishing around the Rio Grande. The conclusion of the message reported that "American blood has been shed on American soil." These words found their way into the president's address, and the declaration of war was almost unanimous.

The military execution of the war was a new high point in the performance of an American army. Taylor invaded Mexico from the north, winning a series of battles culminating in a decisive triumph at the Battle of Buena Vista. Rejecting Polk's suggestions that he continue south toward Mexico City, Taylor rested on his laurels. (A prominent Whig, he would win the presidency for his party in the next election.) So Polk dispatched Winfield Scott and another army to Mexico by sea. Scott's force landed at Veracruz and marched all the way to the capital, winning a series of battles on the way and eventually taking the great city of Mexico. (This, too, is memorialized in the Marine's Hymn in the phrase "From the halls of Montezuma . . .") Other expeditions were ordered into regions that would become New Mexico, Arizona, and California, and all of these met with notable success.

While the American and Mexican armies were armed with similar weapons and led by competent professional officers, American leadership was among the best this country had ever produced. Many famous Civil War generals, including Grant, Lee, Bragg, Jackson, and Sherman, started their rise to prominence during the Mexican-American War. The morale of the American soldiers was also clearly superior, as was the single-minded focus of the troops on their leaders' goals. Manifest Destiny was not simply a government policy; it was very much a popular ideal.

The Mexican government changed hands several times during the course of the war. The territories under dispute were controlled by the Mexican government by virtue of the fact that they had been Spanish territories when Mexico achieved independence in 1821. However, the populations in these territories, especially northern California and Texas, were heavily American, and actively lobbied for the change.

By the time the war concluded in 1848, American arms had succeeded in all theaters. The treaty of Guadalupe Hidalgo, signed in February 1848, ended hostilities. In exchange for a payment of $15 million, the United States acquired Utah, Nevada, California, and parts of New Mexico, Arizona, and Colorado. (This was about half of Mexico's territory.) Mexican families living in the ceded territories were given the option of moving to Mexico or becoming U.S. citizens; the majority chose the latter option.

President Polk had a few more actions to complete during his one term. He concluded a treaty with New Granada (now Colombia) which secured the right to eventually build a canal across the Isthmus of Panama. Finally, during his last address to Congress, Polk declared that an "abundance of gold" had been discovered in California, setting in motion one of the more frenzied migrations in American history. Polk left office at the end of his term, and died a mere three months later.

As to Mexico, her fate can perhaps be summarized by the proverb, often attributed to President Porfirio Díaz around the end of the nineteenth century: "Poor Mexico. So far from God—and so close to the United States."

A GENERAL WHO WILL FIGHT
ABRAHAM LINCOLN AND THE ARMY OF THE POTOMAC

by Douglas Niles

Abraham Lincoln is widely regarded as the greatest president in American history. It is ironic that his very election was virtually guaranteed to start the bloody war that would determine his nation's very survival.

A former Whig, Lincoln joined the fledgling Republican Party in 1856 and became an eloquent spokesman for that party's strong anti-slavery stance. An articulate, intelligent, and extremely witty speaker, the six-foot-four-inch Lincoln was vaulted to national prominence during an unsuccessful Senate campaign in 1858. His debates with opponent Stephen Douglas articulated the abolitionist point of view in a way that captured the enthusiasm of many slavery opponents and appalled numerous citizens in the slave-owning Southern states.

When he won the Republican presidential nomination in 1860, one Georgia magazine stated before the election: "The South will never permit Abraham Lincoln to be inaugurated President of the United States; this is settled and sealed fact." When Lincoln won the general election in November 1860, it was not surprising that Southern states, beginning with South Carolina, began to break away from the Union. By the time of his inauguration in March, Alabama, Florida, Georgia, Louisiana, Mississippi, and Texas had followed suit.

War was temporarily averted when outgoing President Buchanan agreed not to reinforce Fort Sumter, in Charleston harbor, and the South Carolinians agreed not to attack the fort. Lincoln became President on March 4, 1861, and by April he had decided that it was necessary to resupply the fort, which was running low on provisions. That was all the provocation the Confederates required, and they quickly attacked and captured the fort. In the next few days, Lincoln called for seventy-five thousand volunteers and ordered a blockade of Southern ports. Arkansas, North Carolina, Tennessee, and Virginia responded by seceding from the United States.

There is a popular perception in the North that the Civil War was fought to free the slaves, while Southerners often maintain that it was a struggle about states' rights. While neither viewpoint is one-hundred-percent accurate, there was really one specific right in dispute: the right of a state's wealthy citizens to own slaves. Resolution of this question had been pushed under the rug since the time of the Revolutionary

War, but sentiment on both sides had been hardening in the intervening four score plus years. By the time of Lincoln's election, slavery was regarded as an abomination across most of the world. At the same time, Southern slave owners felt that the institution was crucial to their economic survival and they managed to convince the white citizens of their states (the overwhelming majority of whom did not own a single slave) that their regional pride was at stake.

The result was the bloodiest, most destructive war (to America) in United States history. Yet when the struggle began, few, if any, of the combatants foresaw anything but a quick and easy victory. The North had huge advantages in population (twenty million to nine million in the South, including four million slaves), materiel, most of the industrial and manufacturing capacity, as well as virtually unchallenged control of the seas. The South possessed strong morale and unity of purpose, motivated soldiers, and a talented cadre of officers—American army leaders trained at West Point who chose to fight for their states instead of for the federal government.

The next few months were spent in gathering armies and appointing commands. Lincoln offered command of all the Union armies to Robert E. Lee, a Virginian, who decided that he could not fight against his home state. In his stead, General Irvin McDowell became the first commander of the great military force that would soon be called the Army of the Potomac. By July, the Confederates were advancing on Washington, and on July 21, McDowell met them at the small creek known as Bull Run barely two dozen miles south of the nation's capital. The battle was closely fought for a time, but when the Union troops finally broke, they broke very badly indeed. Their panicked flight carried them all the way to Washington, and this very public flogging by the Confederates gave the president and his citizens a foreshadow of the long struggle ahead.

McDowell had done nothing to bring credit to himself during

the debacle, and Lincoln quickly (July 27) replaced him with General George McClellan, who had won a small victory in the western part of Virginia. Never lacking in self-confidence, McClellan wrote to his wife, "I seem to have become the power of the land."

McClellan had significant skills as an army commander: he could very ably train and organize and motivate his men. So impressive was he at restoring the morale and improving the capabilities of the defeated army that Lincoln soon (November 1) appointed him commander of all the Union armies. Said McClellan: "I can do it all."

Indeed, he continued to organize and train as the year of 1861 came to a close. On January 31, 1862, the president spurred the "Young Napoleon" with General War Order Number 1, in which he commanded that a general advance against the enemy begin by February 22. McClellan still was not ready to move, however.

In the western theater, a force under Ulysses S. Grant moved south against two forts guarding the Tennessee and Cumberland Rivers, both promising paths of invasion into the Confederacy. Fort Henry capitulated on February 6, and Fort Donnelson fell ten days later. Based on his response when the besieged garrisons asked for terms, the Union general became known as "Unconditional Surrender" Grant, and was the North's first real hero of the war. He moved down the Tennessee River, through Kentucky, Tennessee, and into northern Mississippi.

Finally McClellan put his own grand plan into operation, moving his army by sea to Fortress Monroe, on the York peninsula of Virginia. From here, Richmond was a short march inland, and the surprised Confederates had very few troops between the powerful Army of the Potomac and the capital of the Confederacy. Spies, reconnaissance, and the president himself were convinced that Mac faced very light opposition.

Not for the last time in his career, however, George McClellan convinced himself that the troops he was facing far outnumbered his own. Even as he pleaded for reinforcements and stressed the vulnerability of his position, he refused to decamp on the road to Richmond. Finally, under direct orders, he began to creep westward. Every dummy strong point and cavalry skirmish, however, suggested to McClellan that he was facing hundreds of thousands of Rebel troops, and as a result he advanced at little better than a snail's pace.

In the west, meanwhile, Grant ran into troubles of his own. Confederate forces surprised his divided army near Shiloh landing; only tenacious defense and the timely arrival of reinforcements prevented a major Union disaster in the two-day battle. Even so, there were some twelve thousand Northern casualties and seven thousand Southern. Together, this two-day tally exceeded all the casualties in all previous American wars combined. Pressed to relieve Grant because of the setback, Lincoln replied: "I can't spare this general. He fights."

McClellan, despite taking careful counsel of his fears, was finally closing in on Richmond by late May. The pace of his advance was so deliberate that the Confederates were able, finally, to muster a sizeable force to defend the city. On May 31, they defeated the Army of the Potomac in the Battle of Seven Pines. The Confederate commander, General Johnston, was grievously wounded, and he was replaced in command of the newly named Army of Northern Virginia by Robert E. Lee.

In late June a series of chaotic battles raged between the forces. Called the Seven Days' Battles, these clashes resulted in McClellan falling back from Richmond. At his usual plodding pace, Little Mac pulled back to Fortress Monroe and, ever so slowly, began transporting his army, by ship, back up Chesapeake Bay to Washington.

In the meantime, Lincoln appointed General John Pope to command the newly created Army of Virginia. Anticipating reinforcement by the Army of the Potomac, Pope began to advance southward. He was met by the fast-moving Lee at the same Bull

Run creek where the first battle of the war had been fought; as it turned out, McClellan had no intention of helping his fellow Union general. Though he outnumbered Lee, Pope was soundly smashed, and Lee advanced to Harper's Ferry on the Potomac. Crossing the river, he commenced to invade Maryland.

With no alternative, and against the advice of much of his cabinet, Lincoln placed McClellan in command of all the troops in the Washington area. Mac was the beneficiary of an incredible stroke of luck when some of his troops captured a copy of Lee's strategic plan, which was a risky gamble in which he divided his outnumbered forces in enemy country. Unfortunately for the Union, McClellan again moved too slowly to take advantage of this intelligence coup.

The vastly outnumbered Confederates were at last brought to bay by McClellan along Antietam Creek. Correctly assessing his opponent as exceptionally cautious, Lee held his ground. Although a general attack would almost certainly have carried the Rebel position, Mac sent his powerful army corps into battle piecemeal, and one at a time they were chewed up by the steadfast defense of the Southerners. (The two corps he held out of the battle actually outnumbered the whole Confederate army.) The result was the single bloodiest day in American military history. Lee's army survived, however, and was able to slip away to the south virtually free of pursuit.

McClellan, convinced he had barely survived a battle with a vastly superior foe, was unwilling to pursue. Lincoln is reported to have remarked to McClellan: "If you don't want to use the army, I should like to borrow it for awhile." In the end, Lee's escape was the last straw for Lincoln, who finally removed McClellan from command, replacing him with one of his corps commanders, General Ambrose Burnside. (Burnside's men had made a plodding, costly, and ultimately unsuccessful attack at Antietam.)

One positive outcome for the Union came out of Antietam: President Lincoln used it as the basis for issuing his historical

Emancipation Proclamation, which was to take effect on January 1, 1863. This bold order banned slavery outright in all territories of the United States. Regardless of the root causes of the conflict, it was now a war to end slavery. On the diplomatic front, the proclamation dissuaded England and France from allying with the Confederacy at a time when such an alliance was the South's only real hope for eventual victory.

General Burnside, the new commander of the Army of the Potomac, was a stolid general, not a poor performer as a division and corps commander, but he was woefully unsuited for command of a large army. (He is probably best remembered for the style of the long whiskers that flanked his cheeks, called "sideburns" to this day.) He consistently failed to properly reconnoiter enemy positions before attacking, and was petulant with subordinates and jealous of his peers. Nevertheless, Burnside took the army on the attack, marching southward into Virginia.

Lee met him at Fredericksburg on December 13, 1862, with the Army of Northern Virginia entrenched on an elevation called Marye's Heights south of the Rappahannock River. Sending his men across the river under withering Rebel fire, Burnside ordered no less than fourteen frontal assaults against the strong enemy position without making a significant attempt at a flanking maneuver. At the end of the day he had more than twelve thousand five hundred casualties, and not a single acre of gained ground to show for the courageous but futile efforts of his brave men.

Faced with a virtual revolt among the Union corps commanders, Lincoln finally accepted Burnside's resignation from army command in January of 1863. As his replacement, he appointed General Joseph "Fighting Joe" Hooker, a general who had displayed the initiative and aggressiveness so lacking in the high command of the army. (Hooker's corps had made the first assault at Antietam, fighting Stonewall Jackson's corps to a standstill; McClellan squandered the opportunity gained by failing to send more of his large corps forward in a timely fashion.)

Hooker's appointment was greeted with relief by the men and officers of the Army of the Potomac, and during the spring of 1863 he succeeded in filling out depleted units, training recruits, and reprovisioning his vast force to go on the offensive. He created an elaborate and imaginative plan to surround Lee's army (which remained at Fredericksburg), employing a large force of cavalry, mapping out a flanking march that did, in fact, catch the Rebels by surprise.

Then, everything started to go wrong. Robert E. Lee was never one to sit still while an opponent gained a march; instead, he decamped, splitting his army once, and then again, giving the appearance that he was running circles around Hooker. When the Union forces finally gained a chance to launch a crushing attack against a part of the Army of Northern Virginia, Hooker seemed to lose his nerve. He failed to press the advantage, and instead took up a defensive position at Chancellorsville, Virginia. Audaciously, Lee detached Stonewall Jackson's corps to launch a flank attack that crushed much of Hooker's army, and sent the rest of it fleeing northward.

Much as had happened with Burnside, the army's corps commanders were appalled at the general's failings, one of them—General Crouch—going so far as to refuse to serve under Hooker any longer. Lincoln was sick and tired of the game of musical chairs that seemed to be going on regarding his major army command, so he did not remove Hooker immediately. But when Lee commenced his second invasion of the north in June of 1863, Lincoln's patience reached an end. A sulking Hooker offered his resignation over a minor matter and, to his surprise, the president immediately accepted it.

Lincoln's first choice as Hooker's replacement was I Corps commander General John Reynolds, but Reynolds declined the offer. As a result, the new leader of the army was another corps commander, George Meade. He was not expecting the promotion, and in fact, when a messenger arrived to inform him of his new job, he assumed that he was going to be arrested for his insubordinate remarks about Hooker. Instead, Meade assumed command of the Army of the Potomac at the end of June, and three days later oversaw the army as it participated in the greatest battle ever fought on American soil.

Gettysburg remains one of the important battles of our history. It represented the turning point of the Civil War, marking the farthest extent of Confederate advance. Afterward, Lee would be forever on the strategic defensive. The two armies were at full strength, and the three days of fighting resulted in more casualties than any American battle until the Battle of the Bulge in 1944–45. However, it cannot be said to be a battle that Meade, or Lee, planned.

It began as an almost accidental encounter between a division of Confederate infantry and another of Union cavalry. Both sides reinforced, and by the end of the first day the Union army had suffered terrible casualties to two corps but had seized and held the key high ground to the east and southeast of the town. For the next two days these strong positions would be held against a series of frenzied attacks, culminating in the great massed attack forever known as Pickett's Charge (though Pickett's was only one of three divisions attacking).

By the end of the battle, the Army of Northern Virginia had been badly mauled. While the clash had been a meeting engagement, Meade had displayed considerable skill in positioning his troops in strong defensive positions. With uncharacteristically poor decision making, Lee had exhausted his army in assaults against these positions. It was a defeat from which the Confederates would never recover.

On July 4, the day after Gettysburg, General Grant's army finally won the Battle of Vicksburg in the Western Theater after a long siege. The fall of Vicksburg gave the Union command of the Mississippi River all the way from Minnesota to the Gulf of Mexico, and effectively cut the Confederacy in two by isolating Louisiana, Arkansas, and Texas from the other rebelling states

In following Lee southward as the Confederates withdrew,

Meade was not able to pursue as aggressively as Lincoln wished, and missed a chance to annihilate the Army of Northern Virginia when it was trapped against the raging Potomac after a period of heavy rain. Lee's army survived, and the war would continue for more than one and a half bloody years.

On October 16, 1863, President Lincoln promoted Grant to command of all Union armies. While Meade technically remained in command of the Army of the Potomac, Grant would remain with the army for the rest of the war, effectively serving as army commander. In the West, General Sherman took over theater command, and would close in on Atlanta and then make his infamous march to the sea. In Virginia many bloody battles remained: at Spotsylvania, the Wilderness, the brutal killing ground that was Cold Harbor, and finally a ten-month siege at Petersburg and Richmond. But Grant was as tenacious as a bulldog, and kept the pressure on Lee, attacking when the Rebel army halted, aggressively pursuing when it moved. He would keep the pressure on the main army of the Confederacy all the way to Appomattox Courthouse, where at last he accepted Lee's surrender.

Grant's tenacity would eventually carry him on an ill-starred march to the White House itself, for he was a better soldier than he was a politician. Above all else, in Ulysses S. Grant, Abe Lincoln had finally found himself the general who would fight.

A SPLENDID LITTLE WAR
WILLIAM MCKINLEY REMEMBERS THE *MAINE*, 1898

by Douglas Niles

At the beginning of the nineteenth century, a wave of revolutions swept through the Spanish colonial empire until, finally, only Cuba, the Philippines, and a few small outposts such as Guam and Puerto Rico remained. By 1895, Cuba was locked in a violent struggle, the majority of the populace seeking the overthrow of the Spanish regime. Insurrections had erupted in the Philippines as well.

Though the United States was not yet regarded as a world power, the Monroe Doctrine established that events in the Caribbean and Latin American countries were very much in America's sphere of influence. U.S. public opinion, aided by a surge of yellow journalism, paid attention to events in Cuba, reacting angrily to reports of atrocities and brutality by the Spanish authorities. As a show of force, and to offer at least token protection to the many American interests in the island that was less than a hundred miles from the southern tip of Florida, President William F. McKinley dispatched the battleship *Maine* to Cuba. (Such interests included more than $50 million in lands and businesses, mostly centered in sugar and tobacco.) A powerful presence in Havana harbor, the *Maine* dropped anchor and stood as tangible proof of American power and American concern.

She did, that is, until the battleship exploded and sank in February of 1898, with the loss of more than 260 U.S. Navy personnel. Though no cause could be officially determined, popular perception blamed Spain. (Later investigations determined that the ship hit an underwater mine.) Americans already sympathized with the rebels who sought to overthrow the Spanish. Public opinion was inflamed by the rivalry between William Randolph Hearst and Joseph Pulitzer, whose New York newspapers, the *Journal* and the *World*, were locked in savage competition. An unconfirmed but illustrative story has Hearst cabling his photographer in Havana, saying, "You provide the pictures; I'll provide the war." As the final straw, a private letter written by the Spanish minister in the United States to a friend in Havana was stolen and published. In it, the minister labeled President McKinley "a weakling" who merely pandered to public opinion.

Even so, McKinley was not as keen on war as the population in general, but he was carried along by forces beyond his control. The newspaper reports grew more lurid, and anger over the *Maine*'s loss, whatever the cause, swelled. On April 19, Congress passed a resolution declaring that Cuba should be a "free and independent state." McKinley signed it on the next day, and Spain felt that she had no recourse other than to declare war.

The conflict was over in ten weeks. An American fleet under Commodore Dewey steamed from Hong Kong to the Philippines and destroyed the Spanish fleet in Manila Bay without suffering a single American casualty. In the Caribbean, the main Spanish battle fleet had crossed the Atlantic to Cuba, but was bottled up in Santiago Bay until American and Cuban ground forces threatened to capture the fort. The fleet sailed and it, too, was destroyed by the guns of the United States Navy.

The troops that landed on Cuba fought several stiff engagements, but suffered far more from malaria and yellow fever than they did from Spanish arms. Aided by the Cuban rebels, they soon overran the island and forced the Spanish to surrender. Another expeditionary force landed in the Philippines and, also aided by local rebels, soon trapped the Spanish army in the capital. In both cases, American forces ended up protecting the captured Spaniards from the vengeance-minded rebels.

In August, a small American force landed on Puerto Rico and captured the island against virtually no resistance. When the Treaty of Paris officially ended hostilities in December of 1898, Guam and Puerto Rico were ceded by Spain to the United States. As an indirect result of the war, American annexed the Hawaiian Islands in 1898. With a string of naval bases extending from Oahu to Guam to Manila Bay, the United States Navy became a major force in the Pacific Ocean for the first time.

Despite American pronouncements of "freedom and independence" for the people rebelling against Spain, subsequent acts served specifically to establish U.S. hegemony over both Cuba and the Philippines. American forces would be locked into an increasingly unpopular counterinsurgency in the Philippines until 1914. As for the Cuban rebels, they weren't even invited to Paris for the peace treaty signing. The United States insisted that the new Cuban nation be specifically banned from forming alliances with other countries. Furthermore, the United States claimed a base at Guantanamo Bay that it continues to hold to this day. Cuba would remain a nation heavily controlled by the United States until the Communist revolution of 1959.

Still during his first term, McKinley followed the Spanish-American War by displays of American power in China (against the Boxer Rebellion) and in gaining territories in Samoa. These expansions of American power were enormously popular, and McKinley was nominated unanimously for a second term. He won the election handily, but an assassin shot him to death before he served even a full year of his second term. He was the third President to fall to a fatal bullet.

Still, his mark was indelible. The major aftereffect of the "splendid little war" was the United States's arrival on the stage of world affairs. For the first time, America obtained overseas colonies, and projected military power against a major power in several broad theaters of war. The United States Navy, in particular, proved itself a force to be reckoned with on any ocean in the world.

A POINT OF ORDER
WOODROW WILSON AND HIS FOURTEEN POINTS

by Douglas Niles

Beginning in August 1914, the most savage conflict in world history (to that date) was enacted across the continent of Europe. The Central Powers, Germany, Austria-Hungary, Turkey, and Bulgaria, were arrayed against the Allies: Britain, France, Russia, Serbia, Rumania, and Italy. Mass slaughter, abetted by machine guns, vast batteries of highly accurate artillery, barbed wire, and trenches, raged for months and resulted in millions of casualties for relatively minor gains in terrain.

For two years, the war was confined to Europe and a few European colonies. Americans, many of whom were immigrants, or descendants of recent immigrants, from the combatant nations on both sides, watched the spectacle with horror, even as the U.S. government steadfastly maintained neutrality. The most highly educated man ever to hold the office of president of the United States, Woodrow Wilson, strongly held to this policy of non-involvement. In fact, he won reelection to a second term in 1916 based in great part on the fact, which became a political slogan: "He kept us out of war."

In fact, Wilson had accomplished a great deal in his first term, and set some precedents for the twentieth century presidency that continue on today. He was the first president since John Adams, more than one hundred years earlier, to give his State of the Union address in person. (For the previous century, the chief executive had written a statement and sent it to the Capitol, where it was read into the record. Ever since Wilson, the address has been delivered as a presidential speech.) He established the Federal Reserve Act, modernizing banking in the United States, and also the Federal Trade Commission. Under his impetus, laws were enacting to protect unions and to regulate child labor.

The major foreign policy focus during Wilson's first term was not Europe, but Mexico. A series of revolutions south of the Rio Grande, coupled with the depredations of the bandit Pancho Villa—who crossed the border to raid New Mexico—caused Wilson to dispatch General John Pershing on a basically unsuccessful mission to corral the audacious Villa. At the same time, Wilson was acutely conscious of the moral imperatives of strength versus weakness, and steadfastly refused to resort to the kind of imperial bullying that had characterized previous administrations' dealings with countries like Spain and Mexico. Woodrow Wilson, for example, took important steps to prepare the Philippines for eventual independence.

But the Great War could not be ignored. The primary threat to American interests lay in the deadly activities of Germany's submarine fleet, which took an increasingly active and brutal role in the Atlantic. When the ocean liner *Lusitania* was sunk in 1915, 128 Americans were among the more than one thousand fatalities. Wilson sternly warned Germany that these kinds of attacks would not be tolerated. For more than seven months, German U-boats backed away from their aggressive tactics in the face of the president's strong statement.

But the war was going badly for Germany, and the Kaiser's military commanders increasingly felt that only an outright blockade of Britain would allow them any hope of victory. The submarine raiders grew more aggressive until, in January of 1917, Germany announced that her submarines would commence unrestricted submarine warfare, sinking without warning any ships engaged in commerce with England. Within weeks, several American vessels were sunk, with significant loss of life. Public opinion was further inflamed by the revelation of a German proposal to unite with Mexico, suggesting that Mexico could regain Texas, Arizona, and New Mexico by invading the United States.

Wilson, ever stubborn and righteous as befitted his strict Presbyterian temperament, had resisted American military preparedness, holding fast to his view of the nation as truly neutral. In great part as a result of this policy, the United States was woefully unprepared for a large scale, modern war. Yet when confronted with this new aggression, he responded with alacrity, immediately ordering that American merchant ships be armed and authorized to fire on any threatening vessels. On April 2, 1917, Wilson addressed a special session of Congress, and asked for a declaration of war against Germany. The resolution passed with resounding majorities in both houses.

Immediately the Selective Service Act was passed, calling for a draft of men between age twenty-one and thirty. Industrial production increased and, by June, General Pershing had arrived in France with the first troops of an American Expeditionary Force that would grow to more than two million men in the next sixteen months. Backed by Wilson, Pershing insisted that the American army function as an intact unit, instead of as a reserve of manpower for the terribly depleted armies of France and England. This determination would pay great dividends during the battles of Saint-Mihiel, the Meuse-Argonne, and other decisive clashes leading to the end of the war.

Even as the terrible war raged through its fourth year, and American strength gradually assumed its place as the decisive balance of power, Wilson was imagining the postwar world through the prism of his powerful intellect and vision. In January, 1918, he addressed Congress with a detailed plan of Fourteen Points, labeling these the "only possible program" for peace. The first thirteen points discussed freedom of commerce, restoration of national boundaries, rights for weaker as well as strong nations, non-punitive treaties, and freedom of the seas. The fourteenth point was perhaps the most crucial: Wilson had the idea to create a League of Nations, a world body that would hopefully prevent the outbreak of another such terrible war.

Finally, on November 11, 1918, at 11 a.m. (the eleventh hour of the eleventh day of the eleventh month), Germany surrendered to the military forces arrayed against her. Wilson was determined to represent America at the subsequent peace talks in Versailles. He would be the first serving President to travel to Europe, but unfortunately he went to France without representatives from the Senate or the powerful Republican Party. At the talks, his idealism clashed with the world-weary pragmatism—and desire for vengeance—of the leaders of France and England. When the Treaty of Versailles was concluded, its harsh terms against Germany had already planted the seeds that would grow into Nazism and the even more terrible specter of World War II.

Nevertheless, Wilson returned home and campaigned vigorously for American acceptance of the treaty, including membership in the League of Nations. But the Republicans had gained control of Congress in 1918, and their isolationist sentiments—not to mention resentment of some of Wilson's progressive accomplishments—proved intractable. When the organization that was Woodrow Wilson's brainchild was at last created, the United States Senate refused to allow the United States to become a member.

Exhausted, partially paralyzed by stroke, Wilson finished his term as an invalid; his wife, Edith, took over much of his work, and carefully controlled access to the president so that the nation was not aware of his disability. As a final honor, he was awarded the Nobel Peace Prize in 1919.

But it was a hollow victory indeed.

A DEMOCRACY GOES TO WAR
FRANKLIN DELANO ROOSEVELT EASES AMERICA INTO WORLD WAR II

by Douglas Niles

With most of the world mired in depression, the 1930s were years of tumultuous challenges in the United States and abroad. In Germany, Italy, Spain, and Japan, forces of fascism gained control of their respective governments, while Joseph Stalin cemented his hold on the Soviet Union, and secured his own grasp on the Communist Party there through a series of bloody purges. China was a chaotic amalgamation of petty warlords and vast population, with no capable central leadership. Democratic governments in Western Europe, most notably England and France, still reeled from the horrific slaughter of World War I, and seemed powerless to cope with the difficulties in their own nations, much less challenge the rise of militancy in Germany and Italy.

Against this backdrop of rising tensions, most Americans wanted nothing more than to be left alone. Certainly they wanted no part in solving the problems of Europe and Asia. The isolationism that marked the Senate's refusal to bring the

United States into the League of Nations after the "War to End All Wars" was further emphasized when Congress passed the Neutrality Act in 1935. Enacted when Italy invaded Ethiopia, the law banned United States businesses from sending armaments to any nation involved in hostilities.

The president of the United States in 1935 was Franklin Delano Roosevelt, then nearing the end of a first term that had been marked by a staggering array of policy initiatives. Collectively known as the New Deal, FDR's legislation—some successful, some not—had given Americans hope that had been lacking since the stock market crash of 1929. While foreign policy had not been his primary concern, he kept a wary eye on developments abroad. He considered the Neutrality Act a bad idea, since it prevented the United States from aiding countries who were victims of aggression just as much as it banned aiding the aggressors. However, the act was popular with the people and the Congress, so he signed it into law.

But it was not in Roosevelt's nature to quietly submit to policy that he perceived to be a bad idea. For most of the decade, Japan had been engaged in military adventurism against China, and in 1937 the Imperial Japanese Army aggressively attacked the larger but much weaker nation. Public sentiment began to turn against the invaders, and in the fall of that year, FDR gave a speech suggesting that aggressive nations be treated like dangerous diseases, in effect, "quarantined."

At the same time, he was quietly increasing the strength of America's pathetically underpowered armed forces. Using his considerable powers of persuasion, FDR got a reluctant Congress to authorize a naval building program to begin the modernization of a battle fleet that had received scant funding and attention since World War I. At a time when most of the world still regarded the battleship as the primary embodiment of naval power, the United States began to place emphasis on aircraft carriers and submarines.

During the next two years, Nazi Germany became increasingly aggressive. In short order, Adolf Hitler's troops occupied without bloodshed the Rhineland (which had been demilitarized since World War I as a condition of the Treaty of Versailles), Austria, and (in two stages) Czechoslovakia. British Prime Minister Neville Chamberlain acceded to these conquests at the Munich conference (1938), infamously proclaiming upon his return to England that his negotiations had gained "peace in our time."

On September 1, 1939, Germany invaded Poland, and World War II exploded into furious conflagration. Roosevelt was determined to support the western democracies, but he recognized that the American people—and the American military—were not ready to participate in the hostilities. Instead, he increasingly flouted the provisions of the Neutrality Act to see that England and France continued to receive at least minimal American support.

The United States was only partially shocked out of its complacency by the stunning Nazi victories in May and June of 1940. In short order Norway, Denmark, Belgium, Holland, Luxembourg, and France were conquered by the German military juggernaut. Paris, which had held the Germans at bay for more than four years in World War I, fell in less than five weeks. With the surrender of France, Britain stood alone against Germany and Italy by summer 1940. Neville Chamberlain resigned his job, to be replaced by the pugnacious Winston Churchill, and Roosevelt immediately opened lines of communication with the new prime minister.

The president was determined to do everything he could to ensure Britain's survival and now, finally, the majority of the population was with him—though Americans were still not prepared to join what was perceived as "another European war." Before the end of 1940, FDR pushed through a deal to swap some fifty old U.S. Navy destroyers to England in return for the use of British bases in the Caribbean. (Even aged destroyers were crucial in protecting merchant ships from the growing menace of Nazi U-boats.)

One of the president's greatest triumphs of preparedness

was the institution, in the summer of 1940, of the first peacetime draft in U.S. history. Thousands of young men were conscripted into the armed forces, albeit—at Congressional insistence—only for one year. These soldiers would form the core of the United States Army during the crucial years ahead, although only after the draft was renewed—by a single vote!—in summer 1941. (If that bill had failed, all of the draftees would have been released to civilian life only a few months before Pearl Harbor.)

In May 1941, FDR proposed and gained passage of the Lend-Lease Act. Neutrality was now a thing of the past, as the United States became the "Arsenal of Democracy," pledging to supply all the nations engaged in war with the fascist powers. Immediate beneficiaries of Lend-Lease were China and England, and when the Nazis invaded the Soviet Union in June 1941, the president immediately extended the offer of aid to Stalin—who was more than willing to accept.

In addition to her adventures in China, Japan took advantage of the fall of France to move against French colonies in Southeast Asia. The war in China was turning into a bloody stalemate, but the military forces controlling the Japanese government remained bent upon expansion. In response, FDR placed an embargo on U.S. exports of steel and oil to Japan. By cutting off these vital materials, the president created an intolerable situation for Japan, and American entry into World War II became inevitable.

Still, the American population was not ready for participation. In August 1941, Roosevelt met Churchill aboard ship in the Atlantic Ocean. The resulting agreement was the Atlantic Charter, which pledged "all aid short of war" to the British. American warships would escort convoys all the way to Britain, and were authorized to fire at U-boats that menaced American ships. Furthermore, and unknown to the public, it laid the groundwork for the strategic war plan that the two close allies would pursue for the next four years by labeling Germany as the most dangerous foe among the Axis nations.

By late 1941, when the Soviet Army had been pushed all the way to Moscow and the British Isles remained the lone bastion of freedom in Western Europe, Franklin Roosevelt had prepared the American military, and the American people, for entry into the war. Some revisionist historians have claimed that Roosevelt knew about the Japanese aircraft carriers drawing close to Hawaii and the U.S. Navy base at Pearl Harbor in early December, but this is a ludicrous charge rooted in the extreme antipathy that this great, but controversial, president still arouses. In any event, an attack against our primary naval base would have aroused American wrath even if it had not been a complete surprise and an unmitigated disaster. Furthermore, it is inconceivable that Roosevelt, a former assistant secretary of the navy, would have exposed his beloved fleet to catastrophe as a mere public relations ploy.

As it happened, Japan's naval air forces attacked Pearl Harbor on December 7, 1941, and the United States was at war from that moment. Yet, even then, the president did not ask for a declaration of war against the other Axis powers. Hitler and Mussolini obliged him by immediately declaring war against the United States.

If they had not done so, it seems certain that the wily FDR would have figured out a way to involve his country in that world-spanning conflict within a very short time frame. Because he was faced with an enemy so determined to engage in conflict and conquest, he didn't have to.

THE BUCK STOPS HERE

HARRY TRUMAN VERSUS DOUGLAS MACARTHUR

by Douglas Niles

By the time the forces of communist North Korea spilled over the border into South Korea in June of 1950, President Harry S. Truman had solidly established his credentials as a staunch opponent of world Communism. He had overseen the creation

of NATO, which stood as a bulwark of democracy against the Soviet threat to Europe. He had authorized the Berlin airlift of 1948–49, when Stalin had tried to isolate that city from its allies in the West. He had boldly announced the Truman Doctrine, declaring that countries threatened by communist invasion or overthrow—specifically Greece and Turkey, but allowing for other targets to be determined as necessary—would receive U.S. aid, support, and possibly troops to aid in the defense.

Korea, however, was not much on anyone's mind during the late 1940s as a potential hot spot. When Japan surrendered following the close of World War II, the United States and USSR had divided the Korean peninsula as a simple means for determining which country's troops would accept the surrender of Imperial Japanese Army units in Korea. The Russians would oversee the land to the north of the thirty-eighth parallel of latitude, the Americans would take the south. It was agreed at the Potsdam conference, among other places, that a free and united Korea would take shape as soon as was practicable.

As the Cold War took shape, however, the Korean peninsula was not exempt. When Stalin's Iron Curtain fell across Europe, it also extended into Asia, forcing the creation of the two Koreas that exist to this day. It was a situation that was satisfactory to neither side. When the fledgling United Nations tried to mediate the matter, the USSR refused to participate in negotiations.

Faced with this intractability, the Republic of Korea was established south of the thirty-eighth parallel, with the capital at Seoul. In the north, Stalin established a puppet government under Kim Il Sung. It was called the Democratic People's Republic of Korea. By summer of 1949, U.S. and Soviet combat troops had mostly withdrawn, both sides leaving a cadre of advisers. The North Korean Army, however, was vigorously expanded and equipped with Russian tanks and artillery. It was supported by an air force of nearly two hundred Russian planes of late World War II vintage. The Army of the ROK, in contrast, was little more than a national police force, lacking virtually all modern military equipment.

On June 25, 1950, the NKA invaded, gaining complete surprise. Seoul was quickly captured, and the mechanized and well-trained North Korean Army pressed southward. President Truman ordered General Douglas MacArthur, who was commanding American occupation forces in Japan, to do whatever he could to support the ROK. Hastening to the front in person, MacArthur concluded by June 28 that South Korea lacked the strength and resources to withstand the invasion. On June 29, Truman authorized the use of American ground troops.

Although four U.S. divisions were stationed in Japan, they were under strength and, softened by years of garrison duty, ill-prepared for combat. Even so, General MacArthur rushed them to the peninsula, and they were thrown into the fight as soon as they arrived. On July 7, MacArthur was appointed commander in chief, United Nations Command. By the end of the summer, UN forces (mainly American and ROK troops) had stopped the enemy advance at a perimeter protecting Pusan, the only port not yet captured by the NKA. As they held onto this little sliver of land, the situation for the UN forces seemed bleak, almost hopeless.

MacArthur abruptly turned the tide of the conflict with one of the great strategic master strokes of twentieth-century warfare. On September 15 he landed an amphibious assault force consisting of one U.S. Marine division and one cobbled-together U.S. Army division, including some 5,000 ROK troops, at the coast of Inchon, very near Seoul and the thirty-eighth parallel. Quickly surrounding the capital, the landing force succeeded in cutting off supplies for the overextended NKA invasion forces, which virtually collapsed, individual units and soldiers simply fleeing into the hills.

United Nations forces pursued quickly and aggressively. MacArthur and Truman were in agreement that the enemy should be pursued north of the thirty-eighth parallel; the implicit goal was the elimination of the Kim Il Sung's regime and a reuniting of the two Koreas. The counterattacking army pressed north, toward the Yalu River that formed the border between North Korea and Red China.

However, the two leaders disagreed on a crucial aspect of the war. Truman, believing along with many of his senior advisers that Europe was the crucial front in the Cold War, was very much determined to limit the Asian war to the Korean peninsula. MacArthur felt that China was weakened by many years of occupation and revolution, and that—if war should erupt between China and the United States—there would never be a better time to fight it.

But the president was in charge, and he made his wishes known. Upon Truman's orders, UN air forces were forbidden to fly over the Yalu, even to perform reconnaissance. Meanwhile, MacArthur's troops continued their northward onrush. Most intelligence sources suggested that the Chinese did not want to get involved in the war. In order to keep the pressure on the disintegrating NKA, MacArthur shifted X Corps, a major component of his forces, by naval transport to the northeast coast of Korea. There it was separated from the rest of his command, the Eighth Army, by the rugged interior of North Korea.

On November 25, 300,000 veteran Red Chinese soldiers spilled out of that mountainous redoubt, smashing both of MacArthur's spearheads, sending the UN troops reeling back toward the south. In a stunning strategic surprise, the lightly-equipped Chinese moved quickly across country, rapidly out-flanking the mechanized—and therefore road-bound—United Nations forces. By dint of tenacious fighting, the America and ROK forces extricated themselves from near catastrophe, but not before they had been pushed south of Seoul, the capital falling to invaders for the second time in eight months.

Through the winter of early 1951, MacArthur's forces clawed their way northward, gaining ground against forces that outnumbered them significantly. But tensions continued to rise between the president and his field commander. Truman still refused to authorize air raids into China, while MacArthur advocated, publicly, that the Nationalist Chinese forces in Taiwan should be engaged against the mainland, while his naval and air forces should be allowed to bring pressure against Manchurian bases and ports.

When MacArthur, whose political ambitions were well known, wrote to Congressman Joe Martin, a Republican from Massachussetts, and declared "there is no substitute for victory," Martin immediately made the letter public. A firm believer in civilian command of the armed forces, Truman felt that he was faced with unacceptable insubordination. He had no choice but to remove the popular general from his command.

The suddenness of the dismissal, coupled with the rapidly growing displeasure with the Truman presidency, resulted in an outcry at home, and even more unpopularity for the president. Yet he acted in the true traditions and spirit of the United States Constitution, and the brilliant but vainglorious MacArthur was forced to accede. In the end, the great general could only stand and give a speech to Congress, proudly declaring that "old soldiers never die. They just fade away."

"HOW MANY KIDS DID YOU KILL TODAY?"
LYNDON BAINES JOHNSON AND THE WAR THAT DERAILED HIS ADMINISTRATION

by Douglas Niles

When President John F. Kennedy was assassinated on November 22, 1963, some sixteen thousand American advisers were serving in South Vietnam. Their mission was to train the South Vietnamese Army (ARVN—Army of the Republic of Vietnam) to resist an increasingly aggressive guerrilla war being sponsored by communist North Vietnam. The war had its roots in many factors, including French colonialism, a desire for Vietnamese

LYNDON B. JOHNSON
1903-1909

independence and unification, and the overarching struggle of the Cold War that had defined United States foreign policy since shortly after the end of World War II.

In 1963, these American troops were not authorized to engage in combat operations, except to defend themselves. By the time, five years later, that Lyndon Johnson declared he would not run for reelection, there were more than half a million American soldiers engaged in direct combat with the Viet Cong guerrillas and the North Vietnamese Army. Casualties were heavy, the enemy was elusive, and there was still no end to the conflict in sight.

Ironically enough, the war that came to define his presidency was a stark counterpoint to the domestic agenda that was Johnson's primary passion. During his presidency, the United States went through a period of dramatically expanded and constitutionally protected civil rights. Medical and financial aid to the poor was expanded. The "Great Society" that was Johnson's ideal had come into focus.

But in the end, his entire agenda was overshadowed by the war in Southeast Asia, and the rising militancy of the antiwar protests at home.

American involvement in Vietnam predated President Johnson by two administrations, with both Eisenhower and Kennedy recognizing the growing communist presence in Southeast Asia. The "Domino Theory" suggested that each country gained by the Communist bloc, whether through revolution or invasion, increased the chances of a neighboring country falling to the same Red Menace. In the case of Southeast Asia, South Vietnam was regarded as a cornerstone in the containment effort, protecting Cambodia, Laos, and a key American ally, Thailand, from falling to communist forces.

Because of the containment policy, Vietnam was a war Johnson felt needed to be fought. But for a host of other reasons, it was a war he never made a solid commitment toward winning. In much the same way that Truman had tried to maintain the Korean conflict as a limited war, Johnson and his advisers banned American forces from striking enemy targets outside the borders of the embattled country. Yet Vietnam was a very different kind of war.

Johnson was not unwilling to engage the communists, and in fact considered it his duty to stand firm in the face of communist aggression. On August 2, 1964, the destroyer USS *Maddox* was patrolling off the coast of North Vietnam, in the Gulf of Tonkin. At the same time, commandos of the ARVN landed on a North Vietnamese island and blew up a radio installation. North Vietnamese patrol boats sortied and launched a torpedo attack against the *Maddox*; no damage or injuries resulted and the *Maddox* withdrew. Two days later, another destroyer, the *Turner Joy*, was patrolling the same area. In a confusing night of sonar and radar images and quirky weather patterns, the *Turner Joy* engaged in a prolonged firefight with targets that were only hazily perceived, but her crew reported numerous torpedo attacks evaded, and considerable ordnance expanded. Her captain, as well as U.S. Navy pilots who had flown above the area, expressed doubts that there had been any enemy ships in the area. Even the president, a few days later, is reported to have said that our sailors "may have been shooting at flying fish."

Nevertheless, Johnson used the incident to push the Gulf of Tonkin Resolution through Congress, authorizing him to engage American forces in direct combat with any enemy forces in the area, without requiring a declaration of war. The measure passed almost unanimously, although many in Congress and the Senate expressed reservations. (The only two "no" votes came from senators who believed the resolution was unconstitutional.) Johnson immediately authorized the U.S. Air Force and U.S. Naval air forces to commence a series of limited attacks against coastal targets in North Vietnam, and attempted to interdict the jungle-sheltered supply route used by North Vietnam to support the Viet Cong guerrillas in the South. This route, the Ho Chi Minh trail, was named after the leader of North Vietnam, and in most places was virtually undetectable from the air.

Between the end of 1964 and most of 1965, the ARVN forces were ineffective and continued to grow weaker because of desertion and poor morale. The last effective president of South Vietnam, Ngo Dinh Diem, had been assassinated three weeks before Kennedy (in a coup backed by American diplomats and the CIA) and for several years the country would veer from one military junta to the next with no effective and stable leadership. Faced with internal disorder and increasing pressure from the communist forces, it became clear that South Vietnam could not stand on its own.

In May of 1965, thirty-five hundred Marines arrived in South Vietnam with the mission of protecting American air bases. By the end of the year, the number of American ground troops, including the U.S. Army and Marine corps, had swollen to two hundred thousand. General William Westmoreland,

American commander in the country, increasingly advocated using these troops in an offensive war. He was confident that he could defeat the enemy, probably in a period of about eighteen months; throughout the next few years he would increasingly call for additional commitment of American troops.

Johnson authorized increasing troop deployments, and went along with Westmoreland's switch to the offensive, but he didn't admit the change in policy to the country or the Congress. At the same time, he was unwilling to risk negative world opinion with an all-out bombing campaign, so targets were strictly limited. Often pilots were forced to ditch their weapons or land fully-armed aircraft because no target had been authorized—or authorization had been cancelled—while the plane was in the air. These restraints crippled the effectiveness of the U.S. military's greatest advantage, it's almost-uncontested mastery of the air.

On the ground, Westmoreland was committed to the concept of large scale search-and-destroy operations, designed to pin down and wipe out enemy concentrations of force. His primary measure of success was the "body count"—the listing of the number of enemy casualties, which Westmoreland took as evidence of the toll the war was taking on the Viet Cong and North Vietnamese.

The enemy, however, proved very hard to pin down, and much preferred operating in small units. When near the borders of Cambodia or Laos, the enemy forces often withdrew into these neighboring countries, which remained as safe havens for their bases because of orders from Washington. The Viet Cong and North Vietnamese forces were often able to pick the ground for their battles, and frequently vanished into the jungle rather than engage in a battle that was not to their advantage.

At the same time as he was heavily engaging the enemy, Westmoreland was neglecting an important strategy: he virtually cut off supply and replenishment to his allies in the ARVN. The South Vietnamese soldiers were still using World War II–era carbines while the enemy was increasingly armed with the lethal AK-47s, and the American troops carried the modern M-16. By neglecting the training and equipping of the ARVN, Westmoreland placed the entire burden of success or failure on the shoulders of the American soldiers and Marines.

Westmoreland's prediction of an eighteen-month war proved unrealistic as operations continued through 1967. Protests at home grew increasingly violent and explosive as public opinion continued to turn against the war. Whether or not he understood the situation on the ground, Westmoreland reported to Congress in late 1967 that "we have reached the point where the end begins to come into view." Meanwhile, protestors outside the White House chanted "Hey, hey, LBJ. How many kids did you kill today?"

Then, in January 1968, the VC and NVA launched the Tet Offensive, a series of attacks that erupted across the entire country of South Vietnam. Battles raged in countless towns and villages; several major cities, including Saigon and Hue, were scenes of savage fighting. Even though the Americans and South Vietnamese defeated every significant attack, inflicting brutally high losses on the communist forces, the Tet Offensive became a major strategic victory for the attackers. Public opinion in the United States swung heavily against the war, as it became increasingly obvious that American strategy was costing the country the lives of very many soldiers with very little to show for that sacrifice.

Shocked and shaken by the display of enemy determination, Lyndon Johnson lost his spirit for waging the war or for running the country. He called a unilateral halt to the bombing of North Vietnam and declared that he would not run for reelection.

But in the jungles of Vietnam, American soldiers and Marines would continue to die for five more years.

18

FIRST LADY FOLLIES

*"And now, dear sister, I must leave this house or the
retreating army will make me a prisoner in it by filling up
the road I am directed to take."*
Dolley Madison

SECOND CHOICE

George Washington was not Martha's first husband. Before she
married George, she had been married to a Virginia landowner
named Daniel Custis. In the era of colonial America, a widow

'remarrying was quite common. The painful fact was that in those times there were a lot of ways to die and people often did.

Three of the first four U.S. presidents were married to widows. These were Washington, Jefferson, and Madison.

FATHER-IN-LAW

Martha's first father-in-law was a difficult person and would likely today be considered deranged. She blamed the early death of her first husband, Daniel, on his father's virulent nature and abuse. When, as a widow, Martha inherited her father-in-law's property, she quickly sold just about every item. Only one thing was kept back. This was the man's prized collection of hand-blown wineglasses. The collection was extremely valuable and had been her father-in-law's most prized possession, but Martha personally smashed every glass.

AYE, AYE MA'AM

No longer willing to bear the separation from her husband, who was serving as minister to France for the United States, Abigail and her daughter, Nabby, made the risky trip across the Atlantic to join him. The story here is in the journey. The weather turned bad almost immediately and Abigail was, at first, continuously seasick. The ship was thrown about so roughly that a cow they had brought along was injured and had to be thrown overboard. Their suffering was made worse by the ship's cargo, potash and whale oil. Both slopped up from the hold and their nauseating odor permeated the ship. The rancid odor meant that the two women could not sleep even with a closed door.

The weather calmed and Abigail was back to herself. She began with the ship's cook, since she could eat again. He was unskilled and produced barely palatable food. Abigail not only took a hand in preparing better food, but taught the cook how to continue to do so. She then began to take an interest in how the ship was run. Fairly soon, she was advising nearly everyone. Finally she could no longer stand the mess and odor caused by the slopped cargo. She, likely recruiting assistance as she could, scrubbed the ship from stem to stern. By the end of the voyage, Abigail Adams was the darling of the crew and the captain was convinced she was after his job.

AH, BACH

What was said to have attracted Martha Jefferson to her future husband Thomas Jefferson was not just his prestige, his wealth, or his intellect, but his talent for playing the violin. The couple both shared a deep interest in music. After their marriage, Martha was gifted with a piano and lessons. Soon the couple would entertain their guests with long duets that mostly expressed their love for each other.

FIRST LADY, FIRST LADY

Because President Jefferson and Vice President Burr had both lost their wives before entering office, the wife of James Madison, the secretary of state, was effectively the First Lady during the Jefferson Presidency, as well as when her husband succeeded to office. But it wasn't only the period when Dolley Madison held this position that caused her to be the model First Lady that even today we judge them against. What really made the difference was Dolley's sense of style. She was elegant in a way that you have to go on to Jackie Kennedy to match. Except during the War of 1812, when she only "bought American," Dolley was the nation's fashion leader, importing the latest European styles. Her turban collection, many jeweled, was legendary and started a fashion trend that swept the nation's upper classes. When you add her open demeanor, kind heart, skill as an organizer, and a sense of the equality of all Americans, you can see why she was the model of those who followed. She also was very much a woman, creating a minor scandal when she adopted the new French-style gowns which featured lots of cleavage.

REQUIRED FLAW

Everyone has a secret flaw. Like the chef who cannot resist White Castle burgers (you know, sliders), Dolley Madison had one really disgusting personal habit. Again, this was a practice that was most trendy in Europe and actually benefited American growers. Dolley took snuff and did so frequently. Now this was a time when most women would never have risked such a habit. The reason for this is the effect that snuff had on the sinuses. The First Lady almost always carried two handkerchiefs. One was a dainty

lace one that she used before using any snuff. The second was, by necessity, a much thicker and sturdier cloth that was needed to deal with the large amounts of mucous using snuff created.

HELLO, DOLLEY

It was the stated intention of Admiral Cockburn in attacking Washington to capture not James Madison, but the First Lady, Dolley Madison. The capture of the popular First Lady would have been much more of a propaganda victory than the capture of her husband. He also came close to succeeding. Dolley at first refused to flee, watching the disastrous rout of the Maryland Militia from the roof of the executive mansion. Only when she received a note from James Monroe asking her to take what she could save, did Dolley leave, only a few hours ahead of the British. The uneaten meal she had laid out for her husband was still on the table when the British entered the mansion. (They ate it before setting the place on fire.) One of the few items saved by Dolley Madison when the White House was burned was a set of heavy, red curtains. In a small way these curtains helped Dolley to get a small bit of revenge. As in the famous scene from *Gone with the Wind*, the First Lady had an elegant gown made from the cloth of the curtains she saved. She then made a point of wearing this gown at victory celebrations.

FAINT, BUT NOT OF HEART

First Lady Elizabeth Monroe was prone to an illness not yet diagnosed, but possibly some form of epilepsy. She would have small fits or faint without warning. One time she had an attack while sitting near a lit fireplace and was seriously burned.

REVOLTING EVENT

Before he was president, James Monroe represented the United States in France. This was a rather challenging job, since he was there at the start of the French Revolution. Americans were well-regarded—our ideas of freedom and individual rights inspired much of the new revolutionary philosophy. The situation presented an even greater challenge to his normally retiring and often timid wife, Elizabeth. But there was one time when she challenged the Directorate and won. The wife of the Marquis de Lafayette had been imprisoned. Lafayette himself was at this time being held prisoner in Austria, likely as a subversive, and his wife was swept up with the nobility and stood in serious danger of meeting the guillotine. James Monroe had actually served under Lafayette, and knew the marquis and his wife well. Elizabeth Monroe went to the prison where the wife of the American Revolutionary War hero was being held and was brought to her cell. She learned that the poor woman was to be executed the next day. But as she left, Elizabeth Monroe announced to the jailers that she would be back for another conversation the next day and expected the marquise to be there for her to speak to. Rather than offend the wife of the American minister, the execution was postponed indefinitely. In the fanatic days of the French Revolution, this was actually a fairly risky action. Just being seen with or consorting with the nobility could get you imprisoned or executed. But in this case, the highly emotional meeting had its desired effect. A few days later Madame de Lafayette was released and allowed to join her husband in Austria. The couple survived the troubles and eventually were able to visit President Monroe and his First Lady in Washington.

BABY SECRET SERVICE

While visiting New York City in 1807, the baby of Louisa and future president John Quincy Adams was snatched from his mother's arms. A maid chased the man, but was unable to catch him. She did see which house he fled into. When confronted at the door by the two women he returned the baby with a lame excuse that he just wanted to show it to his wife.

WORSE THAN FLYING TODAY

In 1814, Louisa Adams was told by her husband to break down their house in Russia and come join him at his new position in Paris. At first, since she hated Russia, this pleased Louisa. The hassles of selling off or packing all their possessions soon took the edge off her joy. The real problem was in the journey from St. Petersburg to Paris. It started in February and the temperature dropped to a recorded 54 below zero (Fahrenheit). Then when she reach Berlin word came that Napoleon had landed and was reforming the French Empire. It was a dangerous time to travel, and no escorts were available. With only a teenage German servant, Louisa and her young son made their way across a chaotic Germany and an even worse France. On occasion, she used her son's toy sword to bluff potential attackers and once represented herself as being one of Napoleon's sisters to French foragers, who were more like thieves than soldiers. The trip took six weeks and it made the future First Lady a phenomenon in Paris.

MATTER OF HONOR

If Andrew Jackson were still alive, I would not be writing about this topic. He was said to be so touchy about this particular problem that he kept two loaded dueling pistols for the expressed purpose of challenging anyone who brought it up. The subject is his marriage, well, actually, *two* marriages to wife Rachel. Andrew Jackson was devotedly in love with his wife. She has been married before to a most abusive man who all his life went out of his way to make things hard for her, even after they were divorced. Fleeing Virginia after having been beaten by her first husband, Rachel Robards met Andrew Jackson. They fell deeply and permanently in love. Fearing to return to Virginia, the couple carefully waited as Louis Robards filed for divorce there and for the required period that followed to make the divorce final. They then got married, but did not live happily ever after. Two years later, for reasons not known, Louis Robards filed a second divorce proceeding in Tennessee. Fearing that there might be a problem with their first marriage, the couple were married again. Today we would think of this as a love story, but in that time, politics were just as nasty and personal as modern mud-slinging elections. When Jackson, a war hero, ran for president, his opponents made much of his moral lapse using the second marriage as proof the couple had been living in sin. Jackson won by a large margin, but did not take this well and it was part of the reason behind one of the most politically rancorous periods.

LOVES LABOR LOST

Despite overcoming the controversy of their two marriage ceremonies, Rachel Jackson never actually lived in the White House. She saw Andrew Jackson elected, but died before his inauguration. Blaming her death partly on the highly personal attacks of his opponents, Jackson never forgave them.

WHO?

Very little in known about First Lady Hannah Van Buren. Not only are there few records, but she is not mentioned at all in her husband's autobiography. That's right, Martin Van Buren wrote an entire book about his life and presidency, but never once mentioned his wife in it.

HIS LITTLE TURNIP

There are no official records, but this was a treasured family tale: At one point in the American Revolution, the father of future

First Lady Anna Harrison felt his daughter would be much safer with her grandparents. The problem was that to get to the grandparents he had to pass through the British lines and onto British-held Long Island. To accomplish this, the father tried a dangerous ruse. He dressed in a British Redcoat's uniform and carried his young daughter in a small sack on his back. When stopped, he explained that the sack contained turnips for the British commander of occupied Long Island. He and the turnips were allowed to pass.

PARTY POOPER

Letitia Tyler hated being First Lady and the social responsibilities that entailed. She was the first wife of John Tyler, the tenth president, and she died while he was president. She refused to attend most of the parties held in the White House, which were admittedly less than somber affairs at which much alcohol was consumed. While the revelers danced and drank, she spent her evening in a wheelchair in her bedroom reading the Bible.

DOUBLE DUTY

Sarah Polk was not only First Lady but also acted as her husband's private secretary. As such, she had a good deal of direct influence on the running of the government. She was said to have done an excellent job. No other First Lady was as involved in the actual day-to-day running of the government except, perhaps, Eleanor Roosevelt. Even the major, if unsuccessful, efforts of Hillary Clinton on medical care are overshadowed by Eleanor's many successes.

PLEASE NO

Zachary Taylor was elected president on the strength of his military record. He was a successful general who had won many battles fighting on the nation's frontiers. That was also where both he and, even more so, his wife, Margaret, were most comfortable. Zachary Taylor's wife shared the hardy life of a frontier soldier with her husband for

almost forty years before he was elected president. She only reluctantly joined him at the White House and avoided all functions of
any sort. What she did do was spend a lot of time in her room. Her
favorite practice while there was to smoke a corncob pipe.

While Zachary could not pass on the honor, each night
before the election his wife would pray he would lose. He won.
But then the gods are sometimes perverse in granting wishes.
A short time after taking office, Zachary Taylor died. The First
Lady quickly packed up and left the city.

RAISE YOUR HAND

Millard Fillmore met his wife, Abigail, as a student in a class she
taught. He was a late-educated son of a farmer and eighteen when
he was attending school. It took some time for the young man
to convince her family to allow him to marry the older woman.
The family kept stalling and their engagement stretched out to
seven years. Finally, in 1826, they felt that Millard had waited
long enough and the couple were married in a simple ceremony.

BOOK OF THE DECADE CLUB

Both Abigail and Millard Fillmore were avid readers. They had,
in a time when books were expensive, accumulated a library of
nearly two thousand volumes before Millard was elected president in 1849. After moving into the White House, the couple
was astonished to discover that there was nary a book in the
building. They finally prevailed on Congress to give them a
$2,000 budget, with which Abigail then bought books for what
was the start of the White House library, personally selecting
each one. This library may be the only positive thing either of
the Fillmores is remembered for.

ANYONE THERE?

Mary Todd Lincoln was an avid spiritualist. She constantly held
séances in the White House, hoping to contact her lost children

and others. When Lincoln was reelected, she also had a strong premonition of his death and often commented on her feeling of doom. When her fears were fulfilled by John Wilkes Booth, she retired to the upstairs of the White House and eventually, because she suspected Andrew Johnson had been part of the plot, virtually squatted there for a month before leaving Washington. Later she let her life be ruled by spiritualism and her unshaken belief in charlatans. They were one of the two of the reasons Mary Todd Lincoln was eventually sent by a court to a mental asylum in 1875. The other was the insistence that she be committed by her last remaining son, Robert.

HANDMAIDEN

Imelda Marcos was not the first. In one four-month period while her husband was in office, Mary Todd Lincoln purchased over three hundred pairs of gloves.

DOUBLE TROUBLE

When a young Julia Grant was a child, she was struck on the side of her head by an oar. This had a permanent effect on the later First Lady's vision. The blurred and double images permanently caused by the accident meant that she had trouble simply walking across a crowded room without bumping into guests or the furniture. To avoid this she adopted a sideways walk that helped only a little. Surgeons offered to correct the problem, but in what was probably a good decision considering the state of medicine at the time, Ulysses forbade any operation.

SEEING MORE THAN MOST

On at least two occasions, Julia Grant gave good reason to believe in the psychic abilities she claimed to have. The first was the day of Lincoln's assassination. An invitation arrived for General Grant to attend the same play at Ford's Theater. Instead she wrote her husband that they should leave Washington immediately. He complied and took her to Philadelphia. Grant was also a target in the assassination plot of John Wilkes Booth. Years later, when the Grants were living in Chicago, Julia had another premonition in 1871 that featured fire and smoke. She convinced her husband to cancel an appearance that night and leave the city. The couple was miles away when the Great Chicago Fire broke out destroying four square miles of the city.

POOL AND THAT STANDS FOR PLANT

The pool table that was brought into the executive mansion by Andrew Jackson, which caused quite a ruckus, was as unacceptable to Lucy Hayes, wife of Rutherford B. Hayes, the nineteenth president, as alcohol, dancing, and other soul-destroying vices. As a devout Methodist, she ordered the table removed and the Billiard Room became a conservatory filled with her favorite plants.

FOR HER BRAINS

The first of the First Ladies who was a college graduate was Lucy Hayes. She graduated from Illinois Wesleyan Woman's College with highest honors in 1850.

PRESIDENTIAL DISCRETION

James Garfield was a model for too many future presidents. His propensity for having affairs and mistresses was notorious. He opened the low moral ground for many of our modern day leaders. Even before he was married to Lucretia (he called her Crete) Rudolph, James Garfield was involved in a number of affairs. Crete forgave and married him, feeling that her own withdrawn nature was part of the problem. It was a pattern that would follow the couple for their entire marriage. As a representative, and even president, Garfield's eye roamed. This was an open secret and well known even beyond Washington. When the president was assassinated in 1881, the long-suffering widow was the object of national sympathy. Over $350,000 was raised in a subscription drive to ensure the former First Lady's financial security and Congress also voted her a $50,000 payment and $5,000 annual pension.

PITY IT DID NOT STICK

On May 20, 1895, while Grover Cleveland was president, the income tax was declared by the Supreme Court to be unconstitutional. Don't you wish they had stuck to their guns? It was reinstituted by constitutional amendment to pay for World War I.

YA BET

Neither U. S. Grant nor his wife, Julia, was the type to hesitate when challenged. Grant proved this on many battlefields. His wife had her own determination. While the presidential party was out west and being shown a Virginia City silver mine, the prominent banker John. W. Mackey bet the president a silver dollar that Mrs. Grant would not go down into the mine and look at the head of the shaft. When the First Lady was told that the wealthy mine owner had bet against her courage, she promptly walked into the mine.

YOUNGER THAN SPRINGTIME

By far the youngest First Lady was Frances Folsom Cleveland, the wife of Grover Cleveland. She was only twenty-one when, in 1886, she married the widowed, forty-nine-year-old president. It was the first wedding ceremony in the executive mansion. She wore a twenty-one-foot train on her gown in a ceremony that was held in the evening before less than fifty close friends. President Cleveland deleted the word "obey" from her vows (women's lib was alive even then). They were a seemingly happy couple and after Grover Cleveland was reelected, Frances gave birth to the first child of a President to be born in the White House.

FASHION STATEMENT

Sometimes a celebrity can have a drastic effect on what others wear. When Clark Gable took off his shirt and had no undershirt on in the movie *It Happened One Night*, the sales of those shirts plummeted. This also happened at the time that the darling of the media was the young and vivacious Frances Cleveland. Everything she did or wore was front page news. But the process reversed itself one long, dull summer. There was simply nothing happening and a reporter needed a story. Editors are rarely understanding by nature. So a reporter made up a story saying that Frances Cleveland had begun defying what had been the current fashion. Specifically, he wrote that she had given up that rather unusual and amusing, to our modern eyes, appliance called a bustle. This backside extender had been part of the fashion scene for several years. Once other papers reprinted the story, women simply stopped wearing bustles. This story was false, but Frances, too, soon stopped wearing one.

FORTY-TWO GUN AFFAIR

When Anna Eleanor Roosevelt married her fifth cousin, the future President Franklin Roosevelt, she was given in marriage at the altar by her uncle, President Theodore Roosevelt.

DOWNPLAYED

Ida McKinley, the wife of the twenty-fifth president, William McKinley, suffered from epileptic seizures. The couple took these in their stride and whenever Ida had a seizure, her very caring husband would place his handkerchief over her face to help her avoid embarrassment and because the lessened light seemed to help her. Once the seizure had passed, the presidential couple would continue on with no mention of it. No matter who President McKinley was with, he always stopped and gave Ida priority when she entered the room.

SLIPPERS

At the end of the nineteenth century one of the major social causes was the welfare of the aging veterans of the Civil War. William McKinley was a major advocate of such charities, which supported thousands of disabled or aging former soldiers from both sides. Ida McKinley did her part and also must have been a lightning crotchetier. The First Lady personally crocheted almost thirty-five hundred pairs of gray and blue slippers to be sold for the veteran's charity.

LAST THOUGHTS

The affectionate relationship between Ida and William McKinley is really a classic love story. All of Washington was charmed by how close they were and how caring both were. After the president was shot, the first thing he said to his secretary was "My wife—be careful, Cortelyou, how you tell her. Oh, be careful."

ONE TIME TOO MANY

In her entire life, Edith Roosevelt made only one public statement. This was long after she had been First Lady. Edith had been a lifelong Republican, but when her distant cousin Franklin ran on the Democratic ticket, everyone thought blood would be thicker than party loyalty. They were wrong; Edith went public encouraging everyone to vote for Herbert Hoover and not FDR. Franklin Delano Roosevelt still won in a landslide.

PIPELINE

On a visit to Hawaii, while accompanying her husband on an official trip to the Philippines, Helen Taft became the first, and possibly only, First Lady to have gone surfing there. But then, Helen had always been interested in leading an exciting life. (Just to cause trouble, when younger she took up the then very unladylike habits of smoking and drinking beer in the local Cincinnati pubs.) On the same trip the couple stopped in Japan. Years later the visit paid great dividends when, in honor of it, the mayor of Tokyo sent two batches of cherry trees to assist Helen Taft is beautifying Washington.

PRODUCT PLACEMENT

Helen "Nellie" Taft was the cause of what is likely the first presidential product placement in the nation's history. The First Lady was frustrated by the refusal of Congress to provide one of the new and modern automobiles for the president's use. While the elite of Washington was riding in new cars, the president was still stuck in his carriage. Her reaction to the rejection was to take action herself. Helen Taft approached the Pierce-Arrow company and asked for a large discount on a vehicle for her husband. To get this, she agreed that the company could advertise that they were the official automobile of the White House.

ZZZ BANG

As a young woman growing up in Georgia, future First Lady Ellen Wilson was an avid shot. Even in later years, sleeping in perhaps the most secure building in the country, the White House, she liked to sleep with a gun under her pillow.

HOW

Woodrow Wilson's second wife, Edith Bolling Galt Wilson, was a descendant of fabled American Indian princess Pocahontas. She was very proud of her heritage, and when allowed to name several Navy warships during World War I, invariably chose Native American names for them. One time, when a snobby French aristocrat snubbed her as First Lady (just a plebeian, you know; elected, not bred), the woman did a one-eighty and gushed all over what she thought was a different woman who was an actual Native American princess.

JUNIOR BIRDWOMAN

The first president's wife ever to fly in an airplane was Florence Harding. Like many women of her day, she was a strong advocate of a greater role for women in all areas. She flew, but insisted on a woman pilot.

TELL HER

The reticent Silent Cal Coolidge was never what anyone would describe as romantic. His proposal consisted of telling Grace that "I'm going to be married to you." While rarely speaking and never demonstrative, he did have a sense of humor, as did the First Lady. When visiting a farm, the First Lady noticed a rooster and hen going at it. She asked the farmer how often that happened and he told her several times a day. She sent him to tell this to the president. On being told exactly that, Calvin Coolidge then asked the farmer, "To the same hen?" and the farmer told him that it was with many different ones. Cal replied, "Tell that to Mrs. Coolidge."

COLORFUL

In 1929, the Ku Klux Klan was a political power in the South. This did not concern Lou Hoover, or her husband. On June 12, 1929, she hosted a tea and one of the guests was the wife of Illinois Congressman Oscar DePriest. The couple was African-American. No one at the tea cared about Mrs. DePriest's race, but the South went bonkers. A week later, just to show this was no anomaly, Herbert Hoover lunched in the White House with an African-American scholar from Tuskegee College. More than his failure to act decisively at the start of the Great Depression, these acts of integration ensured Herbert Hoover would lose the Southern vote when he ran for reelection.

SIGH

"I never wanted to be a president's wife, and I don't want it now." —Eleanor Roosevelt, who was First Lady longer than any other woman in history.

FIT FOR A KING
While First Lady, Eleanor Roosevelt once served hot dogs to the king and queen of England.

NO RETIREMENT
After the death of their husbands, most First Ladies retire from public life. But Eleanor Roosevelt was not like most First Ladies. She soon left Washington in 1945, but only to be the new delegate from the United States to the United Nations. There, she successfully lobbied for and got that body to pass the Universal Declaration of Human Rights. She kept active for the rest of her life. She acted as an adviser to President Kennedy when he formed the Peace Corps. Even more than Hillary Clinton (who is said to have idolized her, and to have heard Eleanor's spirit talking a few times, as well, when she was First Lady), Eleanor Roosevelt was the most active and involved First Lady in the actual business of government—ever.

RESIGNED
When the Daughters of the American Revolution refused to allow the black singer Marian Anderson to appear before their meeting in Constitutional Hall, Eleanor Roosevelt resigned from the organization. She then arranged for Marian Anderson to perform a concert in Washington, suitably, singing on the steps of the Lincoln Memorial. Thousands attended.

JOB PREP
While in college, Bess Truman was a track and field athlete. She often won her best event, the shot put.

BETTER STARCH IN THE COLLAR
Bess Truman was underwhelmed by the services in Washington when she was First Lady. So much so that she had her laun-

dry mailed to be done in Kansas City, Missouri. JFK, who once described Washington as a city with "Southern efficiency and Northern charm," seems to have agreed.

NOT IN MISSOURI

When John Kennedy was assassinated, it was decided to put a Secret Service team on every surviving president and First Lady. Bess Truman made it completely clear that they were neither needed nor welcome in Independence, Missouri, and would not even allow them on her property.

POOR PROSPECT

Mamie Doud had her choice of men when she was nineteen. She was beautiful, from a rich family, and the belle of most of San Antonio's balls. Her father was actually put off when she took an interest in young, poor Lieutenant Eisenhower, who was stationed nearby at Fort Sam Houston. There was a real question as to whether the couple could live on a lieutenant's pay, and no question that the young officer could not keep her in the manner she was accustomed. The first years really were very hard and Mamie had to learn a completely different lifestyle. So much so that she actually once was so exhausted she went into a coma. Then things got even worse, as her husband was shipped off to Panama, a dirty, forgotten posting with no decent housing.

Mamie Eisenhower was determined to make her marriage and life as an army wife work. It took all her efforts and nearly ruined her health, but she learned to adjust and even enjoy. When Ike was stationed in Panama, she took her friends to see the local form of entertainment, cockfights. What impressed the other base wives the most was not the event, but that not only did Mamie seem at home in the strange environment, she also won most of her bets.

PAIN THE EAR

While her husband was off winning World War II, Mamie Eisenhower stayed back in the states. Rumors soon spread that she was hitting the bottle. They were based on those who saw the general's wife weaving or bumping into things at all hours of the day. The truth was that she had Meniere's disease, which upset her balance. Be careful whom you spread gossip about; she might someday become the First Lady.

PRESIDENTIAL PUFF

To her dying day, Mamie Eisenhower smoked. Even while being a leading money raiser for the Heart Association, whose members were some of the first to point out the risks of smoking, she regularly puffed away—but only in private.

GOOD NIGHT?

When Jack Kennedy was suffering after having spinal surgery in 1954, his wife, Jackie, went to great lengths to cheer him up. One effort backfired when she had Grace Kelly dress as a night nurse and prance into the room. Her husband was too bleary to recognize the popular actress (and later Princess of Monaco). Grace commented that "I must be losing it." She may be the only starlet in JFK's bedroom whom he *didn't* get to know much better.

AND A ONE-PIECE, TOO

Such was the scrutiny that Jackie Kennedy was under that when she relaxed on a private beach in a swimsuit, the pictures were shown around the world. By today's standards, the suit was extremely modest, but this was the first time any First Lady had been seen in one. Some conservative supporters were so upset, they picketed the airport when she returned. The irony of all this was that at the same time her husband had the habit of swimming in the buff with a number of young and willing women in the White House pool.

EXTRAS

Pat Nixon, being a true Angeleno, appeared as an extra in several movies, including *Ben Hur* and *The Great Ziegfeld* (not as one of the scantily clad dancers).

CHEAP!

Lady Bird Johnson's wedding ring was purchased from Sears for $2.50. It seems the normally highly efficient Lyndon Johnson forgot to buy one, and on the morning of the ceremony, had to have a friend rush out and grab a selection from the local Sears store, from which Lady Bird picked one. She married him anyhow.

BEAUTIFUL LEGACY

Every time any of us drive somewhere, we owe a small debt to Lady Bird Johnson. As First Lady, she made making America more beautiful a major part of her efforts. This inspired acres of flowers to be planted in Washington. But her real contribution was to encourage a bill that restricted billboards, junk, and junkyards along the nation's major highways. The Highway Beautification Act made and makes a major difference in just how the world looks from our busiest highways. LBJ called it "Lady Bird's bill" and gave her the first pen after signing it in 1965.

ALL OVER

Pat Nixon was not only well-traveled, but an excellent goodwill ambassador. She visited twenty-nine nations while First Lady, and often dressed in the same manner as the people of the country she was visiting. She always did this with apparent cheer, though she had to be more comfortable eating dinner in Paris than on her visit to sub-Saharan Africa. While Pat Nixon might dress in unusual garb while traveling, she was at home a conservative dresser who abhorred the new trend of women wearing pants and never did so.

SHARED INTEREST

One of the things shared by Jerry and Betty Ford was athletic ability. Where Jerry was a varsity football player and team captain, Betty was a talented dancer. She did the choreography for her own dance troupe, and was good enough to study under the top instructors. All her life Betty loved to dance. She often danced with the celebrities who visited the White House. She once posted in the East Wing a picture of her dancing with Cary Grant. Under it she wrote, "Eat your heart out, gals."

WENT PUBLIC

In some ways, Americans can be a bit self-conscious. When Betty Ford was diagnosed with breast cancer and underwent a mastectomy, this was a procedure rarely spoken of in public. Through her efforts and courage during and after the operation, Betty Ford brought the entire topic into the public's awareness. Not only did this help those women who were also facing breast cancer, but the open discussions led to new and expanded research into treatment and prevention of the disease.

PHOTO OP

It is common for local party officials to pose for pictures with the First Lady when she visits a city. In Milwaukee, Rosalynn Carter once posed with a local Democratic Party organizer and donor. His name was John Wayne Gacy.

IN THE STARS

In this case the *real* stars, not her husband's costars. Much of what happened in the White House, at least the timing of it, was determined by the charts and predictions of Joan Quigley, Nancy Reagan's astrologer. Events such as travel and bill signing were changed to those moments considered most auspicious by the California seer.

19

FAMILY CAN BE FIRST FAMILY

By all standards, Teddy Roosevelt was a permissive father. Considering his own behavior, anything else would have been hypocritical. But one time he did get most upset and put his foot down hard. It was when he had to animatedly explain to his son Quentin that one simply does not throw spitballs at the portrait of Andrew Jackson on the White House wall.

Mary Lincoln's brother, George Todd, was an officer and surgeon in the Confederate Army. This led to rumors she was a Confederate sympathizer. Mrs. Lincoln's half-sister, Emilie, was married to Confederate Brigadier General Benjamin Hardin Helm, who died at Chickamauga. When she was captured by Union troops and Lincoln was notified, his telegraphed response was "Send her to me." Emilie then had a long visit at the White House, rekindling all the gossip and innuendo.

RELATED ISSUES:
Our second president, John Adams, was the father of the sixth president, John Quincy Adams.

The ninth president, William Henry Harrison, was the grandfather of the twenty-third president, Benjamin Harrison.

The fourth president, James Madison, and the twelfth president, Zachary Taylor, were second cousins.

While it is now assumed they were closely related, the

twenty-sixth president, Theodore Roosevelt, and the thirty-second president, Franklin Delano Roosevelt, were only fifth cousins.

George H. W. Bush, the forty-first president, is the father of George W. Bush, the forty-third.

Franklin D. Roosevelt was a true blue blood who was related in some way to a total of eleven U.S. presidents, five of them with a blood tie and six through marriage. He was in some way at least a distant relative of Theodore Roosevelt, John Adams, John Quincy Adams, Ulysses Grant, William Henry Harrison, Benjamin Harrison, James Madison, William Taft, Zachary Taylor, Martin Van Buren, and George Washington.

TEDDY AND FRANKLIN

Even though the two presidents were only distantly related and served decades apart, the two men had much in common. They both came from "old money" and saw serving in office as a duty. Both were, as their name suggests, of Dutch descent. Harvard University can claim both Roosevelts as alumni. Both developed severe handicaps—FDR's legs and Teddy's blindness and illnesses—while in office and managed to keep the general public from knowing about them. Both had held the offices of governor of New York and assistant secretary of the navy. Both Teddy and Franklin Roosevelt at one time ran for vice president. And finally, there was an attempted assassination of each Roosevelt.

PROLIFIC PRESIDENT

John Tyler had, by far, more children than any other president. He was married twice, and his second wife, Julia, was three decades younger than the president. Tyler had eight children by his first wife, Letitia, who died while he was in office. After remarrying in a secret ceremony while still president, Tyler proceeded to have seven more, for a total of fifteen presidential offspring.

THE OTHER PRESIDENT

While they did not exactly elope, Sally Knox Taylor, the daughter of future president Zachary Taylor, did rush her engagement and actually was married at an aunt's home in Tennessee, rather than where her father was then stationed as commander of the First Infantry. This led to some strain between her father and her husband. Unfortunately, Sally died a few years later. Her husband and Zachary Taylor served together in the Mexican-American War, and because of the bravery shown by the younger man, they became friends. The husband became a president, too, but of the Confederate States of America. Sally Taylor had virtually run off with, and then married, a young and dashing Jefferson Davis.

GUILT

The fourteenth president, Franklin Pierce, and his wife, Jane, were very religious. They also felt that God took direct actions that affected their lives. Both held the Calvinist attitude that much of what happened to them was punishment for past sins and transgressions. The train taking Pierce and his family to Washington, not long after he was elected, derailed. One car

FRANKLIN PIERCE
1853-1857

detached and rolled down an embankment. The only fatality in that car was the Pierces' only child. Blaming themselves, and even stating that God had taken their son so that Franklin could concentrate on being president, put a tremendous strain on both the president-elect and his wife. While in the train to Washington for the inauguration, Mrs. Franklin could not deal with it and got off to return to their home. She was not present at her husband's inauguration and so missed one of the most depressed inaugural addresses ever given.

WEDDED BLISS

It was truly a wedding to remember. President Ulysses Grant's daughter Nellie was getting married in the White House. It was the event of the season and done sparing no expense. The bride's gown cost over $2,000. To get a good idea of how it compares to today's value of money, add two more zeros. There were more than two hundred guests, a veritable "who's who" of Washington, D.C. The wedding included a sit-down dinner whose menu was printed on satin. Thousands of flowers were rushed by steamer from Florida and filled the East Room. Gifts given the young couple were estimated at having a value of $60,000 (in 1874 dollars)—several million dollars today.

You would have thought this would make a daddy proud, but President Grant could not conceal his grief even at the ceremony. During the Civil War, the closest ally the Confederacy had was unofficial support from Britain. That was where most of those blockade runners like Rhett Butler took their cargos of cotton to sell, bringing war supplies back. Grant's sorrow was that Nellie's husband was Algernon Satoris, an Englishman. Even though the man was of "good family" and wealthy, the president had only reluctantly given his blessing and could not get past the fact his Nellie was not only *not* marrying an American, but an Englishman to boot. Happily, he later visited the couple in England after leaving office.

PRESIDENTIAL BABY

Grover Cleveland's daughter Esther was the first and, so far, only child of a president born in the White House. She soon was the darling of the nation. Until her birth, the South Gate of the White House was kept constantly open. Eventually, the First Lady had to order it locked because too many people were coming through it just to view, and often kiss, the baby. Hard to picture today, but the White House used to be considered every citizen's building and was very much more open and accessible.

TRANSPRESIDITE

Until he was five years old, Franklin Delano Roosevelt's mother regularly made him wear dresses. There are no records of what permanent effect this practice may have had on the president. He certainly was extremely heterosexual and demonstrated this proclivity much more widely than Eleanor Roosevelt approved of. It might have helped him to understand J. Edgar Hoover's personal preferences.

BIG MAN

Some of us are big men from the beginning. Richard Nixon weighed almost eleven pounds at birth.

NAME GAME

When he was born, Gerald Ford was actually named Leslie Lynch King Jr. His mother divorced when he was two and married Gerald Ford Sr. The couple then legally changed the two-year-old child's name.

MAYFLOWER MOMENT

A number of the presidents, three First Ladies, and even one vice president have been shown to be descendants of those who came over on the Mayflower.

These are:

John Adams and also, of course, his son John Quincy Adams
Zachary Taylor
Ulysses S. Grant
James A. Garfield
Franklin D. Roosevelt
George H. W. Bush and his son George W. Bush

Barbara (Pierce) Bush, wife of George Bush, the forty-first president

Lucretia (Rudolph) Garfield, wife of James Garfield, the twentieth president

Edith (Carrow) Roosevelt, wife of Theodore Roosevelt

Vice President Dan Quayle

Dan Quayle? Hmmm . . . the bloodline seems to be thinning.

TWO SONS

Andrew Jackson had no children of his own. He did adopt two sons. One was a nephew who had been orphaned. The western states could still be dangerous places and taking in orphaned family members was common and almost expected. The second son was the child of an Indian woman who had been killed during a battle.

THE COST OF WAR

Teddy Roosevelt was always a bit of a war lover. During the three years World War I ran before the United States joined the allies, he constantly lobbied for us to be in the conflict. His public statements regarding then President Wilson often verged on libel and he regularly questioned the president's personal courage. Once the United States did enter the war, it turned out to be a far from glorious experience for the former president. In 1918, his son Quentin Roosevelt was shot down and killed while flying his fighter plane over the Western Front.

OLD ENEMY

During the American Civil War, the state of Missouri sent about as many volunteers to fight for the Confederacy as the Union. Among those who fought for the South were some of Harry Truman's ancestors on his mother's side. A few were known to have been placed in Northern prisoner-of-war camps, which were horrible places with high mortality rates among the prisoners. This left a lot of very bitter survivors whose families never forgot their ordeal. When Harry Truman became president, his mother came to visit. He offered to put her up in the most prestigious guest room of the executive mansion. Unfortunately this is the Lincoln Bedroom. Martha Ellen Truman turned down his offer, stating that she would prefer to sleep on the floor than in Lincoln's bed.

FORMALLY YOURS

Richard Nixon must have been emotionally frustrating to be married to. He was simply distant and impersonal to just about everyone. The notes he sent to his daughters or Pat, his wife, were most often signed "The President."

HISTORY MAJOR?

Lucy Hayes, the wife of Rutherford B. Hayes, was the first wife of a president to have graduated from a college. She may also have enjoyed being First Lady more than any other presidential wife. Lucy Hayes spent hours every week exploring odd corners of the White House, and unearthing items and odd papers she found in attics, storage areas, and closets. Many of the historical treasures on display in the Smithsonian from the early presidents can be credited to Mrs. Hayes's efforts.

First Lady Lucy Hayes also had a second love, taking great pleasure in flowers. She personally would arrange from a dozen to even several dozen bouquets almost every day. These were sent mostly to friends.

YOUNG AND OLD DADS

The president who became a father at the youngest age was Andrew Johnson—he was nineteen. The oldest president to become a dad was John Tyler, whose young wife gave birth when he was seventy years old. Because of the spread between his and his father's ages, the son of the tenth president actually met with the thirty-second, FDR, and as of 2007 one of his grandsons is still alive.

NAME GAME

It took some time for Harry and Bess Truman to settle on a name for their only daughter. He wanted to name her Mary, but Bess wanted Margaret. Margaret was four years old before it was mutually agreed that was her name.

PERMANENT EMOTIONAL SCARS?

When George H. W., Barbara, and a very young George W. Bush moved west, they had a surprising living arrangement in Odessa, Texas. The apartment building they moved into had a communal bathroom. It was shared by the two future presidents, and a mother and daughter who also worked at an occupation common in oil towns: the two women were prostitutes.

20

STRIPES IN THE STARS

It is unlikely the first presidents thought much about astrology. It was considered a superstition that had been left behind in the Age of Reason. But there was a revival in the late nineteenth century that has carried on to this day. So, were the presidents' fates in the stars?

There is a fairly even spread of presidents and signs.

Aries	2
Taurus	4
Gemini	2

Cancer	4
Leo	3
Virgo	2
Libra	4
Scorpio	5
Sagittarius	3
Capricorn	4
Aquarius	5
Pisces	4

ARIES: Adventurous and energetic, pioneering, courageous, dynamic and quick-witted, but also selfish with a temper, impatient, foolhardy, and a bit of a daredevil. The first Aries president was Thomas Jefferson, who had most of the positive traits listed here. Then again, his love life can be described as rather daredevil for his time. The next Aries president was John Tyler, whose most notable achievement was fathering fifteen children. Okay, so he gets energetic and courageous then.

TAURUS: Patient and reliable, warmhearted, persistent, placid, but also jealous, possessive, resentful, inflexible, self-indulgent, and greedy. James Monroe was the first Taurus to be president. He did not fit the bill too well by type, but if being the most honest president is a Tauran trait, he qualifies. Every trait of stubborn determination attributed to Taurus was manifest in the second Tauran president, U. S. Grant.

GEMINI: Adaptable and versatile, witty, intellectual, eloquent, youthful but also nervous, superficial, cunning, and inquisitive. The great claim of the Gemini was that John F. Kennedy was one. He certainly was a perfect fit for the general traits listed above. I would have thought him an Aquarius though, with the stories of his bedroom frolics. Maybe the cunning part fits.

CANCER: Emotional and loving, imaginative, cautious, protective and sympathetic, but also moody, touchy, and clinging. The skinny-dipping John Quincy Adams was cautious enough, but not very touchy, by any definition.

LEO: Generous, warmhearted, creative, enthusiastic, faithful, and loving, but also pompous, patronizing, interfering, and intolerant. There wasn't a Leo as president until Benjamin Harrison in 1889. He was the coldest, least sociable person to ever live in the White House. His nickname was "White House Iceberg." He missed the first part of the list it seems. The next one, Herbert Hoover, didn't do much better. Shantytowns in the Great Depression were called "Hoovervilles." Going forward from Hoover, you find next William Jefferson Clinton. Loving we got, but missed the faithful part.

VIRGO: Modest, shy, reliable, practical, diligent, and intelligent but also prone to worry, critical, a perfectionist, and conservative. William Howard Taft was a 325-pound bureaucrat and the first Virgo president (in 1909). He somehow managed to make just about everyone in the nation mad at him by the end of his term. Shy? Reliable? Modest? The next one is LBJ, not your typical Virgo it seems.

LIBRA: Diplomatic, charming, easygoing, sociable, idealistic, and peaceable but also indecisive, easily influenced, flirtatious and self-indulgent. Rutherford B. Hayes was the first Libra president and generally botched the job. Basically, take every trait listed for Libra and reverse it and you have Hayes. He was much happier later as a judge. Ike, the next Libra, did a much better job, if mostly from the golf course.

SCORPIO: Forceful, emotional, intuitive, passionate, and magnetic but also prone to be jealous, compulsive, obsessive, secretive, and obstinate. The first Scorpio president certainly had these traits, as it was the Revolutionary hero John Adams. As a Scorpio, James Polk should have been decisive. The truth is that his failure to deal with slavery was one of the eventual causes of a the American Civil War. Teddy Roosevelt was a Scorpio—now that fits. Most Scorpios try to forget that Warren Harding was one too, with good reason.

SAGITTARIUS: Optimistic, good-humored, honest, intellectual, and philosophical, but also careless, irresponsible, and tactless. The first one to hold office was Martin Van Buren; he is mostly known for creating the first modern political machine in the United States and for luxurious living. About honest—see the part about political machine above.

CAPRICORN: Practical, ambitious, disciplined, patient, and careful, but also pessimistic, greedy, and grudging. So all that ambition and patience gave us the first Capricorn president, Millard Fillmore. A case can be made for his being the least effective president to have ever served. A more competent Woodrow Wilson was the next Capricorn. Capricorns have the dubious honor of including Richard Nixon.

AQUARIUS: Friendly, honest, loyal, inventive, and intellectual, but contrary, unpredictable, and unemotional. The first Aquarian president was William Henry Harrison, who spoke almost two hours at his inauguration, fell ill, and died. A bit too friendly perhaps. Abraham Lincoln was an Aquarius, and certainly had many of the positive traits, but then he seems to have had a lot of positive traits. This writer always figured him for a Taurus, the way he hung on during dark times in the Civil War. After all, Grant was. Franklin Delano Roosevelt was also an Aquarius. He led the nation with a near-dictatorial hand through two crises, the Depression and World War II.

FDR does seem to have lived up to the "free love" image, to his wife's chagrin. And who would have figured that Ronald Reagan was an Aquarius? Guess it was from all those years in California.

PISCES: Imaginative, sensitive, kind, and unworldly and very sympathetic, but also idealistic, secretive and easily led. Strangely, George Washington was a Pisces. The next Pisces president was James Madison, a consummate politician and definitely *not* easily led. Never unworldly, Andrew Jackson showed few Pisces traits. Perhaps it was his frontier upbringing.

LONG TIME, SAME PROBLEM

The first time the son of a president was elected president was way back in 1824, when John Quincy Adams, the son of John Adams, was elected. Strangely, both of these men who became president shared one problem. This was that both received less than half of the popular vote and served their term under a cloud.

21

PRESIDENTIAL PETS
by Claire McLean
Curator, Presidential Pet Museum

The curator of the Presidential Pet Museum was kind enough to gather these facts and remembrances of presidents and their pets. You can visit the Museum while in Washington, D.C., or look it up online at www.presidentialpetmuseum.com . For those of you that feel the White House is quite a zoo, it will confirm your suspicions.

GEORGE WASHINGTON
Our founding father was the hero of the dog breeder's domain in early days, having a keen sense of selection of the finest to the finest. He forefathered the American foxhound from the English foxhound, and kept records on his breedings and his animals, which covered dogs, mules, turkeys, and other farm animals. On top of that the story, true or not, is that Martha Washington's parrot was trained to say, "Polly wants a cracker?"

JOHN ADAMS
John Adams built the first stables at the White House and had a favorite horse named Cleopatra. Abigail had two dogs: Juno and Satan.

THOMAS JEFFERSON

This great gentleman was a lover and breeder of French Briards, and is said to have invented the dog license, having asked all landowners to tag their dogs and be responsible for their mischief.

JAMES MADISON

President Madison's wife, Dolley, took the stage at the White House with her society parties and wonderful affairs, but her big claim in the history books is that she and her handlady rescued both the great portrait of George Washington *and* her beloved green parrot from the White House as the British advanced. It is said the parrot outlived both her and her husband, and did not ask for any crackers.

JAMES MONROE

James Monroe's twelve-year-old daughter, Maria, had a spaniel while at the White House, and they both were the objects of much observation and entertainment. One visitor remarked that he was not sure whether Maria or the spaniel wiggled more, nor which was more rude.

JOHN QUINCY ADAMS

One of the most bizarre and yet true stories is how President Adams kept an alligator of questionable size in the East Room of the White House for several months. This well-documented episode tells of how this gift from the French general, Lafayette, managed to provide the President with some amusing and hilarious moments, as many guests would come upon the reptile unaware and show their shock and awe in a variety of ways. To add to his bizarre taste in pets, Louisa Adams kept silkworms in the sitting room and was known to weave their silk into cloth.

ANDREW JACKSON

Andrew Jackson was known as the "racehorse president," as his love for horses and especially for racing them was well documented. His favorite horse was Truxton and another was Sam Patch. It was Truxton, however, that he purchased and put out at stud at his farm, the Hermitage, in Tennessee, and who sired many foals for racing and riding. He loved this horse above many of the others, but perhaps it was because Truxton won so many races for him.

MARTIN VAN BUREN

When he was president, Martin Van Buren fought with the Congress of the United States to keep two tiger cubs that were given to him. They arrived at the White House as cute cubs from the sultan of Oman, and the president was happy to show them off to visitors. He felt they were indeed his property and he could do as he wished with them. But as the complaints began to fly, Congress stepped in and made a decree that such gifts to the president belonged to the people, and therefore the cute cubs, now testy teenagers, went off to the National Zoo and attracted much attention there.

WILLIAM HENRY HARRISON

The story of this president running down Pennsylvania Avenue, chasing his grandson Ben in a runaway goat cart, is the big animal story of the Harrison White House, but it goes much farther than that. Although not well-documented, it is known the grandchildren of William Henry Harrison, just as his children did, had an assortment of small pets and large pets—in particular, the ornery runaway goat, Whiskers. The newspapers carried the story of the runaway goat and some bystanders, aghast at the wildly puffing president, believed it was the president's coachman Willis who spooked Whiskers into his mad dash. Little did they know then that grandson Ben would grow up to be president also, but at that time Ben enjoyed the ride.

JOHN TYLER

Tyler and his wife, Julia, had soft hearts for animals. They had many in their lives and several during his administration, which was fraught with controversy. Tyler was to help pioneer the Italian greyhound in the country when he surprised his wife by ordering a puppy from Naples. When it finally arrived, it was noted that it was rough on furniture and in need of discipline. Le Beau, as he was called, was mentioned in the press on occasions of his misbehaving—mostly in the Tyler estate at Sherwood Forest in Virginia.

ZACHARY TAYLOR

When tales are told of President Taylor, there is usually the mention of his great war mount, old Whitey. A comparison is often made of how they were alike in appearance: an ungroomed, shaggy, and scraggly steed, and his long, lanky rider. Whitey carried the general through hundreds of miles in the Mexican-American War and through many battles to become the most famous horse in the United States. He stayed on with the general when he became president, and while losing many of his tail and mane hairs to visitors at the White House, he joined the funeral procession for his master and found his final resting place at their home in Virginia.

ABRAHAM LINCOLN

Many animals adorned the Lincoln White House, despite Mrs. Lincoln's lack of pleasure in them. The first recorded litters to be born in the White House came on the same day, when Tad's dog and Willie's cat both gave birth at the same time.

Willie took sick with pneumonia and died, and this left the Lincoln family in deep mourning and shock, especially little Tad. Several months later, after other attempts to cheer him up, two goats came to live with him at the White House and went into the history books as heroes. They were Nanko and Nanny. First came a pair of pink-eyed white rabbits, and then came the goats. Tad was a typical rambunctious boy and looked for ways to have fun with his pet goats. He often riled his very stern mother, Mary Lincoln, who did not look upon several of his stunts kindly.

The episode that got Tad in the most trouble was when he hooked up the fun-loving goats to some hall furniture, chairs to be exact, and rode the chairs down the great hallway while the aides and assistants stood aghast. The recorded word has it his father, Lincoln, was amused by his creativity, but Tad was given downtime by his mother. Sadly, Nanny Goat wandered off when Tad and his mother were visiting Vermont and was never seen or heard from again. A long-held suspicion is that the gardener may have assisted in the disappearance, as the goats were notorious for smashing the flower gardens. For some reason, Nanny was often able to escape from the stable and make a beeline for the flowerbed. Nanko stayed on, better behaved and content.

Their famous family dog, Fido, of mixed ancestry, stayed behind in Springfield when the Lincolns went to Washington, but the dog was still very much a part of the family. A formal portrait of this dog can be seen on exhibit at the Lincoln Museum and Library.

ANDREW JOHNSON

During his impeachment process, over which this president prevailed, Andrew Johnson confided to an aide that he had befriended a family of mice that would appear at dusk each night in the Oval Office. He would put out flour or biscuits for the tiny rodents and ponder their plight as he worried late into the night about his own.

ULYSSES S. GRANT

President Ulysses S. Grant appeared to be a genuine animal lover, having had dogs, cats, and horses throughout most of his life. During his administration, he was known to dote on his great racehorse, Cincinnati.

RUTHERFORD B. HAYES

A two-year-old greyhound named Grim, a gift from Mrs. William DuPont of Wilmington, Delaware, gained celebrity status at the White House. He was much admired by the Hayes family and was popular with the public. When Grim met an untimely death by standing his ground in the face of an oncoming train, the public deluged the White House with letters of condolence. Hayes wrote, "The death of Grim has made us all mourn." The Newfoundland, Hector, and the cocker, Dot, both seemed to miss the big guy as well. The Hayeses went on to replace Grim with other adored pets, but with such outpouring of public sympathy, came to realize that their animals were very much a part of their public image.

JAMES GARFIELD

One of the favorite tales told about James Garfield is that of his family dog, Veto, a large black Newfoundland that captured the imagination of the public when the president decided upon naming the big dog.

This story, as sent to the Presidential Pet Museum by Debbie Weimkamer, follows:

James A. Garfield acquired a dog in Washington, D.C., in the spring of 1879, while he was a congressman representing the Nineteenth District of Ohio. He had a home in Washington at Thirteenth & I Streets, but wanted the dog sent to his summer home—a farm in Mentor, Ohio, now the James A. Garfield National Historic Site (aka Lawnfield). The dog traveled by train to Mentor. Garfield sent several letters to his younger sons, Irvin and Abe (who were already at the farm), telling them all about the new dog and to expect his arrival.

Irvin objected to the name that Garfield had given the dog. Garfield had called him Veto because President Hayes had recently vetoed five bills in three months! As a congressman, minority leader of the House of Representatives, and Republican liaison to President Hayes, Garfield had helped the president sustain his vetoes through the House. The name did not win instant acceptance from all of the Garfield family, so they took a vote on it to settle the matter. Garfield was very impressed that his son understood democracy enough to want a vote. The dog's name remained Veto.

An excerpt of the letter to Irvin from Garfield reads:

Washington, D.C.
May 17, 1879

My Dear Irvin,
I have read your letter to Hal [Garfield's oldest son], and I think you are quite right in your view of the way to name the dog. The whole family ought to be heard on the subject; and you may call him 'pup,' or any other name you please until we get home. Then we will hold a meeting of the Garfield family and have the name voted on—each man, woman and child to have a vote. . . .

Affectionately Your Papa
J.A. Garfield

This information can be found in *The Garfield Orbit* by Margaret Leech and Harry J. Brown, Harper & Row, 1978, pages 294–295.

I also have this reference to the dog in *From Mentor to Elberon* by (Garfield's friend) Colonel Almon Rockwell (it appears in J. M. Bundy's *Life of Garfield* and was excerpted in *Century Magazine, 1881*): "The big Newfoundland dog, in memory of the numerous bills killed in 1879 by the executive disapproval, was called by the suggestive name of Veto."

CHESTER A. ARTHUR

While there is no official history or even folklore about President Arthur and pets or animals in his domain, we do know he was a big sportsman and hunter and kept hunting dogs, several of which he considered favorites, and he was attached to them. Because his administration was so secretive, much of his history and documents, journals and government papers were destroyed, so we have a hard time peeking into any personal history of this president and his affinity for (or lack of) towards his four-legged friends. He is one of three presidents to whom no animal or pet can be attributed.

GROVER CLEVELAND

The only president to be married in the White House, big Grover Cleveland, age forty-four, took little Frances Folsom, age twenty-one, as his bride and with her came her Japanese spaniel, a mockingbird, and three canaries. The Clevelands produced five children, one of whom had a famous candy bar named after her, Baby Ruth. The children for a short time began to collect an assortment of pets, none of which took public attention, but this small accumulation of animals, dogs and cats, made way for the other great animal pets to come and live in the White House.

BENJAMIN HARRISON

The grandson of William Henry Harrison, Benjamin had animals at the White House, too, and enjoyed a longer term in office.

WILLIAM MCKINLEY

The invalid wife of William McKinley had a double yellow-headed parrot that she was extremely fond of. By a twist of fate, shortly before the president was shot on September 6, 1901, he was photographed with an unknown black dog crossing his path, as if an omen of something tragic to come.

THEODORE ROOSEVELT

Six children and enough pets to fill a zoo, not to mention the many animals given to the President, which ended up at the

National Zoo. Bleistein was President Roosevelt's favorite horse, and he had horses for all the children. They were called Renown, Roswell, Rusty, Jocko, Root, Grey, Dawn, Wyoming, and Yangenka. General and Judge were carriage horses. Algonquian was Archie Roosevelt's Icelandic calico pony. Pete, a bull terrier, was a favorite pet. There was also Sailor Boy, a Chesapeake retriever. Jack, Kermit Roosevelt's, was a rat terrier, and Skip was a mongrel. Manchu was Alice Roosevelt's spaniel, and she had a snake called Emily Spinach. Quentin Roosevelt also had some snakes, some of which he unloaded on top of his father's desk during a meeting with important people. Everyone scattered as the snakes slithered away; it became a very newsworthy item. Eli Yale was a macaw also belonging to Quentin Roosevelt, and Tom Quartz and Slippers were cats. Josiah was their well-known badger; Dewey Senior, Dewey Junior, Bob Evans, Bishop Doan, and Father O'Grady, were all guinea pigs. The list probably goes further and the Roosevelts can be said to have contributed the most animals to the history of the White House, but the Coolidges can claim a close second and the Kennedys were also high on the list of White House pet owners. A rather famous "pet" story about Theodore Roosevelt's White House is one that describes Quentin Roosevelt taking Algonquian, the pony, up in the White House elevator to see his brother Archie, who was sick in bed on the second floor. Once in the elevator, they had a time trying to get the pony out and it made the news, made the public laugh and the president mad.

WILLIAM HOWARD TAFT

President Taft loved to drink fresh milk. So much so that he had a purebred Holstein cow named Pauline Wayne that he was very fond of, and who had the privilege of often grazing on the White House lawn. It is reported that Taft was so large and drank so much of Pauline's milk every morning at breakfast that on one occasion he became lodged in the White House bathtub and

had to ask his aides to extract him. The White House physician instructed him to lighten up on his milk consumption and, soon after, Pauline Wayne became the last cow at the White House.

WOODROW WILSON

President Woodrow Wilson wanted to set an example of working for the war effort by conserving, and that is why it is reported he had a herd of sheep graze on the White House lawn during his administration. One of the flock was a big ram named Ike, who was fond of tobacco and on several occasions he was reported as the president's "tobacco-chewing ram and pet." The president said the sheep kept the grass in check so the manpower could be off fighting the war. While dogless in the White House, Wilson is known to have said, "If a dog won't look you in the face, you had better look yourself in the mirror and examine yourself."

WARREN HARDING

Laddie Boy, an Airedale terrier, was so popular with the press, the public, and his adoring owners, Warren and Florence, that he stood higher in the popularity polls than they did. He even had his own cabinet chair so he could sit in on cabinet meetings with the president. They threw him a birthday party every year and allowed him to join in on most formal functions. Harding was considered one of our worst presidents, but Laddie Boy was adored by the public. Many newspaper boys across the country contributed pennies to a fund to create a statue of the deceased dog and raised enough for a life-size statue made from copper pennies that is now exhibited at the Smithsonian. The Harding also had an English bulldog named Big Boy and three canaries.

CALVIN COOLIDGE

Calvin and Grace Coolidge had a zoo at the White House. Most famous and beloved was the white collie, purchased from Thomas and Olive Shover, who owned Shomont White Collies. They also entertained and cared for Peter Pan, a terrier, and Paul Pry, an Airedale who was originally named Laddie Buck. Rob Roy was their white collie, and he was originally named Oshkosh. Grace Coolidge loved to change the names of her pets,

CALVIN COOLIDGE
1923-1929

or else she just couldn't make up her mind what name suited the animals best. Also adored by Mrs. Coolidge was Calamity Jane, a Shetland sheepdog. Tiny Tim, a chow, was also sometimes called His Highness. Blackberry was also a chow, but was not as well known as Tiny Tim. The Coolidges also had a rough brown collie named Ruby Rough. They also had Boston Beans, who is mentioned as a bulldog by some reporters but was actually a Boston terrier. King Kole was a police dog of the German shepherd type, although pedigree papers have not been found.

Bessie, a yellow collie, is well-documented, as most of his collies were from the Shomont line. Their stay in the White House also shows that they had a bird dog named Palo Alto, and perhaps for him they added Nip and Tuck (two yellow canaries), Snowflake (a white canary), and Old Bill (a thrush). Enoch was a goose and they also kept a mockingbird for a period of time. Finally there was Tiger, an alley cat; Blacky, another cat; and Rebecca and Horace, raccoons. Mrs. Coolidge loved showing off her pet raccoons and often walked them on leashes around the White House grounds. During Easter week, she would put bonnets on her collies. Then, we must not forget Ebenezer, the donkey, and Smokey, a bobcat. There was also lion cubs, a wallaby, a pygmy hippo, and a bear. Many of these exotic animals were given to them by dignitaries or heads of state from other countries. Many of them helped to populate the National Zoo.

HERBERT HOOVER

President and Mrs. Hoover loved their dogs and kept several with them at the White House. The most well-known was King Tut, who was of German shepherd descent, but often called a Belgian sheepdog. While, in fact, President Hoover was a likable and friendly gentleman, his public image was of an austere and cold machine-like man. It is reported that the circulation of a photo of him holding King Tut up by the paws was so successful in humanizing the nominee, that he was elected. King Tut was a one-man dog and eventually became so protective of the president and the White House grounds that he was sent back to their previous home, where he pined away for his master and died. Another shepherd, named Pat, one of Mrs. Hoover's favorites, tried to take the place of the belligerent King Tut, but could not. Big Ben and Sonny, two wirehaired fox terriers, were fun and pleasure for the couple, and so was Glen, a purebred collie. Yukon was a purebred Eskimo dog, and Patrick was one of a pair of wolfhounds that were also well bred and became well established with the couple. Eaglehurst Gillette, a setter, and Weejie, an elkhound from the famous Hemson kennel of Ski in Norway, were prominent members of the household.

The story goes that the president even adopted an opossum that wandered onto the White House grounds and was thought to be the escaped mascot of the nearby Hyattsville baseball team. Hoover had grown rather attached to the friendly opossum, but rather than have the team think he had "swiped" the mascot, he presented it back to them and they went on to win the state championship.

FRANKLIN DELANO ROOSEVELT

Fala, a Scottish terrier, the most famous pet to have lived in the White House, was the beloved companion of Franklin Roosevelt. His one distinguishing feature was he was never, well hardly ever, groomed. Even his impressive bigger-than-life statue at the Roosevelt memorial in Washington, D.C., shows him to be the shaggy rascal that he was in real life. We are told today that when George W. Bush wanted his Scottie, Barney, shaggy to copycat Fala, it was pointed out that Democrats and their dogs are more untidy and a Republican Scottie should be the epitome of good grooming. So the public sees a very tidy twosome in Barney and Miss Beasley, but they can never replace the incomparable Fala.

HARRY S. TRUMAN

The dog-loving public thought Harry was a dog hater when he sent the adorable little cocker spaniel puppy, named Feller, packing. How could our president not keep such a wonderful gift? Harry had a hard time making up for that blunder, but when the public got used to seeing Margaret, his daughter, with an Irish setter they called Mike, they forgave him. Mike, however, did not thrive, developed rickets, and was sent to a farm before the Trumans left the White House.

DWIGHT D. EISENHOWER

President Eisenhower had two Scottie dogs before he entered the White House, but one of his main pets during his administration was Heidi, a Weimaraner who had the run of the mansion at various times—until she soiled the carpets and jumped on Mrs. Eisenhower when photographers were trying to take her picture. Heidi was sent back to their Gettysburg farm, where protocol was not enforced for dogs. As a hunter, Eisenhower was fond of his many bird dogs, but it was Heidi who got to visit and stay at the White House for a while. At that time the Ghost Dogs, as they were sometimes referred to, got a big boost in American Kennel Club registrations due to Heidi's affection for the president.

JOHN F. KENNEDY

Animals abounded during Camelot. From a white rabbit named Zsa Zsa to a pony named Macaroni, the John F. Kennedy family had more four-legged creatures around than two-legged. John and Caroline had horses, birds, fish, turtles, rabbits, dogs, and more dogs, and then puppies when their Sputnik dog, Pushinka, a present from Nikita Khrushchev, mated with their beloved Welsh terrier, Charlie, and four *pupniks*, as the president called them, arrived.

LYNDON B. JOHNSON

Lyndon Johnson, one of our most dog-loving presidents, learned a hard lesson when showing off for photographers. He became famous for lifting his beloved beagles, Him and Her, up by their ears. "Oh they love it!" But the public thought differently and the outcry over his cruelty was surprising. After untimely deaths, the two beagles were followed by Yuki, a mongrel dog that his daughter, Luci, rescued from the highway. Yuki was the most adored by all and often joined the president for a howling session in the Oval Office.

Lyndon Johnson with grandson Patrick Nugent
and dog Yuki

RICHARD NIXON

Tricky Dicky was famous for his Checkers speech, which he
gave when he was a candidate for vice president, as he had been
accused of taking gifts and gratuities in exchange for favors. He
said he would give a full accounting, but would not give back
their little dog Checkers, a cocker spaniel, whom his daughters
adored. His appeal was so heartfelt, it helped convince Eisenhower to keep him as his running mate. True dog lovers, the
Nixons entered the White House with two dear pets, a Yorkie
named Pasha and a poodle named Vicky. They were joined by
a well-bred Irish setter named King Timahoe. After Richard
Nixon resigned, they all joined the family on Air Force One and
flew back to California.

GERALD FORD

The Ford family entered the White House dogless, but since President Ford had always been an admirer of golden retrievers, it wasn't long before one excellent specimen joined the family. Named Liberty, she was often seen with the president in the Oval Office and on the grounds. Her litter of eight pups at the White House was a very blessed and happy event, but it didn't help Ford overcome the public impression of him as a bumbler. The pups all found happy homes, with one being owned by White House staffer Dale Haney, who served many presidents and was their pets' best friend. Ford learned quickly not to walk Liberty after hours—he was caught by the Secret Service trying to get back in the White House after finding himself locked out.

JIMMY CARTER

The Carters had one noticeable pet episode while at the White House, which the press played to the fullest. Amy Carter got a mixed breed dog that her fifth-grade teacher gave her as a present. Called Grits, the pup was so uncooperative in helping to promote Heartworm Awareness Week that it would not let the veterinarian give it a pill. That, coupled with relieving herself on the Lincoln carpet . . . well, the dog was returned. Everyone breathed a sign of relief, as Grits did not get along with Amy's Siamese cat Misty Malarky Ying Yang. Like Democrats and Republicans, dogs and cats have not carved out a working relationship with each other in the history of White House pets. Even today, Willie, Bush's black cat, tries to hide and avoid the terriers.

RONALD REAGAN

This story comes "from the horse's mouth," as this author had the privilege of being the official groomer of President and Mrs. Reagan's White House pet, a Bouvier des Flandres dog named Lucky. On the occasion of having her formal doggy canine photo taken, I was called to the White House to groom the shaggy, active young puppy. As much of her hair fell to the ground, I scooped it up and into my grooming kit for posterity. The hair from the president's dog! Now *that's* something, and when the photo was turned into a portrait of Lucky, it became the cornerstone of the Presidential Pet Museum thirteen years later. Within a few months, rambunctious Lucky was sent to the ranch, but her short stay in the White House laid the foundation for a museum that tells the story of American history through the eyes of the pets.

GEORGE H. W. BUSH

Millie had puppies at the White House. It was the second litter born since Ford's Liberty, and one pup went on to be a second generation White House pooch when the son, George W., and his wife, Laura, took up residence there. Millie, a springer spaniel, also had a bestselling book, ghostwritten by Barbara, that outsold the president's memoirs.

WILLIAM CLINTON

Socks came to the White House with the Clintons and reigned supreme until the chocolate lab, Buddy, broke on the scene. There was dislike between them, and at the end of his administration, Socks went off to live with President Clinton's secretary, Betty Currie, and Buddy enjoyed his life at Chappaqua, New York, until he was struck and killed by a car. Bill Clinton is quoted as having said his only friends at the time of his impeachment ordeal were his cat and his dog. Socks was so popular with the public she had her own fan club for eight years, and children all over the country wrote to her.

GEORGE W. BUSH

Here comes Barney Bush! He is making history by being the third White House pet in history to have a bronze sculpture made of him. He has been sculpted by famous dog artist, American Kennel Club judge, and professional handler Richard Chashoudian of Baton Rouge, Louisiana. The first is a likeness of Laddie, the Airedale terrier of Warren Harding, made from melted-down copper pennies donated by newsboys around the country to honor his beloved dog, and the second is the great, most famous White House dog of all time, Fala, whose bigger-than-life statue is with his master at the FDR memorial in D.C. While not a "show specimen," Barney is the president's buddy, and though he is a fairly obstinate and tails-down, bad-mannered terrier, he does give the president a softer image. Barney even snapped at the president's mother, and for most photo ops, he would rather be off doing his thing than showing off for the camera. Miss Beazley, on the other hand, is Miss Personality and a happy-go-lucky girl who helps bring a bag of sunshine and good cheer to an administration badly in need of brighter days.

Credit: The White House

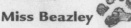

22

PRESIDENTIAL PASTIMES

O kay, you are the most powerful man in the nation, or later, the world. But what can you do for fun? A lot it seems.

PHILATELIST

Because of his crippled legs, Franklin Delano Roosevelt could only indulge in less active hobbies. (No, we are not referring to his wife's assistant, who was his regular mistress.) But FDR took to his hobbies with the same enthusiasm he had for other things. The hobby he enjoyed the most was stamp collecting. He had a massive collection and was often given stamps by other world leaders. It was estimated that he had over twenty thousand stamps in his collection.

FRANKLIN D. ROOSEVELT
1933-1945

SEEDING THE ELECTORATE

For a period early in U.S. history, it was not uncommon for congressmen to give out seeds. This is because of the efforts of the second president, John Adams. Adams was a dedicated horticulturist and during his presidency the Horticultural Gardens in Washington were established. As commander in chief, Adams instructed the officers of the U.S. Navy to gather seeds from useful plants in every port they visited. These seeds were then turned over to the Gardens and often also later to members of Congress. The nation was still very agricultural in those days and every member's district contained many farms. The seeds were distributed to these farmers and many new cotton, rice, corn, and other crops were introduced due to Adam's program.

FORE

President Taft was a workaholic who rarely engaged in sports. That made it a surprise when he accepted a bet on a golf game. The bet was for one thousand dollars (worth $25,000 today), a considerable amount of money at the time. The wager was that he could shoot a score of under one hundred on the Myopia Golf Course near Boston. Myopia was considered one of the most difficult courses in the United States. In the days of all wooden clubs and relatively primitive golf balls, any score under one hundred was considered exceptional. William Howard Taft was not known as a golfer. He was also, to put it diplomatically, large. He knew how to golf, but spent most every day, all day, at his desk. This was one of the reasons his weight had hovered around three hundred pounds since he was governor of the Philippines. What those who bet against the president had forgotten was that he had been, at Yale, a wrestler and on the rowing team. He also enjoyed horseback riding.

When the round of golf ended and his score was tallied, President Taft showed he was not a duffer—he'd scored ninety-eight! The President was so happy with that score, and with winning the highly publicized bet, that this was one of the few time on which the normally retiring man actually kissed his wife in public.

POWER WALKERS

Three of the presidents were serious walkers who would today fall into the power walking category. Benjamin Harrison would often walk for ten or more miles in a night. He frequently started his walks as late as 10 p.m. and normally walked alone. Tell a Secret Service man about that today and watch him shudder. Harrison would return to the White House in the middle of the night, but that was no problem, as the gates were typically left open.

Chester A. Arthur also enjoyed hiking at night. Part of the motivation for the late hours for both men might have been the stifling heat of a D.C. summer. Unlike Harrison, Arthur preferred company and normally had a friend or two accompany him. They often walked late into the night and returned in the early hours of the next day.

The true power-walking president was (it figures) Teddy Roosevelt. He took to walking as he viewed everything: as a challenge and a conquest. Teddy not only walked long distances many days, but planned his walks to encounter a large number of obstacles. The twenty-sixth president often took his sons on the walk and liked to make sure each hike was a challenge for them. The ambassador to France once decided to accompany the president on one of these obstacle walks. It is likely he did not understand exactly what he was getting into or the nature of the course. He followed Theodore Roosevelt off at his normal rapid pace and when they came to a pond was informed of the rules of the march. You could go through or over something, but never around. Having said this, Teddy and the others promptly waded into and through the pond. Not to be outdone, the ambassador, who must have been stubborn or a very good sport, followed. All were wearing their shoes and pants, soaking them. The ambassador finished the "bully" hike a bit worse for wear and even wore his gloves to the end so that he would be properly attired should they meet a lady.

SOME HOBBY

James Buchanan followed the workaholic Franklin Pierce as president. Where Pierce worked killing hours constantly, this next president saw his office as a chance to party. If anything, Buchanan's hobby was having a good time and drinking. The lavish and regular White House parties he threw were notorious for being both ostentatious and alcoholic. This president also liked his liquor more than just about any other. He was known to imbibe all night and rarely even show the effects of the liquor. Larger bottles were his preference and he once chastised a caterer for using too-small bottles for the champagne at one of his many parties (magnums were more his style). To give you some idea of just how much drinking went on in the executive mansion during Buchanan's administration you need just look at how this president bought his whiskey supply. Many Sundays, on his way back from church, James Buchanan would make a short side trip to the distillery of Jacob Baer. There he would purchase a ten-gallon barrel of what he fondly referred to as "old JB."

TEE TIME

Some people think in the tub, others create during walks. Dwight D. Eisenhower appears to have run the United States from the golf course. An avid golfer, Ike spent up to one hundred days a year while president golfing. That is about three days a week. Being willing to accept only victory served Ike well as a general, but as a golfer it made him a sore loser whose temper appeared when he flubbed a shot.

IN DEFEAT

Supreme commander Dwight Eisenhower defeated the Nazis. But once president, he met a foe that he could never win a permanent victory against. This was not the Democrats or even the French. Ike so loved golf that he had a putting green installed on the White House lawn. But despite all efforts, the White House squirrels constantly dug or tore it up.

Ike took his golf seriously and hated interruptions, even when president. While playing a round in Denver in 1955, he was called off the course four separate times on government business. That would throw anyone's game off, and the president spent the rest of the day in a rage. That night he had a major heart attack. The nation worried, and when it got the news, the stock market lost fourteen billion dollars in value the next day.

All Ike's efforts paid off after the president had retired and could really concentrate on his game. On February 6, 1968, former President Dwight D. Eisenhower scored a hole-in-one while golfing in Palm Springs.

23

PRESIDENTIAL YACHTS

By Ginger Marshall Martus

O Captain! My Captain!" is more than a poem commemorating Lincoln. Many of our presidents were ardent sailors. Perhaps it is simply the appeal of the sea. Or maybe it is the fact that reporters can't tag along. Here, a noted yachting historian takes a quick look at the ships beyond the ship of state that past presidents have commanded.

Did you know there have been only seven "official" presidential yachts? Two were "unofficial": the *Lenore* and the *Margie*. The longest was 275 feet, the USS *Mayflower*; the shortest is the USS *Sequoia*, at 104 feet. In 1964, Elvis Presley purchased the USS *Potomac* for $55,000 and then gave it to Danny Thomas for a St. Jude Hospital auction.

USS Mayflower, 1898

There were no government-owned presidential yachts before President William McKinley, who served from 1897 to 1901, when he was assassinated. However, there were unofficial yachts that were almost always available for the president's use. McKinley referred to his as his "presidential ship." Theodore Roosevelt was next to assume office and preferred the term presidential yacht instead of presidential ship, and this term has prevailed.

One yacht was the USS *Mayflower*. This yacht was 275 feet long with a thirty-six-foot beam and was built in Scotland in 1896. She was purchased from the Ogden Goelet estate in 1898. In 1902, the USS *Mayflower* was used as the official presidential yacht. She became the flagship of Admiral Dewey from 1903–1904 and later served in the Caribbean until 1919. Afterward, she was used as a coastal patrol boat by the U.S. Coast Guard. In 1931, she was laid up after being partially destroyed in a fire while at the Philadelphia Navy Yard and was eventually sold to a private buyer. She then was decommissioned by the navy and served as a gunboat in World War II.

The smallest official presidential yacht was the USS *Sequoia*. At 104 feet in length with a nineteen-foot beam, she was built in 1925 at the Mathis Yacht and Shipbuilding Company in Camden, New Jersey. She is perhaps the best known of all presidential yachts and is still with us today. This vessel was originally built for a Philadelphia lawyer, Richard Calwalder, Jr., but was taken over by the Navy and placed in commission in 1933 at Annapolis, Maryland.

The USS *Despatch* was the first *official* official presidential yacht and was used by McKinley. This 174-foot yacht was the only presidential yacht ever wrecked. She sank off Chincoteague Island, which is off the coast of Virginia, and the hulk is still there. Later the USS *Dolphin*, with a length of 256 feet, was also used by McKinley for a cruise up the Atlantic coast to New York City in 1897 to dedicate Grant's Tomb.

USS *Sylph*, 1898

The next official yacht, the USS *Sylph*, was 123 feet long with a twenty-foot beam. She had a long bowsprit, two masts, and a smokestack. The USS *Sylph* was purchased by the government for $50,000 and commissioned in 1898. President Theodore Roosevelt made frequent cruises on her to his home at Oyster Bay, Long Island, New York. Later his distant cousin, Franklin Roosevelt, used USS *Sylph* as well. FDR was an avid sailor in his youth and a former assistant secretary of the navy. He had a great love for the sea and a keen knowledge of ships.

USS *Potomac*, 1936

USS *Potomac*, originally built for the U.S. Coast Guard in Wisconsin in 1934, was 165 feet long with a twenty-three-foot nine-inch beam and formerly was named *Electra*. In 1936 she was renamed USS *Potomac* and was transferred to the navy. For the next nine years, she served as the official presidential yacht. FDR used the yacht frequently, but Eleanor, his wife, rarely came aboard as she did not like the nautical life. However, she did celebrate her fifty-seventh birthday onboard in 1941. Another time she sailed on the *Potomac* was in June 1939. This was a rather special occasion since King George VI and the future Queen Elizabeth II were on board as guests. Franklin Roosevelt, who had lost the ability to walk, had an elevator installed on board so he could be hoisted between decks.

Eleanor does not appear to have boarded when President Franklin Roosevelt entertained Winston Churchill. The prime minister complained that the deck chairs were uncomfortable, even after imbibing his favorite triple scotch and soda. Roosevelt entertained foreign dignitaries and also planned D-Day with General Eisenhower aboard his yacht. FDR did not like to fly and so preferred to travel by train or ship using a government yacht for official travel when possible. He also liked to fish from the stern of the yacht. FDR turned the USS *Potomac* into a "floating White House." He even had a sleeping basket for his beloved dog, Fala. He also had another elevator installed in a false smokestack, which was later removed and today can be seen at the waterfront park in Cambridge, Maryland. The yacht carried two officers and a crew of 54 men. In 1941, she was condemned as unseaworthy but after restoration and conversion was used as a fisheries research vessel from 1946 to 1960; she later was a ferry in the Caribbean. Later in his career FDR also sailed on the USS *Sequoia*, which was also adapted to his disabilities.

After Truman succeeded upon FDR's death, he also used the *Sequoia*, but often in a less formal manner. There was a long scratch on the *Sequoia*'s dining table, which is attributed to

President Harry Truman, the result of a rowdy poker game, one of his favorite onboard pastimes.

The USS *Williamsburg* was built for Hugh J. Chrishold in Maine in 1930 and named *Aras*. She was 243 feet long with a thirty-six-foot beam, and was acquired by the U.S. government in 1941. President Harry Truman used her frequently for long and short cruises, plus entertaining foreign leaders. She carried eight officers and a crew of one hundred thirty.

In 1953, President Eisenhower announced he no longer needed the yacht and had her decommissioned. She was inactive for about ten years until the National Science Foundation acquired her. Then, in 1968, she was damaged in a dry-dock accident, repaired, and later assigned to take rehabilitating wounded Korean veterans on afternoon cruises on the Potomac River.

In 1963, she was sent to Genoa, Italy, for conversion to a cruise ship, which never materialized. Today she is abandoned and listing in Genoa's harbor.

While Nixon was president, he used the *Sequoia* frequently. He stated that being at sea helped while he searched his soul and came to the conclusion he had no option but to resign the presidency after the Watergate scandal. President Gerald Ford also entertained foreign visitors and held cabinet meetings onboard.

President John F. Kennedy loved the nautical life and used the *Sequoia* frequently with family and friends. Together with Jacqueline and the two children, they cruised the Chesapeake Bay and had a surprise forty-sixth birthday party for John onboard.

Perhaps he preferred a simpler life or had enough of the water when he served on a nuclear sub, but it appears that President Jimmy Carter never set foot on the presidential yacht. The ship was put up for auction in 1976 and a private buyer bought the *Sequoia* for $270,000. The yacht changed ownership several times and ended up being mothballed for many years. In 1985, Congress declared the USS *Sequoia* a National Historic Landmark.

In 2000, Washington, D.C., lawyer Gary Silversmith, a presidential memorabilia collector, bought the USS *Sequoia* for $1.9 million and had her completely restored. She is now on the Potomac River and available for charter. There is currently a Presidential Yacht Foundation that is trying to raise funds to buy the yacht from Silversmith and return it to the public as well as make it available to members of the Congress, Supreme Court, and cabinet.

In 1981, the USS *Potomac* was again put up for auction and was bought by the Port of Oakland for $15,000. Fully restored, today she is open to the public and can be seen at the FDR Pier in Oakland, California. In 1990, she was designated a National Historic Landmark.

The next two yachts were "unofficial" but well known. These boats served as "escort" boats.

Perhaps the best known is the *Lenore* (also known as the *Honey Fitz*). This yacht was originally built for Sewell Avery, the chairman of the board of Montgomery Ward, in 1931. She is 92 feet long with a sixteen-foot six-inch beam. In 1935, Avery began serious clashes with the government over President Roosevelt's wage and price provisions, and in 1944, at the age of seventy, he was physically carried out of one of the Montgomery Ward buildings by two soldiers and the government seized his yacht. The yacht was later used as a training ship for submarine crews and also carried Secret Service agents while accompanying the president.

In 1953, President Eisenhower retired the yacht from active service but she was still available for use. When President John F. Kennedy was in office, he used her extensively, and renamed her the *Honey Fitz* after his grandfather. It is said that some of his happiest moments were spent onboard this yacht. The yacht was kept mostly at Hyannisport, near the family summer home.

When President Lyndon Johnson used the USS *Sequoia*, almost twenty years after Truman, he had FDR's elevator converted into a wet bar for cocktail service. Johnson, being one of the tallest presidents, had the yacht's ceilings raised three inches while the floor of the shower room was lowered three inches. Johnson found one excellent use for the yacht: it could leave port and, once on board, he could avoid reporters. The president also retreated to the yacht to assess the impact the assassination of Martin Luther King, Jr., had on the nation. He also sailed on the unofficial presidential yacht the *Lenore/Honey Fitz* on occasion.

By the time Nixon came to office, the *Honey Fitz* was a well-known entity. He renamed the yacht *Patricia*, after his wife, but most people still thought of her as the *Honey Fitz*. In 1970, Nixon put the yacht up for sale. She was eventually sold to Joe Keating, an avid lover of the sea and a great fan of the Kennedys. The boat was restored exactly to the way it had been during the Kennedy administration and Keating placed her in the charter trade in New York City. Keating renamed the yacht *Presidents*, and she was used by private groups as well as for chartering. She was later sold to unknown buyers at the Kennedy Memorabilia Auction for $5,942,000. In 1988, William Kallop, a New York businessman, took sole possession. She then remained "on the hard" in Louisiana and began a slow decline—paint peeling, planks rotting, the staterooms in shambles, the interior stripped bare, and all the once-fine furniture gone. In April 2002, she was moved to a construction yard in Alabama where a complete restoration took place. She is, once again, being used and is in Mobile Bay, Alabama.

The *Margie* was built in 1940 for L. P. Fisher, vice president of Fisher Body Works in Michigan. The War Shipping Administration acquired her in 1942 for Coast Guard use, but she was transferred to the Navy in 1945. She is sixty-four feet long with a fourteen-foot six-inch beam. She was used by the Trumans for trips on the Potomac River and the Chesapeake Bay and renamed *Margie* after their daughter. She was later sold at auction to an unknown buyer. She was never an official presidential yacht, though she was owned by the government. In 1953, Ike renamed the vessel the *Susie E* and used it to entertain dignitaries.

Just in case you wanted to know who sailed on what and when, here is where your tax dollars went to sea:

PRESIDENTIAL YACHTS

USS *Sequoia*, 1931

NAME	LENGTH	YEAR BUILT	PRESIDENT	DATES IN OFFICE
USS *Despatch*	174 feet		W. McKinley	1897–1901
USS *Dolphin*	256 feet		W. McKinley	1897–1901
USS *Sylph*	123 feet		W. McKinley	1897–1901
			T. Roosevelt	1901–1909
USS *Mayflower*	275 feet		T. Roosevelt	1901–1909
			W. H. Taft	1909–1913
			W. Wilson	1913–1921
			W. Harding	1921–1923
			C. Coolidge	1923–1929
			H. Hoover	1929–1933

NAME	LENGTH	YEAR BUILT	PRESIDENT	DATES IN OFFICE
USS *Sequoia*	104 feet	1925	H. Hoover	1929–1933
			F. D. Roosevelt	1933–1945
			H. Truman	1945–1953
			D. Eisenhower	1953–1961
			J. Kennedy	1961–1963
			L. B. Johnson	1963–1969
			R. M. Nixon	1969–1974
			G. Ford	1974–1977
Carter put *Sequoia* up for auction			J. Carter	1977-1981
Potomac	165 feet	1934	F. D. Roosevelt	1933–1945
Condemned and decommissioned in 1941 but restored today				
USS *Williamsburg*	243 feet	1930	H. Truman	1945–1953
			D. Eisenhower	1953–1961

USS *Honey Fitz*, 1961

Unofficial				
Lenore (Better known as ***Honey Fitz***)	92 feet	1931	D. Eisenhower	1953–1961
			J. Kennedy	1961–1963

NAME	LENGTH	YEAR BUILT	PRESIDENT	DATES IN OFFICE
			L. B. Johnson	1963–1969
			R. M. Nixon	1969–1974
Restored in 2002				
Margie	64 feet	1940 (L. P. Fisher)	H. Truman	1945–1953
Renamed **Susie E**			D. Eisenhower	1953–1961
Renamed **Patrick J**			J. Kennedy	1961–1963
			L. B. Johnson	1963–1969
Renamed **Julie**			R. M. Nixon	1969–1974

Ginger Marshall Martus grew up in the family business known as A&R Marshall, Inc., on Manhasset Bay, Long Island, New York. She became a nautical historian and writer. In 1996, she founded the national newsletter Bone Yard Boats, *about saving worthy old boats. She also founded the Nautical Center of the Port Washington Public Library. She is a member of numerous nautical organizations, has presented programs, gives annual awards at four classic boat shows, and writes for* Nor'easter *magazine.*

24

ASSASSINATIONS AND ATTEMPTED ASSASSINATIONS

"Sorry, dear, I forgot to duck."
Ronald Reagan

*T*he first attempt to assassinate a president failed. In 1835, a man who was firmly convinced that the only reason he was not King of America was because of Andrew Jackson, tried to shoot him on the steps of the Capitol. Andrew Lawrence fired a pistol at close range, but it misfired. He fired a second pistol and it misfired as well. He was quickly grabbed, disarmed, and placed in an asylum.

ASSASSINATION ATTEMPTS SINCE 1865

Abraham Lincoln was shot April 14, 1865 at a Washington, D.C., theater by actor John Wilkes Booth, who was bitter over the defeat of the Confederacy. Lincoln died the next day.

James Garfield was shot July 2, 1881, in Baltimore by Charles J. Guiteau, who was a frustrated and likely deranged office seeker, and died September 19. The assassination led to a change in how federal employees were hired.

William McKinley was shot September 6, 1901, in Buffalo by the anarchist Leon Czolgosz; died September 14.

Teddy Roosevelt escaped assassination (though he was shot) October 14, 1912, in Milwaukee by John Schrank, who was found insane.

Franklin Delano Roosevelt, then merely president-elect, escaped assassination unhurt February 15, 1933, in Miami, when Giuseppe Zangara, later found insane, fired five shots at Roosevelt's motorcade. Killed in the attempt was Mayor Anton Cermack of Chicago. It is possible Cermak was the actual target.

Harry S. Truman escaped unhurt from an assassination attempt by two Puerto Rican nationalists, Oscar Collazo and Griselio Torresola, November 1, 1950, in Washington, D.C.

John F. Kennedy was shot November 22, 1963, in Dallas, Texas, by at least Lee Harvey Oswald in what may be the most discussed and dissected assassination in history.

Robert F. Kennedy, candidate for presidential nomination, was shot June 5, 1968, in Los Angeles by Sirhan Sirhan, who felt betrayed by RFK's support for Israel, and died the next day.

Richard Nixon was targeted by Samuel Byck in 1974. Byck planned to crash a commercial airplane into the White House, but was thwarted before it took off. He did shoot both the pilot and copilot before turning the gun on himself. The airspace over the White House is now a restricted zone.

George Wallace was critically wounded in an assassination attempt May 15, 1972, at Laurel, Maryland. The shot left the governor and presidential candidate paralyzed from the waist down.

Gerald R. Ford escaped an assassination attempt September 5, 1975, in Sacramento, California, by Lynette Alice (Squeaky) Fromme, who was a follower of Charles Manson, and later in San Francisco, California, on September 22, 1975, by Sarah Jane Moore.

Jimmy Carter may have been targeted when speaking in 1979 in Los Angeles. Raymond Harvey was arrested carrying a gun just before the president spoke. He later claimed to be part of a larger conspiracy involving Mexican snipers.

Ronald Reagan was shot in the left lung in Washington by John W. Hinckley, Jr., on March 30, 1981; three others were also wounded. Hinckley was said to have been inspired by the movie *Taxi Driver* and had stalked President Carter before Reagan took office. The assassin was fixated on the actress Jodie Foster and actually sent her a letter outlining in advance how he would assassinate the president.

George H. W. Bush was the target of sixteen terrorists working for Saddam Hussein. Their plan was to use a car bomb to kill the senior Bush while he spoke in 1993 at Kuwait University. The assassins were captured by the Kuwaitis before the plot could be attempted.

William Clinton was watching a football game in his executive residence when Francisco Duran fired nearly thirty shots into the White House from the South Lawn. He was firing at a group of staffers he had spotted, under the assumption they were the president and his Secret Service detail. No one was hurt.

George W. Bush was speaking in Tbilisi in the nation of Georgia in 2005 when Vladimir Arutinian threw a hand grenade at him and the Georgian president. The grenade had been wrapped in a plaid handkerchief, which prevented it from exploding.

OTHER THAN THAT, HOW WAS THE PLAY?

The title of this little section is the punch line of a very sick joke. But in reality, it was an appropriate comment for one person involved in Lincoln's assassination. John Parker was assigned to guard President Lincoln the night he was shot. At this time, only one personal guard was on duty at a time. It was the custom of the guard to sit on a chair just outside the door to the president's box. That night, at Ford's Theater, Parker was anxious to see the play, and instead of taking his usual place, he went and sat in the front of the balcony. Since the door to the box was closed, President Lincoln never new he was unguarded.

On that night, the doorkeeper of the theater watched as John Wilkes Booth went in and out of the theater about five times, each time taking another drink to get his courage up. Each time the actor would survey the door and empty chair to see if the guard was at his post. The final time, Booth got up his nerve, rushed into the unprotected box, and shot Abraham Lincoln. Parker later confessed his dereliction of duty to his superior, Colonel Crook, who had guarded the president himself earlier that day. Strangely, with all the blame and conspiracy theories that abounded after the assassination, nothing was said about Parker's failure and no one asked how Booth could have gotten into the box itself. Colonel Crook did not speak to anyone of Parker's failure until after the negligent guard died some years later.

MISSED

The feeling that later led to the American Civil War grew to fever levels during the administration of Franklin Pierce. Trying for compromise, and being basically ineffective, soon led to a situation where just about everyone was angry with the fourteenth president. The crowds that daily grew in front of the White House were a cause for concern that Pierce's life was in danger. For the first time, a personal bodyguard was hired. This bodyguard, one Thomas O'Neil, was supposed to accompany Franklin Pierce at all times. But he was absent when someone finally took a shot at the president. Fortunately, all the attacker used was a hard-boiled egg. Quickly taken into custody, the presidential egger then attempted suicide using a pocket knife he carried. Being a good egg himself, Franklin Pierce eventually dropped the charges against the egg thrower.

GOVERNMENT HEALTH CARE

A frustrated and eventually insane office seeker, Charles Guiteau shot President James Garfield twice outside the Baltimore

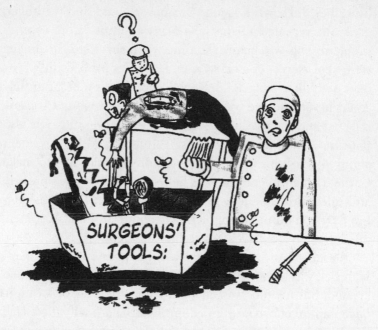

and Potomac Railroad Station in Baltimore. The first shot he fired only grazed the president's arm. But when Guiteau fired again he managed to hit the president in the back, causing a serious but not immediately life-threatening wound. What did kill the twentieth president was a combination of where the bullet lodged and how the doctors reacted.

This was in the days before X-ray machines, long before, as William Roentgen would not discover X-rays until 1895. If they had existed, James Garfield would have recovered easily. The problem was that the bullet was hard to find. And since bullets tended to cause a wound to become septic, that is infected, it had to come out. But in those days, probing for the bullet was a literal statement. Doctors poked around in the wound, tearing up the body even further until they encountered the metal bullet and could pull it out. That is what the president's doctors did. Since they were working on the most public case in their lives, they did so with vigor. But no one could find the bullet, even after repeated attempts. So many attempts led to another problem. This was before the time when surgical instruments were kept sterile. For days on end doctors probed the president with dirty scalpels and blood-encrusted probes. But they could never find the bullet and, surprise, the wound became infected and the president got worse. Worse yet, this was also the time before anesthetics were common and the president endured all of this while fully conscious. Finally, just to make Garfield totally uncomfortable, he was lying there shot, probed, and infected during a summer in Washington. The Washington heat and humidity sapped the strength from healthy men, much less a wounded and suffering president.

Desperate measures were tried. Inventor Alexander Graham Bell was brought in with a metal detecting device he had created, but he, too, was unable to find the bullet's location. Such painful efforts continued until Garfield finally died. Had he simply crawled into a corner or been someone with a lower profile, the doctors might have given up looking for the bullet and he might have lived. But James Garfield got the best care the government could provide—and it killed him.

SELF-DEFENSE

Always a man to do for himself, Theodore Roosevelt, who became president when William McKinley was assassinated, immediately began carrying a handgun somewhere on his person at all times. When asked about it, he replied that he wanted to "have some chance of shooting the assassin before he could shoot me."

25

AND THE OTHER WAS ELECTED VICE PRESIDENT . . .

> "Once there were two brothers. One ran away to sea and
> the other was elected vice president of the United States.
> And nothing was heard of either of them again."
> Thomas Marshall, vice president to Woodrow Wilson

A HEARTBEAT AWAY CAN BE VERY FAR

Until very recently vice presidents of the United States didn't get much respect—and with reason. The position has spent two centuries searching for an identity and meaning. From the first, the vice president has had only three responsibilities: one was to break ties in the Senate, the second to supervise and report the vote of the Electoral College, and the third to succeed to the presidency in the case of the president's death. Until the Twenty-fifth Amendment was passed in 1967, the process of succession was itself mostly undefined and was based on tradition and not law.

The Founding Fathers weren't exactly excited about there even being a vice president. Some of those who helped to write the Constitution were fairly sure the position simply was not needed. One of the representatives, George Clinton, called the vice presidency "an unnecessary position," which makes it mildly ironic that he later became vice president under James Madison. Among the extended and contentious debates that characterized the creation of the Constitution, less than a day was spent on the vice presidency. From this inauspicious start, things went downhill. There was no budget for the vice president other than salary, no staff, and not even an office. The sloppy way the office was created has left doubt to this day as to where, officially, the vice president stands in the government. Is he part of the legislature, since his duties include the Senate, or part of the executive branch, which there is always a chance he might have to head?

FIRST DIBS

John Adams was sworn in and began to serve as the first vice president eight days before George Washington was sworn in as the first president.

At first, the vice president was the man who got the second most votes in the Electoral College. The idea was that he was the next most qualified to take over the presidency. This concept was shown to be a dismal failure fairly quickly. Only once has the vice president chosen to run in the next election against the man he served with. This was in 1800, when Thomas Jefferson, who had been vice president under John Adams, ran against Adams and defeated him. The law was quickly changed to the more familiar election of the president and vice president as a "ticket." It took years for Adams to even slightly forget Jefferson's victory and his defeat and he never forgave him.

Because some presidents have run for a second term with a different vice president, there have actually been four more vice presidents than there have been presidents. Jefferson, Madison, Jackson, Lincoln, Grant, Cleveland, and McKinley all had two different vice presidents. Franklin D. Roosevelt holds the record with three. The difference in the number would have been greater, but there used to be no provision, or even requirement, for replacing the vice president if he became president. There have been several years in the more than two centuries since John Adams took his oath when, for various reasons, there was no vice president.

WHO CARES?

The presidential debates have almost always stirred interest. It wasn't until 1976 that the vice presidential candidates ever met to debate. It was a TV debate between Walter Mondale and Bob Dole. The ratings came in significantly below those of that election's presidential debate.

PAY'S GOOD

If the honor was dubious, it is certain the vice presidents have never been after the job for the money. The pay is okay, though in real dollars it actually used to pay better than it does today. There is also a small expense allowance, which is taxable too.

Here is a quick look at what we paid our backup leaders:

1789	$5,000	($75,800 in today's dollars)
1907	$10,000	($247,600 in today's dollars)
1949	$30,000	(about $300,000 in today's dollars)
1964	$43,000	(about $250,000 in today's dollars)
1969	$62,500	(about $300,000 in today's dollars)
2001	$171,500	
2004	$192,600	

The pay was actually pretty good, since so little was expected of the vice president until recently. Until Walter Mondale was elected, the vice president lived at his own home, some not even living in Washington, D.C. Mondale began the tradition of the vice president having use of the Naval Observatory building (long since converted into a home) as the vice president's official residence. The question is, what changed to make the vice president worth three times as much today as in 1969?

SILENCE IS GOLDEN

Throughout most of U.S. history, the vice president was not encouraged to make policy statements. Perhaps the most memorable non-statement by a vice president came when Wood-row Wilson's vice president was asked what he felt the nation needed. Thomas Marshall's non-political and safe answer: "What this nation needs is a good five-cent cigar."

ODD MEN OUT

Of the forty-six vice presidents, all but two were elected. Only in modern times did anyone hold the office after being appointed by the president and approved by the Congress. These were both the result of the scandals surrounding Richard Nixon. When Spiro Agnew resigned under the cloud caused by his ear-lier corruption, Gerald Ford was appointed to take his place in 1973. Then in 1974, Nixon resigned and Gerald Ford was president, and Ford appointed Nelson Rockefeller to be his vice president. So it took three different vice presidents to fill the job over just a few years in the mid-seventies.

Because he was appointed and not elected to the office of vice president, Gerald Ford was the first and only president to date who was not voted upon by either the people or the Elec-toral College.

TERM LIMITS

Determining how long a vice president can be president is based on the old rule you learned along with fractions: "round-ing up." Anything over half is rounded up and below half a term is rounded down. This means that if a vice president becomes president one day more than two years before the term ends, then he rounds up and he is eligible to run only once more, due to the two-term limit. But if he succeeded to the office with one day less than two years remaining, then the vice president's first term is rounded down and not counted, so he could run twice more. This means that a vice president could, by law, serve for a period of up to one day less than ten years total. (The two years minus a day rounded down to zero and not counting, and then two four-year normal terms.)

SPREADING THE WEALTH

When the Founding Fathers wrote the Constitution, the states were much more independent and jealous of each other. This meant that when they designed the office of vice president it was decided that the president and vice president may never be from the same state.

WINGMAN

Yes, just as any winged aircraft the president flies in is always identified as Air Force One, any aircraft carrying the VP is designated Air Force Two.

THEME SONG

The president is always greeted with the song "Hail to the Chief." He is the only man in the nation for whom this is played. When the vice president appears, "Hail Columbia" is always played.

IRA IRE

Where a former president receives a very generous pension and a substantial budget for staff after leaving office, a former vice president receives only the benefits of his standard government pension plan, no different from that of any federal employee, and not a penny more for anything.

COWBOY HEAVEN

There is nothing more Texan than the Dallas Cowboys, except their name. The city of Dallas was named after James K. Polk's vice president, George Mifflin Dallas, who had been a strong supporter of Texas statehood. Dallas was not even from Texas, but was from Pennsylvania.

HAPPY TALK

Since the vice president oversees and reports to the U.S. Senate the vote of the Electoral College, on four occasions vice presidents in this role have been able to announce to the Senate that the man elected President was *them*. These four are Adams, Jefferson, Van Buren, and George H. W. Bush.

BUMMER

On the same note, there have been times when the vice president had to oversee and report to the Senate a vote by the Electoral College that meant they had been defeated and someone else would be the next president. This has happened only three times so far. The three unlucky VPs were John Breckenridge (Lincoln won), Richard Nixon (when JFK beat him), and recently Al Gore (that he had been defeated by George W. Bush) in 2000.

TIE BREAKER

One of the duties of the vice president is to vote whenever there is a tie vote in the U.S. Senate. This is not a common occurrence. The most times this has happened is twenty-nine, way back when John Adams was VP. (But there were a lot fewer Senators then so ties were more common.) Recently Lyndon Johnson, Gerald Ford, Nelson Rockefeller, and Dan Quayle did not cast a single tie-breaking vote. The most in the last fifty years were eight cast by Richard Nixon in eight years and by George H. W. Bush only seven in eight years, or less than one a year.

SHORTEST TERM OF OFFICE

Since 1967, the Twenty-fifth Amendment makes the provision for the vice president to stand in for the president when he is temporarily unable to serve. Because of the Amendment, Vice President

George H. W. Bush served as president for a total of eight hours in 1985 while President Ronald Reagan was undergoing surgery. This became the record for the shortest period a vice president has served as president. Then in 1988, George H. W. Bush became the first vice president in the twentieth century to be elected president next, and the shortest time record was lost.

LOYALTY

Vice President Aaron Burr fell into disgrace not for shooting and killing Alexander Hamilton in a duel but for plotting to split off a large portion of the Western Territories and create a new nation from them. He hoped to organize the disgruntled frontiersmen and Indians into an independent nation with himself in control and strong European support. The Western Territories were what is known today as the Midwest.

THE DISLOYAL OPPOSITION

After serving as vice president to Buchanan, John Breckenridge left Washington to become first a Confederate senator and then a Confederate general. He has the distinction of being the only former vice president to ever command troops in combat against the U.S. Army.

CHANGING ATTITUDES

The American democracy of today was not a sure thing. As vice president, John Adams was known to be an elitist who distrusted the popular vote as a way to elect leaders. He was of the opinion that the presidency should be a lifetime position and that the seats of the senators should be hereditary, being inherited by the children of the senators and their children.

SO SORRY

When Calvin Coolidge was elected vice president in 1920, he received a telegram from Thomas Marshall, his predecessor. The telegram read simply: "Please accept my sincere sympathies."

NAP TIME

Calvin Coolidge tended to enjoy his rest. He once expressed the thought that he preferred how things had been when he had been the vice president of the United States. Because there were few duties, nothing prevented him from getting his preferred eleven or more hours of sleep per day.

BRIEFLY NOT BRIEFED

In the few months he served as vice president for FDR, Harry Truman received not a single briefing on the war, the Soviet Union and Stalin, or anything significant—this despite the fact that Franklin Roosevelt was known to be in poor health and at risk. Truman was not even aware of the existence of the atomic bomb until he took office and had almost immediately to decide whether to use it. When asked about how he felt about becoming president, Truman replied, "I felt like the moon, the stars, and all the planets had fallen on me."

NOT CLOSE

Dwight Eisenhower was never comfortable with Richard Nixon as his vice president and involved him little in running the government. When once asked if he could identify for a reporter any national policies to which Vice President Nixon had contributed, Ike's answer was, "If you give me a week, I might think of one."

ZOMBIE

When asked to become a candidate for and likely become the next vice president, the famous speaker and political leader Daniel Webster turned it down with the reply, "I do not intend to be buried until I am really dead." Pretty well says it all.

26

THEY SAID THAT?

Presidents can say the darnedest things. . . .

FORWARD MARCH?

Lincoln once commanded a number of Illinois militia as captain in the Black Hawk Indian War of 1832. As a young man, Abe Lincoln was, as he often observed later, notoriously ignorant of even the basic commands. He often recalled how, at one point, he had ordered his men into a line while they crossed a field. The field was surrounded by a stone fence and when they reached the gate, he could not remember the command to form them up to cross through it (form column of two). But he was a quick thinker and, rather than embarrass himself, Lincoln recounts that he simply dismissed the men on one side for a two-minute break, with orders to reform on the other side of the gate when it was over.

LOST LOVE

James Buchanan was a man of strong emotions. Having lost his first love, he never married. He strove for many years to be nominated and elected president. When he finally was elected, he was heard to ruefully remark, "Years ago, I wanted to reward my friends and punish my enemies. But now, after all these years, the friends I hoped to reward have passed away, and the enemies I intended to punish have long since become my friends."

TOOK GOOD CARE?

Shades of Woody Allen. Our twenty-second president, Grover Cleveland, was single when he was elected president. At forty-nine, he married his former partner's daughter, for whom he had been guardian. She was just twenty-one. When asked why he had not married before, Cleveland replied, "I was waiting for my wife to grow up."

OH ME?

Following the footsteps as president after the charismatic Teddy Roosevelt was hard. William Howard Taft once commented, "When they say Mr. President, I always look around and expect to see Roosevelt."

DEFINED

"Conservatism is the policy of make no change and consult your grandmother when in doubt." —Woodrow Wilson

AT SEA

Upon being sworn in as assistant secretary of the navy, a job his cousin Teddy also held, Franklin Roosevelt wrote to his mother, "I am baptized, confirmed, sworn in, vaccinated, and somewhat at sea."

JUST THE TRUTH

It came as a voice in the crowd and became a famous cry. "Give 'em hell, Harry." To which Harry Truman replied much later, "I never gave them hell. I just told the truth and they thought it was hell."

LATINIZED

While Truman got an honorary degree from Oxford in 1956, the citation on it was in Latin and referred to the former president as "Harricum" Truman. When the citation was read out, one Oxford wit promptly cheered back, "Give 'em hell, Harricum."

NOT ALL ADVICE IS GOOD

As a young member of one of New York's most prestigious families, young Franklin Delano Roosevelt was given the treat of meeting then President Grover Cleveland while touring the White House. President Cleveland may have been having a bad day, as he was recorded as saying he had a strange wish for the young man: "It is that you may never be president of the United States."

The advice was not taken since Franklin D. Roosevelt became the longest-serving president in U.S. history.

GOOD ADVICE

The Truman Doctrine began the modern era of American involvement around the world. But somewhere we may have missed the whole intent. In Harry Truman's own words, the idea was that "it must be the policy of the United States to support free people who are resisting attempted subjugation by armed minorities or by outside pressure." Maybe we need to remember what we are supposed to be doing sometime. Good idea?

IT LOOKED GOOD ON PAPER

President Richard Nixon, speaking to Joe Haldeman in happier times before Watergate, was recorded as commenting, "You know, I always wondered about that taping equipment, but I'm damn glad we have it, aren't you?" Haldeman's answer would likely have been different if he had been asked the same question a few years later, after he was freed from federal prison having been convicted in large part from the evidence on the White House tapes.

PAIN AND POLITICS

Lyndon Johnson, when majority leader, could be quite forceful in persuading his colleagues. He was known for poking his fellow senators in the chest, for putting his arm around them and squeezing their shoulders, speaking inches away from their faces, and occasionally kicking their shins to make his point. Hubert Humphrey, after getting just such a pep talk on rallying the vote for a bill, returned to his colleagues and raised his pants to show his scraped and bruised leg to demonstrate just how adamant Johnson was about winning the vote. Everyone got the message and they passed the bill.

TRUE MAN

You get a degree of latitude in what you can get away with saying when you are the *former* president. Sometimes you can just come out and say what others are thinking. Truman showed his dislike for the former California congressmen and later president when, rather unsubtly, not long after leaving office he described Richard Nixon as "a no-good lying bastard."

ON NOTICE

Richard Nixon notified his vice president, Gerald Ford, that he was resigning when the vice president walked into the oval office and the president commented, "You will do a good job, Jerry"—August 9, 1974.

HE DID SAY IT

Lyndon Johnson really did once say about future President Jerry Ford that "Jerry is a nice guy, but he played too much football with his helmet off."

27

WHITE HOUSE WONDERS

The White House is the only private residence of a head of state that is open to the public, free of charge. If you have not yet taken the tour, it is something not to miss.

A ROSE BY ANY OTHER NAME . . . ER, WOULD BE IN THE ROSE GARDEN

At various times in history, the White House has been known as the "President's Palace," the "President's House," and the "Executive Mansion." President Theodore Roosevelt made the White House name official after using it on his stationery.

FIRST IN

The first president to live in the Executive Mansion, the White House, was John Adams. He lived there from November 1, 1800, through the last four months of his presidency. Before that, he had lived most of the time in Philadelphia, where his wife remained.

FOREMAN

Construction began when the cornerstone was laid in October 1792. Although President Washington oversaw the construction of the house, he never lived in it.

COMPETITION

The actual architectural design for the White House was the subject of an open competition in 1790. The winner, James Hoban, had immigrated from Ireland. He won $500 and a lot in the new city. Among the contestants was an anonymous designer listed as AZ. This was Thomas Jefferson who, because he was also the person who had announced the contest, felt he could not use his name on the plans.

SHORT-TERM TENANTS

James Madison and Dolley had only lived there a few years and were just getting the mansion into shape when the British showed up and burned the building. This was in retribution for American soldiers having burned government buildings while invading Canada at the start of the War of 1812.

NO RED PHONE

There is a certain irony in that the War of 1812 and the burning of the executive mansion were unnecessary. The main reason for the war was the impressment of American sailors into the Royal Navy. The British warships, always short personnel, would stop American merchant vessels and take off the sailors they needed, claiming they were runaway British sailors (which some were). The ironic part is that, two days before the United States declared war, the British Parliament suspended this policy. Had there been faster communications, it is highly likely no war would have occurred.

THE ROAD LESS TRAVELED

In 1800, Washington, D.C., was nicknamed rather derogatively "The City in the Wilderness." The U.S. capital had been located in Philadelphia, but in November 1800, the government moved to its new location. John Adams and his wife tried to take their buggy there, and for a while did fine on the well-marked roads.

But when they turned onto the paths that they thought led to the new city, they were soon lost. A friendly local finally guided the President and First Lady to their newly constructed home, today's White House, upon discovering they had already gone eight miles out of their way and had no idea how to find the new capital.

ROUGHING IT

Abigail Adams recorded in her diary just how hard life in the new capital of Washington, D.C., was during the city's first few years. The president's mansion had yet to be called the White House. To Abigail, the winter was cold. When it was warm, it was rainy, and the nearby swamps ensured that warm weather meant a constant threat of disease. In the winter, the new mansion was hard to heat. There were eleven fireplaces, so few that many rooms could not be warmed. Also, the city was new and not enough people lived in the area, so there was no one to chop wood or sell it to the First Family. Eventually, to save on heat, the presidential family closed off over half the building and lived in only six rooms. To keep it from freezing, the First Lady records that she hung their laundry in the East Room. Abigail also found life in the executive mansion solitary. The roads were bad and the nearest neighbor was almost half a mile away. This meant the president and First Lady actually looked forward to when the Capitol building would be finished and Congress would arrive. This is likely one of the last times this occurred.

WHAT COMES ROUND

The East Room of the White House has hosted laundry and many state events, but the best use we have seen for the large area occurred while Hayes was president. It was at about this time that bicycles were the high-tech and "in" new toy for young men. It is recorded that Webb Hayes, the president's twenty-year-old secretary, avoided the dangerous and muddy Washington streets by learning to ride his new bike in the East Room.

ON THE RUN

There was one time when the president of the United States actually had to flee the White House. This came in 1814, after the American militia had been soundly defeated by a British landing force in the Battle of Bladensburg, sometimes referred to derogatorily as the Bladensburg Race, since the poorly trained militia fled virtually without fighting. Having won at Bladensburg, the British marched on the new American capital on August 29, and President and Dolley Madison were forced to leave on very little notice. Their flight was so precipitous that a meal was left uneaten in the White House dining room. The British officers actually sat and enjoyed the presidential food before setting the building on fire. This was less an act of spite than one of revenge. Earlier in the war, American units in Canada had set fire to a number of government buildings and this fire being set by the highly disciplined British Army was considered a response to the American's earlier efforts. The British also burnt the Treasury, State, and Navy buildings for good measure. While all this was going on, President Madison was himself in a forest some seventeen miles away.

Three days after the British burned the presidential mansion, the Madisons returned and were determined to rebuild. A major storm had put out the fire, but the interior of the mansion was completely gutted. Only most of the Virginia sandstone walls still stood. But even those elegant stone walls were now deeply stained with black from the fire and smoke and no one could determine any way to return them to former stately colors. It was then decided to simply paint the walls white to cover the stains. It probably took a few coats, but the result was impressive. It was not long after this that the presidential or executive mansion began being referred to unofficially as the he

"White House," and so it has been called ever since. President Madison and Dolley never returned to live again in the executive mansion. One of the looted items, a walnut medicine chest, was taken by a Canadian soldier and returned to the White House by his descendants in 1939.

PLATED

Florence Harding wanted a higher-class presidency. This was tough to do when Warren preferred to go out tavern-hopping with his friends. Part of her effort to accomplish her goal was to have the White House silverware gold-plated—three times.

FIRE SALE

If the British burned the executive mansion again, repainting the White House would require an estimated 570 gallons of paint to cover its outside. This assumes two coats would be needed as charred rock is hard to hide.

HOUSE PARTY

In 1829, a mob of an estimated twenty thousand inaugural revelers partying inside the White House got violent and destructive. Many were hurt, and after being protected by several of his stout frontier friends, President Andrew Jackson had to flee to the safety of a hotel. Soon the staff set up on the lawn washtubs filled with orange juice and whiskey to lure the mob out.

MODERN APPLIANCE

Until 1850, all cooking for the White House was done over an open flame in a fireplace. Only that year did Millard Fillmore personally purchase and install a cast-iron stove. There were no instructions and the presidential cook had no idea how to use the newfangled thing. So Fillmore went to the patent office and was shown there how to use the stove so he could teach the cook.

BETTER THAN A STOVE

It was only after Abigail Fillmore in 1850 raised a bit of a ruckus and refused to even live in the White House that Congress broke down and paid for indoor plumbing to be installed. Before this, bathwater had been carried in buckets and heated over the fireplace.

TAKING THE HEAT

It wasn't until the administration of Franklin Pierce in 1853 that there was central heating in the White House. Before this time, all heat came from fireplaces spread all over the building.

ROYAL BEST

When James Buchanan was president, the Prince of Wales visited. In order to make sure that Bertie had a room worthy of his station, the president gave him his bedroom and he slept on the couch.

EGG ROLL

The first Easter egg hunt was held at the White House by Lucy Hayes in 1878. "Lemonade" Lucy was a great advocate of morally uplifting events and a great supporter of the Woman's Temperance Union.

COME ON OVER TO MY HOUSE

The White House has been traditionally open to visitors. It was never more so than when Lincoln was president. Or, more accurately, when Tad Lincoln was first son. The young boy would regularly be playing on the streets near the White House and when he got hungry would lead a small mob of his playmates, some street urchins, into the White House kitchen and demand the cook feed them all. This likely upset the kitchen staff's schedule regularly, but they always managed to prepare something for every child to eat.

PILLAGED

It was a mournful and chaotic time after the assassination of Abraham Lincoln. While most of the nation mourned, some saw this as an opportunity. The White House was not guarded at this time. With Mary Todd Lincoln virtually out of her mind with grief, the lower floors were sitting open and unwatched. Dozens of looters or souvenir seekers snuck, or boldly strode, into the executive mansion and helped themselves. Furniture, papers, pictures, and personal items disappeared. The value of the china taken alone would be over half a million of today's dollars.

NOT FIRST ADAPTERS

Even though telegraph communication was widespread and vital during the Civil War, no one got around to installing a telegraph office in the White House until Andrew Johnson took over as president.

LEMONADE LUCY

Rutherford and Lucy Hayes were teetotalers and forbade even wine being served in the White House. There was, at first, a good deal of consternation and concern that the lack would be taken as an insult by visiting dignitaries. The offer of a glass of wine was commonly used to show a person was welcome at an upper class home. But no one did take offense, though Lucy Hayes was nicknamed in the press "Lemonade Lucy," which seemed not to bother the cheerful and very popular First Lady at all.

ZAP

The White House was finally wired for electricity during the presidency of Benjamin Harrison. His wife, Caroline, distrusted the modern invention and refused to touch a light switch for fear of being electrocuted. Actually, the whole family was unsure about the newfangled light switches. They preferred to have the White House usher turn off the lights and often simply left them on all night if he failed to do so. The introduction of electric lights was just one of many improvements. The sorry fact was that by 1889, when Harrison took office, the executive mansion was in bad shape. There was even a discussion of moving the President's official residence to a newer building. Still, the Harrisons were not afraid of change, and added many modern amenities to the White House. Among these was the building's first switchboard, which meant that, for the first time, there was more than one phone line in the building.

PRESIDENTIAL UREIC POISONING

When Benjamin Harrison moved into the White House in 1889, moving in with the president was his wife, their son and his wife, their daughter and her husband, their childrens' three kids, Caroline Harrison's father, and her niece. This is a total of eleven First Family members. At this time, the White House was still just a residence and there was only *one* bathroom in the whole building.

NATIONAL NUPTIALS

Grover Cleveland was the only president to be actually married in the White House. It was an elegant ceremony. Two others, Tyler and Woodrow Wilson, did marry while serving as president, but not in the executive mansion.

ROSE GARDEN

In 1902, Edith Roosevelt, along with the official gardener, Henry Pfister, designed a colonial garden. However, in 1913, Ellen Wilson, the first wife of Woodrow Wilson, replaced the colonial garden with one featuring a variety of roses. The West Garden has been officially and generally known as the Rose Garden ever since. In the Rose Garden you can see not only a variety of roses but also blossoming magnolia trees and Katherine crab apple trees.

NO FUN

During his first term as president, Teddy Roosevelt was walking around the White House grounds and came upon his son Quentin on the latest fad toy, stilts, standing in one of the flower beds. He ordered, "Quentin get out of there." His son's annoyed reply was, "I don't see what good it does me for you to be president." He had a point—what use being a member of the First Family if you can't tear up the daisies occasionally?

HIDE!

Herbert Hoover seems to have been very uncomfortable with the large staff he found was needed to maintain the White House. Or maybe he just was not comfortable in the presence of domestic staff at all. All of the servants, maids, and gardeners working at the White House were under strict orders to get out of sight whenever President Hoover was around. Neither he nor his wife spoke to the White House staff. A series of hand signals was used by Lou Hoover to instruct the servants nearby as to her needs or what to do. Herbert himself preferred not to deal with them directly at all. So how did they keep out of the president's way? Each room or area had a bell system, and whenever anyone heard three bells ring, it meant that the president was coming into their area. Either the service personnel left the area or hid in the closets. Ground staff jumped behind bushes or hurried behind trees. Those who failed to make themselves scarce might be fired, a serious threat during the Great Depression.

CHINESE TO ME

Having spent some time early in their marriage in China, where they were real-life heroes, the Hoovers used Chinese as a secret language to speak privately with each other in front of White House guests.

MONEY PROBLEMS

When Harry Truman wanted to build a porch on the White House he ran into an unexpected expense. The back of the $20 bill featured, and still does, an image of the White House. The Treasury Department had to have a new set of plates engraved at what was likely a greater cost than that of the porch.

TOGETHERNESS

For many reasons, running from diverse schedules to even more diverse bedmates, most presidents and First Ladies have slept separately. The exceptions to this recently were both the Trumans and the Fords, who always shared a White House bedroom.

AT LEAST THE RENT IS LOW

Presidential daughter Margaret Truman call the White House the "Great White Jail," but made improvements on the building that extended its use. The two daughters of LBJ called the executive mansion a "Great White Mausoleum."

ALMOST CONDEMNED

By 1948, it was apparent that the weary White House was either going to have to be virtually rebuilt or demolished. President Truman authorized a $5.7 million project that was to prove both massive and all-inclusive. *Architectural Digest* wrote, "Today there is scarcely a beam in the entire building that has not been bored or cut through dozens of times to accommodate water and sewer pipes, gas pipes, heating pipes, electric and telephone wires, automatic fire alarm and guard signal systems, elevators, a fire extinguishing system and other mechanical innovations. In the very structure of the building itself, generations of architects and builders have concealed the completed mechanical equipment of a modem office building, none of which was provided or even contemplated by the original builders." Without these changes the White House would have had to be torn down and replaced.

PRESIDENTIAL THRONE

The following was in the May 1952 issue of the magazine *The Plumbing News*: "If they offered me any room in the house, I'd take Mr. Truman's bathroom. In the first place, it's big—a spacious grotto of cool, gleaming, green and white tile, where a guy could set up housekeeping if things get tough. Then there are the fixtures all white . . . and a tribute to twentieth century plumbing. Take the bathtub, for instance. None of those squat little bushel-basket-like jobs you see in some modem homes. Our President's tub is a good seven feet long—the kind in which a man can stretch out in when he comes home from the office, all tired out from working over a hot Republican." President Truman's other new bathtub had this message carved in the glass on its back side: "In this tub bathes the man whose heart is always clean and serves his people truthfully."

PLUMBERS

The White House plumbers of Watergate fame were not tradesmen but operatives hired by President Nixon to get secrets from the Democratic National Committee, whose office was in the Watergate Building. Since Nixon had a double-digit lead in the polls and won by a landslide, you have to wonder why he bothered.

A ROSE IS A WET ROSE

There had been marriages before held in the White House, but the first marriage held outside in the Rose Garden was that of Tricia Nixon. It rained.

SAFE HAVEN

When top entertainers appear at the White House, they are occasionally asked to stay there as well. Georgia-born Jimmy Carter was, not surprisingly, a big fan of Willie Nelson. (This was long before Willie's tax problems.) Staying there late one night, Willie Nelson went alone to the roof of the White House. Washington's streets form a pattern, so that many radiate like the spokes of a wheel out from the executive mansion. The view and light show from auto headlights are said to be striking. The view was made even more impressive for Willie when the entertainer, alone on the roof, lit himself what he later described as a "fat Austin Torpedo." He also observed that, beyond the view, no one is going to be up there by mistake, and no drug agents could even get in past the president's security without making a ruckus, so the top of the White House may be among the best and certainly, as he put it, "the safest place I can think of to smoke dope."

DINNER PLANS?

Often employing up to five full-time chefs, the modern White House kitchen is able to serve a multicourse formal dinner for as many as one hundred forty guests or, more casually, hors d'oeuvres to more than one thousand.

JUST HOME

The White House contains 132 rooms, 35 bathrooms, and 6 levels in the Residence. In its walls are 412 doors, 147 windows, 28 fireplaces, 8 staircases, and 3 elevators. Occasionally there was an indoor pool.

Appendix

RATING THE PRESIDENTS

*T*he following statements are pure, unadulterated opinion presented here because such a list is impossible to resist making.

TOP SEVEN

George Washington	Hey, he defined the job, not to mention winning the Revolution.
Abraham Lincoln	Strong leadership in the worst of times.
Thomas Jefferson	Among the best and unquestionably the brightest.
Franklin Delano Roosevelt	Strong leadership through two nation-shaking crises, the Great Depression, and World War II. Many of FDR's New Deal social policies pervade American society to this day.
Andrew Jackson	If for nothing else, and there was a lot, expansion and restoring the government to the common man.
Theodore Roosevelt	Set the nation onto a course that has led to greatness.
Harry Truman	Hard decisions and a common touch. Few remember he led during both the end of World War II and during Korea.
Ronald Reagan	We won! And leading a renewal of spirit and patriotism.

BOTTOM FIVE

Franklin Pierce

If Buchanan's inaction helped to cause the Civil War, Pierce appears to have actively worked to create the problem. He favored slavery and was elected with Southern support. He pushed through the Fugitive Slave Act and used federal forces to return runaway slaves; this quickly made slavery even less tolerable to its opponents and kept it in their face. He was also almost permanently depressed and eventually fell into a bottle.

Andrew Johnson

When not being inept, he worked hard to take away and marginalize the rights of the newly freed slaves. Lincoln's successor, but far from his heir. The first president to be impeached.

James Buchanan

His hesitation, lack of leadership, and unwillingness to deal with the divisive issue of slavery has to be considered a cause of the American Civil War.

Jimmy Carter

He ran as an outsider and remained one, totally ineffective. His lack of strong policy positions, starving of the military, and constant battles with Congress nearly lost America the Cold War. A story is told that one of his advisers appeared before a gathering of foreign policy experts. He began by stating that he was there to explain the Carter administration's foreign policy. A short pause to consult his notes was a mistake. First someone giggled at the mere concept that Jimmy Carter had an actual foreign policy, then the laughter spread until the place roared and this lasted some time. This may not be a true story, but kinda says it all. Until recently, when Carter began to meddle in active politics, some said that he had redeemed himself as one of the greatest ex-presidents ever, with charitable leadership and personal hard work.

Warren Harding

Not too bright, his wife did all the work and ran his campaigns. His administration was marked by few accomplishments and for a shortened term as president, an amazing number of cabinet-level scandals.

DISHONORABLE MENTION

Nixon for style, his own personal really bad style.

BOOKS BY
BILL FAWCETT